# INQUISITION

### By

### Jack Eddinger

"Men are not as they are described by those who idealize them - Christians or other Utopians - nor by those who want them to be widely different from what in fact they are, always have been and cannot help being - ungrateful, wanton, false and dissimulating, cowardly and greedy, arrogant and mean - their natural impulse is to be insolent when their affairs are prospering and abjectly servile when adversity strikes." -- Niccolo Machiavelli – 1505

"All politics is local." -- Thomas P. (Tip) O'Neill Jr., Speaker of the U.S. House of Representatives

*1663 Liberty Drive, Suite 200*
*Bloomington, Indiana 47403*
*(800) 839-8640*
*www.AuthorHouse.com*

This book is a work of fiction. Places, events, and situations in this story are purely fictional and any resemblance to actual persons, living or dead, is coincidental.

© 2005 Jack Eddinger.
All Rights Reserved.

No part of this book may be reproduced, stored in a retrieval system, or transmitted by any means without the written permission of the author.

First published by AuthorHouse 01/22/05

ISBN: 1-4184-7747-8 (sc)
ISBN: 1-4184-7746-X (dj)

Printed in the United States of America
Bloomington, Indiana

This book is printed on acid-free paper.

For , Mary, Lucy, Julie, John, Kim, Jennifer, Jack, Aric, Nifty and All Who Believed

**In Memorium**

Margaret, Joe, Laura, Lou, Jim, Rich, Joe Jr., Liz, Bob, Frank

# CHAPTER ONE
## *Unearthing Paranoia*

Congressman Zachary Taylor Harris entered his apartment in Kalorama Place late after the annual *Fall Follies* at the National Press Club. He stooped for a note shoved under the door. It said to call immediately. Without taking off his coat, he went to his study, put on silver framed spectacles and dialed a number in suburban Maryland. A hoarse voice answered.

"What is it, Robert?"

"It's the hearings, Congressman. We've hit a snag. They want you to reopen them next week," said Robert Bird, his administrative assistant, coughing through a Pall Mall.

"Next week! Impossible! What's wrong with those monkeys over at Justice? They know I just adjourned the committee *sine die*."

"I told them that, Congressman, but there's pressure from the Bureau. The Director's involved. Looks like Nelson and Sterling have gotten to him. He wants them resumed right away. Masters tells me the AG's got a flock of new subpoenas ready to go."

"Sonofabitch, man! I'm up to my ass in provincial politics. Half of Bessemer Steel's management is on the street. You tell that crowd of Micks to back off. I don't care if they want to subpoena the Kremlin. Next week is out of the question. There'll be no hearings, period. Tell them that."

"That's okay, but what do I do about the Director?"

"I'll handle him!"

Harris placed the receiver back on the cradle, took off his glasses and blotted perspiration from the back of his neck with a handkerchief. *It's just like that devious sonofabitch to pull a stunt like this. The headline-grabber has his publicity machine oiled and ready. He's not going to like what I have to tell him. There's no way these hearings can be reopened. Certainly not now.*

Zach Harris was confident he could handle his opponent but the new investigative climate in Hampton County gave him pause. He should have paid more attention, but winding down the SUBACK hearings occupied him all summer and fall. Investigations into public venality by an aggressive politician with reform in his nostrils can always be counted on to produce good newspaper copy. As conducted by the young District Attorney, however, they could lead elsewhere. If certain long-dormant lines were to be unearthed and followed, there's no telling where they'll take him. Federal investigators with sophisticated tools could rip up buried

1

# Jack Eddinger

conduits and cables. Who knows how deep they might go? The quality of the material he saw was first rate; too good to be coming from local sources. It had the fingerprints of the Bureau all over it, especially the stuff from across the Delaware in New Jersey.

He'd have to pay big to get a margin sufficient to offset Ike's coattails, to checkmate Bess Steel's money and to end the snooping of the ambitious District Attorney. No less than 80 percent. A vote that big had never been achieved in the 26th congressional district let alone anywhere in the United States in a contested election. Lloyd Kressman, the man he'd depend on to deliver it, will gag when he hears the numbers.

Before he could make a definitive move he needed time; time to mobilize the District - he could put full faith in Kressman. But his aide's phone call deeply upset him. How the hell would he convince the Director to back off the cockamamie notion that the country needs another round of pointless hearings. The man's as cagey as a magician in a poker game. Plays six hands at once.

He sank deep into the armchair. He put the circuitry of a politically sophisticated mind to work. Somehow, he'd have to motivate the Director to back off. But more than that he needed to know what the investigations were turning up. It would not be easy and it carried a calculated risk. But Zach Harris loved a well-considered gamble. Besides, his safe on the Hill contained the only insurance policy he'd ever need. To get the Director's cooperation he needed to know the extent and quality of information the Bureau possessed. Like the men who understand power in Washington, he knew that beneath the Director's veneer of calculated civility lay an unstable ego. The facade masks a manic instability; paranoia with an intricate and systematic purpose. A grotesque mission, god knows for what; perhaps a weird whiff of destiny.

Zach Harris began mapping a strategy. He had to cut through the hard reptilian shell to soft tissue and lay bare the paranoia at the core. Only when he had the man with his defenses down could he, Zach Harris the insiders' insider, finesse the Director into doing what he wanted. Over the years he'd trafficked in stories about power or perceived power in Washington. He'd chuckle when reading a *Times Herald* or *Evening Star* account of the powerful chairman of this or that committee. "Powerful, hell. The sonofabitch's marinating himself in J.T.S. Brown and wouldn't know a caucus from a cactus." But one man interested him above all others. Any story from the congressional poker circuit about the former clerk, who became the nation's first and only internal security boss, immediately entered his mental databank.

# INQUISITION

In spite of the gangster-hunter, hard-nosed cop image the Director cultivated through his Hollywood friends, seasoned politicians knew otherwise. If Zach Harris trusted anything in Washington, he trusted the superior quality inside information shared over strong whiskey and a well-played poker hand in the smoky rooming houses on Independence Avenue or in the backrooms and rented flats within spitting distance of the Capitol. That's where the real work gets done; legislative agendas midwived and headcounts tallied. Zach Harris was a regular almost from the day in 1933 when he stood in the well of the House with his right hand raised in solemn oath. He learned to sift out the grit and separate muscle from gristle, fact from gossip, and to discount the unctuous flattery that floated over the House floor in roseate clouds. He honed his legislative and parliamentary skills under the tutelage of the swamp rats whose grand-daddies riding with General Nathan Bedford Forrest ripped up railroads, sacked baggage trains and raised general hell six decades before. He handled a whiskey glass with the best of them and could reel off bawdy stories better than any carpet-bagging, funny-talking but god-damned decent Yankee who'd ever paid them mind. He developed a fine set of nostrils for sniffing out fakery. If anybody's to be mistrusted in Washington, his experience taught him, it is the senior bureaucrat. The man who's here year in and year out, wraps himself in civil service protection, owes nothing to nobody; who's never been bloodied in an election, who doesn't have the scent of the people on him. The most dangerous of this breed is the peddler of information from undigested reports, who never surfaces by name, but covers himself with that overworked term, "an official source." He'd seen enough to know. Hell, he considered himself an expert at it.

Zach Harris sank deeper into thought. He plumbed and probed, searching for the disparate pieces that when put together would form a mosaic. Something about the Director lurked deep in the folds of his cerebral cortex. He began a systematic year by year, decade by decade review of the times their paths had crossed - Judiciary Committee hearings on amendments to the criminal codes; support for *Harris-MacNaughton*; testimony on wire tapping, telegraphic interception and mail opening; meetings on the Bureau's appropriation.

The exercise produced nothing specific.

Then he considered the public man. As light breaks down in a prism, he filtered out the spectrum from infrared to ultraviolet. He traced each wave backward in time: the evidence which broke the Rosenberg case; lassoing the 14 Nazi saboteurs from the U-boat off Long Island; the public enemy lists, the evidence that convicted Hauptmann, the Dillinger arrest and the Barker-Karpis publicity; the recorded material which comprised the

# Jack Eddinger

legend. The photographic memory he relied on to produce a parliamentary maneuver that left the opposition muttering oaths; which could produce whole sections of *Roberts Rules* whirred like a movie reel. He reached down deep into his auditory vault. The exercise produced a tangled web of images, words and phrases. They emerged slowly, coalescing into a fixed image. The year was 1950. The place was Madison Square Garden. He was seated onstage; one of six congressmen receiving the American Legion's *I Am An American Award*. The Director was being honored as the Legion Man of the Year. He remembered the deliberate way the man approached the podium; how he paused, never looked up from his text; how he gripped the rostrum with both hands to give the speech they all came to hear. His hard brown eyes blazed; a film of sweat glistened on his chin and upper lip under the merciless television lights. The high-pitched voice was clear, strong and certain even though it lacked the timbre and cadence of a great speaker. What it lacked in polish, however, it more than made up for in intensity; a presence which conveyed the power of certitude to his listeners:

*"Communists have been and today are at work within the very gates of America ... Atheistic materialism is their idol; the destruction of the God of our fathers their goal ... they have in common one diabolical ambition - to weaken and to eventually destroy American democracy by stealth and cunning ... My fellow delegates no less than western civilization is at stake."*

He recalled how the legionnaires, in their blue serge overseas caps, rose, knocked over chairs and stood in the aisles cheering. They whooped and whistled a full ten minutes. Zach Harris remembered thinking if this man were running for national office he'd win hands down. The question was, did he believe this stuff, or was it like his own speeches to friendly partisans hungry for raw meat?

Zach Harris probed for a deeper, more penetrating analysis of the man. He had only pieces of the myth. He needed something deeper, a psychic fragment to support the calculated risk he knew was essential to bring the Director around. With it he would devise a strategy which would not only produce the information, but would keep any investigation in the district at the nuisance level and well outside federal interest. He finally found what he was searching for deep in his own experience; from a long-buried conversation with his political mentor, A. Morton Brodfield, Woodrow Wilson's last attorney general. He remembered the story as if it were yesterday. It was over whiskey and soda on a snowy winter evening at the Willard bar. The old man, now semi-retired, recounted the disastrous decision which denied him the presidential nomination in 1920.

# INQUISITION

Had he relied on his political instincts, Brodfield told his protégé, instead of responding to the importuning of a pudgy, baby-faced underling in the investigations division, he, Mort Brodfield, not the feather duster Cox, would have had the Democratic presidential nomination at San Francisco. America would have been spared the conspiracy cooked up under Warren Harding's nose by Daugherty and Fall. We'd have had Mort Brodfield and Al Smith in an unbroken line instead of the do-nothing Hoover, the old man told him in a long soliloquy:

*A candidate needs a national reputation, which I had. But he needs something else; something that shows he understands the concerns of the little man. I decided we ought to break up the German beer trust. It would reach into every workingman's lunch pail. Well, I launched an inquiry. Anti-German feeling was running awfully high at the time. It was a perfectly natural thing and it certainly appealed to the common man. We'd just finished off the Kaiser and the Huns, yet the working man found the hard-earned money he spent down at the corner tavern going straight back to the Reich. The damned Heinies had all the beer formulas, the licensing and the entire American distribution system tied up. A damnable outrage was what it was.*

*It began as the Hops and Malt Inquiry. The Hearst papers started calling it the Wurzburger Scandal after the German beer. I got a good Milwaukee German, Frank Overmeier, to sponsor the bill. We wanted to show Henry Mencken we weren't out to embarrass German-Americans. Frank opened the inquiry with a set of hearings. I got things started as the leadoff witness. I laid out our argument. I spelled out the specifics of the Kraut's monopolization. I had German maps displayed in color and Gothic type to give them a sinister look, but the thing never caught on. After a month the newspapers went on to other things. We were at a standstill. Then one day this curly-haired young fella who worked down in one of my divisions at Justice - investigations to be exact - got up at a departmental meeting and made what I thought at the time was a very smart suggestion. 'Why waste time on small beer? Go after our real enemies, the Bolsheviks and the Eastern European Jews and Slav bomb-throwers.' He gave us a long, very convincing talk on socialism. He started with Huns and Russkies with unpronounceable names and ended with Lenin and Trotsky. He concluded with sweat glistening on his upper lip and a wild look in his eyes. I'll never forget the weird look on that baby face, Zach. What was taking place in Russia, he told us, would influence politics in this country and around the world for the next fifty years. That was 1919. I've got to hand it to him. He was right on the money.*

# Jack Eddinger

He was up to the minute on everything Red. Hell, half the time I didn't understand what he was talking about. But we took his advice anyway. We went about it systematically. I formed a special investigating force of lawyers, tax agents and customs officers. I had the power under the 1917 Espionage Act. Well, he got me to sign an order letting him carry out a complicated scheme to raid homes and offices of suspected Bolshies. Colonel House and Joe Tumulty were against it, but couldn't block things the way they did when they had the President's ear. Wilson was virtually on his deathbed with his fourth stroke. Our agents picked up thousands of aliens all over the country to start out the new year. We had the Reds on the run. The New York Times had us in headlines and in lights on the Times Square news board. Hearst gave me enough coverage to win the nomination for emperor. I was on my way to the presidency.

Then the roof caved in. Before you knew it, they were throwing bombs and shooting people. The harder we cracked down, the more bombs they'd set off. They blew up old Morgan's bank, and damned near got me. If Millie and I hadn't been out that night, they'd have blown us to the parapets of Jericho. Their bomb blew off my front porch, collapsed our living room and killed the Bolshevik who threw it. Parts of him were hanging in my elm trees. That fellow brought me a lot of grief, Zach. You've got to steer clear of him. I don't know why I ever let him talk me into that damned fool scheme. I'd have been nominated and elected. Now look where he is. I thought he was crazy then, and I think he's crazy today. He has a tendency to go off half-cocked. Something funny about him. I mean deep down inside. I've known many men in the course of my years here, but nobody like him. He has always had this wild gleam lighting up that baby face. You can't trust him. His gol-damned foolishness ended my public career. Mark what I say, Zach, you've got to be very careful in your dealings with him. Personally, I think he's psychopathic. He keeps card files on everybody like the Russian Cheka. And the son-of-a-bitch's a damned hypocrite. Look how he's kept this Red business going. That dad-blamed fool Stone made him a permanent institution. Now he's the country's chief of police and a Red expert to boot. A damned mountebank's what he is.

Zach Harris pondered the old man's words. The exercise cracked open the thick rhino hide of the myth covering the psychic vulnerability he was looking for. Soft pink tissue lay at the core. He would reopen the hearings on terms he was confident the Director would meet. He'd get the Director's agreement by offering him a new assault on his ancient enemies; an assault to be revealed not to 5,000 legionnaires, but to millions of Americans right in their living rooms. He knew it was an opportunity the Director could not, would not, refuse. Television was the key. It would guarantee the

# INQUISITION

Director's passionate commitment and put him in Zachary Taylor Harris's debt. It would pull the plug on young Daley's career.

So thorough an exertion deserved a reward. He mixed a scotch and soda and lit a cigarette. The latter expressly forbidden. *Damned medicos'll deny a man air and water if you listen to 'em.* He carried the drink and an ashtray into his study, picked up the telephone and dialed a number known only to a handful of representatives and senators holding chairmanships of investigative committees. The number was listed in the pocket notebook in which he recorded useful information like his colleagues' votes on certain bills, election results and unlisted phone numbers. He waited. The phone clicked and buzzed, emitting metallic sounds. The line noise and the illusion of distance sounded as if he was speaking over the trans-Atlantic cable.

*Sonofabitch's got his own phone tapped.*

It rang twice. A voice devoid of timbre or resonance answered.

"This is the Director." He sounded automatic like the time and weather voice.

"This is Zach Harris."

"Who?"

"Congressman Zachary Taylor Harris," he said testily.

"Oh, yes. Your man said you'd call. How are you? Sounds like you've got a head cold. Rotten connection. You'd think C&P could do better in the nation's capital."

*Sounds like you've got the damned Army Signal Corps in your closet, you shifty bastard.*

"I've been here reading. Burning a little midnight oil. Lucky you caught me. I was about to turn in. Tell me, congressman, you ever read the analytical works of a priest name of Charles MacFarland S.J. over at Georgetown?"

"Can't say I have. Closest I came to the cloth was debriefing a chaplain we'd trained in intelligence during the war. I used to hear his confession. Why?"

"I've just finished his treatise on Marx. He certainly lays out the disheveled old pervert with clarity. Ever read any Marx or Feuerbach, Congressman? You ought to. Now what can I do for you?"

"To get straight to the point, my man tells me you want me to reopen the security hearings. Frankly, I've got real problems with that, and I want to explore a more realistic timetable."

A long pause.

"You still there?"

# Jack Eddinger

"Out of the question. I want those hearings reopened forthwith, Congressman. I've got fresh evidentiary material which simply cannot wait. Statute of limitations expires, and I want it before the public now. Even a few weeks' postponement will mean work down the drain. Hundreds of man-hours up in smoke and thousands of dollars wasted; taxpayer dollars, Congressman. What's more, my schedule simply won't permit postponement. I expect to be tied up being stabbed and poked over at Walter Reed next week. Then when you people are in recess, I'll be taking my sojourn at Del Mar. That will finish me to the end of the year. During this period, I am available to no one, Congressman, including the President. Those hearings must be reopened at once. Congressman Harris, you and I have an exceptional opportunity before us. I have evidence which places friends and associates of your professor at the center of Communist activity from 1937 on. Matter of fact, I've passed some of this material along to Mr. Nelson and his man. They're all for pursuing it, but they want a signal from you to go ahead. No, these hearings must proceed at once. Absolutely no postponement."

"Look, I can't go into this in detail on the telephone. Can we meet tomorrow? How about four o'clock?"

"Well, let's see - graduation at Quantico in the morning, then Clyde and I will be lunching at the Mayflower, and at three, a retirement ceremony. That will last till well past four, then the Attorney General. Five looks available. I'll shoehorn you between the General and my five-thirty staff meeting. Can you be here at that hour?"

"I prefer my private office in the Capitol."

"Oh, no. Out of the question. I can give you no more than thirty minutes, Congressman and that's stretching it. My meetings start promptly."

*You sonofabitch. Next time you're on The Hill to justify your goddamned discretionary budget, I'll have Flynn put you on hold till your balls ache.*

"All right. I'll be there after the national security briefing.

"I did not know you were in on that briefing, Mr. Harris. Little out of your bailiwick, isn't it? Well, that's neither here nor there. Four-thirty it will be. I've penciled you in, congressman. A good night to you, sir."

Zach Harris held the phone in his fist for a long minute. *"You bastard,"* he spat. The cigarette and drink tasted a year old. How would he explain it to the Speaker, who wanted the Committee adjourned permanently. He thought he'd put an end to things when he gaveled the committee to a close *sine die* that very morning with the professor's cogent summarization and in facing down Nelson and the committee Republicans.

# CHAPTER TWO
## *Sine Die*

Earlier that day Mills Anson Burnham, Ph. D., professor of American history at the University of Pennsylvania and the country's foremost expert on the U. S. Communist Party, had adjusted his trademark black eyepatch and looked straight into the polished convex lens pointed at him from behind the dais of the House Caucus Room. Gray-haired, confident and relaxed, Burnham nodded genially to the press table. With his trim beard and jaunty demeanor, he appeared the avuncular professor ready to enlighten a group of boisterous undergraduates. The only hint of his exploits as an OSS officer in World War II was the small imperial blue ribbon edged with bars of red and white displayed on his left lapel, indicating the nation's second highest award for heroism. So formidable was his academic reputation that only his wife and closest friends called him Andy, his boyhood nickname. To everyone else he was Dr. Burnham. While he had signed numerous petitions over the years protesting the Committee's very existence, he was pleased to be the definitive witness as it passed into history. In spite of significant misgivings, he had accepted the chairman's invitation to offer the historian's perspective on the committee's contributions to American history and law-making. If nothing else, he was contributing to the historical record.

"Mr. Chairman, aren't you going to swear this witness?" protested Representative Glenn Nelson, the committee's ranking Republican.

"That won't be necessary, Mr. Nelson. Dr. Burnham is here at the request of the chair to provide guidance in writing the final report of these proceedings." Zachary Taylor Harris of Pennsylvania brooked no deviation from parliamentary procedure. That way he kept the lid on tight. It was not the first time he rebuked the intense Californian whose reputation as a scourge of subversives, earned in the Committee's glory days, came through the skillful grilling and skewering of even the most truculent witnesses.

"Irrespective of the content of Professor Burnham's testimony, Mr. Chairman, I believe it is simply sound procedure to swear anyone who comes before this committee. As I recall, we've sworn our own members from time to time. It's a precedent we ought to respect."

"One man's precedent is another man's pretext, Mr. Nelson."

"Well, I want the record to show I've asked for this witness to be sworn."

# Jack Eddinger

"Shall I poll the committee, Mr. Nelson?" the chairman cast an icy stare over half-moon reading glasses.

Nelson responded with a smile that lingered between a snicker and a smirk. He turned and whispered into the ear of Ronald Sterling, minority counsel and chief investigator from the 1947-1948 period of the Committee's hegemony. That's when they dragged anybody, from longshoreman to Methodist bishop up to testify. Nelson and Sterling sat at the Republican end of the long, curved committee table. Both wore black suits and vests, white shirts and gold and black striped ties. Although they had shaved that morning, each man's stubble glistened green-black like horseflies' wings under the intense white light. Standing, Sterling towered a good foot over Nelson. The wags in the House press corps called them, Gloom and Glum, the Gruesome Twosome.

"You may proceed, Dr. Burnham." Zachary Taylor Harris adjusted the microphone at the chairman's seat and shaded his eyes with a copy of the *Congressional Record*. The platinum incandescence which flooded the hearing room whitened his hair and etched deep lines in his face like the slash patterns of Waterford crystal. He stopped wearing green-tinted sunglasses after the House Doorkeeper told him he looked like a wop gangster on the evening news. Nature had endowed him with an inquisitorial visage: a mouth that slid as easily into a scowl as a grin, magnesium hard eyes, hair the color of weathered slate and a scratchy baritone that when focused in sarcasm could eat through the armor plate Bessemer Steel Company produced for the United States Navy in the Twenty-sixth District of Pennsylvania, which he represented in every Congress since March 1933. After twelve weeks of hearings he was finally at ease, almost jovial. He took on the thankless assignment against his better judgment. Now he was steering the committee to a close, rationally and with a minimum of acrimony just as the Speaker asked, hell pleaded for. The Committee on Subversive Activities, SUBACK, as the press tagged it, was about to be lowered into the grave, a shadow of the powerful instrument of national policy and political partisanship it had been since 1936, when his fellow Democrat Martin Dies began investigating Nazis. He was in good spirits, considered himself in excellent health and much younger than his fifty-eight years. Only a raspy cough left over from a summer cold nagged at him occasionally.

"Professor Burnham, history will record that you have the unique privilege of being this committee's expert in helping to sort out the meaning of the protracted dramas that have unfolded in this room over three decades." Harris made the observation happy to be the one putting the quietus on the committee. It was an oversight activity he was uneasy

# INQUISITION

with, but occasionally found useful in getting reelected. Eastern Europeans comprised 20 percent of his political base. Subversion, he often told his House colleagues, is the Twentieth Century version of waving the bloody shirt. He pulled a pile of correspondence closer, took out a fountain pen and began signing letters and autographing his official congressional photograph, seemingly oblivious to the witness.

"I am delighted to be here on this historic day, Mr. Chairman. But first, let me preface my text with a compliment to your stewardship. This particular cycle in the committee's history has set a new standard against which investigations past and future will be measured."

Zachary Taylor Harris ignored the comment, continuing to sign papers. Professor Burnham cleared his throat and moved to his prepared text:

"Mr. Chairman and members of the Subversive Activities Committee, legislative inquiry into the perplexing issue of subversion has been with us since the dawn of the Republic. Its roots extend to the Alien and Sedition Acts. We've seen its ebb and flow over the years. Xenophobia rises and falls in combination with societal forces, particularly those from times of heavy immigration, or in the need to find scapegoats in post-war periods. We see it in the rum, romanism and rebellion slogan of Know-Nothingism. We've seen it in many other garbs - the Pullman and Haymarket rioting, the Greenbackers, the Wobblies and the justified calls on the nation's conscience by Eugene Debs and Norman Thomas. We saw it in the Red Scare of 1920 and in the Sacco-Vanzetti case. In fact this Committee has had its own peculiar rendezvous with the issue. However, under your firm and fair leadership, Mr. Chairman, some of the damage has been repaired. Unlike previous hearings yours have been reasonable and restrained, particularly those involving the Department of State in which I served for nearly a decade. All right thinking Americans salute you."

Burnham pondered the irony of congratulating a man whom he held in little esteem and regarded as a political opportunist. *Oh what the hell if I praise Caesar, maybe it'll assure a well-deserved burial for this stain on our national polity*, he mused.

Harris did not look up from his paperwork when Glenn Nelson's palm smote the dais, resounding off the hearing room walls like a rifle crack.

"Mr. Chairman!"

"Mr. Nelson, you will have every opportunity to question the witness. Please proceed, Dr. Burnham.

Nelson scowled, covered his microphone with one hand, turned and whispered angrily to counsel. Sterling got up and left the room through a door behind the dais.

# Jack Eddinger

"Thank you Mr. Chairman. I submit that had the committee entered this thicket in like manner in the summer of 1948, I dare say that the policy-making process both toward the Soviet Union and safeguarding official secrets *vis a vis* individual liberties would be of a wholly different character today. I address this issue precisely in my book, *Test Of A Generation.*

"I..."

"Mr. Chairman!" Nelson insisted.

"The gentleman from California will have every opportunity to address the chair. When I say so. That, I insist. Understood? Please continue professor."

"It is important in the historical view, Mr. Chairman and members of the committee, to realize that the lens we focus on the immediate past distorts the larger view. While I subscribe in general to the view that newspapers represent the first rough cut of history, we need to be mindful that one of the purposes of news coverage is to stir the emotions. Competitive pressures, news cycles, news stand sales and other external factors having nothing to do with the essence of a news event color public perceptions and compromise the historic record. Another factor is the loose terminology employed not only by the press but by virtually everyone associated with investigations such as those conducted by this committee - the conspiratorial mentality, you might say. Take the term 'infiltration.' Communists, the committee has heard repeatedly, have 'infiltrated' the United States government beginning in the New Deal. But the reality is that beginning in 1933, employment in government service was more desirable than working in the private sector. Americans flocked to Washington. There were no loyalty oaths or security programs. These men and women were not 'infiltrators.' They were responding to President Roosevelt's call for people to help run his administration. Many of the individuals this committee has summoned before it were said to have 'infiltrated' government agencies and organizations. They were ordinary job holders, albeit conditioned by the economic difficulties of the times."

While the historian spoke, Congressman Nelson scribbled furiously on a yellow legal pad. He wagged his pencil vigorously toward the chair.

"Point of order, Mr. Chairman."

Zach Harris, a stickler for procedure, gave Glenn Nelson the chairman's full attention.

"Make your point, Mr. Nelson."

"I submit, Mr. Chairman, and it is the view of the minority members of this committee that Dr. Burnham is unqualified to testify as an expert witness. I say this quite seriously and with deference to the chair." Sterling

# INQUISITION

reentered through the rear door, took a seat behind Nelson and handed the Californian a file folder.

"I would like, Mr. Chairman, to bring a few facets of Dr. Burnham's background as an expert witness to the committee's attention. I believe you and the committee would be quite interested in probing certain areas of the professor's personal history, which bear directly upon his expertise and objectivity, before allowing him to continue reading his statement.

"I find it curious, for instance, that his name should appear on a Justice Department watch list of speakers who addressed the Young Socialist League in Vienna in 1936. Perhaps Dr. Burnham will enlighten us about this particular item.

"Moreover, Mr. Chairman, I would like to submit for the committee's inspection, an article our learned witness published in the left wing organ, *Social Policy Studies,* vol. 10, No. 1 dated January, 1940. Its title? *How The Non-Aggression Pact Will Stabilize Europe*." Nelson took a paper from the folder and passed it to the chair.

"I won't ask if he had revised his perspective in light of subsequent events."

Light laughter rippled through the hearing room.

"Are you still on your point of order, Mr. Nelson? I would advise you and the minority that I will not permit any witness to be badgered."

"My point, Mr. Chairman, goes directly to the issue of Dr. Burnham's credentials as an expert, and with all due respect to the chair, I would like to take a few more minutes to elaborate. I certainly do not challenge your wisdom in arranging his appearance, Mr. Chairman. I simply wish to draw the committee's attention to facts that have not previously been disclosed. Now, I realize the committee staff reviewed Dr. Burnham's background. But in many cases our staff cannot do a thorough job of checking current leads much less delving into information from a decade or more ago. I would, therefore, like to share with you and members of the committee a few pertinent facts Mr. Sterling and I have uncovered, which may be helpful in assessing the value of Dr. Burnham's contribution to these proceedings."

"Mr. Nelson, the chair grants you five minutes to make your case." Zachary Taylor Harris, the old prosecutor, winked at the witness.

"Thank you. Paraphrasing you on precedents, Mr. Chairman, let me say that defining the word 'expert' has historical precedents in Dr. Burnham's case. With respect to his so-called expertise, I ask that a series of articles from the *Manchester Guardian* datelined June 11, 1937 Guadalajara Front, be placed in the record. The author, Special Correspondent, one M.A Burns. You will see as you read these articles, Mr. Chairman, and fellow

# Jack Eddinger

members, that the author describes the arrival of, quote, Soviet Volunteers, unquote, to support the Spanish Loyalist forces as something akin to von Steuben's arrival at the Battle of Trenton. I might add that the entire series was subsequently published by the *The New Masses*, a publication its former editor, Mr. Eastman, acknowledged before this Committee as nothing more than a reprint service for the Comintern.

"For the record, sir. Is the name M.A. Burns familiar to you?"

"Yes, Congressman Nelson. It was my pseudonym at that time."

"Why, sir, was it necessary to use a pseudonym? Why were you hesitant to use your own name?"

"It is common practice in publishing, Mr. Nelson. No other reason."

"Is that a fact? I wonder if it might be that you used the false name to hide your identity as a member of the Abraham Lincoln Brigade or one of the other leftist entities you served in Spain?"

"Mr. Chairman, I resent the innuendo here. The pseudonym was used to separate my reporting from academic publishing, no more, no less. There was no misrepresentation whatever."

"Thank you, Dr. Burnham. Mr. Nelson, you may continue, but I believe you're headed into a First Amendment thicket with this line of questioning. Dr. Burnham's a scholar, before that a reporter, covering a war. He may write and publish whatever he wants." The chairman made the statement obliquely. His eyes were on the reporters seated at the press table.

"Now Mr. Chairman, I am not questioning the witness's journalistic credentials or his right to publish what he wants. I believe I speak for the other distinguished members of this committee when I tell you that Mr. Burnham's publishing record admits to a certain partiality for things Red.

"Let me be specific. Here are the opening words of one of the articles I alluded to earlier: *'Loyalists are battling the Fascist forces of Generalissimo Francisco Franco to a standstill on the vast plain surrounding this fortress city, thanks to an infusion of tough young volunteers from the dusty villages of the Caucuses ...'* Or this one from another dispatch by the same author, *'Vladimir Okhsarshadze is a 22-year-old descendant of hard-riding Cossacks who shed his blood and honor for the cause of Spanish freedom on a sparse and rocky plain a thousand miles from his peaceful village on the banks of the Don ...'*

"Shall I go on? I ask you, Mr. Chairman and members of the committee, does this sound like the sentiments of an impartial observer or the slants of a clever propagandist?

"Let me add one further item in support of my point of order. Dr. Burnham's affiliations. His official biography is peppered with the acronyms of the Left - the ACLU, the ADA, the AAUP, the ILO. He has

# INQUISITION

served two terms as president of the Philadelphia Chapter of the American Civil Liberties Union, an organization which has long been sympathetic to leftist causes and has defended known subversives. He serves as chairman of the speakers forum of Americans For Democratic Action, which as you know, Mr. Chairman, first attempted to defeat, and failing that, worked diligently to repeal, the *Harris-MacNaughton Act*."

Zach Harris stopped signing correspondence. He glared down the long dais at Nelson and Sterling. *The MacNaughton-Harris Immigration Control Act of 1952*, as it was officially known, was the greatest achievement of his nearly thirty years in Congress. He crafted 150 provisions into a bill establishing the official immigration and naturalization policy of the United States for the balance of the Twentieth Century. He set the schedule of hearings and hand-picked the witnesses to establish an impeccable legislative history. He personally authored its strong anti-subversive provisions and managed the bill to passage on the floor with no help from the Speaker. He picked off opponents from organized religion, the educational establishment and labor unions with his surpassing knowledge of parliamentary procedure and deft editing. He dragged a reluctant Senator Patrick J. MacNaughton of Nevada, chairman of the Senate Judiciary Committee, along by placing his name first, waiving the precedent on bills originating in the House. Then he got Dan Flynn to agree to conference language on the Reclamation Bill to include a $250 million dam on the Humboldt River and a clause in the construction contract to keep Mexican labor off the project. Before Zach Harris stepped in, MacNaughton could get nothing out of Sam Crump of Mississippi, chairman of Senate Appropriations. The pair had tangled in the Senate cloak room, after Crump called MacNaughton a yellow-bellied canary for crowing to the press about the secret deal he cut with Harris in the House-Senate conference to gut the civil rights bill of its enforcement provisions.

"Mr. Nelson, your comments are very interesting, and I am certain Dr. Burnham is eager to respond in detail. However, nothing you have said is germane to your point of order. I personally reviewed Dr. Burnham's credentials with the majority members. We find him to be a bonafide expert on all things Red. The majority does not share the minority's view on this. Besides, I think I'm still an honorary member of the ADA in spite of my differences with them. Clark Clifford sent me this when we approved the Marshall Plan. Said I might need it if I ever gave a speech in New York. Never thought I'd have any use for it."

He fished a dog-eared card from his wallet and held it up for the photographers. He grinned the grimace of a trapper who'd cornered a skunk. He knew he'd be on page one of the nation's newspapers the next

# Jack Eddinger

morning. Nelson and his carping would be buried ten paragraphs into the news story wrapping up the committee's work. Smiles broke out all along the press desk.

"You may proceed, Dr. Burnham."

"Thank you Mr. Chairman. I have no association with the International Labor Organization. The ILO reference on my vita is to the Indian Lake Organization, a property owner's association in Maine to which I must say I pay considerable dues. I am indeed, Mr. Nelson, president of the Philadelphia ADA Chapter. I dare say that city has seen a few dissenters in its time. And although I opposed *Harris-MacNaughton*, Mr. Chairman, I was simply carrying out the wishes of my constituents, something that is not quite unknown in these parts."

Light laughter.

Zachary Taylor Harris tapped his gavel gently.

Unfazed, Congressman Nelson whispered animatedly into Ronald Sterling's ear. For the next 30 minutes Professor Burnham reviewed the history of the Communist Party in the United States. He traced its beginnings from the Comintern letter to American radicals in 1919, urging them to organize Communist cells among returning soldiers and sailors, and to arm the proletariat. He described the abortive meeting in the summer of 1922 in the woods at Bridgman, Michigan and the CPUSA's organizing days under Earl Browder and William Z. Foster; its involvement in the labor organizational wars and civil rights activities of the Twenties and Thirties; its embrace by W.E.B. DuBois and Paul Robeson, and finally to past and current attempts by the United States Government to define it, grasp it by the throat and eliminate it from the body politic.

"In the final analysis, Mr. Chairman, like all movements which alter the course of human events, Communism has had a romantic hold on the imagination of many American intellectuals. Lenin was one of the seminal figures of this century. Zinoviev, Trotsky, Bukharin et al were intellectual contemporaries doing battle with the forces of reaction. But, there's a major difference. The American intelligentsia's flirtation was principally of the armchair variety with the exception of a handful of individuals like John Reed, who participated in the events of 1917 and immediately thereafter. There was the interlude of the mid-1930s. American intellectuals and activists of all stripes rallied against fascism. Many were caught up in the Popular Front, calling for the CP to cooperate with liberal and left-wing factions to oppose fascism. American infatuation with international communism faded - our notoriously short attention span - as Stalin gathered power. It was all but dead by the time of Kirov's assassination and the Purge Trials. Interestingly, Mr. Nelson, there was a time when your

# INQUISITION

party and the Communists cooperated, though that appears hard to believe today. The America First Committee with its odd assortment of socialists, pacifists, fascist-nationalists, and progressives among others was the catalyst. They even recruited John L. Lewis's daughter, and in 1940 backed Wendel Willkie for president. The GOP went so far as to place an anti-FDR advertisement in *The Daily Worker*. That should exhibit some balance as to my *New Masses* article, Mr. Chairman. The final coffin nail was driven when Molotov and von Ribbentrob initialed the non-Aggression Pact. Of course, there were some American hangers on ..."

"Mr. Chairman!" Glenn Nelson broke in.

"Mr. Nelson?"

"Mr. Chairman, this is an outrage. If the views advanced by this witness as to the docility of the Communist Party USA are as he would have us believe, then we are all candidates for Gullibility 101, a course he seems to be at home in. I don't mind saying sir that I find your so-called scholarship to be superficial and insulting to every member of this committee and to the American people. Perhaps Mr. Burnham would be more in his element on the faculty of Moscow State University? I remind the witness that were he under oath, he would be flirting with contempt of Congress. What makes you believe that you are the final arbiter on the Communist Conspiracy, professor? It was testimony before this committee, sir, which sent communists and their bedmates to jail. The denigration of its work in this alleged summation insults the hundreds of Americans who jeopardized their lives by testifying as to the extent of Communist penetration of our government and society. It is this committee that evoked the chilling testimony of Elizabeth Bentley and Louis Budenz, the glib sophistries of Owen Latimore and the profound revelations of Mr. Whittaker Chambers. Mr. Chairman, I move that the testimony of this witness be stricken in its entirety."

"Is there a second?

Nelson's motion was seconded by Roush of New Hampshire.

"All in favor, aye. Opposed, nay.

"Six nays and five ayes. "Motion defeated."

"You may proceed, Doctor."

"Actually, I have concluded, Mr. Chairman. I thought Mr. Nelson was delivering a philippic, which of course is his right."

"Mr. Chairman, I move that the committee convene in executive session to take up further information that has come to my attention in this matter."

"I'm sorry, but that's not in order, Mr. Nelson. There's no need for an executive session. We have achieved our purpose. Dr. Burnham, I thank

## Jack Eddinger

you on behalf of the majority members of this committee. I wish I could say the same for the minority. Your material will be incorporated into the record.

"There being no further witnesses, this committee stands adjourned *sine die*." Congressman Harris slammed the gavel twice.

The chairman moved through the milling crowd toward the press table. Other members of the committee exited through the rear doors. Reporters crowded around Professor Burnham.

"Well gentlemen, do we have a quorum?"

Zachary Taylor Harris took extra care in cultivating the House press corps. Late on summer afternoons when the clerks yawned through Cotton Montgomery's monologue to an empty chamber about price supports for peanuts, rice, sorghum and sugar beets; or when the nickel-squeezer, Butz of Iowa, was on the floor lacerating the State Department for spending two million on embassy tennis courts, Zach Harris headed for the press gallery. He'd round up a squad of regulars and lead them up the narrow, winding stairway to his hideaway office just below the Capitol dome. With its sweeping view down the Mall to the Potomac, he always referred to it as the office with the second best view in Washington. He believed in keeping the press stuffed like a *foie gras* goose. No scraps or crumbs. Good stuff, like why a chairman suddenly took his hold off a bill he'd bottled up for a year; how a Foreign Affairs statesman can't get a bill out of Rules if he crawled into Howard Smith's office on his hands and knees; which liberal voted to kill oil depletion then wrote the conference report keeping it alive. Sketch out the turf battles and ego dysfunctions. Give them a solid lead to a story, like when to expect the Justice Department to move against the Bessemer Steel-Toledo Bearings merger, or how Dan Flynn got that $30 million railroad for the Luzerne Weapons Depot and put the heat on the Army to burn Pennsylvania anthracite in every barracks in Europe. Produced a thousand jobs and maybe three times as many new votes back home.

Like a pathologist tracking systemic malfunctions, Zach Harris enjoyed performing autopsies on the august Lower Body for his friends in the press. No outsiders. Only the regulars, and definitely no women. Bring the boys inside and chances are you'll snag 'em. Tell an AP, UP or INS man something solid, and by God, it will be on the front pages from Ipswich to Yakima the next day. Their appetite is insatiable. They read the House as if it's a fever chart. Connect a few lines and they'll put your diagnosis in their copy. Take away their sources and you've taken the gun out of their hands. Zach Harris knew their needs, right down to the

# INQUISITION

deadlines and the daily cycles that drive the wire services. He worked hard to keep the press well fed.

He rarely held a press conference. When he did, it was usually with other members, or with the Pennsylvania Congressional Delegation. Too damned many strutting peacocks. As chairman of the subcommittee on criminal law and immigration, he could make news anytime. Hell, he knew more about the inner workings of the investigative bureaucracy than any member of Congress.

But things were changing. Ever since the television cameras began poking into the practices and procedures of Congress, Zach Harris sensed a sea change. He tried gamely but failed to get the old curmudgeons like Carl Vinson and Bull Andrews to stop fighting progress. He knew that television was a phenomenon that would shake Congress to its foundations. But neither the senior committee chairmen, nor the Speaker would hear of it. They regarded television as a heathen intrusion into the Holy of Holies. To the Speaker and his chairmen, televised hearings breached the unwritten compact that holds the foundation in place - no member shall outshine another member, least of all a powerful chairman. They preferred doing business in private. To clutter their baroque hearing rooms with cables, lights, tripods, cameras, wires and hordes of unkempt technicians was unthinkable. The real power radiated from the iron control over all aspects of legislative life exercised by committee chairmen. They ran the United States House of Representatives the way their confederates back home ran the faded, backwater court houses of Calhoun, Pickens and Jefferson Davis counties. No detail was too insignificant - who gets offices with a view of the Capitol, which new members are assigned to the choice committees and what is expected of them; which offices get an annual coat of paint or leather arm chairs and settees. With great certitude, they believed the public would turn back to the newspapers once the cameras focused on the arcane procedures and calculated monotony by which they conducted the country's business.

The Speaker kept television crews on a very tight leash. At the request of his friends in the press, Zach Harris made the first breach in the old Texan's stubborn resistance. No amount of rational argument or ego stroking could have brought Ham Clayburg around to even a minimal accommodation. It was horse trading pure and simple. The Speaker agreed grudgingly to go along with very limited coverage of a few important committees. In return, the Pennsylvanian would have to chair and wind down Subversive Activities.

Harris protested. At a time when seniority's supposed to bring comfort, such an assignment would send him bobbing toward a treacherous shoreline; one which glowered out of the sea mists like the Cliffs of Moher. The Speaker would loosen the reins on television only if Harris brought the Subversive Activities hearings to a close quietly and uneventfully. No other member, the Speaker told him, had the parliamentary skills, mastery of procedure and knowledge of the chemistry which binds more than 400 egos together. If that Committee comes unstuck in a replay of the past, the Speaker advised him, this place will be a god-damned livestock auction with every goat, heifer and sow kicking, pushing and gouging to get attention.

"You've got to wind this thing down, Zach. We've got to get this communist stuff behind us and get on with things. Nelson and his man Sterling are a two-man lynch party. I need someone who'll run them off the range. You're the only one I can trust to steer the wagon around the boulders out there. By God, Zach, do this for me, and I'll see ya get want ya want."

With the Speaker's assignment now complete, Zachary Taylor Harris relaxed and invited his friends in the press to exercise their powers of second guessing him.

"Did I understand you to say the hearings are finished? No more *Sturm und Drang*?" asked Art Blake, the AP's veteran House correspondent. He had one leg over the arm of the big leather chair. He sipped a bourbon and water, and put the glass on the floor next to his chair. Other reporters sat on the edges of tables and sprawled over the room's government-issue furniture. There were about eleven altogether.

Congressman Harris stretched both legs across his roll-top desk. His glasses were shoved up on his forehead. He tipped back in his chair and waved his glass at the assembly. He regarded his drinking companions with narrowed eyes, the way he did witnesses.

"That's right, Blake. No more hearings. The histrionics are over. I had a patriotic duty to end this business. Congress has enough on its plate to keep busy for the next two years. We need to get serious about organized crime, and we need to begin thinking about some movement on civil rights. The natives are getting restless."

Laughter.

"What *about* organized crime, Congressman? I've heard rumblings from Government Ops that they don't want anyone on their turf. I've been told they've asked Flynn to kick up legislative appropriations so they can beat your criminal law subcommittee to the TV cameras. They want the limelight and their own spot in the news hole."

"I'll gladly defer to Chairman Flynn. But, as you fellas know, don't try to second guess the Barrymore of Wilkes-Barre. We go back a long way.

# INQUISITION

And I'd be damned careful about writing a story about budget projections for the next session. Criminal Law is the natural place to begin taking a look at what I believe is the real menace facing the country, not this weary retread of the Red Scare."

"Suppose Nelson finds commies in academia? He really went after your professor today. Will you reopen SUBACK if he does? What about funding the committee?"

"I'll think about it. Now, you know better than to ask about funding. Next thing you fellas'll want to know is who we're subpoenaing. My crystal ball is good, but it doesn't have night vision. I'm just delighted these hearings are over. I took on this assignment on one condition - produce legislation or fold up the tent. Hammurabi himself could not make enough sense of that hodgepodge of testimony to write a law. Did you hear Nelson today? Jesus, he'd make Brer Rabbit sound like Torquemada. I'll be damned if I'm going to bail out the Republicans. It's their witches brew. Let them partake of it. Look at Pardee, for Cripes sake. If the horse's ass hadn't used the U.S. mails to collect kickbacks, he'd still be chairman of the committee, the GOP would hold the majority and Joe Martin, one of the finest men I've known, would be the Speaker. He wouldn't let them try to bludgeon us with this phony Red issue to keep control of the House. Poor 'ole Pardee'll be hammering license plates in Danbury for the next ten years.

"Look, I thoroughly enjoy chairing immigration. We made a real contribution. The Act is one of the few things we've passed since the war that makes sense for the country. It's meant more jobs, and it's already putting a brake on expenditures for everything from schools to welfare checks."

"Congressman?"

"Yes, Beech? What's new in the collective consciousness of the *New York Times*?"

"Can I get you on the record? You were one of SUBACK's biggest detractors when the Republicans had the majority. I believe you made a floor speech about 'trampling free speech with Gestapo boots' during the *Amerasia* hearings. Are we to interpret today's adjournment as a signal that the Committee has closed the book on this sordid chapter of history?"

"Oh, I wouldn't go that far. Let's just say the book is not salable as fact, but may have some value as fiction."

"Aren't you likely to get the right wingers - the American Legion, say - into a lather over what they are sure to say was your cavalier treatment of Mr. Nelson? He has a point, you know. And if the right storms back,

# Jack Eddinger

how are you going to keep the liberals happy? Seems to me you've got a delicate balancing act to perform, Congressman."

"You know my rules, Beech. Nothing for the record. Now, even if I were on the record, I'd have trouble responding. I don't entertain questions framed in the structure of a dilemma. Rhetorical snares aside, let me just say this: I've been in Congress for 25 years, and was a Justice Department attorney before that. I've studied this Red business for longer than I care to remember. Hell, I had a first hand peek at the alien lists thirty-five years ago. I think I know what I'm doing. As I see it, we can bring some sensible thinking to this issue. That's what's been lacking. I'm not for one minute writing off the security of the United States. But I've got to have facts, dammit, not wisps of smoke. The House isn't run by a bunch of left-right hand signals. You fellas put too much credence in ideology and liberal versus conservative political theory. Hell, this isn't the House of Lords. The only left and right we've got in the House is in the washrooms. The hot's on the left, the cold's on the right. It all comes out of the same spigot and the chairmen run the water. As most of you know, I'm certainly not a dues paying member of the ADA. As the professor noted, they opposed me every step of the way on *Harris-MacNaughton* until I rounded up the votes to override the veto. Since then it's been all sweetness and light. Their supporters proved more interested in jobs and money back home than in ideology. As for your conservatives, Beech, I've known most of them since they came here. They're small businessmen from the outback who can't tell a Communist from a Congregationalist. A lot of them think you fellas are commies. I work both sides of the aisle. The reactionaries want someone who'll listen to them; someone who'll hold their paws and rub their fur. The hot-heads like Nelson want the same thing. Most of the time you can reach them by rational argument. If not by reason, then by greed. Take New York State, Beech. Ever think of how many aircraft engines the G.E. plant turns out in Schenectady? Brooklyn may be the cradle of leftist theory, but there are 25,000 jobs up there at the Navy Yard. A few unkind moves by the old segregationist who runs Armed Services would panic the New York delegation. They'll bring their most overheated hothead into line. Except if one of them is a loose cannon like Nelson. To him it's all ego. The shifty-eyed sonofabitch's got his eye on something else. I'm not sure what, but give him a forum and he'll give you a performance worthy of Macbeth.

"When I took on this thankless assignment, I told the Speaker I'd be unsparing in my investigation of real subversives like the two British pansies who gave Stalin the A-bomb, or traitors like Fuchs and the Rosenbergs who wouldn't have been in this country if we had *Harris-MacNaughton*

## INQUISITION

a decade or two sooner. But I've seen nothing to convince me that we need another spectacle. The public's had enough from that lunatic over in the Senate. They're fed up with steely-eyed, smart-ass Harvard lawyers tangling with their brethren from NYU. The country's seen enough exhibitionism. I function in the real world, Beech. Politics levels all. I'd say the chances of reopening these hearings are remote. But I don't underestimate the bloodhound passions of people like Raymond Nelson."

"Congressman," Blake of the AP stopped him. "My sources also tell me you specifically asked the legislative appropriations subcommittee to test the idea of holding televised hearings outside Washington. What do you have in mind?"

"Blake, I'd be damned certain of my facts before you put anything like that in a story. You know the Speaker is simply adamant about widening the sphere of influence opened by the TV cameras, and I don't blame him. You can't legislate effectively in front of a bank of cameras and klieg lights. Yet, someday we're going to have to confront all kinds of new public information issues, and televised hearings outside of Washington are on the list. I asked Flynn for a study with an authorization attached. An appropriation is a long way off, but I think we ought to be prepared. Don't you?"

"Can I quote you?"

"Nope. But I'll let you know when you can. Just report that it's under consideration."

"Congressman, Bill Jones, State News Service. On another subject. My desk wants to get your response to two questions ..."

"What's that, Jones?"

"What are your thoughts about State Senator Marcel's campaign for your congressional seat? He says Bessemer Steel's backing him all the way, and will give him everything he needs to win. And, two, what can you tell me about some kind of investigation that's underway in the district? I've heard rumors that the DA's trucked off a ton of files from the Hampton County office building. Everybody in office up there's jittery."

"Jones, you're new here. Where's Charlie Miller?"

"My desk moved me up from the Statehouse beat. Charlie's been up at Harvard taking a public policy course. He's back next month. I'm assigned to the delegation till then."

"Charlie Miller at Harvard? That's like Frank Leahy at Southern Methodist."

"You may recall I covered one of your campaign speeches two years ago and interviewed you afterward. It was at the USW clambake in Bessemer City."

# Jack Eddinger

"Hell, I can't remember every reporter who's interviewed me, Jones. Steelworkers, eh? That's the one where everybody's oiled by the time the speeches begin. I'm glad you remember, Jones, because I sure as hell don't."

Jones wrote rapidly on folded copy paper. He did not look up.

"Put your notes away, Jones. Anything that's said here stays here. Before I respond to your desk's questions, let me tell you a story my colleague from Maryland, Tommy D'Alonzo, likes to tell. Seems a smart young *Sun* reporter came into his office one day when he was mayor of Baltimore. Now, this young fella tells Tommy: 'Mr. Mayor, my desk told me to ask you why you are putting an advertising tax on the newspapers.' Well, Tommy was never one to beat around the bush, so he comes out from behind his desk and tells the young fella: 'Kid, I got a desk, too. It's a beauty ain't it? Good place to put your feet up on and relax at the end of the day. I want you to go back and tell your desk I gave your question a lot of thought. Tell 'em I talked to the Solicitor and the City Council. Tell 'em I even consulted *my* desk and listened for an answer. After long deliberation, tell 'em, my desk told me to tell your desk to kiss my ass."

Raucous laughter.

"Now, let me take your desk's questions one at a time. The senator is a good Republican who does what he's told. His party, I must admit, is certainly imaginative. Over the years they've thrown corporate executives, silk-stocking lawyers, used car dealers and county clerks at me. Now, they've come up with a state senator of wide repute. Do you know what Marcel does for a living, Jones? Calls himself a business man, Why, he's a god-damned hair-dresser! Looks like they're going for the female vote this time. Tell your desk I'm running scared, Jones; running like hell. That I will fight him in the wash basins and under the drying machines. I will take my campaign into his perfumed salons and defeat him among the finger waves, the bouffants and the permanents."

More laughter.

"Mr. Eugene Garrett Palmer of Bessemer Steel Corporation, however, is quite another matter. He's never forgotten the Navy hearings. We went after him on the defective armor plate he stuck the fleet with. Caused him a lot of grief. And he never has gotten over the '34 campaign when FDR came into the Lenape Valley. It was the year of the 75-day steel strike. I worked the picket lines outside Bess Steel's gates. The President told the steelworkers that he'd personally see to it that Palmer would never again earn a million dollar paycheck with the country in the middle of a Depression. It was a bitter strike. The workers pushed cars into the Lenape River. Palmer got his friends in Harrisburg to okay the use of force. They

# INQUISITION

had the State constabulary on horseback swinging truncheons and running down picketers. It was mean. Roosevelt brought the entire Pennsylvania House delegation with him. It gave me a big victory. John L. Lewis sent me a letter. I still have it. He quoted Moses, Shakespeare and Eugene Debs. Palmer's never forgiven me for disturbing his serenity up there on Mt. Sinai. Thinks he's the Republican Party's burning bush. Wants to repeal the progressive legislation we passed since 1933. Tell your desk I take any threat seriously, especially one coming from the top floor of *Iron Mountain*. Now, on your second question. Yes, I've heard the same rumors. They were serious enough to warrant my own inquiry. Here's what I can tell you, and this is not for attribution, strictly background. I had two of my subcommittee investigators check every Federal inquiry under way in Eastern Pennsylvania. They expect a break anytime on the organized crime front. The Attorney General tells me it's confined to Philadelphia and the Scranton-Wilkes Barre areas. Hell, that's nothing new. They've been at each other's throats since Prohibition. Turf wars again. We picked up some intelligence on the District Attorney of Hampton County. His eye's on the U.S. Senate. Seems that an investigation of police corruption he launched last summer led nowhere. Now, to advance his aspirations, he's going after what he calls political intrigue in the county court house. Hah! That Byzantine place'll occupy him for a while. That's all I know."

A knock on the door ended Zachary Taylor Harris' monologue.

"Well, it's my old sidekick, the majority leader. What's on your mind, Mr. Leader?"

"Sorry, to interrupt gentlemen, but I need someone to turn around a few votes if we're going to have a trade bill. You're tying up my main weapon fellas. Let's go, Zach."

"See you boys at the press club tonight," Harris said as he ushered them out.

# CHAPTER THREE
## *Quid Pro Quo*

Overnight, Washington's predictably warm early autumn turned unpredictably crisp. Pavement vents poured white clouds of steam into the October morning. Overcoats and hats sprouted along Connecticut Avenue. Furs were about to make their appearance at Embassy Row receptions. Late in the afternoon Zachary Taylor Harris waited to be announced on the third floor of the granite fortress of Justice at Ninth and Pennsylvania. He was clearly irked. He twirled his grey fedora and waited. At precisely four-twenty-five, a woman in a turquoise cardigan sweater ensemble and flared, ankle-length woolen skirt greeted him. She had a pleasantly pink face. Blue tint highlighted her neatly coiffed grey hair.

"Congressman Harris? Will you come with me please?" She led him through a set of heavy plate glass doors. The Bureau seal on both sides reminded him of decals on the bottoms of the cheap ashtrays sold in the House stationary store. She escorted him to a windowless office. A man in shirtsleeves bent over paperwork. He wore a cop's holster strapped to his torso like mountain climber's suspenders. Except for his friendly blue eyes and starched white shirt with French cuffs secured with Bureau cufflinks, he might have been a hired gun packing a Smith & Wesson snubnose police special.

"Hello Congressman Harris," he virtually sang in a jovial brogue filtered through South Boston. "It's a pleasure to see you, sir. I'm special agent Donegan." He held out a hand in greeting. Donegan showed the deference a junior officer has for command. Zach Harris gave him his best campaign greeting: direct, warm, and a firm handshake with just the right amount of masculine pressure.

"I'll take over, Miss Royston."

Zach Harris watched the sway of her hips disappear down the long corridor.

"Right this way, Congressman." Donegan led Harris to a small anteroom before a set of oak doors with highly polished brass knobs. The Bureau seal was set at eye level in inlaid walnut.

"Crazy weather out there. Get out to the Redskins game yesterday? That new quarterback from Notre Dame's got a great arm. Nothing like Sammy Baugh though."

"No, I rarely get out there any more if I can avoid it. Opening day's about it for me. Get splinters in my butt every time I sit down. You need an

# INQUISITION

iron arse for that place, Donegan. They ought to tear it down and replace it with a junk yard."

The agent smiled. "Aww, c'mon, Congressman, you don't really mean that. Griffith's one of the great places in the country to watch a ballgame. Well, I'll leave you to your thoughts about our old ballpark, Congressman. Director'll be with you shortly." By Donegan's pronunciation the word was "shotly."

"He's been on the phone for the past hour. Here's this week's *U.S. News*. You ever read David Lawrence, Congressman? Required around here." Donegan winked.

"No, I'll just wait. What's keeping him? John Dillinger back in circulation?"

"Big shakeup. He's cleared out one of the field offices. Two guys axed outright. He put another on the bicycle - Boise, Galveston, Richmond, Fresno. The poor guy's wife's threatening to leave. God, don't tell him I told you that. He'll have me peddlin, too. Nice meeting you, Congressman. Hope to see you again, sir."

The agent left through the long hallway. Looking down the paneled corridor reminded Zach Harris of squinting through the opposite end of a telescope. Agents, secretaries and clerks moved in and out of offices. The hallway gave the illusion of stretching to infinity.

*Damn! I wonder if he's got the Paraclete caged up somewhere in this eyrie.*

Behind the closed doors, a clock chimed softly. On the final strike, the door swung open. A short, sun-tanned and powerfully built man in his early sixties with the swagger of a Latin American dictator appeared, smiling. He approached Zach Harris with regal, almost papal, bearing.

"Good to see you, Congressman. My God, it's been a while." The Director embellished his cordiality with the jauntiness of a ward politician at a Knights of Columbus breakfast. He extended his right hand, as if offering the ring of St. Peter.

Harris ignored the gesture.

"Last time was a year ago in executive session on your supplemental."

"That's right. I'd almost forgotten. You're a member of Mr. Flynn's committee, aren't you? Won't you come in?"

They entered the oak paneled room. It looked like a miniature version of the Explorers Club lounge. An immense spotted blue marlin with shiny green gills and a pink mouth hung in an alcove behind the Director's desk. The desk itself stood on a platform six inches higher than the floor. Flynn'd raised holy hell when he found out what it cost the government

## Jack Eddinger

to remodel and furnish the Director's office, let alone the taxidermist bill. The theatrical Irishman shredded the GSA people for circumventing regulations. A Wall Street patron of the Director quietly paid the $75,000 bill after Flynn waved it at an assistant director during a closed hearing on a special funding request by the Bureau for 1955. He threatened to give it to the newspapers if it wasn't paid immediately. For his performance, Flynn earned five asterisks, like a *Guide Michelin* grande luxe restaurant in the Director's special file. Until then, no one had earned more than three. Black and white framed photos covered the walls. They were signed by generals, admirals, viscounts, business executives, athletes, cinema stars and a few faces in yellowing photos in old black-rimmed frames. Harris recognized officials of the Harding and Coolidge administration. A dark and brooding oil on canvas, as if by Velasquez, of Harlan Fiske Stone in full Supreme Court regalia occupied an entire wall, befitting the shrine of a Christian saint. It was Attorney General Stone who draped the mantle of state security chief over the Director. The Roosevelt-Truman years were sparsely represented. Standing on a pedestal near a tall casement window, a bust of the Director in white marble scowled up Pennsylvania Avenue to the graceful hill a mile away. The chairman of a distilling company commissioned the bust and underwrote its cost in celebration of the Director's twenty-fifth year at the helm. It was identical to the translucent busts of American vice presidents and statesmen set in the walls of the ornate reception room and halls outside the U.S. Senate chamber in the Capitol.

"Cigar, Congressman? The Prime Minister's favorites. Scotland Yard ships them from Havana every Christmas along with several bottles of choice spirits. You might say it amounts to partial re-payment of Lend Lease. Never touch the hard stuff myself. Usually pass it along to the Cabinet. They go in for that sort of thing. It gets their attention, and costs me nothing. Pays dividends when I need one of them to stimulate some of your parsimonious colleagues at budget time."

The Director clipped off the end of the big brown corona, rolled it around his lips, lit it and blew a small firestorm at his visitor. The smoke momentarily clouded Zach Harris' line of sight. It curled around the mastiff face, giving the Director more than his usual aura of calculated toughness. His hair was sleek and black with a touch of gray at the temples. He wore a 35-year federal service pin in the lapel of his dark blue suit, and a small American flag in the other. The gold and black bars of his tie, the white shirt and the neatly pressed white handkerchief squared off at the top of the breast pocket gave him the look of a small town haberdasher. Everything reflected Presbyterian rectitude. That is everything except the

# INQUISITION

eyes. They disclosed not light but opacity. The hard red-eyed indifference of a rhinoceros. Pinpoints buried in folds of flesh. Something primordial lay behind the black inexpressive pupils.

"What keeps you in town, Congressman?" the Director drew on the long brown cigar and examined his fingernails. "I understand you're in quite a tough election up in Pennsylvania this year. Who's minding the store?"

As did no other man in the history of the republic, the Director occupied a place at the core of the national government which made him infinitely secure and immune to all influence. After more than a quarter century he had achieved hegemony. With it he deflected and occasionally blunted presidential power. Change, he told his new agents assembled in the Bureau auditorium before being dispatched to field offices throughout the country, is the fatal flaw of democracy. It must be managed and channeled to be effective. The public must be led and instructed at every turn. It is the mission of this organization to not only protect society from its enemies - subversives as well as the criminal element - but to set the example of moral leadership. Left uninstructed, voters will too often send buffoons, or worse, fools, to Washington. The twin temple at the top of the Mall too frequently produces nothing but compromise and mediocrity.

"I'll be completely frank with you," Harris replied with the irritation of a proud politician inconvenienced by a bureaucrat, "I'm not about to reopen these hearings with a very difficult election staring me in the face. Eisenhower's exceptionally popular in my District. That translates into turnout and votes for my opponent. I simply haven't the time. They'll have to wait until the new congress convenes in January."

"Congressman Harris, as I told you, sir, it would be the height of irresponsibility to put off this inquiry. It must go forward immediately, election or no election. I'll not compromise on this, sir."

"I've come down here to tell you why they cannot proceed. I wish to hell the only factor was a tough election. That, I can handle. What I cannot allow to go unanswered are unfounded accusations. It's a damned shame. A man can come to Washington, work hard for a quarter century, assume the chairmanship of major committees and bring prosperity to his District, only to be confronted by an opportunist with an agenda containing every tenet of left wing radicalism. I needn't remind you that power concentrated in the hands of an inexperienced and opportunistic prosecutor is the most pernicious of all threats. It used to be that our leaders advanced up the ladder of public service, balancing personal ambition against the party's objectives. But now, sad to say, that democratic process has given way to egomania. The ambitious prosecutor in my congressional district is an unrepentant liberal, who has refused to accept the decision of the ballot box."

"Sounds like your standard, garden variety politician to me, Congressman."

"He's standard all right. Standard calumnist and slanderer. I'm depending on your sense of priorities. Do you want me or some ADA professor of social theory setting the Judiciary Committee's agenda after January 5? Do you want to deal with Daniel P. Flynn on substantive issues, not to mention your budget in the 83rd Congress? He's just behind me in seniority and will take over if I don't return."

"But, Mr. Harris why is your congressional career in jeopardy simply because some political acolyte decided on a kamikaze run? After all, and correct me if I am wrong, his opponent was a popular two-term governor. I don't see the connection or follow your logic."

"Logic hell. Politics. Political sophistication is not an unknown commodity to the mind of the one man in America who's probed, mastered and laid bare the psychopathology of criminal behavior better than anyone in law enforcement. Or am I wrong about that?"

"Please continue." The Director's imperious demeanor shifted. Zach Harris perceived it at once.

"Let me lay it out as simply as I can. Without a daily output of pseudo-news this fellow remains completely obscure. He has no statewide or precinct organization, and but for a few contributors of the Hebrew faith, has no campaign treasury. In short, he is a creature of publicity. He must rely on it constantly. But the more he uses the press, the more he becomes shackled to it. He must continue leaking investigative information. Stuff that looks good to reporters who have only part of the picture. You know as well as I that a prosecutor commands the information situation in a given investigative scenario. Not even a grand jury enjoys that kind of power. The selective use of investigative information represents the ultimate abuse of power. I'm here to tell you that this ambitious individual finds raw, undigested material an irresistible tool for career advancement. I am particularly interested in a vicious story that's circulating - this is what I've been told - that your field office in Newark has begun some sort of investigation which reaches into my congressional district. If this is true, and as chairman of the operative committee of Congress, I demand a briefing."

A tiny light flickered in the pupil of the reptilian eyes then went out.

"Why that's absurd, Congressman. No it's downright contumely. It displays a complete ignorance of the Bureau's operating procedures."

# INQUISITION

"That's exactly what I'm telling you," Harris answered. "The man's a loose cannon."

"First, let me say this to you, Congressman Harris: no one has earned the country's gratitude more than you have, sir. I regard the *Harris-MacNaughton Act* as one of the most critically important tools law enforcement has been given in a very long time. The provision removing the courts from alien deportation proceedings and placing them under the Immigration Service, with whom we work closely, was a stroke of genius. Harris-MacNaughton is one of the supreme deterrents to alien ideologies."

The Director's reference to the country's principal immigration law by its correct title was not lost on Harris.

"You know, I appreciate that. I don't get much recognition. Only abuse. *Harris-MacNaughton* is an effective public policy achievement. It is designed to block foreign influence, which leads to foreign entanglements, which lead to foreign wars - principles as old as George Washington. The liberal editorialists have been relentless in trying to discredit it. They have their claque in Congress, Republicans as well as Democrats. It's the same thankless crowd who begged me to arrest the chaos in our immigration policies. And their fellow travelers in academic circles and foundations stand ready to do their bidding. We ought to strip them of their non-profit status. They seem to forget that this law saved many DPs in Europe. They forget my record in Congress was New Deal. I put the finest legal minds in the country to work drafting that bill. It's the best and most orderly law in a long, sad history of immigration compromise that has seen our country mongrelized by radical social theory."

"Congressman Harris, I could not agree with you more completely. I've always believed that a small coterie of radicals stands at the center of this conspiracy. They and the leftover Wallaceites are poisoning this country's political dialogue with their behaviorist theories. They're stirring up the Negroes. And that collection of classroom socialists on the Supreme Court is pushing for more and more liberalization. Soon we will have the coloreds in public office and we'll be a step away from turning this country into a nation of mulattos. They're already eating at our restaurants here in the District. I'd never thought I'd see that day. Your assessment is prescient, Mr. Harris."

The Director's fist tightened. Big purple veins showed through the taut translucent skin. He slammed his desk, knocking papers to the floor. "Now this business of investigations, Congressman. When we move, we move by invitation of local authorities. We've had none. Who is supplying this false information?"

# Jack Eddinger

"Let's just say I've got excellent sources both inside and outside government and leave it at that."

The reptilian eyes regarded Zachary Taylor Harris coldly. The Director bent over, whisked up the papers and delivered them to his in-box in a sweeping motion.

"If the Bureau is to cooperate, I must have full disclosure of any and all information you possess about press leaks of investigative material. Slandering a member of Congress is a felony violation of Federal statutes. It warrants investigation. I'm prepared to staff this up immediately."

"I'd go slow on that. This fellow is smart enough to keep it at the level of innuendo rather than outright slander."

"What makes you think any of this has come to my attention?"

"As a man who relies on receiving and evaluating information, you will understand that I cannot give you anything piecemeal. As to Bureau involvement, my subcommittee investigators have told me as much."

"It is true, I have authorized our field offices to share on a very limited basis certain types of investigative information with local authorities. Professional courtesy, you might say. However, my standing order clearly mandates that only the chief law enforcement official of a local governmental unit may view files on an 'eyes only' basis. If what you say about leaks in your District is correct, I will immediately inform the field office in that jurisdiction to break off any and all contact."

"I can only advise you to judge for yourself. Daley's in the news with new allegations several times a week. They certainly cannot be backed by evidence generated by his own efforts. No, these charges have to be from raw investigative files developed by a sophisticated law enforcement organization. If this were only a political maneuver, I wouldn't be here. I'd handle it politically. But this goes far beyond politics. We're looking at an array of sinister factors. First, we have rumor and innuendo running rampant. No indictments or charges, mind you. Only unsubstantiated allegations. Second, we see history running away from democratic principles toward worldwide socialism. Third, we have naked political ambition. Finally, we have the cynical manipulation of investigative resources."

"I must say, Congressman Harris, you are a perceptive and articulate man. Up to now I doubted the strength of your commitment to ferret out subversives. Your grasp of this incipient conspiracy surpasses any analysis I have heard or seen from your colleagues. With the exception of Mr. Nelson, they are lukewarm schoolboys in the end game being played out in back alleys and barrios from East Berlin to Guatemala City. The pattern is unmistakable. Insinuate rationalist-behaviorist social theory into our laws and institutions. Get the support of the intellectuals and so-called opinion

# INQUISITION

makers. Set race against race, generation against generation, class against class, the rabble against established authority. And like your professor, discredit the legitimate concerns of government about subversion. Now, I can assure you of one thing. There is no manipulation of Federal investigative resources, period. You have spoken eloquently of this threat, congressman. Let me tell you what needs to be done." The Director puffed vehemently on the burnt out cigar stub. "We must go on the offensive. We need a revived campaign to dig out the roots of this tree of subversion."

Like a climber who has been blown off the pinnacle only to return again and again, Zach Harris felt the winds shift. He moved instantly.

"If you agree to a postponement. I will agree to hearings immediately after the new Congress convenes in January. I will widen their scope: labor unions, research laboratories, academe, wherever the scent of *Evening in Moscow* takes us. Furthermore, I will expand the very limited television coverage we have given this subject to date, and will see to it that we have gavel to gavel coverage. We will open in Philadelphia with our professor. Only this time, I'll have Mr. Sterling conduct the interrogation."

"But, Congressman, you know very well that House rules prohibit televised hearings off the Hill. I made the very same recommendation to the Speaker a few years ago. He turned thumbs down. He's adamant about it."

"As a committee chairman, I have the right - hell, the duty - to conduct hearings wherever the evidence takes us. If it means outside Washington, that's where we'll go. The Speaker's writ does not extend beyond the Potomac. I will be chairman of the Committee on Committees come January. That means I will have the support of the chairmen and all senior members. The Speaker is a reasonable man; he can count votes. Hell, he still lives in the 19th Century, but I assure you he'll see it our way on television. I will conduct hearings in every city associated with the radical movement - Philadelphia, New York, Detroit, Chicago, Milwaukee, San Francisco. They will be conducted in federal court rooms in each city to give them the impact of criminal proceedings."

The Director's facial firmament glowed as if lit by two red dwarf stars.

"This project will require a major investment of resources," he said. "We must go to the roots; to the theoreticians, and to their life's blood in the tax-exempt foundations. You will need a full array of investigative resources - records, data, manpower, archival sources, contacts with foreign intelligence and law enforcement services, counterintelligence. I can put these at your disposal, congressman."

# Jack Eddinger

The Director's sudden cordiality brought Zachary Taylor Harris up short with not a little twinge of chagrin. If his peers ever learned of this compact, he'd be drummed out of the club.

"I wouldn't want you to cancel your examination or holiday on my account," he countered. "I need your help, of course, but my office will organize the hearings."

"Oh, I'm not so concerned about my ticker that the EKG cannot wait till spring, and Southern California isn't going anywhere - unless they have another earthquake. Had I any idea you would make such a consequential proposal this meeting would have been entirely unnecessary. My resources are at your disposal."

"Now that's decisive. What can I do for you on the Hill?"

"That's kind of you, congressman, but in view of your proposal, what can I do for you, sir?".

"Frankly, I'd like you to give me a fix on what, if anything, is under investigation in my congressional district."

"From my vantage point, Congressman, we have a great deal of unsubstantiated allegations, as you so perceptively noted. You are fully aware through your subcommittee, I believe, that we have had a long interest in racketeering activities that have moved across the Hudson into New Jersey. I would be remiss if I did not tell you there has been spillover into Eastern Pennsylvania. The area is too lucrative to keep them out. However, there is nothing in our investigations, which as far as I am able to discern, involves prominent figures. Perhaps a few persons with whom you might have had innocent contact. Not so for one of your former colleagues, I am sorry to say. Perhaps he's felt the cold blast of conscience, and has stirred up the congressional rumor mill. You know how that works. Someone hears something and before you know it they have created a fiction worthy of Erle Stanley Gardner. Should anything develop that I think you may find interesting, you'll hear it from me directly. Should problems arise - of any kind - I'll see that the Bureau does what it can."

"Well hell. I'd like more of a commitment than that. My credibility's on the line. Perceptions get more attention than facts in this town. Even the most innocent reference can turn into a public hanging."

"Well now, I think we can reach a mutually satisfactory understanding."

"No, sir! Zach Harris shot back, "Mutual satisfaction leaves too many loose ends. If Flynn gets wind of a Federal investigation anywhere in Pennsylvania, he'll upstage you with his own Government Ops inquiry and he'll hang you up with demands for everything including your agents' meal and room checks. You and I may think he's a fool with those capes and scarves and his waxed mustache, but don't underestimate him. He runs his committees and the state delegation like the College of Cardinals, and he's the Pope."

"Very well then." The Director's voice became imperious, intense and menacing. "I want two very specific legislative items from your subcommittee; items I have had great difficulty convincing your colleagues the country needs."

"Item One: pre-clearance of every appointment to the Federal bench. Not just background checks. I want judges sympathetic to a strict interpretation of constitutional rights; men who are not afraid to limit individual liberties for the greater good; experienced jurists who are not out to rewrite American history and the criminal code. I want men who will stand up, who harbor no bleeding heart anguish in applying the death penalty. I want defendants dealt with the way I handled the Rosenbergs. No leniency.

"Item Two: I want legislation declaring interstate travel for the purposes of ideological conspiracy a federal offense. To support it, I want a sound wire-tapping law with no loopholes, a law that will not undercut our work in gathering electronic evidence. And I want freedom for my people to operate; to go into homes and offices clandestinely, if necessary, to gather substantive evidence from which to prosecute subversives, including psychiatric and medical records. These are within your committee's purview. You can accomplish this."

Zachary Taylor Harris listened carefully. He thought of old Mort Brodfield's admonition. But it was too late. The wild look and the glistening upper lip were fixed in his memory. Neither, however, were there. In their place was an exceptional aura of intimidation which put the lie to the Director's congressional cloakroom reputation as a staff-driven lightweight. Zach Harris felt an iron grip on his throat. He wondered how he could possibly manipulate the full Judiciary Committee let alone its counterpart in the Senate to invest in the Director's agenda. It was the same approach the Speaker took when he asked him to chair Subversive Activities. He was extremely skeptical. Everything the committee'd done in its various permutations contributed nothing to the law of the land. The monkeys hadn't proposed a single amendment, let alone a complete bill. He tried to bring reason and rational procedure to its work, but that failed. Then the liberals began squeezing harder and harder to torpedo *Harris-MacNaughton*. What the hell do they know about the sweat that went into getting that bill enacted and overriding the veto? They're not going to undo the work of a lifetime.

# Jack Eddinger

"With these tools, Congressman, we will have a set of surgical instruments to excise this cancer from the body politic."

Zachary Taylor Harris barely heard the Director's words. "Uh. Well, you drive a hard bargain, but these things are good for the country and I'll stand behind them. Our campaign begins in Philadelphia the day after the Mummer's Parade."

"Excellent choice." The Director's adrenaline was pumping hard now. His cordiality reappeared.

"Did you know, Mr. Harris, that the last Congress of the First International was held there in 1876?"

"Where? Independence Hall? Sounds like the cradle of liberty's the cradle of Communism, if you ask me."

"I will instruct all relevant field offices to begin preparations immediately. A telex will go out tonight. Meanwhile, I'll have the Attorney General void the present subpoenas and issue new ones."

"Good. I'm flying out of here in the morning. Is there anything else?"

"No, I believe this understanding covers everything. Inasmuch as I sincerely admire you, Congressman, I see no need to commit anything to paper. Too bad. The historians miss all the real background to government decision-making, don't they? But that's the nature of this business in this day and age. I like your idea about television. Never thought about your off-campus approach, so to speak. Original. Excellent idea. It will establish a whole new dimension, a different kind of public record. Perhaps I shall be one of your witnesses."

The Director pressed the Congressman's hand in a cold, reptilian clasp. Zach Harris felt as if he were grasping a rattlesnake.

"It's always a pleasure to have you down here, Congressman Harris. I look forward to working with you. Feel free to call me anytime day or night. Good day to you, sir." The clock quietly struck the hour. It was 6 p.m. Zach Harris nodded and pulled on his raincoat.

*You, sir, are an evil bastard.*

Congressman Harris nodded and smiled faintly as he passed the front desk receptionist. Washington's fickle autumn weather had shifted back to a standstill summer. The warm air was to hang over the capital for days. In spite of the change, Zach Harris shivered beneath his raincoat.

The Director sat at his desk in silence. The tall case clock ticked softly. He lifted the Dictaphone and began speaking in a low monotone. Then he removed the belt, unlocked the armor-plated industrial safe and rolled out a file drawer. He carefully flipped through celluloid tabs until he came to the one he wanted.

# INQUISITION

It was marked: HARRIS, Z.T., U.S. House of Representatives, 26th D., Penna., 1933 - as if on a graveyard headstone.

# CHAPTER FOUR
## *View From The Hill*

It was after seven when Harris returned to his office on the third floor of the Longworth Building. The staff had already left for the day. He reached into the cabinet behind his desk, took out a bottle of Haig & Haig and poured a double shot into a glass. He downed it quickly, and tried to think clearly about his meeting with the Director.

His office took up an entire corner of the stately white marble building and looked out across Independence Avenue to the Capitol. The floor to ceiling casement windows opened on a small balcony. His seniority and legislative and parliamentary skills had earned him a key position in the hierarchy of the House of Representatives, and an office to go with it. It combined 19th Century tycoon extravagance with the clean Graeco-Roman lines the founders preferred to embody the ideal of a republic of virtue. Lower-ranking members envied his view of the great Bernini dome of the Capitol and of the Palladian elegance of the House Wing with its clean lines and fenestration. His was the Capitoline view of official Washington; the Washington of postcards, photographs and movie sets.

When Congressman Harris sat in the big leather swivel chair behind his mahogany desk flanked by the flags of the United States and the Commonwealth of Pennsylvania, visitors were presented with the stuff of myth. He arranged it that way. He loved the unspoken authority conveyed by soft lights, thick carpet emblazoned with the Great Seal of the United States, old leather, and the exceptional back-lighted view of official Washington presented to anyone seated before him. The walls contained black-framed photographs of House and Senate members. One photo stood out from the others. A smiling FDR sat in the front seat of a 1939 Lincoln convertible, cigarette holder pitched at a jaunty angle, *pince nez* in place, a gray fedora with a sharp crease down the center sitting on the great leonine head. It was signed, "To My Good Friend, Zachary Taylor Harris - FDR." Wood carvings and miniature sculptures presented to him by admirers and foreign dignitaries were scattered about on tables. A marble fireplace, its coal box filled with shards of Pennsylvania anthracite, dominated one side of the room.

In his fifty-eighth year of life and twenty-third year in Congress, Zach Harris stood in the waning light reflecting on the agreement he had committed himself to with the Director. He gazed across the wide avenue to the Capitol. Waxy green magnolia leaves broke up the long shafts of October sunlight. Washed out reds of dogwoods and maples riffled in the

# INQUISITION

breeze blowing off the Potomac. Russets, golds and yellows, the brilliance of Indian Summer, contrasted with the alabaster tomb-marble and spilled over balustrades and down steps splashing everything with color from the palette of an Impressionist's autumn. The green sweep of lawn extended to the elliptical reflecting pool flanked by the crystal pavilion of the Capitol Botanical Garden. High on a marble pediment with the capitol dome as backdrop, Ulysses S. Grant, garbed in weather-greened bronze and mounted on a powerful black stallion, rode grim visaged and implacable toward the killing fields of eternity.

Congressman Harris's mood was out of synch with the Indian summer scene beyond the window. The autumn twilight brought stirrings of concern and discontent. The trajectory of his twelfth campaign was as flat as the electrocardiogram of a corpse. No momentum, no inspiration, no push. It was going to be exhausting and expensive. To get the kind of victory he needed to blunt Palmer's money, Kressman's god-damned acquisitiveness, the potential dangers posed by Daley required a campaign unlike any he'd waged. It would be a war with no peace. It required concentrated effort and his own complete commitment. He could count on no one. Robert Bird, his chief aide, was competent but uninspired; the perfect Capitol Hill operative conversant with the intricacies of committee politics and legislative detail. As office manager, he made the trains run on time and kept ambitious young staffers at arm's length. Bird was a good hired hand, loyal to a fault. But he lacked guile and had only a surface understanding of the 26th District. That's the way Zach Harris preferred it. Don't open doors. Keep the staff occupied with constituent mail, casework, answering phones, running errands. Robert Bird believed, as do so many congressional staffers who never leave Washington, that election victories are directly proportional to the press coverage members of Congress receive both at home and in the nation's capital. A stack of news clippings from home, a front page story in *The Evening Star* or an editorial in *The New York Times*, he believed, produced more mileage than the endless meetings with job-seekers, court house politicians and political hacks like Lloyd Kressman.

Kressman made Bird's life particularly miserable with unending requests for favors. The congressman's aide had little appreciation for and less understanding of how Zachary Taylor Harris won elections, except what he could attribute to public relations and news coverage. In his view they were one and the same. For Zach Harris the election of 1956 held elemental importance, more perhaps than any since 1932. He had the Library of Congress research House records to determine the all time vote getter. A big victory with big numbers would mean that he, Zach Harris and not the

# Jack Eddinger

Democratic Party would carry Pennsylvania for Adlai Stevenson in 1956. But more importantly it would end Daley's flimsy investigations. While the gears and flywheels of the city machines in Philadelphia and Pittsburgh were being monkey wrenched by factional war; while Ike's distaste for patronage and his insistence on military discipline in appointments down to the state and local levels gave the professional politicians fits; while suburban and rural voters knocked each other out in a statewide vote split, Zach Harris's 26th District would pull the wagon home for Adlai.

The victory he had in mind, which would swing Pennsylvania's 34 electoral votes behind the Stevenson-Kefauver ticket would make him the state's prime mover. He'd approve U.S. Attorneys, postmasters, bridge and customs commissioners, U.S. Marshals. You name it. It could also be his ticket out of the House and on to better things - Secretary of the Navy perhaps, maybe serious consideration in 1960 or '64 for vice president when the professionals get into ticket balancing. He knew it was a long shot. But he liked long shots. Harry Truman was the longest shot of all, and look what happened. He'd be perfect with Lyndon Johnson or Estes Kefauver or Stuart Symington. A solid northerner, he would balance things nicely for any Southern presidential candidate. To win a reelection victory that would position him nationally from a House seat meant an unprecedented effort. It called for every tactic, every feint, every subtlety he'd employed in 25 years of hard campaigning.

He poured another scotch. The elixir warmed him. The tension receded. He slammed a fist into his open palm. Dammit, never send a pawn to do a knight's job. Parrying the Director's thrusts did him a world of good. He felt his back stiffen and the old stamina flowing into his legs. By god, you gotta have good legs to haul the political baggage-train. A mule may be a dumb animal, but it's the mules that win elections even though some of them turn out to be jackasses. Hell, its the party's symbol. Elephants are fat boys with big ears. They're nice, but don't count on 'em when the lions are loose. Getting into the thick of electoral combat held deep rewards and satisfactions. It was like mastering the battlefield. You know the enemy's out there somewhere behind the smoke and barbed wire. Go after him, challenge him, draw blood, get him to venture into no-man's land, then tear him apart with concentrated gun fire. His weapon was rhetoric; flint-hard, polished and honed by a savage wit to inflict a pitiless bite.

If Zachary Taylor Harris possessed one strong trait it was his insistent, implacable belief that he could out-perform anyone or anything thrown at him. That's what brought him to Congress and sustained him for nearly a quarter century. It could still carry him to the national prominence he craved. He not only sustained himself in this belief, but on something

# INQUISITION

deeper; something that always pumped vitality and animal power into his political cardiovascular system. It was his ability to move people; to get them to do what they did not want to do. He could move them in the face of almost any odds, like the way he got the Director to back off.

It wasn't the first time he'd heard rumors and backbiting. Hell, that came with the job. He knew how to handle it. Always did. Proved it again and again. His thoughts raced back to the kick off of his twelfth campaign. The day started at 4 a.m. in the darkness outside Bessemer Steel's plant gates as the shifts changed. By 8 a.m. he was chattering in Pennsylvania Dutch with farmers at the produce stalls of the South End Market. He was in high spirits in mid-morning delivering his announcement speech to the built-in crowd on the steps of the Hampton County Court House.

In a rare appearance his wife stood at his side smiling and waving. Marion Harris rarely accompanied her husband on his political safaris. She preferred privacy. It was different in the early days. But then so was her life. She still made appearances for causes she believed in - civil rights, equality for women, curbing world population growth, and for her consuming interest, the United Nations. Her husband's reelection assured her own re-appointment to UNESCO's board of overseers by the House Foreign Affairs Committee. At noon the congressman was basking in the accolades of the Board of County Commissioners after making grand rounds: Judges Chambers, the Register of Wills, Prothonotary, Recorder of Deeds, Tax Collector, Assessor, and Sheriff. He visited his old basement haunts from the days he served as county attorney. The only office he passed up was the prosecutor's. He jawboned with clerks, bailiffs and maintenance employees. Then it was a flyby at the Uptown Chamber of Commerce and back to the gates for the change of shifts at 3 P.M. The day ended with a traditional Zach Harris rally before a friendly labor union. This year it was District Eight, International Ladies Garment Workers.

The camera of Zach Harris's mind's eye zoomed in on a tight close-up of his face. He was at his best and everybody knew it. He stood loose and erect at the microphone, one hand in his coat pocket, the other slicing through a blue light shaft of tobacco smoke. He hammered away. First, unconscionable corporate profits, then big business, next the Republican Party's failure of economics: depression, despair and disillusion. Finally, his own special distillate: communist subversion. Scare hell out of 'em. Throw 'em language out of a secret intelligence report. Slam the do-gooders; the League of Women Voters, the ACLU and the county's misguided District Attorney for the naive belief that only they could interpret the public interest. End with raw meat; a broadside against

# Jack Eddinger

sellouts in Washington, throw in Mindzenty. Tell 'em Ike blew it in '45 by not going all the way to the Danube, as George Patton urged. That always brought Bessemer City's Poles, Czechs, Ukrainians, Hungarians and other Eastern European chauvinists to their feet. Hell, half of them never set foot in a Captive Nation, but that's all right they vote their guts. Never mind the irony that he wrote the law limiting the flow of uncles, aunts, cousins and grandparents to a mere trickle. If to his colleagues in Washington he was the patrician parliamentarian and reluctant chairman of the Subversive Activities Committee, in the ethnic wards of Bessemer City's South End he was the little guy's equivalent of the Grand Inquisitor. The Washington press corps was unaware of and could care less about his hometown image.

It was the Zach Harris of old, the Zach Harris people came out to see, to hear, to cheer; defender of the Democratic Faith; the little guy's hero; the Democrat of all Democrats; the man who brought jobs, flood control and prosperity to the Lenape Valley with Franklin Roosevelt and Harry Truman, and kept cheap foreign goods, cheap foreign labor and cheap foreign ideology out. The man who called Bessemer Steel's CEO, Eugene Garrett Palmer, a cut-throat to his face. The precinct captains had done their job. The ballroom teemed with campaign workers: door-knockers, telephone callers, drivers, poll watchers, anybody involved in getting out the "Harris Vote." Before going to the rostrum, he took his leaders aside, nicked them in the ribs with a friendly fist and told them, "Boys, this is the big one, the one that'll put Old Zach at the top of the Party. Bring this one in big, and I'll take care of each of you." He never looked or sounded better. Like summer lightning, flashes of the old oratorical fire sent his thoughts back to earlier campaigns when his entourage of staff, reporters and political workers followed him into grimy saloons and taprooms outside the black iron gates of Bessemer Steel Company's flagship plant, which sprawled for ten miles along the Lenape River. He'd buy drinks around, climb up on a barstool or balance himself on a table-top and begin his routine denunciations, starting with his opponent, whoever he might be, in the raw imagery the steelworkers reserved for the supervisors and foremen in the mills and foundries of Bess Steel.

The night of his mind's eye was special. Every inch of the South End Hungarian-American Club, which everybody in Bessemer City called "Hunkie Hall" undulated and rocked. Female hips heavy from years at the stitching machines, pattern tables and steam presses of Bessemer City's clothing district hung out over wooden and metal folding chairs. The voter turnout was the largest by far of any of the 26th District's precincts.

He warmed up his audience in his well-rehearsed method.

# INQUISITION

"Y'know, there's a world of difference between the House and Senate, ladies. How can you tell? It's all in the way we handle our affairs. We're two completely different bodies. Different as day and night. You know why? Well, in the House we have a committee we call foreign affairs. Over in the Senate, theirs is foreign relations. We have affairs; they have relations. And with that crowd of prima donnas, their relations certainly are foreign."

District Eight, of the ILGWU exploded. Zach Harris delivered speeches that went beyond language. His special alchemy was in the cadence of delivery; the inflection he put on a word, a phrase a syllable; the lifted eyebrow, the grin; the embellishment of a long and deadly pause; the short, swift chops of his left hand.

"You gals have turned this place into a pleasure dome for Old Zach," he winked. His eyes followed the red, white and blue streamers cascading from a brass chandelier the size of a conestoga wheel hanging in the center of the room. "Why, you make me feel like a sheik among his concubines."

He loved to fool with the language, developing incongruities, mixing metaphors, concocting a steamy mixture which barely skirted the vulgar and profane.

Maroon draperies sealed off air circulation and had a hermetic hold on the scent of Bessemer City politics - sweat, cigar smoke, whiskey and F.W. Grand Co. eau de toilette. Black and white blow ups of FDR, Harry Truman and Adlai Stevenson looked out benignly over the assemblage from the rear of the hall. The men in attendance stood along the bar which stretched across the width of the place at the back. Precinct and ward bosses, courthouse officials, numbers runners, bookies, and newspaper reporters co-mingled and shared political gossip. Others - Italians, Syrians, Jews and Lebanese - in silk suits of iridescent blues and greens, chewed on unlit cigars. Known to everyone locally as "Kourkorian's Kollectors," they wore wraparound sunglasses and watched the congressman perform in the mirrors behind the bar above tiers of whiskey bottles. The reflection of Zach Harris worked silently and efficiently. Ignoring the politics, the men talked business: collegiate and professional football point spreads, who'd go down in the sixth round at St. Nick's, and variations and combinations needed to hit the big payoff races at Garden State, Pimlico and Gulf Stream. The Mediterraneans ran the package stores, greasy diners, jewelry shops and showbars of the South End. Their whorehouses and numbers operations kept them busy twenty-four hours a day to the rhythm of Bess Steel's three-shift workday, year in and year out. The businesses camouflaged high volume gambling. They took $5,000 a day

# Jack Eddinger

of the mills and rail yards 365 days a year. Everybody had a favorite: numbers, horses, prize fights, baseball and football pools, craps, monte. Name it, you play it. If you were short on cash, they'd arrange a fast loan with up to a year to pay, starting next payday, 50 percent interest. If you made a deal, your name went to the top of lists scrawled on the backs of envelopes. Next to each name was a number sometimes a letter or two. Some mornings you wished you'd gone straight through the gates into the plant instead of stopping for coffee, the Daily News or to play a number you liked at Sam the Clam's or One-Eye Johnny O'Brien's. But maybe, just maybe it was your day to hit.

Fats Kourkorian, a hulking Lebanese in a filthy white suit, collected the weekly take from his lackeys, doing business every Friday afternoon from the back seat of his powder blue Cadillac. They hated his surly attitude but made their payments, knowing he was skimming 10 percent. They also knew the man from Union City was clocking him. It was only a matter of time before he'd descend to eternal damnation. The Bessemer City *Star-Times* railed against corruption, but in the backrooms and lofts along Diamond and Anthracite streets the monetary and carnal action continued unabated. Police raids were predictable. Advance warning got everything out minutes before Chief Rocco Di Lupo's axe-wielding sergeants splintered pine doors and window frames. Di Lupo ordered his men around on the loudspeaker of his squad car. He usually appeared on the scene as the newspaper photographers arrived.

"Sorry boys," a sergeant would explain to the disgusted bookies and their runners. "Only following orders." The biggest complaints down in the streets were not against the raids or the editorial carping or Di Lupo's bullhorn, but against the high costs of replacing doors and windows. Action resumed within an hour of every raid.

Zach Harris scoffed at the newspaper complaints and the police raids, telling his listeners that the real scandal was in the padded payrolls, expense accounts and luxury suites of *Iron Mountain*, the tall soot-blackened building overlooking the Lenape River, which housed the executive offices of the Bessemer Steel Corporation.

"The little guy needs some harmless wagering to break the drudgery and monotony of the mills," he'd tell USW audiences. "If that newspaper wants to uncover corruption, mismanagement and abuse in this town, let them look into the 18th floor suites with their private bars and soft leather settees."

As Zach Harris gave the ILGWU his best, Charlie Miller, the *Star-Times* political writer, scratched on his notepad. He stood at the bar taking notes and sipping a beer. A flurry of sparks rose from his corncob

# INQUISITION

and settled in a fine white ash on the shoulders of his jacket. "Ah," he mused, "Zach's finessing the good ladies of the swatch tonight. Always at the top of his form with Dubinsky's lovelies." As he wrote, his eye caught the hand-lettered sign taped to the mirrors behind the whiskey bottles.

It read:

ATTENTION GARMENT WORKERS
KEEP Z.T. HARRIS
IN
CONGRESS
He's Kept the Reds
Out of Our Govt.,
Our Union, Our Schools.

A photograph about ten years out of date completed the poster. It was a black and white portrait like those in the *New York Times* announcing an executive appointment or highlighting an obituary. In print, "1946 photo" would appear in agate type in the lower right hand corner of the picture. The handsome, if arrogant, features stood out. Only a slight turning down at the corners of the mouth presaged the facial trait that was to become more pronounced with age, giving him an almost constant scowl. Charlie Miller had covered Zach Harris for two decades. He made a specialty of it. His stories about the Democrat from Pennsylvania who was rising into the House leadership gained both men ascendancy in their profession. Many of Miller's stories moved on the state and national wires. He was one of the few non-Washington newsmen to be offered membership in the National Press Club, and was greeted by his first-name at the men's bar. Zach Harris clipped and read Miller's stories, putting at least four a year into the *Congressional Record* and sending copies to Miller and his editor, Rufus MacManus. He kept a Charlie Miller Reference File in his office. Late at night he'd pour a glass of scotch, put on his reading glasses and go over them carefully. He'd rethink the steps that went into a legislative play or political move. Or he'd use Miller's insights to anticipate public reaction to a speech, a floor statement, a committee initiative or an investigation. Though he once considered it, he'd never hire Miller. He could never fool the little gamecock.

Miller watched the Congressman's eyes pass over the audience. He immediately noticed something different in the congressman's demeanor; something he could not quite pin down. The mannerisms were all there - the cagey invective, the thrust for the jugular, the pitch for votes. But there was more, and Miller chastised himself because he could not put his finger on it. It was an impression. He made a mental note, and continued writing.

"I see the Fourth Estate is with us tonight, ladies," Harris intoned. He squinted at Miller, Arnold Mason of the *Evening Sentinel* and two young reporters getting their first exposure to Zachary Taylor Harris. They stood with the men at the back of the hall.

Boos.

Harris used the trick whenever the press attended a speech, or when it served his purposes to point out the reporters covering the story. Miller heard it frequently over the years. It began when Rufus MacManus became editor of the *Star-Times*. The irascible Scot nudged the conservative newspaper to the left. The newspaper-of-record in Pennsylvania's 26th district and its congressman often tangled. They went at each other on *Harris-MacNaughton* (which always had the names reversed in news copy); MacManus from the editorial page, Harris in the Letters-to-the-Editor column and in floor statements carried in the *Congressional Record*. He mailed reprints throughout the district. When the *MacNaughton-Harris Immigration Act* became the law of the land in 1953 after the House overrode President Truman's veto, The *Star-Times* carried an editorial bordered in black. It damned Harris for rounding up the two-thirds vote to override. Zach Harris had it framed and hung it on his office wall. Later an uneasy truce prevailed, but neither Harris nor MacManus could resist an occasional gratuitous tweak. Charlie Miller dismissed it as an ego game; posturing by his editor and cheap shot speechifying by Harris. He told them off from time to time in his weekly column.

"I'm told these fellows believe my opponent will be elected to Congress. Why, just the other night I read that Mason of the *Sentinel* thinks I've lost touch with the voters of the 26th District. Now, I ask you ladies is this an apparition you see here, or is it a countenance to rival the Great Barrymore?" Harris turned in profile, his nose in the air.

Cheers.

He pulled a news clipping from his pocket, put on his glasses and began to read. Arnold Mason shifted uncomfortably. Harris read from his *Around The County* column of the previous week, hitting every typo and pausing on each transposition and garbled phrase. The errors went out in the first edition before Mason corrected them. Zach Harris made sure he had the uncorrected version in his pocket .

"It says here and I quote, 'Congressman Harris has never been more valnuerable' - I don't know whether to take that as a compliment or a slur. 'Chances of his firt defeat appear better today than ever as State Senator Hornry' - that's what it says, ladies, Hornry! - 'Marcel's campaign picked

# INQUISITION

up its first real world endorsement as Bess Steel's Joseph P. O'Neill said the company will support the Hampton County Republican financially and with an organization. Moreover, there are murmurs of political scandrel' - I guess that's scandal - ' Meanwhile in the Democratic Party organization, Dist. Atty. Tom Daley, has announced an investigation into political corruption in the Lenape Valley.'"

"Motherfucking typesetters," Mason grimaced at Miller.

"Murmurs! Scoundrels! Hornry! Why ladies, a score of Hollywood gag writers couldn't do better."

Mason was in agony.

"Let me tell you something. I knew that little beautician when he wrapped himself in silk bathrobes like a damned sultan, and sidled up to the Republican ladies of the West End under the name of Mr. Henri! I'll bet none of you could afford Mr. Henri's cute coiffeurs." He pronounced it coyfers. "Why, I remember when everybody called him Frenchie," a sly smile crept across his face, "from the days when he racked balls in the pool rooms down here in the South End. Mr. Henri! Hah! ... I like Hornry. That fits him better. He's hornry all right; horny for that window decorator he travels with .... Ladies, I believe Mr. Henri, pardon me, Hornry, is a queer!"

Zach Harris's technique in dealing with an opponent was by label, epithet or an invented nickname. Sometimes he just told the truth. Imagination did the rest. He took great pleasure in skewering a challenger on some peccadillo. He'd resurrect an unflattering scrap, and fine-tuning his audience, develop it to the point of evoking humor, then derision, then contempt.

"Who's kept the Corporation out of your pockets?"

Zach has!" someone yelled.

"Who's kept the coolie-labor rags off our clothes racks?"

"Zach has."

The ladies of District Eight picked up the litany.

"Who's kept the riffraff out of the country?"

"Zach has!" They were all chanting now.

"Who's got the communists on the run?"

"Zach has!"

"Who's gonna win Nov. 2?"

"Zach will."

He used no text, no notes. He spoke quickly and forcefully occasionally running a string of words together like Republicanbigbusiness. Or he slowed to a rasp, as if sharing a confidence, dwelling on provocative words for effect. He let the accents fall like a trip-hammer.

# Jack Eddinger

"First, I want to say I have no argument with the President. He's a fine old fellow who's had his day. He's just had a helluva lot of bad advice from Wall Street lawyers and moguls like Old Presbyterian Dulles and Charlie Wilson. "

Jeers.

"I don't even have an argument with our friend, What's 'is name? Hornry!

Laughter.

"But I do have an argument with the jackals and political opportunists who have nothing better to do than smear the good name of people we admire and respect here in the Valley. Let them investigate all they want. When they're finished all they'll have is what they started with, a string of unsubstantiated accusations. Do you know what's at the center of this fraud?"

Silence and attention.

"By controlling Pennsylvania's two U.S. Senators, Mr. E.G. Palmer commands the votes to keep his corporate profits up and your wages down. He's been getting away with it for years and by supporting Daley, in the primary election against our best Senate candidate, Palmer's drained the campaign treasury of an assured vote-getter with the general election only a few weeks away.

"If you don't vote for Governor Stevenson for president and George Lerner for the Senate, for me to represent your interests in Washington, for a new team in Hampton County and the straight Democratic ticket, we're going to have economic depression, and prosecutorial witch hunts like you've never seen before. Nobody needs to tell you who goes first when Palmer decides to cut back production when his so-called experts tell him the country's economy is in a downturn. Downturn! That's Republican for saying 'Sorry, we couldn't predict this business falloff, so we're asking you to take an indefinite vacation without pay."

Booing and jeering.

"But I didn't come here tonight to tell you I've had a finger on the pulse of the working man and woman. I didn't come here to tell you that I've battled to keep the courts of this land free of sleazy corruption. Nor did I come here to tell you that we are restoring Europe and building a new economic order.

"I came here for your support and for your votes."

Spiked heels clattered.

On the platform Zachary Taylor Harris, stood rigidly at attention as if he were Julius Caesar reviewing his legions. The lights burned deeper lines in his face.

# INQUISITION

"Finally, ladies, I want to raise a subject which gives me no great pleasure."

The room fell silent.

"I must counsel you to reject an individual whom I once held in high regard, a young man I considered might one day succeed me as your representative in Congress. I'm talking about a man born and raised in Hampton County, whose election to the powerful office of District Attorney I not only encouraged, but nurtured and supported. Now we see him using the most influential office in government to carry out a vindictive political agenda. I say to you that a prosecutor has a solemn obligation; no, a duty, to stand above politics; to use the extraordinary power the people have entrusted to him in an even-handed and impartial manner. When a man takes up the office of prosecutor, he assumes a responsibility far beyond that given to any one of us. What he sees and hears but above all, what he presents to a grand jury is one of the few legitimately secret processes permitted in a free society. But it can do irreparable damage to ordinary citizens if allowed to trickle out in gossip, hearsay and rumor. He must regard the information that comes to his attention as a priest regards the seal of confession. He walks a thin line, a line which, if he steps over out of arrogance or political ambition, can inflict life's harshest pain on the innocent."

Zach Harris had his man in the crosshairs and began squeezing the trigger.

"I submit that we are witnessing an ego out of control. What's more he has aligned himself with a handful of individuals whose purpose is to put forward an elitist agenda in this country. They are afraid to come forward and present themselves to you the voters. Their names are unfamiliar to you. They are the liberal clique which induced Mr. Daley to run for the Senate to help them enact their left wing agenda and to repeal laws like *Harris-MacNaughton* which have put them and their bedfellows - I should say Red fellows - on the defensive. And if you think I'm exaggerating, take a look at the sources of Daley's Senate campaign funds. It's a guidebook to the Left:

"Americans for Immigration Reform, $250. A liberal group that believes we should repeal *Harris-MacNaughton* and throw open our doors to anybody.

"The Friends of Free Migration, $500. A lunatic fringe group advocating one-world nonsense and open immigration.

" World Watch Institute, $1,000. Another gang of southpaws, atheists and scientific humanists headed by - you guessed it - Mr. Eugene Garrett Palmer.

# Jack Eddinger

"The list goes on. Not a penny raised locally. Combined with the contributions of Palmer and his lackeys, Daley was handed the money that could not be offset by the party treasury, forcing a good man, George Lerner, to exhaust his financial resources in a purposeless primary. His double dealing must not go unpunished."

As the congressman recited the campaign fund litany, a commotion stirred in the lobby. District Attorney Tom Daley and his campaign manager entered the hall and stood at the rear. Daley with legs wide apart, face grim, an overcoat draped over arms folded across his chest stared directly at Zach Harris.

"I'll have more to say about this in the coming weeks," Harris said, pausing for a sip of water and squinting through the tobacco smoke with disbelief straight at Daley. Charlie Miller noticed the minuscule change in the congressman's demeanor; a change measured in milliseconds. Daley and the congressman were separated by 60-feet, the distance between home plate and pitcher's mound. The prosecutor's cold, hard stare cut through the congressman's rhetoric. It threw Zach Harris off stride. Charlie Miller could not recall an instance when the congressman's composure flickered. In eyeball-to-eyeball contact with Zachary Taylor Harris the other fellow always blinked. The chairwoman of the Hampton County Democratic Committee reacted quickly. She spoke briefly to Daley and ushered him and his companion to a waiting room behind the bar. He'd be given five minutes to speak after the congressman left the premises.

Zachary Taylor Harris always performed well on the stump. But what he normally would rate a premiere performance before the ladies of District Eight, was lost in Daley's steely stare. It threw off his timing. He could read a crowd like a theater critic. He did not get the response he wanted. He expected long, sustained applause like in the old days when he could throw away lines against cheering and whistling that swept a room. Whatever he said in such a situation rarely mattered. What the hell was Daley doing here anyway? He didn't like it one damned bit. The officers of District Eight promised him an exclusive. They told him no other candidate was to be in the room. What the hell was Daley and the woman discussing? Damned liberal bitch. He was uncomfortable attacking the fellow then having him walk into the middle of his denunciation. It was amateurish, bad form for a political pro. Daley on his prosecutor's stallion means he'd have to rely almost exclusively on Kressman, a thought he hated to contemplate. The wily Dutchman would get him the vote he needed to trounce Marcel and to elect Daley's opponent. Kressman ran the Republicans as if they were cows in milking stalls. "Only gentle pressure, Zach. Pull their tits too hard and they get sore." He'd have to pay dearly for the old man's connivance.

# INQUISITION

Kressman handled the GOP's minimal patronage jobs and appointments in the Lenape Valley. He controlled a handful of jobs and always wanted more. How they were parceled out spelled control. The Congressman's aide, Robert Bird knew nothing of the nature of the Harris-Kressman relationship. Bird considered Kressman a nuisance the Congressman tolerated and passed off to him to handle. The quintessential staffer Bird kept Kressman happy and never asked questions.

But this election would take more than Robert Bird's indefatigable effort. Palmer and his top lawyer, O'Neill, were now in the act. O'Neill poured on his Irish charm and had the reformers and do-gooders raising campaign money and putting volunteers on the street. Marcel was charging him with abandoning the subversive hearings and Daley was playing the corruption card - issues Zach Harris had always owned. Was he losing his nerve? Was his indignation about running against an inferior candidate, blinding him? What will Palmer's money and O'Neill's manpower do for his opponent? A close election was something he was loath to contemplate. The Hampton County Republican Party might not be willing to take a walk as in past elections with Palmer's money behind Marcel. To stay off the defensive and win decisively required a new strategy with new tactics to support it. He'd need all his powers of persuasion to convince the always prickly Kressman to start moving immediately.

"I want to conclude, ladies and gentlemen," he said clearing his throat.

The room grew silent.

"I want to end by telling you to get everybody out to vote - family, neighbors, friends, other unions, churchgoers - everybody. Tell 'em Zach needs 'em. But more important, tell 'em the Democratic Party needs 'em. America needs Governor Stevenson and Senator Kefauver and they need a Democratic Congress that'll work to get what you want. That will take nothing short of a victory big enough to drive turncoats out of our Party."

His uneasiness subsided as he attacked. "Don't bother reading the newspaper voter guides, or the bias masquerading as analysis on the editorial pages. Don't waste time with that list of approved candidates from the League of Women Voters." He dragged out the words with consummate scorn. "That's do-gooder garbage. What do newspaper editors know about subversion? What do country club matrons know about politics? Go into the booth on November 2, close the curtain and pull for the Democratic Party."

Applause.

Congressman Harris stepped down from the rostrum, his gray eyes blazing. He coughed and slaked the fire in his throat with a long swallow

# Jack Eddinger

of ice water. In spite of the fervor of his speech a restiveness edged back in preventing him from enjoying the moment. Charlie Miller watched Harris extend both arms into the crowd. He brushed the outstretched hands slightly, pausing to talk when he recognized a campaign worker or member of District Eight's rank and file. He moved through the aisle created by a wedge of South End precinct workers.

Outside, an unseasonable northwest wind in synch with his mood skimmed a damp chill off the Lenape River and whipped the trousers of passing steelworkers hunched low in mackinaws on their way to the fire and clangor of the mills along the riverbank. Chief Di Lupo's motorcyclists spewed exhaust into the night as a cold misting rain began. Goggled and wearing leather jackets, white crash helmets and shiny black boots, Di Lupo's Dandies revved the vehement little engines till they were a pack of terriers barking in unison. At the curb, Sam McBryan, the congressman's driver, held the door of the black Lincoln Continental open. Passersby stopped on the sidewalk to warm themselves in the gamy humidity that poured out of the hall. Zach Harris saluted the small crowd. A precinct worker handed him his overcoat and black homburg. He draped the coat over his shoulders like a cape, cocked the hat slightly to the right and climbed into the back seat of the limousine, which bore Pennsylvania license plate ZTH 26. "Wait a few minutes, Sam. The boys in the press may need a ride uptown."

Back in the hall Charlie Miller, one hand covering his left ear, was dictating his story for the final edition from a wall telephone. Arnold Mason took notes as he talked with Frank Comstock, Daley's campaign manager, nodding frequently. District Attorney Daley ascended the platform. The agreement was five minutes, no more. Ignoring the congressman's attack, he asked the ILGWU to remember his prosecution of the Hawk Shirt Company for hiring teenagers below the hourly minimum, and the unfair labor practices case he brought against the Lenape Throwing Mills and took all the way to the Pennsylvania Supreme Court and won for them. They listened in silence. From the back someone yelled, "G'wan home, ya turncoat;" another, "Run with the Republicans, rich boy."

A projectile, launched from the vicinity of a raw bar arched over the chandelier and landed on the speakers' platform with a slap. Daley took the microphone from its stand and walked slowly across the platform dragging the cord. He stopped and stood solemnly over the spot where the projectile landed, looking down, as if turning up a long lost object. Then he bent over and picked something up. The men at the bar stopped talking. The room went silent. He walked slowly to the rostrum then consumed a minute or two fastening the mike to the stand. He looked out at the crowd,

# INQUISITION

and stared. He held up his catch. "Well now," he said with a devilish grin as he rotated a smoky-eyed Louisiana red snapper under the spotlight like a fish monger, "I wonder if this is what Harry Truman had in mind when he took the 80th Congress to task for throwing a red herring into the political stream?"

Two women stood up and tentatively, very tentatively, began to clap. A few more joined in. Others got up. Then more. Some began blowing kisses. In minutes the girls of District 8 engulfed the platform. They were the bobby soxers of their youth, swooning as Sinatra crooned to them at the Paramount. They grabbed at his pinstripe suit. He reached into the crowd to touch hands, which mussed up his dark hair. He stood motionless under the spotlight with a big Will Rogers grin on his face. It was a turnabout worthy of a Neapolitan mob curling upraised fists into prayerful clasps as the blood of St. Januarius performed its annual liquefying miracle. The entire performance took only five minutes.

Charlie Miller was on his tiptoes watching the performance while dictating into the phone. "That's it, Ethel," Miller told the *Star-Times* dictationist. "Tell MacManus it's nothing short of the loaves and fishes. Too bad there's no photo to go with this fish story. Then again, there never is. Right, Ethel? I'll file more later. I'm going up to the McKean with the congressman. And Ethel, tell him to keep that red herring quote at the top of the story." Zach Harris's speech would be lost in Miller's droll fish story which led the morning editions. What was not captured on film was more than manifest in Miller's colorful writing.

The big black Lincoln eased down the steep hill and followed the darting red tail lights of Chief Di Lupo's motorized terriers yapping into the mist. Whenever Congressman Harris came up from Washington, Rocco DiLupo took personal command. The congressman's safety was of intense concern to the squat, flat-nosed police chief. Harris suffered the chief as one of the petty irritations that men in public life must endure. DiLupo assigned his parade motorcyclists, and hand-picked the detectives who escorted Harris whenever he moved around the Lenape Valley. It appealed to his innate caution as well as to his *carabinieri* passion for *spectacale*. To Chief of Detectives John Maggio it was ass-kissing of the first magnitude, especially when he had to pull a detective off an investigation. Maggio fumed. DiLupo rode in the unmarked police car which cruised discreetly behind the caravan. To the radio dispatchers at headquarters it was Mussolini and his Riding Monkeys. But most of the time, they referred to him as *Il Boca*, the big-mouthed sonofabitch.

# Jack Eddinger

Swiftly, the limousine moved into the flow of headlights on the industrial highway between the Lenape River and the steep escarpment known as "Slav Town." On the hilltop, as if flung by some celestial Cyclops, the steelworkers' houses were strewn about and scattered and stacked atop each other. In them lived the men who supplied the brawn, sinew and skills to convert iron ore, limestone and scrap to steel, then roll, hammer and squeeze it into armor plate and ship bottoms, suspension cable and reinforcing rods, beams and turbine spindles, tools and dies, wire and nails for Eugene Garrett Palmer and Bessemer Steel. On the surface of the river an eerie incandescence reflected the fiery plumes of burning gases, casting light and imagery, as if in a worn strip of black and white film spinning on its reel. Engine hum and vibration engulf the ear. Traffic thinned into a continuum of tail lights on the wet streets. The reflected light on black tarmac resembled a school of luminescent fish swimming in a time-lapse photograph. The congressman's limousine sped under a railroad trestle. Overhead, battered and rusting hopper cars shunted cargoes of ore stripped from rich seams deep in South American and West African iron ranges. The cars disappeared into a maw of corrugated metal. Clam shell buckets the size of small houses dipped into storage bunkers, hoisting and dripping ravenous bites of ore the color of chili powder, depositing it in self-dumping cars which transport it to open-hearth and electric furnaces. Phantasmal silhouettes of foundry and forge, mill and cooling tower sulked against the night sky. Sulfides mingling with the stench of oil, ozone, and burning gases - coke, coal tar and bituminous residues - spewed a malodorous fog across the landscape, simulating a World War I gas attack. A fine ocher powder coated buildings, walkways, streets and parking lots.

Within ten minutes, Zachary Taylor Harris, Charlie Miller, Arnold Mason and two very junior reporters slipped into red leather armchairs in the McKean Hotel's Pemberton Room. Local history held that Washington and Lafayette met on the same spot in an 18th Century forerunner of the McKean. Two waiters stood by solicitously. The congressman plucked a thin silver timepiece from his vest pocket and snapped it open. "Excuse me, boys. Gotta make a call. Order me the usual, Charlie."

"Well, waddya think?" Arnold Mason said, as Charlie Miller ordered two double bourbons and a scotch and soda for the congressman. Mason ordered two fingers of Three Feathers and water; the younger men, beers. "I don't know," Miller said, stroking his mustache. "Something's bothering him, and its more than a virus, or even the beginning of old age. On the way up he sat staring out the window. Didn't say more than three words. It doesn't jibe. Never mentioned the campaign and that's not like him."

# INQUISITION

"Yeah, he'd've told a couple of bullshit stories," Mason said. "Maybe the man's just tired. The SUBACK hearings are dragging out. I wonder if he'll finish before the election like he says. Marcel ain't the turkey Zach'd have his listeners believe. He's a shrewd, tough old bird. Ben Franklin might've been right wanting it as the national symbol. Plus Zach ain't gettin any younger. What's he, about sixty-three or four?"

"Fifty-eight," Charlie Miller corrected Mason. "And a young 58, too. A couple a things got me puzzled. Why's he going after Palmer. Marcel, I can understand. Political rhetoric. By the way, I disagree with you about Marcel. He's got about the survivability of a fart in a windstorm. But it just doesn't make sense for Zach to be tangling with Palmer. He's too smart for that. He knows it can only hurt him. So the question is why? The other thing is his vehemence about the D.A. Sure, he's irked by Daley's grand-standing, but this has vendetta written all over it. What's Zach Harris got to fear? Certainly nothing to do with street crime or the syndicate. He put damned near every guinea crook in jail when he was D.A. They don't want any part of Harris. If he as much as sneezes from his sub-committee, they catch cold in Palermo. I tried to get him on the record in the car coming up here but he just clamped his lips. You're an old police beat hand, Mason. You think this investigation scuttlebutt has any substance?"

"There's nothing on the record anywhere that we can find from either the cops or the DA's office," one of the young reporters interjected.

Mason glowered across the table.

"You're supposed to listen, kid. Who the hell would tell you anything?

"I got it straight from the chief."

"Look asshole, the only time you ever ask Rocco DiLupo anything is when you want it broadcast up and down the East Coast.

"Charlie, I talked to Comstock tonight. He says he can't comment but I figure they're on to something. I've done some digging and found that the grand jury keeps pushing Daley for more evidence. As I understand it, the Feds had a wiretap on Fats Kourkorian, but they aren't about to share it with Daley. Without it he can't prove that Fats's paying off anybody. He's come up with a lot of stuff, but nothing tangible enough to produce an indictment. The grand jury's getting impatient. The Palmer thing's more simple. Zach knows Palmer put Joe O'Neill to work for Marcel and he's really pissed, because he respects O'Neill. By the way Joe told me he tried to get Kressman behind Marcel, but got nowhere. Zach knows Joe's a pro. He's worried about what he can do for Marcel with Palmer's dough."

# Jack Eddinger

"That Comstock stuff's interesting," Miller said. "I'll talk to John Maggio."

"Dawson!" the congressman called, as he re-entered the room. "Now, where the hell did that little shine get to? Dawson ..."

The Pemberton's ancient head waiter appeared in the doorway. " 'scuse me, Mr. Zach. I was around front in the lobby."

"Did those apes order my drink, Dawson?"

"Oh, yes sir, Mr. Zach. It's waitin on you. You gonna dine with us this evening?"

"Yes ... I'm sorry for shouting, Dawson. Yes ... yes, the usual."

Rich mahogany paneling burnished the soft light casting an amber Rembrandt glow on the faces of the men dining. The three older men looked younger. No one else was in the room. A barman in a short white jacket polished long-stemmed wine glasses. Brooding, be-whiskered portraits of the city's colonial founders and 19th Century merchant fathers gazed down glacially from their Olympian summit. A white-coated waiter lounged at a table near the door waiting; hoping the group would order quickly and leave so he could forget the night, the cold and the man and go to sleep.

"Well, boys this has been a helluva satisfying day," Harris said slipping into a chair. "Long, but it ran smoothly. Usually a few snafus on opening day. Both Miller and Mason noticed the change immediately. He was either genuinely relaxed or it was an exceptional performance.

"Good news. Just talked to the committee counsel. We'll have our final week of hearings and wind it up *sine die* on Thursday. Then I'll be back here to show that French faggot how to campaign. What did you think of my speech tonight?"

"It was great, sir," said one of the young newsmen.

"I'll give that little bastard a run he won't forget," Harris said, ignoring the young man. "When I finish with him, he'll forget who he used to be. Charlie, you remember what I did to Haggerty in '48, don't you? Well, I'm going to plow that little Frog so deep he'll have to consult the election board for his name, address and party affiliation."

Zach Harris picked up his glass and sipped the scotch. Miller and Mason spoke simultaneously.

"Excuse me. What were you going to say, Charlie?"

Miller frowned and looked into an empty bourbon glass. He reached for the second. "I was going to ask Zach why he's waging World War Three, when a Mexican Border Raid would do," Miller replied, lighting up his corncob, his eyes twinkling.

"I'd like to know what Palmer's thinking," Mason countered. "Why's he backing Marcel?"

# INQUISITION

"Wait a minute. One at a time. Charlie, the answer to your question - and you should know better - is they're all tough. I know that's not going to satisfy you, but dammit when I get mad, I run hard. Mason, you know full well Palmer'll do anything to hang on to control of the state government. Sonofabitch's put thousands on that little bastard. He, the manufacturers association and the GOP think they're the godhead, and Marcel's the man they created in their image. They've always wanted me out. Sorry for putting you on the griddle tonight, Mason, but that column you wrote's unadulterated horseshit. Daley give it to you? By the way, who's that funny looking fellow with Daley?"

"Name's Comstock, Benjamin Franklin Comstock. Goes by Frank. Was an assistant U.S. Attorney in Philly before signing on to run Daley's Senate campaign. They were classmates at Penn Law. He's smart and knows the political terrain pretty well. Joe O'Neill got him the job running the primary for Daley. When Daley lost to the governor, Comstock joined the DA's staff. Now he's running Daley's reelection campaign. I don't think Knowles can touch Daley, do you?"

"Well, he's dead wrong if he gave you any of the stuff you put in your column, Mason. A hundred and eighty degrees wrong. You tell him that next time you see him. I meant what I said tonight. Hell, you fellows're always looking for some deep interpretation. You look for fireworks and I gave you a few sparks," Harris winked at the two young newsmen.

Dawson distributed the dinner plates. Each bore a hefty steak. The waiters worked quietly, unobtrusively as the congressman spoke.

"Dawson, just a salad with oil and vinegar," the congressman said then attacked the T-bone. "Tonight, boys, let's talk about the days when politics meant something around here." Charlie Miller shifted uncomfortably. He'd known Harris to regale his listeners with political stories. Mason, munching on a roll, looked up from his plate quizzically. The two young men waited anxiously for the congressman to continue. Both senior newsmen wanted to talk strategy. They wanted to put serious questions to the chairman of the Subversive Activities Committee; the man who at his ease was a clever storyteller and drinking companion, but became instantly opaque when anyone tried to analyze his motives. The two newsmen knew that once started they could not interrupt a Harris monologue. Both owed him. As independent and objective as they truly believed themselves to be, both had placed themselves in his debt. He treated them as part of the political landscape as he did the precinct captains and poll workers. "You help me, boys, and I'll take care of you. Maybe you'll win one of those newspaper awards they're killing themselves for at the Press Club." He was true to his word. Arnold Mason received a Front Page Award in 1944

## Jack Eddinger

for a series on waste and mismanagement on Navy contracts in Bessemer Steel's armor plate division at the company's big tidewater plant near Baltimore, courtesy of Zachary Taylor Harris. It raised Eugene Palmer's ire several degrees. Charlie Miller was Pennsylvania's Newsman of the Year in 1950 for his *Inside Pennsylvania Politics* columns analyzing the Steel Triangle. Miller traced GOP patronage from Palmer's executive suite on *Iron Mountain* to the State Capitol to the Senate Finance Committee in Washington. Zach Harris suggested the columns and paved the way for them with Lloyd Kressman's devious assistance. Kressman harbored deep resentment toward his party's leaders' iron lock on GOP patronage in the Lenape Valley; something Kressman ached to get his hands on, but could not pry loose from Bess Steel's control. Miller, of course, never got anything about Kressman's alternative route to political patronage and largesse via Zach Harris.

"What about the Daley investigations, Congressman?" Charlie Miller asked casually. He figured he wouldn't get a straight answer but his professional pride made him ask. If nothing else, he was in the familiar off-the-record terrain Zach Harris used to mix conjecture with fact. Sometimes Miller was able to mine a nugget buried in an aside, but for the most part, it was *terra incognita*. But the congressman's mood had shifted. He spoke confidently, affecting the demeanor Miller and Mason knew so well - the inside source. He was massaging them with material they knew they'd have no chance of verifying. They could take it or leave it. They had no way of determining how much of what he said was valid. Harris, they knew, moved in Washington's rarefied circles, where information is legal tender, and is held close like gilt-edged securities. Few, if any newsman, let alone a local one, could assess its accuracy. Enterprise didn't help much either. Smart reporters sought an appraisal by an independent source, or checked it through the not-always-firm interpretations of a well-placed staffer. Yet, there was always a nugget in whatever Harris passed along, something that when panned and assayed usually spelled news.

"Y'know what I think, Charlie? They're shallow. Daley and his friend haven't developed a single shred of evidence a grand jury'd accept. Not only that, he's going about it ass-backwards."

"What do you mean?" Miller said instantly. Zach Harris responded with equal swiftness.

"Let me lay it out for you. Don't forget I was once pretty good at force-feeding grand juries. They've got nothing. Maybe some small time numbers writing and betting operations. Who's he kidding? Hell, look at his investigative resources, a couple of grab ass detectives and DiLupo's

# INQUISITION

parade marshals. They couldn't get a conviction against Sacco and Vanzetti if the defense lawyer spoke pidgin English.

"Off the record, my sources at the Justice Department say there's nothing that resembles organized crime in the Valley. Not enough action. I'd be happy to talk to both of you privately about what they told me when I'm back here for Marion's dinner next week. Take it from me, there's just nothing there and young Daley knows it. He's in over his head politically with his debt to the liberals. Maybe, I was tough on him in my speech tonight, but god-dammit both of you know he's using this non-issue as a springboard to run statewide again. But he's making the classic mistake a politician in law enforcement makes. Views everything through the smoky lens of suspicion and conspiracy. He's made an even bigger miscalculation by leaking unverified information. Problem is he doesn't understand the dynamics of news. Anybody can make headlines with accusations and posturing. Initially, it'll attract plenty of ink. But, he sure as hell better be able to back it up. He's got to produce hard evidence; something that spells indictment. If he doesn't, it's only a matter of time before MacManus sics you fellas on him. You guys'll turn him into dead meat. But the way I see it is this: his real interest is in running for the Senate in 1960. He's got an inflated view of himself. Daley's got nothing but misplaced ambition; lots of it. That's why the primary challenge. He knew he would lose, but challenging the party will get his name across the state. Sounds like a smart strategy to position himself for the Senate two years from now. He'll use the District Attorney's office as a pulpit to promote himself to the public. I've got news for him and for you, Mason. Remember, you heard it here first. Daley's going to lose. His opponent, Arthur Knowles, is no pushover. I'm surprised you two haven't pushed Daley and his sidekick to the wall. Get them to defend these failed indictments."

"Can we quote you on that, congressman?" asked one of the young newsmen.

Mason winced.

"Sure you can quote me. None of you remembers when political discipline was the cement that held everything together. Today, any prima donna with a baritone and a pompadour thinks he can get elected. Never mind putting down a solid base and working your way up. That's too tough. Today, its the Big I technique. The Big I of image and irresponsibility. Hell, it's enough to make an old man weep and yearn for the days when politics meant accomplishment. A man can go down to Washington for a quarter century, bring millions of dollars and countless jobs into his district and they thank him by investigating his friends and running a fourth-rate frog against him. Where's the justice in that? Thirty-five years in public life

## Jack Eddinger

and I'm still battling whores, only now they're faggots. But I said we weren't going to talk about that tonight, didn't I?"

Miller caught the congressman's eyes momentarily and noticed them flutter. His body shook. His face turned crimson. He gasped for air. Instantly, Miller was over him slapping his back.

"Zach ... Zach ... Are you okay?"

Congressman Harris's eyes rolled up. He fell backward holding his throat.

"My God ... Dawson, call a doctor. Quick ..." Mason yelled to the waiter.

"No! god-dammit," Harris rasped. His head was down on the table, but he had one eye open. "Don't do a god-damned thing. I'm all right."

"Get him a drink, god-dammit. Get him a fuckin drink," Mason shouted.

They stood at the table stunned. Miller massaged the congressman's shoulders. Harris's contorted face moved through rapid changes: pink, red, ashen, but with Charlie Miller's massage, his color was returning. With a prodigious summoning of will, he drew a breath, coughed and extended his hand to receive the glass of whiskey. He gulped it down then slumped backward in the armchair holding his throat and gasping

"Mason, I don't care what the congressman says, call a doctor. No, call an ambulance."

"The hell you will," Harris spat. I'm all right. It'll pass. It's the god-damned asthma."

Mason stared across the table, his eyes bulging.

"What the hell are you looking at?" Mason's eyes dropped. The white tablecloth was stained with steak juice, sputum and flecks of blood. The congressman uttered something incoherent. After minutes of awkward silence Zachary Taylor Harris regained his composure. "It's the asthma complicated by this damned cold," he said. His eyes were bloodshot and spittle rolled down his chin. "This damned climate's worse than Siberia. This stays right here. I want none of this in your newspapers. Understood?" He blotted his face with the starched white napkin.

Zach, you gotta get some medical help. I'll call Sam. He'll drive you over to St. Helena's emergency room."

"Sit down and be quiet, Charlie." His vitality began to return. "I'm not ready to go yet, either prematurely or tonight. Remember, not a damned word of this to anyone."

# INQUISITION

Two short rings on his private line jolted Zach Harris out of his remembrance of things past. His meeting with the Director ran longer than anticipated. He looked at his watch. It was close to seven-thirty.

"This is Congressman Harris."

"Oh, Zach darling, you're still there. I was hoping you were on your way. Is there something wrong?"

The silken voice of Lenore Price triggered a sensual twinge deep in the bio-neural source of his finely-tuned lust. Thoughts of lilac perfume, long slender legs wrapped in a violet skirt clinging at the hips, which gave her walk a sensuous curl, and of full breasts spilling into the low neckline of a violet angora sweater aroused him from the melancholia that had gripped him since his meeting with the Director.

"Sweetheart, you know not to call me here. Lucky everybody left early. Damned place is like a Baptist quilting party with those two old hens out front lifting their eyebrows and clucking every time a good-looking woman walks into the office. They'd have apoplexy if they ever saw you." The tough-minded always guarded, Zachary Taylor Harris disappeared to be replaced by a human being of warmth, geniality and solicitude, traits he'd not known he possessed before he met Lenore Price.

"I called several times, but no one answered. Between those old maids you employ and the parade of witnesses you've been listening to, I'm afraid you're becoming conspiratorial, darling. But I won't press your obligations if you promise there'll be no shop talk all weekend. It's going to be very special. I've planned everything, darling, starting with your favorite dinner here tonight and a wonderful French wine. I'm looking forward to the drive down to the Greenbriar tomorrow. It's supposed to be a glorious day. Let's leave early and take the Skyline Drive down aways from Front Royal. The colors will be spectacular. We'll have a wonderful weekend together, darling."

"There's nothing I'd like better, Lenore, you know that. But this damned election's giving me fits. I've got to be back in that rathole no later than tomorrow afternoon. That means we only have tonight. When this is over, my dear, I plan to take you down to Sea Island. I've a long standing invitation to review the fleet at Savannah with the Chairman of Armed Services. We can drive over to the Cloisters from there." He wished he was holding her instead of wasting time on the phone. "Some important business at the Justice Department held me up. I'll leave now and be there in 10 minutes. Mid-town traffic's gone by now. I was getting ready to call when the phone rang, and there you were, my sweet."

"Hello? Lenore are you there?"

# Jack Eddinger

It happened before; numerous times. She learned to contain her disappointment. But this was different. He did not sound like the same sweet cynic she came to know so intimately. Something was bothering him. She could tell by the subtle distance he was putting between them. She wanted to ask him about it but she knew he hated being psychoanalyzed and certainly did not want the woman he loved worrying about him. She never probed and pried. It was a trait he liked about her.

When Lenore Price smiled her green-eyed greeting that day in 1954 at the Democratic National Committee's annual meeting for state party leaders, Zach Harris knew instantly he would pursue the committee's new secretary. What he did not know about the tall, intelligent 36-year-old brunette from New Mexico was how hotly he would pursue her, and how she would consume him. He liked everything about her that day she took his coat, smiled warmly and led him to the speakers platform. He was among the congressional leaders addressing the delegates who came from the far reaches of the republic. They listened closely as their party's elected leaders explained how they could take back the White House in 1956 with Stevenson and Kefauver against Ike and the despicable Nixon. The professionals who ran the elections, however, had already written off 1956, and looked to hold seats in the Senate and maybe add more in the House. She watched delegates rise and applaud as the senate majority leader, the Democratic national chairman and the Honorable Zachary Taylor Harris, chairman of the House Democratic caucus took their seats on the speakers platform.

Zach Harris enjoyed the company of beautiful women, beginning with the college girls and agency secretaries he'd invite up to his digs during his last year of law school at George Washington. In the summer of 1918 he put on the classy white Ensign's uniform of a Navy Department lawyer. While doughboys of the same age were tangling with the last of the Kaiser's reserves in the mud and gore of the Meuse, Zach Harris was pursuing his bachelor's prerogatives in Washington with persistent ardor. He kept his liaisons discreet - no married women. The thought of a cuckolded husband pursuing him with a pistol conjured up images of Harry K. Thaw doing in Stanford White. Occasionally he was tempted by the bored spouse of a bibulous hunt country squire on weekend outings in Maryland and Virginia, but he always managed to put them off. Never could tell which Senator was screwing her regularly. He did not want to spoil a career in politics before it started by having a Senate grandee spreading the word that he had trouble keeping it in his pants. Overt sexual profligacy stood just below public drunkenness on the unwritten list of prohibitions that could wreck a prospective national career. Later at the Justice Department,

# INQUISITION

he managed to juggle several steamy affairs, but duty and politics tempered his appetites. Sex played a subordinate role in his quest for power.

After his marriage to Marion in 1922, he settled for conjugality sobered by the prospect of procreation. The latter was a thought he did not wish to contemplate. By mutual consent and for reasons of career interests - he politics, she the care of a father domineering even in his feebleness - they would postpone having children immediately. Soon after their wedding he put aside an interest in raising a big family like so many of his friends. He channeled his unfulfilled desire into the reputation he was building as a shrewd lawyer and prospective leader. He tightened his personal mores. He knew he could be wiped out instantly by criticism from the chancels and pulpits of absolutist Protestant, absolutist Catholic Pennsylvania for the slightest indiscretion. He confined his carnal urges to the marital bed.

A daughter, Pamela, was born in 1927. He did not see much of her due to his expanding law practice. Marion, following the practices of families of wealth, left the baby's care and pre-school education in the hands of a succession of nannies.

Pent up animal desire reappeared the instant he was confronted by Lenore Price's high-spirited sensuality. Lust long latent burned in him again. It was not simply her physical attractiveness which she possessed in abundance. It was chemistry, biological affinity, mystery. They shared the same raw carnality.

"Oh, Zach. When are we ever going to be free together? I realize your obligations must come first, but, darling, I need you so. I really planned everything around your last free weekend. It's so difficult for me to share you with the crowd. I know I shouldn't put myself before your duty, but I was so looking forward to this time together. I'm terribly disappointed. Can you come over and cheer me up?"

"I'm on my way."

Within ten minutes Zach Harris's bony finger pressed the buzzer of Lenore Price's mailbox. It was greeted by five short accented bursts of code, which he translated instantly: "shave and a haircut." He responded with his usual, "two bits." She waited for him at her doorway half way down a long corridor. He liked the shadowed slatternly look she presented. As soon as the apartment door clicked closed, he tossed his grey homburg on the sofa, slipped off his suit coat and pulled her to him. They embraced pressing hard against each other. His hand moved behind her neck and under her soft brown hair, working the zipper of her dress slowly downward. She massaged him with her long, slender hands. They moved into the bedroom, disrobed slowly and made love.

# Jack Eddinger

"Why must you go back this weekend, darling? Weren't you there just a week or so ago." Lenore Price sat up in bed and lit a cigarette, barely concealing her disappointment. Earlier that day, she had picked out a sexy black sheath at Garfinckel's then stopped by the French Market in Georgetown for bread, veal and escargots for the special dinner she planned for her congressman. She made a quick diversion to Plain Old Pearson's for the wine. A clerk with a New York accent suggested a bottle of *Chateau Haut-Brion* 1950, a vintage *Mercier Cuvee* champagne and a bottle of *Martell Cordon Bleu*, his favorite cognac. "With these libations, dear lady, I guarantee you a superior evening," the clerk told her. On her way home she stopped at Magruder's for fresh strawberries, ice cream and a pungent square of Pont L'Eveque, *le fromage exquisite de Normande*, as the hand-lettered store sign proclaimed. It would be a very special evening.

Congressman Harris relaxed completely in the company of Lenore Price. He regarded her as among the true political *cognescenti*, and listened attentively to her views on national issues. Sometimes he'd say things he'd otherwise regard as revealing too much or that he'd have to backtrack on later. He took great pleasure from her doting concern for him.

"Things have gotten complicated, and if I'm not there to sort them out and bang a few heads, nothing'll get done," he said with feigned exasperation. "You'd think politics would settle into routine after twenty-five years. No rest for the weary. I have to put in an appearance at the Democratic Women's fund-raiser tomorrow night. Can't duck it. I'm the honoree. I've always said that whenever you start getting the honor instead of giving it, you better look at who's calling you a statesman, which is a way of referring to your age without saying as much. Next thing you know there'll be a credible young and vigorous opponent instead of the broken down jackass the GOP's put up this time. I believe 1960 will be the year for change; one of those watershed years of generational change."

"Darling, I'm surprised at you. Since when does Zachary Taylor Harris worry about an opponent or the future. You're head and shoulders above anyone in Congress, let alone anyone in Pennsylvania. You could be Speaker or Majority Leader or Secretary of State in a Democratic administration. It's not like you to be overly concerned," she said taking his hand and looking deeply into his gray eyes.

"Well, y'know, Lenore, I'm not getting any younger - 59 next August. Even a politician as successful as I've been has to begin thinking about retiring. Sometimes I think there's nothing I'd like more than an ambassadorship - Switzerland. Now, that's my cup of tea, or should I say snifter of *Poire Williams*? Y'know, maybe it'll be doable in a few years," he

# INQUISITION

lied. "How would that be? I've got just the place. Berne isn't so hot. Spent time there after the war. Been in and out of Zurich. Gives me headaches, all that dampness and chill off the lake. I prefer the south. I've had my eye on a place in the hills above Lugano overlooking the lake. We'll stay at one of the most beautiful small hotels in Europe. Villa Castagnola. It's charming with its green lawns and wraparound porches under bright orange awnings. Very English in spite of its name. Just down the road from Villa Fiorentina. Maybe I can get Baron von Fricke, to give us a tour of his art collection. It's the finest private collection in Europe, perhaps the world. I helped him when the Allies were trying to break up his steel interests in the Saar after VE Day. He's a gay old lecher. I understand he has a world class collection of pornographic art. Asked me to look him up anytime. Maybe he can help us find the perfect little house on the mountain side. I've been eying an appointment to a new international commission being set up in Geneva to monitor refugee movements around the world. The House will name several of the members. My seniority and work on immigration will be sufficient to land one of the appointments. I'd like you to serve as an administrative assistant to the commission at an executive secretary's salary tax-free. I will also set you up with a *pied-a-terre* in the diplomats district. We can use it as a base and spend weekends in Lugano while we search for a permanent place in the sun. What do you say to that my striking Miss Desert Flower?"

"Ohh Zach, how absolutely marvelous; how exciting. I adore Ticino. My grand-parents took a lovely lace-curtained chalet in Orselino above Lake Maggiore when I was a little girl. I'll never forget seeing snow on the Alps through palm trees. It's so romantic. I'd love to be with you. And the Italian Swiss. They're so full of life. Nothing like their stiff-necked German cousins in Zurich. And the little towns like Ascona and Brissago along the lake are so charming and clean. Lugano's just perfect. And working with you in Geneva! How exciting! A girl's dream come true. I love you, darling."

"Well, I want you to know I'm giving a lot of things serious thought. Running every two years is a drain on any man, no matter how safe the district. But before that can happen, I've got to get reelected, and that means roadwork, sweetheart; raising money, plugging candidates and winning big. I figure I've consumed enough stringy chicken and steel peas at $50-a-plate dinners over the years to gain a place in the Poultry and Pea Pickers Hall of Fame."

"That's original, Zach. You ought to ad lib it in your introductory remarks tomorrow night. Who is the main speaker? Anyone famous?"

# Jack Eddinger

"Oh god no; a career diplomat name of Masters. Assistant Secretary of State for African Affairs. Assistant secretaries of anything are a humorless lot, Lenore. Dulles must have recruited this guy straight out of the ministry. I had him up to the office on a courtesy call before his confirmation. He spent most of the time unraveling the longest damned tobacco pouch you've ever seen, and fidgeting with his pipe like a damned English vicar. He's opaque. Africa's the perfect place for him. Belongs in Sierra Leone or Liberia or one of those godawful holes on the Dark Continent."

"I read in the *Post* this morning that Adlai's making headway in the polls, Zach? I just adore him. Do you think he can win?"

"I think on the whole the Democratic Party's stronger than '52. But even with his health problems, Eisenhower's still awfully popular. He brings out a vote that you could normally count on staying home on election day. Makes it tough on all of us. That's why I'm running harder and spending a lot more money. Sometimes you wonder whether it's still worth the effort. The House isn't what it once was. These newcomers want everything overnight, grandstanding and grabbing the microphone at every opportunity. Even the subversive hearings have been anti-climactic. I was committed to winding them down in this session, but just this afternoon that damned fool at the Bureau has requested new hearings in January. Claims he has new evidence involving the professor I had up before the committee today. Thought we were finished. Damn, how I'd really like to put it all behind me and get on with our lives."

"Will you be seeing Marion tomorrow?"

Lenore Price longed for the opportunity to confront Marion Harris. She wanted to talk candidly with her; to reach a reasonable understanding like mature women. But he always found a way to deflect discussing the subject whenever she mentioned a divorce. He told her nothing of his wife's situation other than their mutual agreement to present the appearance of a long and faithful marriage, but to go their separate ways. She accepted his explanation as an arrangement not unlike Eleanor and Franklin's. Even though their affair was private, to Lenore Price it was open and honest just as she believed herself to be. Theirs was a discreet relationship between two adults whose emotional and psychological needs blended surpassingly, and de facto voided the marriage contract which had already been breached in fact, if not in law. She accepted the situation as a problem that would soon be resolved. He spoke vaguely about filing for divorce. Being from the Southwest, where male-female relationships possessed a quality of impermanence, Lenore never fully grasped what she considered Eastern priggishness about divorce, particularly in a loveless marriage.

# INQUISITION

"We've got to appear in public together, Lenore. The voters' think there's no estrangement. Look what's happening to Stevenson, and he's been divorced for more than a decade. Nixon and the Republicans are shoving the stiletto in every chance they get. I don't want to give anybody the slightest reason to vote against me. This will be the last campaign. Two years from now, you and I will be out of their range. Just be patient with me for one more term. And don't forget we'll soon have Geneva together. It could be as early as next year. After that, who knows, maybe Mr. Ambassador?"

It was a lie. He could never leave politics. It defined him; it gave him his place in the universe; it provided the fuel necessary to keep going. He needed the confidence of the comrades, as well as the adversaries he'd shared the legislative harness with for nearly three decades. Like them and all who preceded them, he was defined by forces, which he truly believed only the elect could interpret, clarify and channel into the great stream of American history. Yet, he truly loved her and enjoyed the warmth and tenderness she showered on him, but to which it was impossible for him to surrender, or to open himself to vulnerability. To him his relationship with Lenore Price was in perfect balance. He'd just like to leave things that way.

# CHAPTER FIVE
## *The Connection*

A vast, swirling storm front spread over the Atlantic seaboard. Inland and to the west, across the Appalachian Divide the first light snow of the season sifted down on dark spruce and hemlock forests. To the east along the coastal plain, mixed rain and snow turned an ugly evening miserable. It was good to be indoors. The truce in Korea was in its fourth year and holding. Drew Pearson predicted that Adlai Stevenson and Estes Kefauver would be buried by the Eisenhower-Nixon ticket in the 1956 election - now only a few weeks away - under a landslide bigger than FDR's defeat of Alf Landon twenty years before. Earlier that summer, President Eisenhower landed troops in Lebanon and told the British and French to get out of Suez or the U.S. Marines would escort them out.

In the Lenape Valley, U.S. Representative Zachary Taylor Harris was ending an exhausting but satisfying campaign kickoff. In the coming weeks he'd be hammering at his opponent at rallies and campaign stops throughout the 26th congressional district. He could not resist tagging Marcel, "Palmer's little hairdresser." He was getting laughs and cheers everywhere until the Barbers and Cosmeticians union told him to knock it off.

On the same night Congressman Harris was addressing the ILGWU in Bessemer City, eighty miles to the east in Union City, New Jersey, four men - three middle aged, the fourth about 25 - sat at a table in a low-roofed cinder-block building. They listened intently to the man at the head of the table. He sat behind rolls of blueprints, specification drawings and the backed-up paper work of a thriving construction company. His small, almost delicate hands played an expressive glissando to an impassive face. A lacquered fingernail traced an arc in the parchment glow of a desk lamp. The yellow light shaped the lower part of his face, cheeks, nose and mandible, into a mask flecked with the blue-black residue of gunpowder. Floor to ceiling draperies insulated the room against the throb of traffic. Tractor trailers grinding into low gear, entered the long downhill grade outside the building. A window air conditioner hissed *soto voce* in the background.

"*Amici miei*, you've given me the benefit of your knowledge and skills many times. I want you to know they've been of great value in the formation of our enterprises," the man said. "Now, once again, I need you to advance our interests. Stefano Maglie brings me very distressing news. Our enterprises, Maglie informs me, are experiencing the very same

# INQUISITION

difficulty we corrected five years ago. Each of you understood what was required. What I want now, *amici, es finalimente. Giuro vendetta."*

It was not the leaden face or the hooded eyes, or the speaker's expressive hands that commanded respect, but the animal power lurking in his low, throaty voice. It imparted the measured rationality of a man at ease with power and manipulation. It held the capacity to persuade by inference; the ability to make others see the exquisite rationality of a plan, and the necessity to carry out its most minute detail. Enunciated precisely, the Italian language possesses exceptional strength, beauty and clarity. When spoken with the slurred inflection of the northwestern quadrant of the island of Sicily it plunges into imprecision and mystery. Facial expression and gesture dominate. Long silences slice into the psyche and test the capacity to endure.

"The services I require, *amici,* are those which you performed in *Febraio Nel Mille Novacento Cinquantuno.* This time *niente concezioni. Una conclusione sodisfacente.*"

The men smoked in silence. Each understood exactly what was expected. Truck traffic on Highway 22, the four-lane ribbon slicing across New Jersey's shoulder blades, pounded eastward to the wharves and piers along the Hudson at Weehawken, Hoboken and West New York. In the rear of a men's clothing store a mile from the cinder block building, two men in shirtsleeves, ties askew, listened with headphones as the reel of a Wollensack tape recorder rotated. They had been listening to the private conversations of Gaetano Cavalieri Russo for six months. At the Federal Office Building in Newark they replayed the previous day's tapes in the dismal green-walled office of Frank Jordan, special agent in charge of the Federal Bureau of Investigation's field office for northern New Jersey. Jordan headed the Bureau's special electronic surveillance team he code-named, Operation Garibaldi, just for the hell of it. The name stuck and was used in official reports on the comings and goings of visitors to the Cavalier Construction Co.

Jordan sipped his coffee and made notes on a yellow legal pad. Had the men in the cinder block building the benefit of fluoroscopic vision, they might have noticed the tiny but powerful electronic listening device embedded in the knotty pine paneling just above eye level. The knots were sanded smooth and lacquered to match the wall. Frank Jordan listened intently as he had listened on previous mornings, then he went to a gray file cabinet, unlocked it and rolled out the drawer. His eyes skimmed over the plastic tabs. He found the one he was looking for, then rooted through the drawer until he found the others.

# Jack Eddinger

"Here they are." A smile crawled across his angular face. "Reads like a textbook of Renaissance villainy. Gaetano Russo, *Il Duco*, Salvatore DiFrancese, *Il Comandante*, Joseph Zaccardi, *Il Cocchiere*, and Robert Basilico, *La Torcia. Uomini respettato, et Spirito Santo, Amen.*"

"Henderson, run a check of the regional file for *Febraio Mille Novacento Cinquantuno* - February, 1951 to you non-Latins. See what we've got. I want everything: police reports from all jurisdictions, newspaper clippings, radio tapes, fire calls, ambulance runs. Whatever. And get back up here ASAP. "Miss Ellison, hold my calls, unless it's Washington. Get yourself a cuppa coffee, Foster. I want to hear a segment of that tape again. Frank Jordan lit a Chesterfield, picked up one of the folders and began reading aloud. Special Agent Albert R. Foster, a ten-year FBI man trained in electronic surveillance closed the door, turned his chair around, straddled it and sat down.

"Wadd'ya think, Frank? We got anything?"

"I don't know, but I will say that from the records on this trio, Russo isn't planning a street festival for St. Francis of Assisi. Looks more like the invasion of Sicily.

The tape continued.

*"If we have learned one thing,* amici, *it is that when a year has produced inferior wine, with no prospects for improvement in the next growing season, we must harvest what's left, prune back to the roots and burn the old vines. But before we can begin grafting, we must assure that our root stock is free of disease - no foreign matter."*

"Shoulda hit 'im four years ago."

"No, amico, quella 'e la cosa guista da farsi. Niente accommadante. Finito.

"*Va bene. Action. Remember when we whacked the little guy? Joe hadda tire iron around his throat. I stiffed 'im in the* coglioni *five, six times. He goes down and comes up again.* Fantoccio a Molo. *Up down, up down; up down. Joe hit 'im again and again. Nose is bleedin, eyes comin outa his fuckin head. Up, down; up, down. Then he pukes and croaks. Sonofabitch, little as they are, they struggle."*

"Amici, *I want Mimi to handle our basic concern. I expect it to be executed with skill,* con esatezza. *Bobby, you know what to do. Giuseppe, I want a clean work site. Above all,* niente rintracciare. *Tell me what you need. You are to work through Stefano Maglie. No one else. If complications arise, he'll work things out. See him for* i vostri pagamenti.

"I gotta have un pagamento anticipato *for some new stuff I heard about. My source wants the money up front. What do I do?*

"Quanto?"

# INQUISITION

"Uno mille."
*(Silence)*
"Cinquacento. *See Maglie for the rest.*"
*"Mimi?"*
"No. Nuthin. Later."
"Giuseppe?"
"Si?"
"Che cosa le serve?"
"Niente."
"Buono. *I expect the job to be completed in the next five days. Bobby, if you have problems, I want you and no one else to handle them through Maglie. You are not to return here under any circumstances. Now, you are my guests tonight at La Casa Lucca. Enjoy."*

End of tape.

At 1 a.m. three men walked to the wet parking lot outside the Casa Lucca restaurant on U.S. Route 22 in Union City. A black Ford coupe, a red Thunderbird classic and a battered and rusting gray Dodge pick-up truck were lined up under the glare of floodlights. Salvatore Di Francese belched loudly got into the coupe, and wheeled around. "Fuckin peppers. They give me gas." Tires shrieked on the damp asphalt. He turned into the eastbound lane of the divided highway and roared away, passing through a neon-lit strip with signs flashing the incessant commands of all-night truckers' meals and cut-rate gasoline. He sped past a discount clothing store in the shape of a trans-Atlantic liner, and a drive-in movie showing the last scenes of an Elvis Presley double feature to a deserted concrete amphitheater. Bobby Basilico and Joseph Zaccardi stood in the light rain talking for ten minutes. Then they got into their vehicles and drove away. Half an hour later, Bobby Basilico locked the door of his 1953 T-Bird, and tightened the belt of his camel's hair polo coat. He tossed the car key's in the air, caught them jauntily and walked towards Il Ceppo's in midtown Manhattan. He pushed his way through the crowded bar, waving to the bartenders. They nodded towards the rear of the restaurant. Bobby Basilico was a suave mixture of paten leather and innocent blue eyes. Women found him irresistible. The next afternoon he drove to a maritime pier under the West Side Highway. A forklift operator negotiated a 50-gallon oil drum from the rear of a sheet metal building and lowered it into the trunk of the T-Bird. Bobby handed the forklift man five one hundred dollar bills then drove away.

Joseph Zaccardi pulled his beat up pick-up into the gravel driveway of a repair garage on a dead-end street that backed up to the Pennsylvania Railroad tracks in Linden. He walked up a flight of wooden stairs which

# Jack Eddinger

creaked and swayed under his weight. He stretched for a light switch at the top. The words, "Calabrese Bros. Truck Repairs," came on with the lights. He tossed his sweat-stained cap on a chair, went to the refrigerator and took out a gallon jug. He poured himself a glass, flipped on the television and sat before the blue glow at a fold-up tray holding the jug of red wine. The label had a picture of an old man and a donkey cart. The picture reminded him of Calabria and his grandfather.

Gaetano Cavalieri Russo completed his paper work and took his golf clubs from a closet. He slung the bag over his shoulder, picked up his spiked black and white wingtips and shouldered off the lights. He put his clubs in the trunk of a white Sedan de Ville, and looked up into the darkness. He saw a few stars, and knew daylight would bring one of the better weekends of the fall for 36 holes of golf at the Kenilworth Country Club. He'd tee off at 8 a.m. sharp with the usual foursome consisting of himself, the President of the First Federal Bank of Union City, the Mayor of Newark and former Congressman F.X. O'Hara, chairman of the Essex County Democratic Central Committee. When the penetrating Arctic cold rolled in off the Atlantic in January and February, he'd pick up the tab for his foursome every fourth weekend in Miami. His white sedan with New Jersey license plates GCR-1, was familiar to every attendant who worked the VIP parking lot at Newark International Airport.

"Let's take these guys one by one, said Frank Jordan.

**"DI FRANCESE, SALVATORE** - Little Mimi to those of you who follow the comics. Except he's no comic book character - is 55. Lives in West New York. Occupation, laborer. Sandhog on both tunnels in the 30's, a gang boss on the G.W. Bridge job, and performed masonry duties on the Sing Sing rock pile."

An index card held Salvatore DiFrancese's extensive involvement with law enforcement agencies: Born, Pescara, Italy, 3-5-00. Naturalized U.S. citizen, 6-21-28.

1. Bootlegging - eight charges, one conviction.
   Two years Sing Sing Federal Penitentiary,
   Ossining, New York, 1930-32.
2. Assault - five charges, 1929-35. No convictions.
3. Armed robbery - four charges. One conviction.
   Sentenced State Penitentiary, Dannemora, 1940-45.
   Recommendation for deportation stayed by order U.S. Department of War, Jan. 13, 1945.

# INQUISITION

4. Extortion - charged in three-count indictment, 1949. Grand Jury dismissal, lack of evidence.

What the concise FBI profile of Salvatore (Little Mimi) Di Francese did not show was his extensive service as a hit man. He was, in the words of the agent who compiled the report, "an animal on a leash. Unchain him and he will kill just for the fun of it."

A frown wrinkled Frank Jordan's forehead and moved across his baldness. He opened the second file.

**BASILICO, ROBERT**, a/k/a Bobby Brown. White
male. 30, Newark, N.J. Born 8-11-30.
Occupation unknown. One year service Newark City Fire Dept.,
Level-1 Firefighter. Enlisted U.S. Army,
1948. MOS, Ordnance Specialist (Explsvs.) Hon. Disch., PFC, 1952

1. Arrested disorderly conduct (drunk) 12-26-50.
   Guilty Plea, Essex County District Court.
2. Paid $50 fine. Traffic Division, N.J. State Police,
   arrested 9-20-51, speeding NJTP (Subject driving 125 mph).
3. DWI, 11-17-51. Charge dismissed, faulty transcript;
4. Speeding, 1-20-50, S. Carolina Highway Patrol.
   Guilty plea. Paid $100 fine at JP hearing. NFI.

A file in the open cases section at New Jersey State Police Headquarters, Trenton, doubtless would have been of great interest to Frank Jordan. It reported the details of a three-alarm fire the night of January 18, 1953. Three buildings of a suburban shopping district in Morristown were burned out - a dry cleaners, a clothing store and a jewelry shop. This single act earned Bobby Basilico professional respect. So complete was the burnout that the police could not determine the precise loss for days. By then Bobby Basilico had turned the sapphires, emeralds and diamonds into a wad of $1,000 bills at a jewelry shop in midtown Manhattan. Then he turned his T-Bird south toward the Miami sunshine. Jewelry dealers got the word around - a new talent had arrived on the street. Gaetano Cavalieri Russo, who savored an exceptional skill even more than jewels and Florentine antiquities, sent word that such talent was in demand and would be handsomely rewarded. Because his specialty had not yet received wide acclaim, the FBI file in Newark was silent.

# Jack Eddinger

Frank Jordan lit another Chesterfield.

**ZACCARDI, JOSEPH**, a/k/a, Joe Calabrese. White male, 43. Occupation, operator, truck repair garage, Linden, N.J., Class AA chauffeur's license, heavy equipment permit. Born Reggio di Calabria, Italy, 9-8-12. Naturalized U.S. citizen June, 1936. No record of arrests. Information source, U.S. INS, 90 Church St., Manhattan.

"Don't bother with Russo's pedigree," Foster told Jordan. "Clean, except for lottery charges he beat years ago before he surfaced and seemingly went legit. He's been in just about everything since - used cars, leasing - owned a couple of buildings over in Sheepshead Bay and was hauled before the Price Stabilization Board during the war for jacking up rents. Then into roofing, paving, general contracting. Now this construction operation. I hear he has interests in antique shops, too. How's that for a well-rounded portfolio? No criminal record. The only thing we've come up with is civil stuff - liens for lousy construction work and a damage suit on a school job default. Beat 'em all."

"Yeah, and he must be a helluva negotiator. At a time when construction operations are shut down every other week, he's got labor peace. Tells you something about his executive abilities, huh," said Jordan.

A ledger entry in a big black registry - the kind used to docket official proceedings - kept by the United States Immigration and Naturalization Service during the 1930s might have made a man of Frank Jordan's impatience call his wife and cancel their anniversary dinner. An entry in September 1934 noted the admittance of a 22-year-old Sicilian through the Port of Brooklyn by authority of a personal privilege bill passed by the U.S. House of Representatives. "Naturalization hearing waived, 73rd Congress, House of Representatives Committee on the Judiciary, recommendation of the subcommittee on immigration." The statement appeared next to the name of one Gaetano Cava of Castellamare del Golfo, Provincia di Palermo, Italia. The entry was written in long hand by some retired or deceased immigration clerk whose writing showed the strain of recording the long lines of European émigrés standing before his desk. The notation was unexceptional. Routine matters, as they so often do, fall between the cracks, and cracks open chasms. Alien registry papers and supporting documentation had never been filed. It was congressional privilege pure and simple. No immigration clerk or reviewing officer would question an Act of Congress. A young refugee from Mussolini's bully boys brought in under congressional fiat was a simple, charitable act of a generous nation.

# INQUISITION

Plenty of Jews were getting in. An Italian now and then will balance the books. They're hard workers, they keep their mouths shut and will put something in an envelope for you. Nice and clean - no language barrier on that. The only supporting record was the index card. It identified the young man's sponsor as one Giordano Della Notte and gave an address in Brooklyn's Red Hook section. The author of the special legislation was not given but a check of the *Congressional Record* for that date would show that Rep. F.X. O'Hara, of New Jersey, reported ten personal privilege bills to the floor. The originating documents plus information from Italian authorities were locked away in an impenetrable safe. Nor was there a record that the surname, Cava, had dropped away like a chrysalis to be replaced by Rosso, metamorphosed to Russo, Red.

Frank Jordan and his eavesdroppers had been monitoring the activities of Cavalier Construction Co. and its influential president for nearly two years. But telephone intercepts do not tell the story of a man's life. Only another Castellamarese could fully appreciate the special events which preceded the long journey of a lad from Castellamare del Golfo to New York in the summer of 1934. Don Cava would know. But the old man rests now in a grave on the peaceful hillside which looks northeastward over the fishing village into the intense blue of the Tyrennhian Sea. It was the last month of the old man's life. He summoned young Gaetano to the austere upstairs room of the whitewashed Villa Cava. There, he sipped the earthy, dark Segesta and watched little fishing boats coming and going far out on the gulf, while his father spoke of his friends in America. Often, the boy would remember this time with his father. He drew strength from the old man even in his infirmity. He would recall the day his father asked for his complete trust. He was told to pack a single *valigia*. He was to make a long journey. It was no longer safe for the first son to remain in Castellamare del Golfo. That retribution for his father's intense rivalry with Don Calo and the insult it provoked would be visited upon the son, went unquestioned on the island of fire, volcanic ash and subterfuge. His father's friends in America would protect him, and would put his good mathematical mind to use.

"You are too *intellegente* to be tending vines and planting wheat, *mia figlio*," his father had said. I am too old for what lies ahead, but the honor of the Cavas will be defended and upheld. This island shall see the last of one generation. It shall not bury the sons of a new one. You must leave Castellamare tonight."

The old man embraced his son and kissed him on both cheeks and on his palms. *"Bienvenuto, mia piccolo Gaetano."* He was never to see his father again. He wept and thought of the farewell when Zio Giordano brought word of the old man's death a few months later. A peaceful death is a blessing, but his father was to know neither. In New York Gaetano thought often of his father and the stories his father told him of America. When Gaetano was a lad of ten, his father told him of the life they once lived together in the great land across the sea. He told his son that one day the boy would leave the choking dust of their village and take up a new life in America. The boy often went to the hilltop above the sea and strained his eyes to see the land of his father. Gaetano would be puzzled by the words stamped across his father's papers from America:

**DEPORTED 6/8/12; UNDESIRABLE ALIEN**

The boy knew only that his father was *e uomo di rispettato*, who held the allegiance of many men from the provinces of northwestern Sicily who came seeking favors at the Villa Cava. In Red Hook Gaetano lived at the house of his father's cousin, Giordano della Notte. The house stood on the edge of the vast basin with its oil and fish smells. The merchant navies of the world deposited their cargoes with the help of cranes and trucks and olive-skinned men from Castellamare and Catania, Reggio de Calabria and Napoli, Provenza and Casteldeluccio. He worked long hours for small wages. But it was good work. Work he enjoyed. Work with men he liked, and who liked and respected him. Work that he would one day use to great advantage. Many men had no work at all. They came to the office of Zio Giordano for help. Giordano della Notte received them with respect just like Don Cava. Zio Giordano and the boy would help the men find work in the basin, perhaps only for one day out of ten, but work. Giordano Della Notte always acknowledged their gratitude, nodding and pointing to the boy. He told them to remember that Gaetano was the son of their friend, Don Cava. Like the boy's father, Zio Giordano was a man of respect.

The events of his arrival in America were always with him. It was a warm, brilliant spring day when his father's first cousin met him at the foot of the gangplank of *L'Isola d'Elba*, kissed him as his father had done, took his *valigia*, put an arm around his shoulder and walked with him toward the office of the Italo-American Fruit Shippers. The office was a second floor loft in a wharf on a dilapidated pier with large dark openings. Railroad tracks ran into the darkness and disappeared. Zio Giordano saw the black sedan burst out of the darkness. Instantly, he pushed the boy to the ground covering him with his bulk. A flash exploded out of the back seat. The pellets shattered the boy's jaw and tore skin from his face. He lay in quiet terror under Zio Giordano's inert bulk as the car sped away. The sisters at Mater Consolata Hospital prayed each day in their small chapel

# INQUISITION

asking God to guide the fingers of the surgeon attempting to restore the beauty of the young man's face. They were only partially successful.

Later, when the bandages came off and the skin grafts were less frequent, Gaetano was no longer afraid. He was grateful to Zio Giordano's first son, Salvatore, who cared for him, and who spoke to the immigration official who visited him in his hospital room. Salvatore spoke in the dialect of the Napolitani and handed the official an envelope. The boy was asked to sign his name many times on the papers. His eyes passed over one with an eagle inside a circle at the top of the page. It was not a *Fascisti* eagle as he had seen in Castellamare, but one with pointed sticks in its claws and a Latin phrase he was able to read. Under the circle was a language he did not understand. Many years later, he would bring other young men to America just as his uncle's family had brought him; men who were of great value to him in organizing his enterprises. One day when he came to know his father's friends and their work more completely; when he was able to read and speak the language of the eagle paper with only a trace of the accent of the Castellamarese, he had Stefano Maglie, his *consigliere*, sign new papers, which would bring great respect, respect even his father had not known. Across the table in a Manhattan hotel room sat a man whom he was told held great power and influence; a man who could assure protection for his businesses.

Special Agents Frank Jordan and Al Foster spent the next five hours sifting through records and documents from two years of pulling apart the diverse enterprises of Cavalieri Construction, Inc. At 3 P.M. Special Agent Tom Henderson took the elevator six flights to Jordan's cramped office. From the thousands of pieces of law enforcement and public record information that flowed into the center in the early days of February 1951, Henderson was looking for a fragment, which in the hands of skilled investigators might penetrate the intricacies of the Sicilian mind; a mind genetically shrouded over the centuries in a secrecy which folds itself in mists, like the fog that crawls into mountain valleys of the Alto Adige, burying forests and villages, and holding light unto itself. One thing was in his favor. Mid-winter meant a low level of traffic on the teletype network linking fifty police jurisdictions in the region covered by the FBI's Newark office. The clerks were told nothing of the purpose of their search. Henderson wanted only information on significant activity: murder, robbery, larceny, aggravated assault, auto theft, or about items involving the use of firearms or explosives. Henderson was interested in incidents reported from four New Jersey counties - Essex, Morris, Hunterdon and Warren, and two across the Delaware River in Pennsylvania, Hampton and Lenape. Together, the six political jurisdictions comprised the territory,

## Jack Eddinger

which the United States Government identified as the domain of La Famiglia Russo, one of the invisible governments operating in the eastern United States like those which rule with impunity in Palermo, Partinico, Gela and Agrigento.

"Waddya got?" Jordan asked.

"Not a helluva lot. First off, I cut out most of the local stuff, figuring Russo's had it pretty tightly controlled with his own people. It's not likely he'd allow too much to get out of control in the back yard."

"You're right there."

"So I began tracking reports from the two western counties and the two over in P.A. Lots of routine stuff: something like 75 burglaries, a cartload of auto thefts, a bank robbery outside Somerville, a hijacking in Phillipsburg, a few routine gambling raids over in McKean - dice, monte and a fair numbers bank. Then I ran through ambulance calls. Just the police stuff. Added up to less than a handful - a couple of knifings; a shooting in Bessemer City, black-on-black; a slew of muggings and domestic assaults. Nothing we'd be interested in. Newspapers had very little. This is the only thing I found. Not much."

Henderson shoved the news clipping across the desk to Jordan.

It read:

*Bessemer City, Pa., Feb. 7 (AP) - A spectacular gas line explosion early today tore apart a popular night club-restaurant and office complex here causing $90,000 in damage, police reported. There were no injuries. The explosion occurred at 3 a.m. and demolished a kitchen and office, and leveled the main dining room of the Blue Peacock in East River Twp. five miles east of this steel center. Police tentatively attributed the blast to a ruptured gas line. Officials of the East Penn Gas Light Co. were unable to confirm the cause, but said the line could have burst as a result of the recent cold snap which has sent temperatures plummeting to below zero. The restaurant owner, Anastas L. Kourkorian, referred all questions to his attorney. He could not be reached for comment.*

"I don't know," Jordan said passing the clipping to Foster. "It doesn't look like a god-damned thing to me. Bank robbery and hijacking are more their style - 'very special services, *amici*.'"

"No, the bank heist was in broad daylight, two jigs in stocking masks - as far as I know Russo hasn't integrated yet," said Henderson. "The hijacking? Possibly. Three goons. Involved a shipment of dresses and furs out of Reading to Bergdorf Goodman. Could've been a Russo operation. A piece of cake. They got about $100,000 worth of good goods."

# INQUISITION

"Is every Armenian named Anastas?" Foster interrupted. Jordan looked at his wireman as if he'd just asked for six months leave.

"What in hell does that mean?" Foster had broken Jordan's intense concentration with the obtuse remark, and the boss didn't like it one bit.

"Nothing. But it seems like every time I see an Armenian name, the first name's always Anastas. Like that little Russian with the big mustache. What's 'is name. You know, McCoy, or somethin. He's always behind Khrushchev in the pictures. He goes back a long way. Started in the 1920s with Stalin." Foster pronounced it Staleen.

"That's Mikoyan. Anastas Mikoyan. He's been around since the Bolshevik Revolution," said Henderson. "Their last names always end in I A N or A N. Like Saroyan, William Saroyan. He wrote *The Time of Your Life* or was it The Skin of Your Nose? Something like that."

"*Skin of Your Teeth*, Shakespeare," Jordan growled. He wrote it in 1946. Thornton Wilder wrote, *The Time of Your Life*."

"*Anastas L. Kourkorian*," Foster intoned. "*A man who'll ne'er pay a whore again. Why won't he do it? Not everyone knew it, but he'd banged her before she was one of 'em.*"

"Not bad, Al. With a little practice you'd qualify as official latrine laureate," Jordan snapped. "Let's knock off the literary exercise and get some work done, dammit."

"Nothing literary about Anastas L. Kourkorian, Frank. He's the owner of the Blue Peacock or what was left of it on the morning of February 6, 1951. That's what it says here." Foster slid the news clipping back across the desk.. Frank Jordan clamped his lips.

"I'll be god-damned. Al, hit that rewind switch. There's something on that tape I want to hear again."

"Huh?" asked Foster.

"Play it again, Sam. Maybe it's nothing, but you got me thinking with that Armenian business."

"What d'ya mean, Frank?"

Foster pushed the rewind button sending the tape backward then sped it forward in a whir of bird twitter. It took several minutes before Jordan found what he wanted. "There. That's it. Run that through again."

"... *our vines. But first we must remove all foreign matter.*"

"Zip it back again."

"... *we must remove all foreign matter.*"

"Dammit, that's it."

The two agents looked at their boss puzzled.

"I don't get it," Foster said. What do you mean?"

# Jack Eddinger

"Look," Jordan said, "These Sicilians use all kinds of nuances, metaphors and hidden meanings. You gotta learn their code. When you crack it, it makes sense."

"Great, but what's grape vines got to do with a couple of heavies pullin a job for Russo, boss? I thought we were lookin for ..."

"It was there all the time," Jordan said.

"C'mon, Frank. What was there? How about sharing the secret."

"Tell you what. I want you two literature majors to do some research for me. Al, see if our Philadelphia office has any tape on this hotshot wop lawyer, Maglie. I'll take anything they got."

"Henderson, I want you to run Kourkorian through your files downstairs. I want anything you got on him. Get crackin."

"I don't see what some skin joint operator over on the Pennsylvania border has to do with what we're looking for in Jersey, Frank."

"Do it, will ya."

After his two agents left the room, Frank Jordan sank into deep contemplation. His reverie was short-lived. "Double whammy down in Philly, Frank," said Foster pulling the door behind him. "Turns out our brethren in the City of Brotherly Love have had taps on two very unlovable guys sixty miles up the road. Dammit, we need central files on this stuff. I hate going through the back door. Director's hell on sharing things in the field. Anyway, here's what Philly gave me on the q.t.- they say Maglie doesn't report to anyone in their territory. They got taps up everybody's ass from the Susquehanna to the Delaware and all points in between. The action down there's run by Fat Tony Strello. Maglie's not exactly Tony's dish of pastafazool. A guy that goes to the barber every day, has his nails lacquered and wears french cuffs ain't South Philly. Dress code at 9th and Christian is blue suede shoes, shiny suits and duck-ass haircuts. The line on Maglie is he belongs to Russo. Kourkorian's pigshit. Runs numbers for Maglie. Mostly, dime store stuff in the Lenape Valley. Russo's given the whole operation to Maglie. He's the buffer between Strello and the Buffolinis upstate - Scranton-Wilkes Barre. The Buffos and Strello're always muscling each other. The Pocono Council put Russo between them. Russo's got a lot of action going. My guess's he'll outflank 'em both."

Henderson strolled through the door with a big smile on his face. He waved a file folder while whistling, *On The Street Where You Live*. "By damned you were right, Frank. It says here this guy's a two-bit numbers jock in Bessemer City. But you're only half right. Kourkorian's Lebanese. His mother was Armenian. Says so right here. Naturalized, 1938. I'll bet he's the foreign stuff Russo's talkin about on that tape. You know why? He's the only operator Russo's got who's not a guinea. The Duke's got him

# INQUISITION

on a choke chain. These are old files - nothin's up to date. But the stuff that's here's good enough for me to put a couple taps on him."

Frank Jordan snatched the file from Henderson with the sniff an adult gives an impetuous adolescent. Inside was the extensive police record of Anastas Lhouris "Fats" Kourkorian along with a fingerprint record and a police mug shot. "Here he is. And he's a beauty," Jordan said holding up the smudged card containing a front and profile view of the head and shoulders of a man of about 50. He held it at arm's length with two fingers, and wrinkled his nose, as if to say "skunk bait." By the thickness of the neck and the flaccid face he appeared to weigh in the 300 pound range. Closely set rodent's eyes were framed by tinted black-rimmed glasses. His thick black eyebrows blended with the frames. Unshaven and with his white shirt open at the neck, Anastas Kourkorian looked every inch the Levantine flesh merchant.

"I think we got our who. Now all we need is the what, why, where, how and when," said Frank Jordan. "And that could come anytime in the next 72 hours, if I got Russo's timetable down."

Two days before summoning Salvatore de Francese, Bobby Basilico and Joseph Zaccardi to the meeting in Union City, Gaetano Cavalieri Russo listened closely to Stefano Maglie's news. He appeared bored, even unconcerned. He moved his right hand, as if flicking a cigar ash. It had been exactly three years and eleven months since Anastas Kourkorian's first breach of faith. In dealing with that infidelity Gaetano Russo showed he was a man of strategic vision. A prince, in amassing great domains, must act in ways inconsistent with appearance. Anastas Kourkorian had succumbed to the first temptation that presents itself to men given responsibility beyond their capacities. The spring from which Anastas Kourkorian's hubris flowed was the irresistible magnetism of the small, red-eyed, fat-bellied idol of greed. It whispered in his ear that with wealth he would be the great man he knew he was. Indeed, wealth was his right. In his heart Anastas Kourkorian knew he deserved great respect and remuneration beyond the trifling sum he received for his considerable services. After all he was descended from Anatolian chieftains. An enlightened business pays handsomely for expertise, and Anastas Kourkorian's collecting, accounting and banking services demanded he be treated with equity and respect by Stefano Maglie, for whom he had little respect. Anastas Kourkorian began making adjustments. He levied a tax of one percent on all moneys collected from his operatives in the mills and lofts of Bessemer City's South End. They worked the back rooms of taverns and magazine stands along the streets and alleys which backed down to the Lenape. It was a paltry sum.

# Jack Eddinger

Instead of reporting his one percent commission he would raise it and make it grow by reinvestment. The previous year, 1950, produced remarkable results. His levy generated more than $50,000, which when added to his retainer would bring him respect and influence. With it, he would challenge the fraudulent Maglie. Gaetano Russo was a man of fairness and subtlety, but above all he appreciated the value of instant return on investment. He would understand. And Anastas Kourkorian, a man who understood the uses of flattery, would replace Maglie in Bessemer City and all of Eastern Pennsylvania.

    Gaetano Cavalieri Russo played the role of merchant prince with care and circumspection. Anything that would delay his plan to achieve a balanced and consolidated portfolio would create unnecessary problems. Eastern Pennsylvania was a promising vineyard. With skillful cultivation under a benevolent sun, in only a few years good wine would flow. For more than a decade this domain had appealed to his orderly Sicilian mind. At the meeting in the big fieldstone lodge in the high Poconos he argued forcefully to his associates that Eastern Pennsylvania's Lenape Valley be placed under his care and direction. They discussed it for an hour privately, then announced that the Lenape Valley would separate the Strello and Buffolini families, and henceforth and forever would be a province of La Famiglia Russo. He managed his new domains with considerable skill. They soon ranked second only to Newark. Under Stefano Maglie's careful cultivation, relentless attention to detail and unerring judgment, the Lenape Valley acquitted itself remarkably. As the duchies of Bayonne and Jersey City generated revenues from construction and labor contracts; Long Branch, Perth Amboy and Phillipsburg from package stores, taverns, restaurants and brothels, the Lenape Valley stood next to Newark as a rich satrapy of gambling in all of its permutations. At the century's midpoint, Gaetano Russo read the emerging American consumer psyche as Venetian traders read Christendom's hunger for material goods. Bessemer City and the Lenape Valley could be relied upon to return a high yield on a minimum investment. Weekly earnings exceeded $50,000 with annual untaxed profits of $2,600,000. Put to work in new businesses - vending machine companies, shopping centers, car wash garages, trucking companies, refuse hauling, funeral establishments, cocktail lounges and nightclub-office combinations like the Blue Peacock - it was returning a princely rate and extraordinary public and private influence to the man from Castellamare del Golfo.

    With characteristic precision Stefano Maglie carried out all aspects of Gaetano Cavalieri Russo's new writ. He put in motion the guarantees, which would extend the growing enterprise from its base in New Jersey.

# INQUISITION

He negotiated the agreements which opened investment opportunities for the family's newly acquired wealth, he settled labor disputes, and made it known that he would pay well for any service he required. Stefano Maglie had been his *consigliere* and confidante from the beginning in the 1930s. He came highly recommended by the Gargagno Family of Red Hook, whom he served as *avocate*. Maglie handled all legal matters and business contracts for Cavalier with firmness, efficiency and discretion. He was of special value in the political realm with his intimate knowledge of public projects and his broad contacts with the men who administered them. He understood the subtleties of recurring contracts and how they are enforced. The initials "**SM**" on a document guaranteed the full faith, credit and backing of the Cavalier organization. But his greatest coup came when he initialed the agreement guaranteeing freedom of operation to La Famiglia Russo in its lucrative new sphere of influence. The fulfillment of this extraordinary assignment placed him first in familial succession.

The year 1951 was a time to build, a time to consolidate; a time to invest, a time to arbitrate. Like a judicious Florentine prince Gaetano Russo would extend clemency even to thieves and brigands. He made it unmistakably clear that clemency, the prerogative of princes, must never be mistaken for weakness. To underscore this point, he commissioned a single, yet unforgettable demonstration. In the early hours of February 6, 1951 emissaries were dispatched from Union City. They would persuade the resident manager of the Blue Peacock, Anastas Kourkorian, to recognize his error, to do penance, to make restitution and to amend his ways. Only then would limited absolution follow. It was an exceptionally cold and blustery February morning when Anastas Kourkorian tearfully and with overwhelming remorse declared himself schismatic. On his knees like Henry at Canossa he confessed and pledged eternal fidelity to his magistrate. Temporal punishment came in the form of full payment of his indebtedness. Payment was to be made from the proceeds of the casualty policy on the late Blue Peacock held by Anastas and Marie Kourkorian, owners of record. A new loan would be committed from family funds along with transfer of title to GCR Associates, Union City, N.J. A handsome new Blue Peacock, which included offices and small shops, soon rose from the ashes. For form and procedure, Anastas Kourkorian retained the outward signs of proprietorship. Under the arrangement drawn up by Stefano Maglie, his name would also appear on Hampton County tax rolls and on all food and beverage licenses. In return, he would be personally liable for the face amount of the reconstruction loan provided by GCR Associates at 150 percent annualized interest. Stefano Maglie would function as trustee for this arrangement. All details of the transaction were recorded

# Jack Eddinger

in a ledger locked in a safe deposit box at the First Federal Bank of Union City. The official interest rate on Hampton County building records was listed as .03 percent.

One day after the arrival of the Eastern States Fire & Indemnity check in Anatas Koukorian's mail box, a white Sedan de Ville appeared in the circular driveway of Anastas Kourkorian's big field stone ranch house. In the back seat Anastas Kourkorian opened a briefcase containing $500,000 in neatly arranged packages of $50 and $100 bills. The two visitors counted the packets slowly and meticulously. Stefano Maglie made notes of the meeting. When they finished, they smiled and asked Anastas Kourkorian to step from the car. The gray-haired executive rolled down the car window. Like a priest granting absolution he told him that he would return to Bessemer City only to attend the funeral of a family member. Anastas Kourkorian stood in the driveway and watched the big fan-tailed automobile blend smoothly into traffic, accelerate and disappear. His legs bounced and jumped uncontrollably as if they'd just been unhooked from the elastic braces holding up his hose. Sweat soaked through the jacket of his suit. He had great trouble breathing. His head pounded. On the winter-burnt lawn a pink cement flamingo danced on one foot. A sparrow walked across the ice of a mirror-inlaid bird bath with a base of encrusted sea shells. He wished he were a sparrow or a pink flamingo. He turned and shuffled slowly into the dark cavernous house. The blinds were drawn. He slumped into a red velvet sofa trembling.

Now, four years later, Gaetano Cavalieri Russo listened intently as Stefano Maglie related the story of Anastas Kourkorian's second and final fall from grace. A small fire burned in his gray-rimmed brown eyes.

*"Egli e morte."*

Stefano Maglie nodded. Gaetano Cavalieri Russo filled their glasses once again with Segesta. They sipped the warm Sicilian wine in silence.

Frank Jordan finished reading the file on Anastas Kourkorian. The record stretched back to 1939. It showed one conviction for operating a lottery. Other charges were dismissed by the court for lack of evidence. "Gives his occupation as restaurateur," said Jordan. "It ought to be escape artist. Who's his lawyer, Clarence Darrow?"

"INS records show he was under a deportation order a year after he took the oath of citizenship. Order was rescinded by direct intervention of U.S. House of Representatives Committee on the Judiciary, Hon. Charles E. Muncie of New Jersey, chairman. Ever hear of him?"

"Yeah. Been dead about ten years," said Henderson.

"A lot of good that does?" Jordan replied.

# INQUISITION

"Al, you're familiar with Eastern Pennsylvania. Who can we trust over there?"

"It's pretty shaky turf. Our Philadelphia office pays it no mind. Scranton's a frontier outpost with two agents. It's wide open. The U.S. Attorney's office is useless, populated by civil rightsers, lefties and Ivy Leaguers. I keep an eye on it from here for the eastern regional office. Except for a few contacts I don't have a handle on it at all. All I know is Bessemer City police department's headed by a dago named DiLupo. When he's not struttin around, he's kissing ass. The only one I can vouch for confidently is a detective, John Maggio. He's tough. He's honest and he don't back off."

"That's a recommendation we oughtn't to take lightly," Jordan smiled. "But he's a wop, too. Right? What makes you think he'd help us?"

"Hey, you call him wop and he'll rippa you head off. Roman. Lex, legis; loves the law. He once told me nothing would give him more pleasure than to castrate half the males on Bessemer City's South End. Considers 'em all greasers, black-trash ginzos from the Mezzagiorno, who're blackening the good name of every Italian-American. Plus, he's a combat veteran. Won two Silver Stars and the Purple Heart killing guineas and krauts in the Italian Campaign. He's a graduate of our police training center at Quantico. We tried to recruit him, but he likes what he's doing. Says you get results fast. I schmooze with him every time I'm over there. He's got the pulse."

"I wish I knew this guy Daley, the D.A., a little better," Frank Jordan said. "I've had a few conversations with him on occasion. I get hot and cold readings. Some of our people swear by him. Others say he's a hot dog. My gut tells me to stay away from politicians. What's your detective friend think of him?"

"I haven't talked to John for awhile; he's got a thing about politicos. Thinks they're all crooks. But, as I recall, he has a grudging respect for Daley. Taking on the county courthouse over there alone has to be to his credit. Maybe he's not Frank Murphy, but he's got guts. When he moves prosecutions, he gets convictions, and it's not just run of the mill stuff. He's a bulldog on political corruption. Two months after his election, he indicted the sheriff, the Recorder of Wills and six of their clerks. No convictions yet, though. Jury's still out on the guy, literally. Three years of young Turkdom does not a D.A. make.

Looks real good on paper. His old man, Tad Daley, was a local legend; a helluva man, according to some of our old agents. I've listened to their stories. But he was found in his car with a .32 slug in his brain. That was 1938 or 40, somewhere around there. The son may not have the old

## Jack Eddinger

man's reputation, but he's got a pretty good pedigree. Lafayette College. Penn Law. Reopened his father's law office. Mostly civil practice. Some pro bono work. Assistant D.A. for a couple of years. D.A. for the past three. Well connected socially. Married the grand-daughter of the guy who invented the I-beam. Don't know whether he's got tough testicles when things get nasty. Never had his family threatened. We've fed him stuff from time to time, but I can't recall his acting on anything specific. A lotta newspaper stories, but not much in the way of results."

"Sounds like a law professor to me," said Jordan, "Personally, I find him a little too liberal. How about the mayor?"

"Retired doctor. Holland. The Plague of Women Vultures pushed him into public life. A non-entity."

"Okay. We gotta act. Looks like your man Maggio's all we've got. Get a telex out right away. We've got one big problem, gentlemen," Frank Jordan said closing the folders. "Operation Garibaldi is dead in the water on this thing. No Federal statutes involved yet. And I don't want my ass on the rug. Director's hell on keeping us out of things we don't belong in. So, our hands are tied. We've got no statutory authority to go in there. All we can do is alert the locals. I'm afraid we'll have to watch Detective Lieutenant John Maggio, pride of Rome, tangle with The Duke of Castellamare from the Coliseum bleachers. First quarter score: Russo's Lions 50. Maggio and his Christians 0."

The FBI telex arrived on Lt. John Maggio's desk at precisely 11:35 a.m., Friday, October 26, 1956, according to the electronic stamp. He was reviewing paperwork on an indictment for rape and aggravated assault he expected the Hampton County grand jury to hand up on the basis of his testimony within the hour. Maggio was six feet four, had the shoulders of a linebacker, the forearms and biceps of an Olympic discus-thrower and the face of a wounded basset hound. His round head carried the advanced stage of baldness which bestows a unique machisimo. His big, earthy laugh came from deep in the gut. He was open and earnest, if not solicitous, to everyone, traits which earned him instant respect, even affection. Only his cool, pale blue Siberian eyes, probing and piercing, offset the image of the gentle giant. To his fellow detectives, he was a tough and fair company commander who worked harder than any three of them.

The keys tapped out the coded message:

# INQUISITION

EXPCT MJR O.C. ACTIV. E.PA W/I 72 HRS.
PTL. VTM <u>A.L. KOURKORIAN</u>, OPR, BLUE
PEACOCK CLUB, U.S. RT. 22. SUBJS: 3 WHT.
MLS (DESCRS FOLLO). PSBL HOMCD W/FRMS
& EXPLSVS. INFRM SCR CVL AUTHS. ON  RECPT.

John Maggio tore the dispatch off the teletype machine and took the stairs three steps at a time. "Jolly Old St. Fats. God Damn!" He put through a call to the mayor' office. "Honey, this is John Maggio. Get your boss on the line, please. I need his ear for one minute."

"I can't interrupt him, lieutenant, He's with the council on the budget."

"Tell him it's me and it's urgent, sweetheart. I only need three minutes."

Maggio waited five minutes for Mayor John Holland to answer the phone.

"Yes, lieutenant?" It was the soft voice of the working class city's non-working class mayor. "I'm with Council. I am really tied up. Can't it wait till I'm finished?" The mayor was irked by the intrusion.

"No, sir. I need to see you immediately."

"Very well. Give me fifteen minutes to get them out of my hair. Come to the rear door. Miss Lewis will let you in."

"Roger. I'm on my way."

At 11:55 a.m. John Maggio was ushered into the teak-paneled office on the third floor of Bessemer City's municipal-red-brick city hall. Mayor Holland was seated at his curved desk like the slot man on a newspaper copy desk. He wore a sweater-jacket in the maroon and white of Bessemer City High School's state championship football team and puffed on a curved Sherlock Holmes pipe.

"Your Honor," Maggio said, sliding into a chair in front of the mayor.

"What now, John? Another Di Lupo vice raid? He's making an ass of himself and a laughing stock of the city. I cringed when I saw his picture on the front page of the *Star-Times* last week in that doorway with an axe in his hands. Can you imagine what one photo can do to us when the wire services pick it up and carry it around the country? I am constantly mortified whenever I attend a Municipal League meeting. They ask me if he dives for pearls, too."

Lt. Maggio choked back a guffaw. "Shit, Mr. Mayor, I don't know whether he dives for pearls, but I do know you can cast them before him."

# Jack Eddinger

"It's no joke, dammit. Our image as a progressive city is on the line. I'm a busy man. What do you want?"

"More bad news for our image, I'm afraid. I just got a classified FBI wire from Newark. They want you to know Fats Kourkorian's been spotted to get whacked sometime in the next 72 hours. They don't know where, when or how, but they know he's in the crosshairs."

"What do you want me to do? Substitute for him? God, how I hate this business. If it isn't vice and gambling, it's underworld intrigue. Our city's reputation suffers irreparably every time one of these incidents occurs. I've spent four years and countless thousands of dollars advertising us as an All American City. Walter Winchell told the nation a few years ago that if you want to commit murder, do it in Bessemer City, because nobody will do anything about it. Can you imagine that, lieutenant? What more can a man do? What is your advice, lieutenant?"

"I'm handling this myself. I need your support when push comes to shove with DiLupo. I've got to have your assurance that this information will travel no further than this office. If I have your word on this, I guarantee that all your hard work won't be in vain. It'll give me the time I need to crack open the mob's gambling nut and scoop up the worms that wriggle out. I don't want to appear to undercut my boss, the chief of police, but we both know how he'd handle it."

John, you've got my 100 percent support and cooperation. Tell me what you need."

"I've got to find out when and where they're going to hit him. I've got to let them get far enough so I can beach these goons, and nail Fats with his ledgers down. They know he's skimming the weekly take. I've got to get my hands on his paperwork. Without it I got no case to take to the grand jury. Give me this support, and I'll pull up what you call the underworld by the roots. I guarantee you there'll be no more nasty remarks by Winchell or anybody else about Bessemer City, P.A.

"Who else knows about this?"

"Nobody. Just you and me, That's the way I want it."

John Maggio played by the rules, except when he knew rules wouldn't work. He ran his own shop. He gave Di Lupo only the sketchiest information on the cases he handled. The chief knew better than to meddle. Giving him anything about the Kourkorian hit would have reporters outside his office instantly. No, this time John Maggio was going to do it his way. He'd solved cases simply by waiting things out, never volunteering information, even to the District Attorney. He'd wait for an opponent to commit, then hit him hard. No chance to recover and no possibility of counter attack. Make them play your game. That's how he and his pals, Ed Franco and

# INQUISITION

Vince Lombardi, played the line at Fordham for Johnny Dell Isola. The same principle guided him in law enforcement. He considered Mayor John Holland to be above the vintage organization politics practiced with virtuosity in Bessemer City's ethnic wards and neighborhoods, particularly on the South End where the old goat Kressman stamps out the votes on his assembly line. By rights Holland shouldn't even be mayor. Who'd of thought the League of Woman Voters could elect anyone, let alone an Independent. He respected the 55-year-old surgeon's intelligence, idealism and reasoned approach to government. He interpreted Holland's even-handed and open administration as a sign that Bessemer City was capable of being governed well. At some point, he believed this intelligent man would turn the searchlight of professionalism and competence on the Bessemer City Police Department and sack its blustery chief.

Maggio knew nothing of Dr. Holland's tortured compromise. The distraught young women who came to him in tears moved him as they would any understanding father. His compassion was rooted in a deep belief in his Hippocratic Oath. Since his residency days at Bellevue, he vowed that he would use his talents as a surgeon in the service of others even if they could not pay. Too often he had seen the results of botched abortions and tried to correct the dismal results. If he turned away from what he perceived as a moral duty, the girls and their families would find a butcher somewhere who'd gladly take their money. They would pay, of course, for the rest of their lives. His surgical practice grew to the point where he could take on two assistants to handle all but the most complicated procedures. He became a wealthy man, but remained the social liberal he had been since college, medical school, internship and residency. He began performing the surgery quietly and without payment if the young woman's family made a personal appeal. He took particular pride in the victims who learned from their personal tragedies, and heeded his lectures about contraception. His compromise began with a fourteen-year-old five months into a difficult pregnancy. The girl and the baby died on his operating table at Doctor's Hospital where he saw indigent patients once a week.

Dr. Holland panicked. But the proprietors of Doctor's Hospital had handled situations with similar complications almost routinely. They brought in their private counsel, Stefano Maglie. Maglie put Dr. Holland at ease with his explanation that this was a tragedy, which a brutal, unsympathetic and Church-backed public would one day change. But till then, these procedures are an absolute necessity. The death certificate filed with the Hampton County Coroner's office fixed the cause of death as a ruptured appendix during emergency surgery. There was no report of a birth; no autopsy and no inquest. The funeral and burial at a weed-choked cemetery in Bessemer City's working class South End went unrecorded except for an entry in Stefano Maglie's black book. Two years passed before Stefano Maglie put a proposal to Dr. Holland. Such a highly respected physician who had arrived at financial independence and fully supported society's need to assist the poor and disadvantaged would be an ideal candidate for mayor of Bessemer City. Reform was in the air. The League of Women Voters was on the warpath. An independent, incorruptible, citizen-politician was a perfect match for the public mood. Six months later John S. Holland M.D. took the oath as Bessemer City's twenty-first mayor. Later, in Union City Gaetano Cavalieri Russo showed his esteem and fraternal affection for Stefano Maglie by bestowing upon him the title, *capo di tutti capi di la Famiglia Russo,* with full responsibility for all new enterprises and initiatives in the new domain across the Delaware, and immediate access at all times.

"How long are we to keep DiLupo in the dark, John?" Mayor Holland asked. "You know I cannot withhold information of this nature. At some point, I must apprise him of this development."

"Give me 48 hours. With the kind of intelligence I'm getting, if I don't break this thing open, I will personally hand my badge to you and DiLupo at a public ceremony at high noon in front of City Hall. Telling him any sooner will blow everything. He'd take over the investigation and completely fuck it up."

"Very well. But remember, John, easy does it. I don't want this to break prematurely in MacManus's newspaper. He's keeping the city's image black enough with sensationalism. I cannot have another ten-part series on Bessemer City as the nation's small town crime capital. It will absolutely ruin our efforts in tourism and conventions. And, John, please handle this non-violently."

"I can't promise that, your honor. But you've got my word on personal supervision. I don't want blood in the streets any more than you do."

"Please keep this at low visibility."

"Right. I'll give you a report within twenty-four hours."

When John Maggio left, Mayor Holland told his secretary to inform the City Council he would reconvene the meeting at 9 o'clock the next morning. He slipped out the rear door, descended a back stairs and drove to his mid-town apartment as he did every day at noon. He dismissed his housekeeper and went to his study. He placed a telephone call to Stefano Maglie's unlisted number.

Lieutenant Maggio, experiencing unusual emotional lift, called the District Attorney's office as soon as he got back to his office. "But the

# INQUISITION

boss needs you on the stand in ten minutes, Madge," importuned Assistant District Attorney Frank Comstock.

"Look, counselor, all I can tell you is something I've been developing is ready to break. He'll have to go without me. Put me over a week. Hell, the grand jury can wait. We're not making a case against Jack the Ripper."

"If we don't go today, we've got a serious civil rights problem on our hands, Lieutenant. It means I'll have to release this defendant. The court's already ruled on it. We've got to be absolutely scrupulous on defendant's rights. Morally, there's no other way."

"Horseshit! This spick you feel morally bound to raped a fourteen year old child, counselor. Look, I'll make you a deal to get you past your scruples. You make the presentment and I'll send Browning over to make the case. He's worked it with me, and can handle the evidence. That's the way it's gonna be, counselor. I'm outta here. See ya in Orphan's Court."

John Maggio laid out his plan. He detailed four men on eight hour shifts to Anastas Kourkorian's peregrinations. Two others, on twelve and off twelve, kept the Blue Peacock under surveillance. Maggio positioned himself behind the steering wheel of a 1947 Chevy junker in a used car lot down the hill and across the highway from Kourkorian's big stone rancher he'd dubbed, Villa Fats. Maggio considered the irony of the situation many times during his vigil. Seven men and god knows how much money assigned to protect a third-rate asshole we already have a complete book on. There are at least fifty better things to do on a weekend. By midnight his breath iced the windshield. The surgical steel inside his right femur and at the hinge of the kneecap throbbed and pulsated in the polar cold. Winter sank its fangs into his feet, fingers, cheeks and nose. Over the years he trained himself to handle physical discomfort by focusing his mind on his experiences in combat along the shin of Italy starting at Anzio. He focused on the wide sweep of Ligurian beach, and the hot wind that seared his face as the big steel door of the LSI carrying his infantry company crashed into the clear blue sea. His introduction to the land of his father's birth was howling pandemonium and sickening carnage. He was completely unprepared for it after the easy landings of North Africa and Sicily. They were fighting about 200 kilometers from Rome, which produced the only civilization that mattered to First Lieutenant John Maggio. The sudden, viscera-tearing explosion split his ear drums and tossed his body in the air. Splinters of steel ripped into his legs, tearing through muscle and bone. The medic, who found him, tried to free his right leg but it was twisted and folded back under the weight of his body. With two morphine needles stuck in his thigh, he dragged himself up the beach and over the dunes. He took out two German machine gun bunkers with hand grenades and stayed

# Jack Eddinger

in front of his men until he passed out. They carried him to an aid station, then put him in the same LSI that brought him for the return trip to the Hospital ship anchored five miles offshore. It reeked of urine and vomit. Later, when the American Army entered Rome, he would go frequently on crutches to the Sistine Chapel. Ignoring the strain on the muscles of his back and shoulders and the pain which blazed in his leg, he'd spend hours studying Michelangelo's *Last Judgment*.

At 3 a.m. John Maggio was jolted from his mental meandering by the tail lights of a car turning into Anastas Kourkorian's driveway. He recognized it immediately. It was Kourkorian's powder blue Cadillac. If they're gonna hit him, it'll be when he gets to the front door. John Maggio's '47 Chevy came alive. It roared out of the used car lot and up the driveway, arriving at the top simultaneously with the Cadillac. John Maggio jumped out and yanked open the driver's door.

"Police. Out, asshole." As John Maggio pulled the door open a second car then a third roared up the driveway and across the snow-crusted lawn, knocking over the flamingo and bird bath. Four detectives sprang out, weapons drawn.

"Hey, wait a minute. Where's the fat man?" Maggio screamed into the driver's face. The driver shrugged and motioned over his shoulder with his thumb. "Trunk." He handed the keys to Maggio. One of the detectives sprung the trunk and shined his flashlight. A huge undulating clump lay crammed inside. It took the combined strength of Maggio and three of his compatriots to turn it over. The stiff, bloodied and decapitated body of Anastas Kourkorian resembled a beef carcass at the first stage of slaughter.

John Maggio looked at his watch, it was ten after three. Seconds later an explosion shattered the frozen night and shook the ground under him like a salvo of the 36-inchers that softened the beaches for the Fifth Army. For an instant Anzio rushed back at him. A crimson glow lit up the eastern sky, as if the sun were coming up. Within fifteen minutes a firestorm engulfed the Blue Peacock obliterating it in an incendiary maelstrom. Firefighters could not control it with water. Hours later the site lay smoking like the center of Dresden in 1945.

At 3:20 a.m. a Cavalier Refuse Company truck with three men in the cab trundled across the Delaware into New Jersey. They paid the .75-cent truck toll at the plaza and roared away.

Three detectives spread-eagled the driver over the hood of Anastas Kourkorian's Cadillac. Lieutenant Maggio removed the badge pinned to the lapel of his overcoat and slipped it into a pocket. He grabbed the man's collar and in a single, fluid move turned him over like a bundle of rags. He

# INQUISITION

took his .32 caliber pistol from his shoulder holster, pried open the man's mouth and shoved the nickel barrel in up to the trigger guard, breaking off teeth.

"Italian roulette, prick. I spin. You sing."

"They pulled up in a garbage truck when Fats was closing down," the driver blurted, spitting blood and bone. "and blocked off the back door. I had the motor runnin waitin for Fats. One of them, a guy about five-five, had a sawed off shotgun. Another guy maybe 27, 28, was carrying a gym bag. The third guy stayed in the truck. The first two busted in the back door. Then the truck driver spotted me in the car and shoved a shotgun through the window. I had it down a crack because the engine was idling. I heard a shotgun blast and knew they hit Fats. Two of them dragged him through the snow, pulled me out and made me open the trunk. The little guy went back inside and comes out carryin somethin in his hand like it was a dirty rag mop drippin water. I almost threw up. It was Fats's head. Then he starts swinging it through the air over his head like a lariat and then hook shots it into the back of the garbage truck. The driver got in and gunned the engine. I watched the blade come down. Then the three of them picked up Fats and threw him into the trunk. The guy with the gym bag went back in. He came out in about fifteen minutes without the bag. Must of put torch stuff around the place, because I saw him pulling a reel of wire out the door. They put a gun against my head and told me I was lucky. I was scared shitless. The little guy shoved me back into the car, and told me to drive to Fats's house or he'd blow my head off. I got outta there faster than I ever done nothin. Them bastards was mean."

# CHAPTER SIX

## *A Winning Proposition*

### MARCEL CLOSING GAP WITH HARRIS
### POLL SHOWS CONTENDER MOVING UP;
### KNOWLES GAINING IN D.A. RACE

The headline in 24-point type appeared over a story by Charlie Miller the day after Congressman Harris met with the Director. The story mentioned nothing of the congressman's dinner table attack two weeks previously. The District office secretary dictated the 10-paragraph story to her counterpart in the Longworth Building. The story's effect in Robert Bird's cubicle hovered between consternation and disbelief. Zachary Taylor Harris read it with predictable ire. "I'm going to teach the little SOB the difference between polls and politics," he resolved, as he read Miller's piece for the third time. "Robert, come in here, and bring your notebook." He shouted through the doorway at his all-purpose aide. "I've got a plane to catch at National in an hour. The Committee will renew the security hearings in Philadelphia when Congress convenes in January. I want a witness list within two weeks. Work with Donegan at the Bureau and the minority counsel. Between them they'll turn up Reds from the far side of the moon. Work carefully with Sterling without going into too much detail. Just tell him the congressman agrees with Mr. Nelson about further hearings, and wants as much background as he can provide on the pinko professor from Penn. Check with me before finalizing anything. I want these hearings precisely orchestrated."

"Speaking of precision, Congressman. How do you want me to respond to this poll that shows Marcel gaining? I've been fending off calls all morning - AP, UP, INS even the Philadelphia papers. What do I tell them?"

"Now, let me see. What's an appropriate response? You know your history, Robert? What'd Jack Pershing say when he found himself surrounded by krauts in the Argonne?"

"I'm sorry, Congressman, I'm not too smart when it comes to history, especially ancient history. I was a journalism major," Robert Bird said with a pained smile.

"ATTACK! Dammit! Attack!" Tell 'em I haven't begun my campaign. I'll hit him with everything in the last ten days."

"Marcel's turning into a handful. Did you expect the polls to be this close?"

# INQUISITION

"Hell, if this borderline pneumonia hadn't laid me low, the polls would show something quite different. I'm going to reverse things starting immediately. Tell that to your friends in the press. Now, I want a release out on the hearings - full field hearings starting January 2 in Philadelphia. It'll be page one news here and around the country. I want you to keep this thing stoked for the next two months. Focus on a new angle every week - Justice Department conferences, results of your meeting at the Bureau, witness lists, etc. Be sure Charlie Miller gets it firsthand. The wire services will pick up his story. As for the site, get hold of the U.S. Commissioner in Philadelphia. Tell him I want the grand jury room in the Federal Courthouse. It's the only one big enough to accommodate the TV people. Tell him to make it easy for them. They'll want camera platforms, power outlets, extra cable, the works. Then inform the networks and the Philadelphia news desks."

"Television! Christ, Congressman, the Speaker'll go crazy. That's the one thing calculated to drive him bugeye. He's tough enough about TV here on the Hill. Even the networks have had a hard time getting him to go along. He still believes the pencil press is the best way to get the news out - must be all those weeklies in his district. I heard he ordered one of the network guys out of the caucus room when he showed up with cameras and lights to cover the committee reorganization meetings. I also heard he blocked Adam Clayton Powell from holding a televised press conference in the Ways and Means Room, but the reverend slicked him and held it in the Cannon basement on the fly. Don't you think you' should reconsider ... ?"

"God dammit, the Speaker can claim turf all he wants, but when a chairman decides on a course of action, the chairman prevails, Speaker or no Speaker. I've rounded up plenty of votes for him in tough situations over the years, and sheltered his rectitude by sponsoring Tidelands Oil. He'll see it my way. These hearings are on my turf. He has no jurisdiction beyond the House floor. We are expected - hell, mandated - to do the job as we see fit. Nobody challenges a chairman. Every Speaker since 1900 - Cannon, Longworth, Rainey, Garner, even Joe Martin - upheld their chairmen. We elect the Speaker. We're dealing with House precedent here. My hearings will be the first in history to be televised from where the people live. This is history, son. I don't think the Speaker is up to taking on the whole republic. I intend to bring the question of subversion out to the locales to let the people decide for themselves. Either it's there, or it isn't. There's been too much of the smell of the carnival about this thing here in Washington. No more Washington exclusivity. Someone has to show leadership."

# Jack Eddinger

"I've got to admit, congressman, you're a genius at tactics and precedents. But the Speaker won't like it one bit."

"As I said, I'll handle him. Now next item - get on the phone to Max Bronstein at the Democratic National Committee, Sam Becker, Barney Steckel and Lloyd Kressman in the District. Have 'em distribute tickets to their people. I want our crowd in that courtroom every day."

"But what if the Commissioner balks on separation of powers? I'm sure you're aware he's under the judicial branch. Suppose he won't guarantee us the space?" said Robert Bird looking up from his notebook.

"Dammit, Robert if God made pessimism a virtue, you'd be it's patron saint. You may be the best detail man in Washington, but sometimes I wonder where your political education got side-tracked. Who do you think put him in that job? I took a lot of heat from the state delegation on that appointment. Flynn wanted McLaughlin."

"Speaking of Congressman Flynn, sir, I just know we're gonna have trouble getting him to approve the appropriation for your hearings. He's very upset over the Lenape Dam bill. We have a major problem here. I couldn't get a seat at the AA's table in the cafeteria for weeks after the conferees wrote our language into the conference report to build the dam in the 26th District. They say you stiffed Flynn by doing it in the public session. He was off guard. You may have sidestepped things for now but it could cost us big."

"They said that, did they?" he said dryly. "Well, when you staff people start instructing us about our duties and responsibilities, that's when the dishwashers begin running the restaurant. I'll handle the great god Flynn."

Congressman Harris coughed violently into his handkerchief twice and cleared his throat. He looked at it for several seconds before putting it back in his pocket. Flecks of blood remained. "I want releases out every day and make sure you distribute them fairly. I don't want somebody's back up. Start with the flood control and soil erosion money in the agriculture appropriation. Then do a rundown of projects I've sponsored over the past two years. Have the Library of Congress get employment figures and economic data. Stress my role in preserving those funds. Show how the multiplier effect is creating jobs. Keep it subtle. The average voter'll get my message."

"I'm a step ahead of you, Congressman. They're ready to go."

"Good. Next, mail out that issue of the *Harris Letter* we've been holding back. The one highlighting these projects and my amendment to the trade bill putting quotas on the cheap stuff coming out of the Far East. Get it in the mail by the end of next week, and get a couple thousand

# INQUISITION

copies to Steckel and Kressman. They'll have 'em under every door in the District."

"Lloyd Kressman? I thought we were avoiding him."

"Look, I know Lloyd can be a pain in the ass. But the one thing to remember, even though he's a Republican, he's always been for me. Besides, he knows Marcel's owned by Palmer and Bess Steel. He knows full well that if that non-entity is elected, the Hampton County GOP has had their last pull on the Federal teat. Think about it. Kressman'd lose every minority member of every federal commission in the Lenape Valley, not to mention the federal funds he channels into Republican banks. Don't worry about Lloyd. He can be a bastard, but I own him."

"Okay, but I don't want to deal with him personally. He's a dirty old man. Usually has an off-color comment about the girls out front every time he's in here. They told me to keep him away. Plus, he literally stinks. Does he ever change his underwear?"

"Been wearing the same union suit for as long as I can remember. What're the latest circulation figures for the Sunday *Star-Times*, Robert?"

"About 75,000 last time I checked. It's moved up in Hampton County. Jumped about a couple of thousand since I was there. Now it's neck and neck with *The Sentinel*."

"Regard everything up to the Sunday before the election as the softening up barrage. The Sunday editions will finish it. I want both papers carrying my announcement of the Lenape flood control project. Make sure Charlie Miller and Arnold Mason have it well ahead of the embargo. Get the Corps of Engineers to provide aerial photos and schematics to illustrate the main story. Lt. Col. Armistead over at the Pentagon is your man. He's got the details."

"But what about Congressman Flynn? That area belonged to the 40th District for sixty years before the last census. His AA says he wants his name on it."

"So Flynn wants his name on it. Well, I agree. He should get it - posthumously. That's more than enough. I lined up the Interior Department and had the funds earmarked by Public Works. He played a very marginal role. God dammit, even the Pope doesn't get everything!"

"I'll finesse it so we get maximum coverage, Congressman. The weeklies'll run it on election day, and the jerkwater radio stations up country will give you coverage on every news break. They'll eat it up. They can't give you enough coverage since we sent out that *Record* insert on Christianity and country music; God, patriotism and Hank Williams. You, Hank and Jesus control the airwaves. But, just remember there are some influential constituents who're up in arms. The landowners in the upper end

## Jack Eddinger

of the District have been holding meetings with the preservation society all summer. Don't forget, Marcel's supporting their lawsuit. They're trying to get a hearing in Federal court. They're madder'n hell. They're putting out this story about developers coming in and selling lakefront lots for $250 a front-foot after they've been forced to sell their adjoining land to the government for $750 an acre. They're complaining about traffic on the local roads. But the hidden agenda's New York. They see Puerto Ricans, niggers and Jews descending in clouds every weekend of the summer. Sam McBryan spent last week up there and says that's all you hear in the taverns. They're all pissed-off. It's a mean scene."

"Sonofabitch, man! Don't you ever stop fretting. I can't be concerned about a handful of hay shakers. The dam's the biggest thing that's come down the valley since the '36 flood. The votes are in the valley, not up there in the outback. Mason'll write columns on the dam for the next six weeks. Miller'll give it a ride in the Sierra Club newsletter. He's the secretary, you know. His byline on that piece is worth hundreds of votes."

"Nevertheless, I'd be cautious. They never endorse candidates, but they can mobilize the Grange people."

"How many Granges up there, Robert? Two, five? If there were five hundred, I wouldn't care. There isn't a Harris vote among them. And, as you say, those radio stations're ready to declare the Second Coming."

"All well and good, Congressman, but I'd still be careful. It's not just the opposition to the dam," Robert Bird persisted. "They could start cutting into our base. Sam's been there every weekend since Labor Day checking with our people. Marcel's been working that whole upper-District area, telling anybody who'll listen that you can be beaten by their vote. He tells them he's cut into your home turf vote. Says he's the only GOP candidate that can swing Labor, especially the Teamsters. He's been hitting you hard on the Longshoreman hearings. He's saying roughing them up last year shows you're no friend of Labor. He's telling them the Teamsters could be next. Don't forget half the men up there drive rigs for a living, and they have brothers and wives and cousins and uncles and aunts who vote. Some of their leaders are starting to listen. Sam says the county GOP's asking for no labor endorsement of you or him. That cuts into bone."

"Look, son, I'll handle the politics. Just do what you do best and keep the press well fed. I'll handle the Reds, the Teamsters, the farmers, the conservationists and all the rest of them."

"Okay, I just want you to know the scenario," Robert Bird said almost contritely.

"Now Robert, if you do your job and keep your eyes and ears open," Harris told his aide in a conciliatory tone. "There'll be a time in the

# INQUISITION

foreseeable future when Zach Harris will close the book on all of this. And that day may not be far off. Then it's up for grabs. I'll help you as much as I can. Hell, even you could whip Marcel with the right kind of tutoring." It was the first and only time Robert Bird had heard Zachary Taylor Harris acknowledge the possibility of his impermanence, let alone imply that his administrative assistant might succeed him. Many other AAs had done it. Harris knew the hint would send Bird back to his cubicle with warm feelings about his future; that the boss was human after all. Bird threw himself into the job, arranging the security hearings, writing releases, dictating them to the wire services and spending hours on the telephone with government bureaucrats lining up the details to include in the press releases he'd issue during the next three weeks.

Zach Harris was leaving Washington as the Federal city settled into the quiet season. Roads, driveways and plazas of the Capitol were deserted, the summer crowds of tourists and visitors were long gone. Telephones, typewriters and mimeograph machines, the ordnance of congressional combat, were silent. Darkened hallways of the Cannon and Longworth Buildings - even the Capitol - resembled the anterooms of mortuaries. The principal occupants were out across the land, serving up their special intoxicant to voters in the biennial balancing of scales. They returned to prairie town and tidal flat, ghetto and suburb, county seat and township, ward and precinct, to plead and cajole, and to scold their opponents and the rival party. They stirred up a purely American brew of cant, hyperbole and bluster. The recipe would produce the votes to send them back to work the levers and winches of the republic for another two years. Their performances were played out with rhetorical flourish at sequined and tuxedoed testimonials on the creamed chicken circuit; in sweaty labor halls and party clubhouses heavy with the rank smell of tobacco smoke and flat beer; in stifling tobacco barns and cluttered country stores crammed with hunting and fishing gear, dried hams and walk-in ice boxes; in the pathetic charnel house wards of Veterans hospitals, and in stuffy, cabbage-scented basements of church suppers and social club gatherings. They worked the crowds at county fairs and showed up at plant gates at each change of work shift. On city streets sound trucks blared out their cacaphonic messages. They marched in parades, attended funerals and graduations and made presentations between the halves of high school football games. They jawboned in post offices and filling stations. They toured old folks homes and school rooms; nibbled baloney sandwiches and hunks of processed cheese; pitched horseshoes and hurled baseballs at fake milk bottles; kissed fat ladies and bent over wailing children. They trudged the dusty roadbeds

## Jack Eddinger

of strip-mined towns sliding down the shoulders of Appalachia, rode farm tractors and combines, milked Holsteins and pitched silage. They listened intently and nodded in serious affirmation. They laughed a lot and agreed with everyone's observations. They stood stoically as their well-heeled contributors outlined agendas promoting unattainable utopias, or offered solutions to the republic's problems, each with a tinge of fascism. When it was over and with the electoral grail safely restored, they took their seats under the great dome of the republic alongside more than 400 others to record their voices in the swelling pages of *corpus juris Americana*.

Representative Zachary Taylor Harris was strapped into a first-class seat as the late October sun glinted off the silver and white Colonial Airlines Super Constellation, which lifted off the tarmac of National Airport and bumped up through fat, low-hanging clouds. Below, the Federal city stretched bone white in patches of autumn sunlight, looking to Congressman Harris like a well cared for cemetery. The sepulchral geometry of the federal architecture, the white shaft of the obelisk, the funerary elegance of the temples memorializing Lincoln and Jefferson, and the long emerald sweep of the mall stretching to the Capitol gave the appearance of a baroque necropolis. Down on the river glistening in the sunlight, a pair of racing sculls pulled against the hard, swift Appalachian current, darting like millipedes past Georgetown gothic and the gray eminence of the National Cathedral. As the airplane climbed northeastward, he flipped through the morning newspapers and was slightly discomfited by the *Post's* editorial praising his handling of the Committee on Subversive Activities, urging its retirement from the peculiar place it occupied in the American polity for nearly a quarter century. He wondered how the editorialists would treat its resuscitation in just two months.

Ninety minutes later with the newspaper rolled up under his arm, Zachary Taylor Harris stepped into the haze and smog of the Lenape Valley Airport. The prop wash beat at his raincoat and flattened his trousers. He squinted, held onto his hat and paused at the bottom of the retractable stairs seeking his district office manager, driver and all-purpose aide, Sam McBryan. McBryan had the congressman's Lincoln continental parked on the edge of the runway. He was at his leader's side in seconds, grabbing the congressman's two-suiter and leading him to the automobile. The ten-mile drive to Bessemer City took them through low pre-Cambrian hills. Zach Harris never had an eye for landscape, picturesque or ugly. It was something to get past quickly. This eccentricity might have resulted from an innate uneasiness about what had been done to the land during a century of industrialization.

# INQUISITION

The Lenape Valley, bedrock of Pennsylvania's 26th Congressional District, is tucked into the vest pocket of northeastern Pennsylvania between parallel chains of worn down piedmont. Once thick with oak, elm, flowering cherry, white and yellow pine, blue spruce, white ash and sycamore, the valley now lays in a perpetual haze. In the limestone and cement towns street lights burn at noon, and a fine white ash from the cement kilns coats the land like an early snowfall. On the clearest days ocher clouds swirl skyward from a multitude of smokestacks, forming a shifting Rohrschach skyscape. Spoils heaps and slag dumps, piled with the detritus of steel production, stick up out of the smog like the burial mounds of a lost tribe. Deep ravines of exhausted stone and slate quarries and sand and gravel pits gouged into the earth a century ago, their mineral wealth exhausted, scar the land like tissue over an unsutured wound.

Anthracite, which the Lenni Lenape tribes called "stonecoal," lay undisturbed for eons in vast basins deep in the glacial folds of northeastern Pennsylvania. The War of 1812 forced colonial entrepreneurs to improvise. They turned to the native anthracite when they found that when blown and air-blasted it could melt iron to stoke the forges for producing muskets for the Continental Army. The slow-burning, hard and compact rock with the brilliant luster fueled the young republic's industrialization. The Lenape River was the first thoroughfare for the flat-bottom boats and barges carrying their sulfurous cargo out of the hills. Soon, a better waterway was needed; one which would support shipping hundreds of tons down river on a single vessel, to Philadelphia and eastward to New York. Later coal and iron entrepreneurs began digging the Lenape Canal upgrade into the Appalachian wilds starting at the point where the Lenape empties into the Delaware. Within two decades the canal builders turned their engineering skills to railroad construction. They laid out the route of the Lenape Valley and Philadelphia and Northern railroads along both banks of the Lenape. Following the remnants of Indian foot paths and mountain trails, they laid track with theodelite and plumb line first west then north, hacking through slate cliffs and laying track like commanders of great armies on the march. Battalions of swearing Irishmen, grunting Germans and grinning, uncommunicative Swedes got 50 cents a day for driving spikes, setting rails, cranking winches and flogging the small mules hauling the barrow-trains of rock and mortar for the vaults and arches of viaducts which carried the rails over and around gorges, moraines, unfordable streams and the rubble and debris left by retreating glaciers of the Ice Age. The tracks followed the curves and bends of the slow-flowing river. Seventy-five miles north-northwest, they crossed the Appalachian Divide into the anthracite fields on wood-truss bridges and timber trestles. Titanic locomotives pulled lines

## Jack Eddinger

of gondola cars stretching to infinity, each overflowing with shiny black anthracite. Rusting steel, disintegrating ties and washed-out ballast choked and overgrow with brush are all that remain of the once powerful track beds. The mines abandoned and filled with water and junked automobiles, and the tailings of a century of pillage scar the landscape. The land lay exhausted and broken and smoldering like a desolate battlefield. Coal seams burn interminably, fueled by inexhaustible sources deep within the earth.

The congressman's black limousine climbed the steep grade over the mountain and descended into Bessemer City. Smoke stacks, cooling towers, ventilator housings and the soot-covered sawtooth rooves of Eugene Garrett Palmer's mills emerged out of the sulfurous smog.

"To the office, Congressman? "

"No, I want to see Kressman. Drop me off at his place, but be back in exactly one hour. I don't want to spend a minute more than necessary with the old buzzard." He snapped open his watch. It was five-thirty.

In the years after his election to Congress in 1932, one man opposed him implacably year after year. In the bitter aftermath of defeat his opponent, Lloyd Kressman, made a vow to unseat the self-important young congressman with the social-register wife no matter how long it took. Lloyd Aaron Kressman was as stubborn a Pennsylvania Dutchman, as only that race can produce. He kept the pressure on Zach Harris year in and year out. Congressman Harris knew that a truce with his antagonist regardless of its indignity would free him from the embarrassment of being regarded as a regional politician concerned only with his political base instead of a man with potential for national office. In 1938 Zach Harris found the resources he needed to acquire Kressman, as he would a piece of real estate. In return for a monthly stipend of $1,000 and a pick of New Deal jobs in the Lenape Valley, Kressman agreed to end his opposition. Lloyd Kressman craved recognition almost as much as he craved money. In spite of his enmity for Harris, he came to silently and grudgingly admire him. He liked the toughness, the quick sense of humor and the congressman's willingness to reach an accommodation. Their agreement guaranteed whatever number of votes Zach Harris needed to win in the future. In return, Kressman controlled the GOP's local destiny with federal jobs. It also put some of Bessemer City's best real estate within his grasp. Zachary Taylor Harris concluded that now was the time to test the limits of Lloyd Kressman's fidelity.

The old Dutchman's value lay not only in his ability to manufacture votes, but in Kressman's mortal hatred of the power, influence and money of Eugene Garrett Palmer, CEO and chairman of the board of The Bessemer

# INQUISITION

Steel Corporation and a senior contributor to the national Republican Party. Palmer cast a long shadow over Zach Harris's political ambitions and thwarted Kressman's own ambition to head the Republican Party in Pennsylvania. Palmer followed the legacy established by Simon Cameron, the man who is credited with electing Abraham Lincoln president and stood for decades as Pennsylvania's first true political czar. Like Cameron Palmer exercised control with money supplied by the state's business interests. Cash went into GOP campaigns for the presidency and both houses of Congress, as well as those for the state legislature and governor. Steel hardened the powerful patronage sword he wielded in company with his steel-making brethren across the state in the Monongahela Valley. They considered the Commonwealth of Pennsylvania a wholly-owned subsidiary of their enterprises. They continued a second century of ownership through their legatees, the two leaders of the Pennsylvania General Assembly, the Speaker of the House of Representatives, and the president *pro tem* of the Senate. Their offices on the second floor of the state capitol in Harrisburg brought together divers traffickers in political commerce from the far corners of the Commonwealth. Nineteenth Century ornamentation accented by cold marble, gilded ceilings, brass fittings leftover from the gaslight era and shiny spittoons greeted visitors to the Speaker's office - a Gilded Age saloon frozen in time. On campaign tours through Pennsylvania in 1936, FDR's special train whistled through the long green valleys and hazy gray mountains of the Keystone State. So important were the state's electoral votes to his reelection that at every stop the President dragged his crippled legs out onto the platform at the rear of the Ferdinand Magellan, his private coach. He preached baroquely to clusters of working men in crumpled caps and soiled overalls with big CIO buttons pinned to their shoulder straps. They'd waited for hours with their wives and children along rusting sidings and in mill town depots. At every whistle stop the President warned that a vote for the Republicans was a vote for E.G. Palmer and his economic royalists, who deliberately kept workers' wages low to line their own pockets.

Eugene Garrett Palmer reached his position in life, not by compromise and accommodation but by mastery of detail, a willingness to get the dirty red residue of steel-making on his shoes and to do anything necessary to advance the fortunes of Bessemer Steel. Combined with a hard-nosed balance sheet ruthlessness and a withering, stone-cold demeanor before which his senior executives trembled, E.G. Palmer built Bessemer Steel relentlessly over fifty years through good times and bad. Bessemer's sales force fanned out across the globe, bringing in contracts for Austrian gun barrels, Japanese naval ordnance and the world's largest order for steel

## Jack Eddinger

- rails stretching across the steppe from Moscow to Vladivostok. When the Great Depression descended upon the Lenape Valley, Eugene Garrett Palmer was drawing a bonus of one million dollars a year. At the same time, his managers were earning theirs by cutting mill wages to 20-cents an hour. Bessemer's stock climbed throughout the 1930s when industrial production in the country slackened then went cold. When Adolph Hitler put Nazi arms at the disposal of the Spanish Caudillo, Palmer saw opportunity. He went to London to call on the First Lord of the Admiralty with blueprints and contracts to rebuild the Royal Navy. To consummate the deal, Palmer needed influential members of Congress to get him past the Neutrality Act. He would allow nothing to stand in the way of re-fitting the king's navy in Bessemer shipyards. The contract for three battleships, eight heavy cruisers, six light cruisers and 20 destroyers along with ordnance, fittings and spare parts would trigger a major transfer of wealth from George VI's exchequer to the treasury of Bessemer Steel Corporation. The contract for £50,000,000 would produce jobs and economic benefits in twelve states with Bessemer plants and shipyards. The inflow of capital, Palmer augured, would provide the resources to accomplish a move he'd been considering for nearly a decade, the acquisition of Toledo Bar, Sheet and Bearings, Inc. With TBS&B Palmer would have his long sought opening to the American heartland and the automobile industry, making Bessemer the world's largest steel producer.

To accomplish the merger, there could be no congressional meddling; no investigations like the armor plate hearings which angered and tormented him after the World War, and above all a compliant Judiciary Committee. For that he needed the simple majority he'd painstakingly put together by campaign contributions which put him - through the Committee on Rules and Administration and its arcane processes for establishing the makeup of committees - directly into the engine room of the U.S. Senate. As news stories began to surface about Harris's interest in running for the U.S. Senate, Palmer passed word that Zachary Taylor Harris in the Senate was unacceptable today, tomorrow or anytime. Palmer signaled that it would cost Harris a million dollars to finance a losing campaign, and that he had better reconsider. No opportunistic New Deal congressman would sup at his table while breath stirred in him. Maneuver, deception and an unerring sense of timing constituted the theology by which Zach Harris arranged his professional life. Aristotle's virtues of prudence, patience and fortitude his compass. After long and agitated consideration, he realized he could not win against Palmer's opposition. He announced that he would seek another term in the House of Representatives. Eight painful years would pass before an opportunity for retribution would appear on his radar screen. After his

# INQUISITION

reelection, he was no longer greeted as a member of the leadership club. He was very nearly an ex-congressman, whose ambition for the Senate did not sit well with the old chairmen. He would have to prove himself all over again. The war provided the opportunity. The Speaker approved a leave of absence. Zach was commissioned a full commander in the navy assigned to fleet logistics in the South Pacific. He returned to the House in 1945 with a citation signed by Admiral Nimitz for outstanding contributions to planning the invasion of the Philippines, and as a naval attache' at the San Francisco Conference. The Speaker embraced him, brought him to the well of the House and gave him the microphone for fifteen minutes to describe the purpose of the new international organization. This single act of respect from the Speaker restored his place in the House firmament. The subcommittee on immigration had lain defunct for years. He asked the Speaker to dust it off and start looking ahead to a time after the war when immigration overhaul would be needed. But the Democrats lost the House the following year. Things brightened, however, when Joe Martin, the new Republican Speaker, merged the judiciary subcommittees on criminal law and anti-trust and gave them a new purview - immigration reform and stronger oversight of monopolistic practices, which had been neglected during wartime. Zach moved up to ranking minority member in 1948, and on January 5, 1949 became chairman as the Democrats won back the majority on Harry Truman's short but stiff coat tails.

In March 1950 Eugene Garrett Palmer, flashing an uncharacteristic grin, announced the acquisition of Toledo Bar, Sheet and Bearings Company by Bessemer Steel Corporation at a news conference at the Century Club in Manhattan followed by lunch with investment analysts.

Chairman Harris read the *New York Times* story with great interest. He leaned back in his swivel chair and said to himself aloud: "Now that is a profoundly stupid move. I gave Palmer more credit." He called in aide Robert Bird and told him to "get Charlie Miller on the phone." Miller's page one lead in The Bessemer City *Star-Times* was a masterpiece of second-day reporting. Instead of focusing on the New York press conference, Miller's story, which was picked up by the wire services, got the reaction of the newly-minted chairman of the sub-committee with oversight of the nation's anti-trust laws.

The import of Miller's story pushed the merger off page one to the business page. The 32-point headline over the story by *Star-Times'* chief political writer, Charles J. Miller, gave newsboys up and down the Lenape Valley something to shout about:

# Jack Eddinger
## HARRIS BLASTS BESS STEEL-TOLEDO MERGER CALLS IT MONOPOLISTIC

The story cascaded in a two-column spread down the right side of the newspaper. It was highlighted by a two column photo of a stern Zach Harris gaveling a hearing to order. Never mind that it was a morgue photo of a hearing dating back several years. It made its point. A *Star-Times* editorial denounced the merger as a public swindle. Pandemonium broke out the minute the bale of newspapers landed in the green marble lobby of *Iron Mountain*. Eugene Garrett Palmer read the story in a steaming rage. He fired his public relations man on the spot for dragging him against his wishes into the press conference. He put through a call to the master Wall Street fixer and public relations guru, Sam Lee.

"Lee, I want this under control tonight. I can't have our stock move down even a tick. I want this situation contained now. Get up here on the next train. Better still, I'll send a car for you. See me immediately you arrive." Lee and Palmer's lawyers from Thatcher, Simpson & Bartlett calmed the investment situation, but they had no idea what awaited them, as the new chairman of the House anti-trust subcommittee announced a full investigation of the merger. During the next three months the subcommittee tied the deal into knots, embarrassing the president of the Toledo firm into admitting that he was unaware that the merger had anti-trust ramifications, and backing Bessemer Steel's high-priced legal team into a corner. Palmer was traveling in Europe at the time and refused to return to testify. One day after the hearing concluded Palmer stormed into Congressman Harris's office in the Longworth Building. He demanded to see the chairman. But the meeting was to be no encounter between a repentant monarch and a lordly churchman. Alone, behind varnished oak doors emblazoned with the seal of the United States House of Representatives, the Adam Smith laissez-faire Republican and the Wilsonian, anti-trust Democrat, glared at each other with consummate contempt.

"I see we are going to have a problem, you and I, over this acquisition and merger business which you call beneficial and economically sound for the country, and I say is a naked ploy to create a monopoly," Harris began.

"Mr. Harris, you may make your pronouncements as you wish, but I admonish you, sir, to consider the consequences. For if you persist in your efforts to have this consolidation rescinded, you and I shall meet not in these halls, but in the courts of this land. I am prepared to fight you to the Supreme Court. Furthermore, I assure you the Bessemer Steel Corporation, whose workers you need to return you to office, will not sit

# INQUISITION

idly by. We will see you defeated, sir. That is not a threat, but a simple statement of reality."

"Just a minute, Palmer," Harris snapped. No one at Bessemer Steel or anywhere else dared refer to Eugene Garrett Palmer by his surname. The initials, "E.G.," were off limits, even to confidantes and peers. "E.G." was his newspaper name. It appeared in the news columns of *The Wall Street Journal*, or on the business pages of the *New York Times* under a somber Bachrach photo accompanying his year-end "State of Steel" report as President of the American Iron & Steel Institute. To everyone: workers, office girls, executives, steel barons, prime ministers and kings, it was always Mr. Palmer. Eugene Garrett Palmer gave Zachary Taylor Harris his most twisted sneer and practiced snort of contempt, turned on his heel, and stalked out, pulling the door behind him with so resounding a force that it reverberated for minutes down the halls of the cavernous Longworth Building.

"I'll be damned," Zach Harris said aloud to an empty room. "The old iron master's lost his grip. Well, for better or worse, the battle is now joined."

Eugene Garrett Palmer swore a second oath. His version of Rome's blood oath against Carthage, became simply, Harris Will Be Destroyed. He would wait until the time was right for vengeance. Meanwhile, Bessemer Steel's lawsuit against the Justice Department's anti-trust ruling blocking the merger worked its way interminably through the federal court system. The election year of 1956 gave Palmer his first, clear opportunity for retribution, and he relished it. Of a soft May evening when the pastels of dogwoods and azaleas wrapped the tired landscape of Pennsylvania's Lenape Valley in vernal effulgence, Palmer convened his senior executives around the big oak dining table at Calypso Hall, his Georgian mansion atop Spyglass Hill. Its sweep of green lawn broken by shade trees, rose beds, Italian water gardens with fountains, fish ponds and Graeco-Roman statuary, stretched down to the swift-flowing Lenape river.

After a dinner of lobster, pheasant and roast beef Palmer and his subordinates convened in the library with crystal snifters of a shimmering 1708 Fonseca Port and exquisite Cuban cigars. Palmer announced that each would contribute $12,000 in monthly $1,000 deductions from salary toward a new action fund the Company had established to educate the public to the interests of The Bessemer Steel Corp. The Company, he told them, would advance campaign funds to worthy candidates by monthly checkoff.

"Gene, by God, this checkoff system is what I'm trying to get Dave McDonald to back off of out in the mills. How do you expect me to get

# Jack Eddinger

a contract with the USW, if we're using the same payroll checkoff we're denying them?" said Joe O'Neill, his general counsel, grimacing through the blue haze of cigar smoke. Palmer did not appreciate the comment one bit. Irony was his province, but O'Neill was his reliable trouble-shooter and labor lawyer, and the only member of management who called the boss by his nickname. Years before, Gene Palmer pitched for Joe O'Neill's Lenape University ICAA baseball champions. Palmer brought his former coach to Bess Steel to be his sounding board with the workers, trade unions and local politicians. O'Neill was Belfast Irish Presbyterian; quick of wit, charming of manner and with a whiskey glass accenting a clever story, the supreme raconteur.

"God-dammit, Joe, this will go no further than this room. If it does, I'll have all of your hides, yours included. This corporation and its people will no longer sit on the sidelines. From this point forward, we will take an active part in the campaign for our congressional seat. As of this moment we are supporting Mr. Henry Marcel, our distinguished state senator."

O'Neill's grimace widened. "Aww c'mon Gene, Henry's a total horse's ass and you know it. We can't support him."

"Henry Marcel may indeed be that and more, but he supports our interests. It is your job, Mr. O'Neill, to make him into a thoroughbred. Understood?"

"Chrissake. I shoulda retired a year ago when I had the chance. Now I'll never get back to Ballyronan. The fish of Loch Neagh will receive a full reprieve. Henry Marcel. Jesus. Harris'll … But then again, anything's possible. Okay boss, but I've got to do it my way. Lloyd Kressman's the wild card here. I need to find a way to get him behind Marcel, whom he despises almost as much as us. Maybe there's another way to do this."

"I expect you to persuade Mr. Kressman that his interest lies with us," Palmer told O'Neill. "That's the only way it will be. Understood?"

"Yes, sir."

Lloyd Kressman pushed through the squeaky wooden gate separating his office from a long wooden bench where his clients sat. He extended a callused hand to the congressman.

"*Wie gehts*, Zach. By golly you don't look so good. The bug gotcha? Just catching up with things around here while I got some peace and quiet." He put a gnarled, arthritic claw on Zach Harris's shoulder. "What brings ya all the way up from Washington, Zach? Frenchie's gotcha worried, I'll bet." His voice rose and fell in the singsong cadence of Pennsylvania *Deutch*. Declarative sentences sounded like questions. Kressman's value lay in the Fifty-Fifty Club, the political organization he commanded. It

# INQUISITION

consisted of 50 Democrats and 50 Republicans. He had his people in the field 365 days a year. Hundred's of birthday cards went out every day. Turkeys, geese and chickens were delivered across the two counties on Thanksgiving and Christmas. Fruit baskets, flowers and boxes of candy went to hospital rooms every week. Dollar bills stapled to newspaper clippings went to youngsters who excelled in sports or dramatics or made the honors list or were spelling bee finalists. If a sports team or individual brought particular distinction to their school or neighborhood or borough, a bank sack containing 50 silver dollars arrived along with a letter of congratulations from Lloyd A. Kressman, counselor at law, to be posted on their school or church bulletin boards.

Kressman drew political wisdom from Simon Cameron's legatee and political heir, Matthew Stanley Quay. On his rise to U.S. Senator, Quay raided the state treasury to create the machine that dominated Pennsylvania's politics for over 50 years. Quay's formulation was simple: "Politics is the art of taking money from the few and votes from the many under the pretext of protecting the one from the other."

Kressman came from a nearly extinct breed of lawyers like Quay who had qualified for the bar by reading the law in a long apprenticeship of writing briefs, of interminable hours in the courthouse vaults searching land records, of reading probate papers and taking on any and all assignments, including running errands for judges and senior barristers. Kressman's office reminded Zach Harris of a remnant of the American frontier. A sheriff's office, perhaps, or a newspaper publisher's or the territory physician's. Smudged calendars for the past five years with pencil strokes through each day marched across one wall. A green metal lamp shade on a frayed cord dangled over an ancient roll-top desk. Crannies and pigeon holes were crammed with pen nibs, ink bottles, worn-out erasers, pencil stubs with deep teeth marks, paper clips, rubber bands, balls of twine, lead soldiers, canceled postage stamps, brown-edged penny postcards, the innards of a pocket watch, broken shoelaces and flakes of chewing tobacco. A goose-neck telephone stood on a pedestal of dusty out-of-print law books. A heavy oak table running along a wall held blue-backed petitions for zoning exceptions, orphans court filings, wills and deeds of trust with bright orange tax stamps, and immense ledgers recording mechanics liens and real estate transactions. Entries were written in a spidery script in black ink. On the floor next to the desk within range of the tilt-backed swivel chair, a leprous broth stewed in a spittoon. The chair's leather seat, shiny from wear, was rent by a slit, exposing white cotton stuffing. Framed and hanging on a wall was Simon Cameron's famous quip that "an honest politician when bought stays bought."

# Jack Eddinger

"Jesus, Lloyd, this place looks like the ass end of a yak herd," Zach Harris said, his gray eyes twinkling. "When's the Board of Health going to tack the quarantine sign on your door? Why don't you move into one of those office buildings you own uptown? It'd be a lot healthier than this." Zach Harris was one of the few individuals from whom Lloyd Kressman would tolerate any easy familiarity. Harris made the mistake of underestimating Kressman only once. Pennsylvania Dutchmen, he learned, have long memories. Befriend them and they'll go to the grave with your secrets. Cross them and you pay for it long afterward.

"Me, move. Naaa. I don't like them fancy places with the big windas ya gotta pay to have washed every week. Hell, I make $10 on every winda my girls clean," Kressman said. "The old lady'd be waggin her finger, tellin me the girls that come in and clean up the place'd distract me from my work. Not that I'd mind it, but hell, I'll never move outa here. They'll hafta carry me out. Well, Zach, tell me. How's things goin in Washington these days? Seems like we never see muchaya anymore now that you're one of the big shots down there. Boy, that's a bugger of a cold ya got there. You need a shota schnapps. It'll warm ya up, once. I got some good stuff right here in the desk. Nuthin but the best."

"No thanks. I'm taking pills. They may not mix with that moonshine."

"What brings ya in? Us Republicans givin you a tough time, huh? This little Frenchie, he's gotcha worried I bet."

"Lloyd, you know better than that. How long's it been? Twenty-five years? When have I ever let a hay shaker worry me? Not when I can depend on you. Where did you dig him up?"

"Well, let me tell ya. I didn't have nothin to do with it. Some of Joe O'Neill's people from the Steel came to me. They said I should help Joe, because he's a Republican like me. They started in about how Joe's family lived here before the Hunkies and Polocks got here; that his grandfather was one of them smelters they brought over from Belfast to the old Iron Works down by the river. They said us Republicans need to stick together. When I told them I was for you, they said that's the reason we don't get anybody elected anymore. That's all I needed to hear, Zach. These *ein, zwei, drei schies in der hosen jungen* think they can buy their way into the party. I'll tell ya it ain't like the old days. Today they put on a suit, a white shirt and a Dobbs hat, spend nine-to-five pushing paper, drink fancy cocktails and tell us they know what's best for the party. They don't set foot in none of our clubs like the Red Men and the Knights of Pythias. They go out to the country club and hit the little ball across the grass. The next thing they told me was they'd raise a lotta money for this fella, and

# INQUISITION

I better get on the team, because if I didn't, I'd be sorry. Frenchie's told them he can beat you Zach, and you know, these buggers believe him. Well I told them what they could do with their money. They're a bunch of no good *schieskophs*! Told 'em they'd be safer investing it in Mexican whorehouses. Then they threatened me. Said they'd take their real estate and zoning business to that little Jew, Piskoff. I saw red. Nobody threatens me, god-dammit, particularly with a kike. I threw 'em all out. I don't need their charity or their Jew boy."

Zach Harris knew the Dutchman's single-minded objective was to show everyone this *auslander* who hadn't been as far as the fifth grade was not only their equal, but their superior. Nearing the age of 75, he was closing in on his goal. He'd soon be a millionaire. One day soon bankers and lawyers all over the valley would awaken to learn that to accomplish anything in the public arena; to purchase even the smallest piece of strategically located land required the acquiesence and approval of Lloyd Kressman, zoning lawyer-conniver without equal.

"Lloyd, you know how much I appreciate your support, but this time I need an exceptional effort. And I'll subsidize it completely with enough left over for you. We've been together a long time but I can't remember an election like this. It's not Marcel I'm concerned about, or O'Neill or even Palmer's money. It's this young fanatic in the District Attorney's office. He's cocky, Lloyd, damned cocky. As you know, Tad Daley was the best friend I ever had in politics till you came along. His son's grandstanding with these phony investigations are causing a lot of understandable turmoil at the court house. He's got the whole place in an uproar. You remember what he did to Ed Weiss two years ago. Bribery, hah! We both know nobody could bribe Ed. Dammit, Lloyd this fellow is dangerous. We've got to get him out of there. It's time he's taught a lesson."

Lloyd Kressman tipped back in the wooden swivel chair, ran a hand through his thick, gray Von Hindenburg brush and pushed his rimless bifocals off the tip of his nose. He spat the cud he'd been chewing into the spittoon and took a red and green pouch containing the bronze visage of an Indian chief from a pigeon hole and extended it to his guest. Congressman Harris winced and held up a blocking hand. He had important business to transact. On another occasion he might have taken a pinch.

"Lloyd, I want you to cut Marcel's vote out from under him. I want to carry the District by 80-85 percent. I need that kind of margin to reorganize the party and put the quietus on that young fella's ambition once and for all. I'm prepared to give you two appointments to the Toll Bridge Commission. They pay $12,000 each."

# Jack Eddinger

Zach Harris knew the old man wanted more than a few throw away political appointments. It was a starter for getting Kressman's real price to deliver the election numbers he wanted. Kressman dug into the pouch. He brought out a stringy wad of Red Man chaw big enough to choke a goat. He packed it into his jaw, chewed contemplatively then spat.

"Bejeebers, Zach, that's a tough one. What can I get outta a couple a bridge appointments? Forget 80 percent It's gonna take a lot of hard work to get you fifty-five. I can't do it for jobs alone. I'd need at least fifteen thousand dollars to give you a vote in that range, and that won't be enough. Hell, I'll have to scrap the ballots I just printed. We'll need new ones half with your name on them; half without it. And that ain't the half of it. What am I gonna tell our candidates running for alderman, justice of the peace, burgess, election judges, constable, councilman and other local offices? It'll take time and a helluva lot of work to convince them you'll put money behind them against your own party. It'll take five thousand for new ballots even if I can get them printed in time. You know I don't use a union shop. Everything for you has to be union. Most of my people hate labor unions, especially the *hemlocks* in Allendale. What am I gonna do for election day cash? I need hand-out money for drivers, poll watchers, canvassers. This is a big job, Zach. You ain't makin it easy."

"I can have $15,000 cash to you in a couple of days. I'll throw in an extra ten to cover your loss on the ballots. You can pocket what's left. Don't worry about labor. They'll do whatever I tell them. How about it?"

"Well, not so fast," Kressman demurred, pulling an earlobe. "I want to think it over."

"Hell, what's there to think about? Remember, the highway appropriation is coming in January. There's a nice piece of land in the north end that will be an interchange when I put the Bessemer City Connector in next year's bill. It's off of the Old Towpath Road. A modest investment now will return you a good profit."

"Zach, I want to be cut into the Lenape Dam project.."

"Now wait a minute, Lloyd. God-dammit! You know I can't work you into those contracts. Highways're different. Nobody cares. The dam's another story. That money goes through the State Treasury."

"Ya, ya. I know that. What the hell do you think I was doing in Harrisburg this week? My people want to help, but they say it's out of their hands. And that's where I need you. Zach this county'll never see the kind of money that's comin in here for the dam. You're the only man I know can get a new bank chartered quick. I want you to charter me. I'm gonna show those buggers who the hell's boss. Whaddya say?

# INQUISITION

"Jesus Christ. How can I pull that off?" Zach Harris said feigning surprise until he could consider the Dutchman's request. "I'm not on the Banking Committee."

"Yeah, but the chairman's your friend, Zach. Don't bullshit me. I know what you can do. Zach, if you want them votes, you better find a way to get me chartered."

In that instantaneous blur that is human intelligence: reason, memory, concentration, insight, intuition, judgment, which no computer or cryptographic machine can duplicate, Zachary Taylor Harris subjected Lloyd Kressman's proposal to an exacting analysis. His mind went to work turning it over, breaking it down, pulling it apart, filtering out the subtleties. How will it cost me? Can it be traced? Any IRS problems? Will I get burned? How can I capitalize on it? Will it put this old buzzard in my pocket?

After completing his calculations, he had to suppress a chuckle. It surprised him that Kressman would propose so attainable a favor in return for what he deemed a tough, damned near impossible election assignment. Once he had the Dutchman's word, he knew he had his votes. He'd get Kressman chartered with a phone call to Wade Hance, chairman of Banking. He needed an acquiescent contract review board to approve the transfers. Flynn'll go along if I let him fill the majority seats with his people. Kressman can name the two minority members.

"Make the bastard squirm."

"Jesus, Lloyd, I don't know ... the IRS and Treasury police those charters pretty close. They'll want chapter and verse on you, and they'll want to know about stockholders, directors, assets, liabilities, accounting procedures - everything," he said gravely looking at a spot on the floor next to the spittoon. Out of the corner of his eye he saw the old man's cheekbones working and the yellow ends of his mustache quivering.

"God-dammit, Zach, I know that! I ain't no crook. I got everything in order. Come around here and let me show ya."

"Hell, Lloyd. All I need's your word. You may get some questions about it. Then again, they may just let it slip by."

"Good ... Good! Then it's done, huh?"

The 80 percent margin was crucial. Numbers like that will furnish the muscle to realign the party and put an end to Daley's meddling. Kressman will parcel out the legal work to assemble the land for the Bessemer City Connector project. Greedy lawyers make good political allies.

"As good as money in your bank," Zachary Taylor Harris said firmly. "Now, you can pour me that shot of schnapps."

# Jack Eddinger

The two men chuckled, raised their shot glasses to eye level and downed the fiery rye. Zach Harris made a wicked grimace. He took out his black notebook and penciled in a notation.

Sam McBryan, the congressman's driver, appeared in the doorway, looking at his wristwatch. "It's 6:30 congressman. You don't want to keep Mrs. Harris waiting."

"Okay, that's it then. I'll have my man talk to Flynn tomorrow. Now do what you have to do to get me my 80 percent."

He shook hands with Kressman and left.

"Stop by the District office. I've got to call Washington." Within minutes Congressman Harris was greeting the two now middle-aged secretaries he'd hired a decade before. They upheld the reputation of an office known for its immediate and precise constituent service. Their typewriters hummed throughout the day, and they stayed around till the work was done. He went directly to his office, closed the door put on his reading glasses and dialed for a long distance operator.

"Person-to-person, operator; Mr. Robert Bird in Washington at FEderal 9-5000, extension 200."

"Is that Washington, New Jersey, sir?"

"D.C., operator. Washington, D.C. This is Congressman Harris. *Christ, I'm glad I'm not calling Moscow, Idaho.*"

"Yes, sir."

"Hello, Bob Bird."

"Where do we stand on the hearings, Robert?"

"We've hit a snag, Congressman. I was getting ready to call you. You'll have to make the judgment as to its extent. Flynn's office says no deal on the funding to move the hearings off the Hill, unless ..."

Harris cut him off.

"That sonofabitch! I dragged his ass out of every legislative blind alley he went down this session. Why the hell is he doing this to me? I thought I left it cut and dried?"

"His AA says the only way his boss'll go along with the supplemental is if he gets his name on the Lenape Dam bill. Says they want no trouble with the Speaker by tacking the hearing funds on the legislative appropriations supplemental. Routine stuff's, okay. But he told me that something special like this requires cashing in some big chits. He said Mr. Flynn's awfully upset that you're writing the dam bill. Don't forget his view that it's still in his District."

*The key to this is Flynn. Even with my best effort, he's completely unpredictable. One day he's on the rampage about some jackass on the committee he thinks double-crossed him. The next day he's got his arm*

# INQUISITION

*around his shoulder telling him how he's going to make him a hero back home with soil erosion money.*

"Listen, Robert I'm relying on you to finesse this thing. If you're ever going to understand Congress, you got to know when to make a move. Suggest to Flynn's people that as caucus chairman I'll support moving Buck McAndrews off Agriculture and over to Government Ops. And, I'll see to it that he can take his seniority with him. Tell him Billy Yates told me he won't run after this term. That means Post Office and Civil Service will be free. Buck'll be chairman. Flynn knows what that means. Tell him I'll cut him in on everything we do on the dam publicitywise. Hell, man, use the good horse sense I taught you. Dammit, Flynn's seat's the safest in Pennsylvania. I'm the one with his ass uncovered.

"Robert, I've got a fund-raiser in one hour. Get Flynn's man on the phone and lay it out for him exactly the way I told you. You can tell him you're speaking for me. Tell him the congressman's got to understand my situation, but that I appreciate his feelings, and I'll make it worth his while. Use those precise words. Tell him I've got the entire State Delegation behind a resolution to put his name on the Dam. It will be named the Daniel P. Flynn Dam and Watershed the day he retires. Between you and me, Flynn'll interpret that as a move to get him out of the House. Now this is crucial. Tell him I intend to let him name three of the five members of the contract review board. Tell him that. Dammit, he can't want more than that, unless he wants to wear his vaudeville getup to the press conference. I'd even go along with him on that."

"I think he'll go for the package, Congressman. They've been on my butt about the board ever since the public works bill passed."

"Okay. I'm leaving it in your hands, Robert. Get him to sign off on this thing. I don't want to hear any more about it. Nail it down, son."

"Yes, sir!"

Flynn can always be counted on in a package deal, especially one that gives his ego a massage. Crazy sonofabitch puts every penny into his broken down political machine. Thinks he's the last of the Gaelic chieftains. He'll go to bat for the hearings. And if the Speaker wrestles him down on TV, Flynn'll put the full appropriation in the Bureau's budget now that the Director was inside the tent. In the event of trouble Robert Bird acted without authorization. No one could prove otherwise.

Grand slam! He'd bagged them all - the Director, Flynn, Palmer, Kressman and the upstart D.A. Not a bad day's work.

# CHAPTER SEVEN
## *Marion Hanson Harris*

Marion Hanson Harris, smoking a cork-tipped Benson and Hedges paced across the black and white marble foyer of the elegant, ivy-walled Georgian house on Bessemer City's Prospect Hill. She wore a satin evening dress the color of bright emeralds. A sable fur piece draped over her slender shoulders. The ice in her blue eyes made frostier by the dazzle of diamond pendant earrings and silver-grey hair pulled back in a severe chignon, chilled her always theatrical greeting.

"Well, the great man home from the hunt." The husky Finishing School accent he once found appealing evoked a frown. "What, pray tell, brings him out of the forest when he might be flushing partridges from the brush? Or cocking an ear for the legendary Prothonotary warbler who'll tell him who's the reddest bird in the kingdom?"

"Save your ornithology for the Audubon Society, my dear. I'm here. That ought to be sufficient." Zach Harris never argued with his wife. He took her sarcasm in stride. Had it come from a witness, the poor weasel would be facing a contempt citation. Over the decade since her treatment for acute depression, his wife's permanent mental state, it seemed to him, was typified by mood swings ranging from despondency to breezy self-assurance. It allowed him to play the long-suffering spouse. It resulted in an unspoken agreement that took them along separate paths following World War II. He never asked and she was unable to remember. That's the way it was in recovering from deep depression, and that's how they left it. Only her dearest friend, Anna Daley, knew the full story. Returning from the South Pacific to a life radically changed, Congressman Harris decided not to push matters too far. The situation, he reasoned, might be beneficial to his career, and would free him to pursue his political ambitions not to mention amorous diversions. The appearance of a proper marriage could not be sacrificed to a wartime peccadillo or whatever it was. Had it not been for her independence and inherited wealth, the episode might have led to divorce a long time ago. It was over, forgotten, buried. Life would go on. It left him free to pursue other relationships unfettered by maudlin sentimentality. His career proceeded rapidly after the war. He moved into the House leadership. Eleven years after his discharge from the Navy with the rank of captain, he was on the upward trajectory he knew would place him in a strong position for national office.

They gave up their elegant Tudor mansion on Kalorama Circle with its leaded glass mullioned windows set in sandstone and timber during

# INQUISITION

the war. She returned to the Lenape Valley and purchased the handsome octagonal Georgian residence on Prospect Hill out of her legacy. He found a rent-controlled, cramped *pied a terre* in the old Washington neighborhood that suited his immediate needs. The arrangement matched their marital situation. Neither had raised the prospect of divorce. Their concession to each other was to project the image of a successful marriage, successful careers and self-sufficiency in both. Marion Harris emerged from depression only after several years of therapy. She continued to face periods of manic agitation characterized by feelings of deep remorse and inadequacy. Alcohol seemed to ease her anxieties. On special occasions like tonight they were partners of convenience. They would appear together, as the political bedfellows the public believed them to be. Months before, he allowed his wife to commit him to be guest of honor at the Democratic Women's gala fund-raiser for the Stevenson-Kefauver ticket. He held his nose when he was forced to ask the Democratic National Committee to send her liberal pinup boy, the Assistant Secretary of State for African Affairs to deliver the keynote address scheduled for 8 P.M. in the grand ballroom of the McKean Hotel. He'd never measure up to Zach Harris's standards of a statesman.

"Oh, compose yourself, darling," she said through a veil of blue smoke rising from her cigarette her long slender artist's fingers. "Anyone on a steady diet of Arthur Krock needs a good stiff drink. What can I get you? I must say you really are beginning to believe everything that's fit to print. Next thing, you'll be violating your own standards, and begin believing your press reviews. I'm sure you noticed *The New Republic* favored you this month as one of the ten most reactionary members of Congress."

"I take anything coming from that Commie rag as a left-handed compliment. Scotch. I haven't changed my drinking habits, as I see you have." He took two empty fifths of Fairfax Gentleman from the liquor cabinet, and held them up to the light. Looks like Lee's army's been through here."

She ignored the comment, stirred a scotch and soda and left it atop the small bar. "Anna, not Robert E. for your information, congressman. I had the gala committee over for cocktails." She could not have known that her husband found a drained bottle of rye under the dust ruffle of her dressing table on his last trip home. She prided herself on how well she handled alcohol. Had she known of his discovery, her response would have been less breezy. It was all right to park a whiskey bottle anywhere but there. Carelessly, she had forgotten about it. Getting slightly tipsy at dinner parties did not bother her. She always had the situation under control. It would bother her deeply to know that he knew she drank alone.

# Jack Eddinger

Marion Hanson Harris had never fully escaped the dark shadow cast by her father, whose every move in life as in business was calculated to produce a pre-conceived outcome without the uncertainty of risk. A wealthy man at the age of 30, Buchanan Hanson measured all men - he never considered the possibility of female independence - by the worldly equivalent of the economy of grace. He harbored the capitalist's belief that he had been pre-ordained to create wealth. To do so required a singular strength of character and a mind for commerce. God infused such traits into but a handful of the elect. He had been tested and found worthy. At age 16 he began his quest as a telegraph clerk for the Pennsylvania Railroad as the Civil War spread north. Sam Hanson, the older brother he admired and loved, caught a rebel ball through the brain and died in a muddy creek bed at Antietam in 1861. His younger brother grieved and vowed to use his skills to help crush the rebellion, not by musket and cannon, but by knowledge and logistics. His knowledge of telegraphy, freight movement and the fastest routing schedules made him the equal of men twice his age. His superior, Col. Horace MacPherson, joined Lincoln's War Department, headed by Simon Cameron, and brought young Hanson with him to Washington to coordinate military rail lines in the East. The young man did the work of ten men, and stayed on the job until his tasks of dispatching food, horses, fodder, cannon and ammunition were completed. Never was his work more frantic than in getting the Army of the Potomac re-supplied and headed south after Gettysburg.

Buchanan Hanson was one of the many Northerners who put the organizational skills they gained in the military and the war economy to work converting Jefferson's agrarian democracy into the industrial republic of Grant, Hayes, Garfield and Harrison. Beginning with a $600 loan from his benefactor, Colonel MacPherson, he started a company to produce iron bridges and rails for rebuilding and modernizing the North's railroads. As steel making replaced iron smelting, he formed the Hanson Coal & Coke Co. to bake soft coal into coke for Andrew Carnegie's Pennsylvania steel companies. By 1871, he owned 50 coke ovens and 300 acres of bituminous fields. Nine years later he owned 1,000 ovens and 3,000 acres of coal fields.

At the age of 47 with his business interests consolidated he married a member of the Carnegie household. Miss Kathleen McGinley followed her sisters from Dungloe, County Donegal, to America to serve in the homes and mansions of the emerging nouveau riche. She began as an upstairs maid at *Balmoral,* the Carnegie estate near Pittsburgh. Kate worked her way into her employer's confidence, becoming the equivalent of the Scot's favorite niece. Having no children of his own and as a fellow

# INQUISITION

Celt without pretensions, Carnegie made the vivacious young woman his social secretary. It was at a gathering at Balmoral that Kate met and fell in love with Buchanan Hanson, who was nearly twenty years her senior. The year was 1888. Carnegie opened Balmoral's gardens and grounds to their wedding and gave the bride away. Morgans, Vanderbilts, Garys, and Astors mingled with, Fricks, Garretts, and Sayres and one thousand less luminous guests. Pennsylvania's two U.S. Senators, J. Donald Cameron - Simon's son - and M.S. Quay attended. Matt Quay brought wedding greetings and a small gift from President Harrison, whose campaign he had managed. Quay purchased the gift in Philadelphia for another purpose and slipped the president's card inside the wrapping.

Buchanan Hanson moved his business to Bessemer City to supply Carnegie's protégé and steel-making heir, Charlie Schwab, with inexpensive coke for the furnaces of a new company, Bessemer Steel Corporation. A son, Alec Cameron Hanson, was born in 1890. Buchanan Hanson committed the boy's care to his wife and a succession of nannies and tutors. It soon became clear that Alec would never grow up to be a captain of industry. Hanson blamed Kate for this unpleasantly conspicuous oversight. A dark and menacing mood descended upon their marriage. The arrival of a daughter, Marion McPherson Hanson, nine years later sent him into fits of fury and prolonged hostility. They drove his young, blue-eyed wife into a tryst with his business manager, Stewart Legrange, the son of a middling family descended from French Huguenots. Attentive, witty and congenial with a warm smile and easygoing nature, Legrange, a man of generosity and charm, was everything Buchanan Hanson was not. Kate Hanson's infidelity unfolded slowly over the next decade. Marion, now twelve, was confused by her mother's mood changes. When her father was present, her mother avoided contact. She acted aloof and otherworldly. She joined a weekly seance group and spent most of her days away from *Strathclyde,* the dank and austere mansion her husband built on a hilltop overlooking the Lenape River. Whenever she returned from her mystical meanderings, Kate took to her room until the mandatory appearance required of her at dinner hour. Dinners were unbearable. Silence prevailed, broken only by the clink of china and silver or by Buchanan Hanson's habitual throat-clearing or by the kitchen help's muffled footfalls. But in her father's absences, her mother's demeanor shifted. Kate was always younger, happier, prettier and as chirpy as an Irish songbird. Growing into young womanhood, Marion was perplexed by the changes. Kate's radiance returned whenever her husband was away and Stewart - Uncle Stewart - appeared. Legrange brought frivolity and delight - alien emotions - into the cold-walled Hanson mansion. To Marion it was something new and

## Jack Eddinger

different; something not to be fully trusted. Stewart Legrange seemed to be guided by a different sensibility than her father; one which went beyond talk of coal and iron ore, mines, men and money. It puzzled her. Marion wondered why she enjoyed being in his company. His charm, however, could not provide the warmth, security and integrity she craved. She bore a heavy guilt for what she considered her inability to please her father and command his love.

In his senior year at Princeton Alec Hanson established himself as a leader among a small group of campus socialists, mainly from the northern Midwest, which his father could not fathom. Buchanan Hanson wanted his son to excel in engineering, start at the bottom of the family business and work his way up to the riches awaiting him. Alec quit engineering in the second week of his Freshman year. He studied English literature, attended Professor Woodrow Wilson's lectures on American government, and talked about working for newspapers. He wanted to cover wars, murders and write stories like Stephen Crane and Richard Harding Davis. His father recoiled at the prospect of a son in a calling populated by rogues, vagabonds and confidence men. The rift widened. Alec began writing short stories and with two of his closest friends and with money sent by Kate started a small literary quarterly that became a publishing outlet for the scant handful of radicals, which Princeton tolerated with resigned exasperation. Alec became editor of *The Daily Princetonian* in the same year. Near the end of the term he and a classmate, whose uncle ran the copy desk of *The New York Journal American*, were given an insider's tour of Hearst's most influential daily from copy rim to hell box. They were recruited on the spot and told to report a week after graduation. Beginning salary would be $15 a week with a nickle-a-word for any scandalous story they could dig up on their own time and at their own expense. Subjects were limited to lust, avarice, anger, envy and any shameless morsel they could unearth. After graduation Alec's affinity to alcohol, horse racing and women intervened. Two of the three were passengers in the yellow roadster he'd purchased the previous September with winnings from his best day ever at the track. At 60 miles an hour Alec could not bring the car out of a sharp bend on a two-lane back road north of Trenton. The roadster jumped an embankment, plunged fifty feet downhill and overturned into the South Branch of the Raritan River. Alec was dead at the scene. His companion died on the way to the hospital.

Alec's death sent Marion into a state of prolonged despair and anger. She fantasized that if she were with him, he would still be alive. She blamed her mother's estrangement from her father for her brother's lack of self-control. Growing up under her father's austerity, Marion regarded

# INQUISITION

the few males she knew, including Stewart Legrange, as inadequate. Her self-image appeared as a dim reflection in an old and faded looking glass, blackening at the edges and with spidery lines on its surface. She had a recurring dream. In it, she saw Alec embracing Kate as both glided through the mirror in a passionate dance. As she approached, the images dissolved into the visage of her father. His handsome bearded image, arrogant and worldly, appeared over her shoulder. But he was always out of reach, as she tried to touch his short, neatly-trimmed beard. She began to believe she was the true reflection of her father. Soon she began to regard all males as lesser men. She made her mother pay a heavy price for her relationship. She informed her father of Legrange's frequent appearances during his absences, and how when out of sight, her mother mocked and belittled him. A harsh confrontation between husband and wife, and a brutal caning of Legrange sent the lovers fleeing. The divorce was made more fearful by the power of the Hanson fortune from which Kate was cut off irrevocably. He told Legrange he would never hold another position in business anywhere and would live out his days in penury.

Later with his wife banished and his brother and only son in early graves, Buchanan Hanson began to take an uncharacteristic interest in his daughter. The dinner hour, once grim and distant, began to produce animated conversation. It started slowly, and built into a genuine dialogue something which neither had previously allowed. Marion rekindled an emotion in him that he had buried in the deepest recesses of his psyche. Her bright-eyed intelligence, eagerness to learn and absence of fawning reverence peeled back the scar-tissue over the deep wound of his youth. He was astonished to find that she not only had his dead brother, Sam Hanson's, blue eyes and handsome face, but her voice had acquired traces of Sam's thoughtful speech and manner. It was in the way she ended a sentence, and in the pauses between thoughts and words. He was overwhelmed with an emotion which had been submerged for nearly a half century. Buchanan Hanson's black mood lifted. He took over the supervision of his daughter's life, the way he took over a competitor's business. It would begin with a superior education: Lenape Seminary for Girls then Bryn Mawr College. Summers abroad - Crete, Mycenae and Delphi; Alexandria and Cairo; Pompeii and Herculaneum. She followed his arched back deep into Etruscan caves and down wet and slippery stairwells of Germanic castles. They climbed the hill towns and towers of Tuscany and strolled the galleries of Florence.

In personal relations, he taught her, weak-willed men deserve contempt and domination. It was the Hanson family trait to command. On his sixty-seventh birthday he called in his lawyer and dictated a new codicil to his will, making her sole heir to an estate worth nearly $50 million. She was

# Jack Eddinger

sixteen. She also made the powerful psychic discovery which launched her immediately into adulthood - a quick wit and exceptional intelligence. It opened doors leading down new and interesting corridors; corridors containing rooms filled with art and poetry, design and texture, sound and light. It dominated her college years at Bryn Mawr and blossomed into Phi Beta Kappa. Had Cecil Rhodes recognized women, she would have spent the next years studying Renaissance art at Oxford University.

But Washington, not England, was to hold the key to her heart and mind. Her first visit to the White House was not as a tourist like most Americans, but as the guest of President and Mrs. Wilson. The scene was a cloudless June day in 1919 on the South Lawn. Edith Boling Wilson presided over one of her summertime soirees for the Cabinet and financial contributors to her husband's election campaigns. Buchanan Hanson had been courted by Wilson in 1905 to build the new graduate school of business at Princeton. Hanson responded with a donation of $2 million - more than enough for the school. Hanson liked Wilson's quick mind and strong Scottish character. By 1912, he was convinced the governor of New Jersey and former professor of history was a reasonable Southern Democrat. He would be flexible on the tariff. The idea of the trust-busting damned cowboy in the saddle again after a four year hiatus terrified him and his fellow Union Leaguers. Though he leaned to William Howard Taft, Hanson knew the heavy and ungainly President would not be reelected in spite of trimming his girth. The right kind of Democrat - not a Bryan or a Champ Clark - annoying as it might be, would be acceptable. He put his skepticism aside and helped raise the money Wilson needed to win the presidency.

Hating social affairs of any kind, Buchanan Hanson sent his bright and exceptionally attractive daughter to Mrs. Wilson's gathering in his stead. The President spoke to her with warm cordiality, as if she were his own daughter. Her father, he told her, helped make him president, and her late brother was one of his brightest students. On that brilliant day on the South Lawn the dim outlines of the partnership that she believed might one day bring her to Washington as First Lady came into sharp focus as she extended a white-gloved hand to a young Justice Department lawyer on loan to the U.S. Navy to handle ship-building and armaments contracts. She knew immediately that she had met her father's equal. He was 22, severely handsome and the possessor of an acute intelligence. He had a presidential name, a presidential mind and presidential ambition. She was instantly captivated by the young naval officer and lawyer, Zachary Taylor Harris. At the punch bowl, Harris introduced her to his boss and mentor, A. Morton Brodfield, the Attorney General of the United States.

# INQUISITION

In June 1923 Zachary Taylor Harris took the hand of Marion McPherson Hanson in holy matrimony at the Episcopal Cathedral of The Redeemer atop a hill overlooking Bessemer City. In the Cathedral's Bethlehem Chapel the Rt. Rev. Francis Steers, coadjutor of the Episcopal See of Pennsylvania, presided over a union of commerce and public service. White-bearded in wing collar and morning dress, Buchanan Hanson gave his radiant 25-year-old daughter with only slight reluctance to the handsome young lawyer with national political ambitions.

Buchanan Hanson's positive attitude toward his son-in-law lay in his deference for the Harris family lineage. Like the Hanson progenitors, Harris's were Anglo-Saxons who settled in Pennsylvania before the Revolution. The English Harrises were land rich. They started at the confluence of the Lenape and Delaware rivers on a land grant from Charles II. They accumulated more land on patents granted by William Penn, whose agents assembled hundreds of thousands of acres in the vast Northeast Kingdom of the Algonquin nation. The land originally settled by the Lenni Lenape, a stouthearted tribe of Algonquins, came under Penn's writ in a foot race to obtain land, engineered by the saintly Quaker's son and a group of unsaintly trappers and woodsmen. Harrises were among the agitators for independence as early as 1750. They helped Washington's disorganized militia by raising money for gunpowder, shot and jerky beef. As brigadiers and ensigns, Harrises fought from the beginning of the Revolution and were on hand at Yorktown to see the world turned upside down. Less than a century later, their grand-sons commanded Union artillery on Cemetery Ridge. The family produced clergy and educators, physicians and soldiers, scholars and lawyers. All committed themselves to Penn's principle of enlightened public service, and Ben Franklin's dictum: *all wealth earned by the individual is a consequence of the opportunities afforded by the larger society ... The instinct of the wealthy to protect their property at the expense of humanity is the beginning of tyranny.* By the 20th Century Franklin's principles were encumbered by acquisitiveness and opportunism like the green moss that spreads over ancient tombs. While he regarded a career in public service skeptically, Buchanan Hanson nevertheless saw promise in his son-in-law; promise fortified genetically by the shrewdness and thrift of his forebears. The safeguard of that promise, and against any profligacy, was the ironclad trust he established for his daughter. No one would have access to the Hanson wealth without her agreement. Veto authority was vested in the power of attorney lodged with the J.P. Morgan Co., of New York.

The Hanson-Harris wedding surpassed even the wedding feasts of Newport. Carnegie's fete of nearly a half century before could not compare.

# Jack Eddinger

Marion's wedding displayed the adornments of a feudal banquet set in a country garden. Buchanan Hanson built his gray-walled Scottish-Norman manor house he called, *Strathclyde*, in honor of his clan on a promontory overlooking the Lenape River. It had many of the appointments and accouterments of Carnegie's manse, particularly the gardens and grounds. Like Carnegie he invited his fellow gentry to celebrate with him. He chartered trains from New York, Pittsburgh and Philadelphia to carry financiers and industrialists to Bessemer City. Guests disembarked on a special platform provided by the Lenape Valley Railroad. It led to a long stairway arched by a canopy of red, yellow and pink roses. The stairway opened to a grass terrace behind the mansion with a panoramic view of the surrounding hills and forests. The lawn sloped gracefully down to the banks of the Lenape. Townspeople waved from canoes and flat bottom boats. It was a scene awaiting expression in the soft rounded lines and pastels of Renoir. The House of Morgan's wedding gift proved the sensation of the day, a Bavarian carousel with carved winged horses, dancing bears and mirror-inlaid coaches choreographed to the cadence of a steam calliope. To her father's consternation Charlie Schwab, the gregarious chairman of Bessemer Steel Co., astride a prancing wooden horse cajoled everyone to board the carousel. Lacking a master of ceremonies, Schwab took over introducing guests. He introduced the newlyweds to his young lieutenant just back from straightening out Bessemer Steel's ore fields, Eugene Garrett Palmer. Palmer, dour and stiff in a white linen suit and boater, bowed to Marion Harris and shook hands with her husband. Zachary Taylor Harris disliked him instantly.

Like an Old Testament prophet Buchanan Hanson surveyed the scene from the edge of the terrace, gazing like Moses out across the green valley which stretched before him. Within 18 months he was dead.

The couple spent the first 24 hours of wedded bliss at the Astor in Manhattan. At noon the following day they boarded the Queen Mary and sailed to Southampton. They spent a week trudging about London. They put up at Brown's Hotel in Mayfair. They slept late and passed up tea much to the displeasure of the lady concierge. Zach Harris managed to stir her undisguised animus for Americans by filching two pieces of Brown's best crystal. They sat on the quay along the Thames, feeding the pigeons and drinking Glen Barnach neat from Brown's finest. Madame spotted the two bulges in his coat pocket later and asked him to surrender their contents or be charged double for breakage. Zach Harris paid her from a bulging packet of five pound notes and flicked cigarette ashes across the reception desk. They glared at each other. The next morning the Harrises crossed the Channel and by mid-afternoon were aboard a French express

# INQUISITION

bound for Paris. They sipped absinthe neat like their Thames scotch. They arrived at Gare du Nord before 6 P.M. Rank humidity stifled the great pavilion, which smelled of drive-wheel grease, bituminous fumes and garlic - a scene far-removed from the impressionistic elegance of Camille Pissaro. Theirs was a ten-week honeymoon of *Guide Michelin* days and Latin Quarter nights. They walked the Boulevard Montparnasse, joining their contemporaries in the cafes and brasseries of St. Germaine du Pres. Later, they caught the Simplon Express to Venice. It wound through long dark tunnels and across towering stone viaducts. They looked down on the tops of black spruce forests, roaring mountain streams and into deep gray-walled canyons before easing out of the alpine Valhalla onto the Veneto Plain.

But that was all behind them now - very ancient history. Much had passed between them - several lifetimes - since that romantic suspension of time and reality. Tonight, however, called for new beginnings for Marion Hanson Harris. It was her party, her doing, her triumph. She would do her part for her husband by accompanying him and giving the appearance of amity, but her real interest was in electing the man whom she idolized and sometimes fantasized at a distance as a lover, Adlai Ewing Stevenson of Illinois. He reminded her of another Princetonian she knew in those halcyon days in Washington between the wars.

Overnight, the grand ballroom of the McKean Hotel became a Caribbean Elysium lavish with royal palms, rubber trees, fake banyans, eucalyptus, oleander and hibiscus imported from a New York theatrical warehouse. Macaws, parrots and yellow-beaked Tucans of extraordinary color and plumage screeched and beat stiff wings against the mesh screens that kept them a safe distance from the bare shoulders, bosoms, white-gloved arms and tuxedos that gathered in clusters below. No other social affair in Pennsylvania held the flamboyance of the annual candidates' dinner of the Eleanor Roosevelt Democratic Women's Club. It was organized by a group of self-propelled matrons, who considered themselves Marion Harris's visionaries. They wanted to change the name to the Eleanor Roosevelt-Marion Hanson Harris Women's Democratic Club, but she told them that would be unwise.

"Well, Marion when do the natives arrive with the stew pots? I haven't seen anything like this since the invasion of New Guinea," Charlie Miller smiled a broken toothed smile. He sidled up to the Harrises, who had just finished greeting guests. They were moving slowly to the dais, stopping at tables and chatting on their way. He directed a young cameraman with a Speed Graphic to get a picture of them in front of an ice-sculpted replica

## Jack Eddinger

of Diamond Head. "Freeze folks. Need to balance that piece we did on Marcel yesterday."

"I placed the clipping next to his tuxedo tonight, and waited for Vesuvius to erupt," Marion Harris winked at the newsman. "Sure enough, right on time. I was not disappointed."

"Any comment, Congressman?"

"Hear those birds sqwuaking up there, Charlie?" Harris squinted up at the caged ceiling. "I couldn't give you a better response to that puff piece," Zach Harris grinned.

"Let's go Mrs. Congressman."

Miller watched them walk arm-in-arm to the head table. He noticed Zach Harris's lack of attention to her as he worked the crowd. It was as if she were not there. Charlie Miller always looked upon Marion Harris with a vague feeling of sadness. It wasn't well-drawn, but words like frail, delicate, fragile formed in his mind. He'd always held her in high esteem. They enjoyed talking and sharing experiences over the years. He gave her a look at Bessemer City's underclass, something she, with her superior education, could relate to only from sociology texts. He was not a scholar, but with his journalistic pedigree formed on the police beat and criminal court long before he became the *Star-Times* political expert, he provided insights she could get from few others. Surely not from her husband. She always sought Miller out on the political banquet circuit. She laughed at his stories, coughing her smoker's hack through a bourbon highball. In that frame of mind, she always promised to share some cherished memories with him, but it never happened.

"Ladies and gentlemen, take your seats, please." Barney Steckel, the Hampton County Democratic chairman, looking like an overstuffed armchair, big and leathery in a shiny tuxedo, called the gathering to order. It took five tries before dinner chairs scraped and china began to clink. "A few announcements before we begin: Let's give Myra Liebowitz and her committee a big hand for the fine job on decorations. Aren't they grand? (Loud applause) ... There's a lavender Skylark convertible with Pennsylvania tags blocking the driveway outside. If it's yours, you better claim it fast. Chief Di Lupo's been eyeing it for his next parade (laughter) ... The centerpieces were donated by Allied Florists - let's hear it for Allied. Oh, and before you start fighting for them, ladies, we got a numbering system based on your tickets. Check with the gals at the desk before you start pulling hair, girls. (Smiles). And finally, I want to read a telegram. It's from California and I quote, 'Campaigning hard in the West. Sorry I can't be with you. Hampton County will lead the Democratic Party to victory in Pennsylvania. Sincerest affection for one of the Democratic

# INQUISITION

Party's noblest, most courageous ladies, Marion Hanson Harris. With warmest regards, Adlai E. Stevenson.' How 'bout that folks!." (Sustained applause). Zach Harris noted the snub. Stevenson knew he was guest of honor and involved in a tough reelection campaign but never mentioned him. He'd let him know about it next time he wants the national committee to pick up his god-damned personal expenses.

"Now, if you'll all please stand, we'll have the invocation by Father Frank Cavanaugh. He brings us a special Irish prayer before meals that's been guaranteed Kosher by the rabbi of Dublin. As you can see Father Frank is sporting his green yarmulke ... Father." (chairs rumbled). "Incidentally folks, the equal time principal is in effect. We'll have dessert and benediction by Rabbi Goldman." (chuckles).

Marion Harris, sparkling and clear-eyed, sat next to the keynote speaker, Assistant Secretary of State G. Glenn Masters, one of the few Democrats to hold a position in the Eisenhower Administration. They were talking animatedly about a new idea circulating in Washington - sending American youth into the Third World to work in villages, tenements and barrios. Far down the table Zachary Taylor Harris looked ten years younger than the bored chairman of SUBACK in white shirt, bow tie and tuxedo. The ensemble accented his gray hair, gave his shoulders an athletic lift and highlighted the manly, if arrogant, features of his pink face.

The clatter of tableware and china, the clink of wineglasses and the buzz of conversation pervaded the big ballroom as waiters in white gloves glided among the tables weighed down under trays of prime rib, Potatoes Anna and broccoli vinaigrette under the watchful eye of a small, mustachioed and gravely serious maitre d'. The orchestra played a Cole Porter medley. The evening held the stuff of perfection. After the main course, the waiters returned with flaming dishes of Baked Alaska followed by a second echelon of waiters pouring Laurent Perrier Brut grand ciecle. Barney Steckel, everybody's toastmaster, rose.

"We want to move this along because we're in for an outstanding evening, ladies and gentlemen. So, if you don't mind, we'll get right down to business while you're sipping that soda pop they're pouring. It gives me a distinct pleasure to introduce a great ... a truly great American and Democrat; a man who needs no introduction to this audience, because he is in the vanguard of Americanism here in our community, in our country and around the globe. All of us know him for his commitment to democracy, and for his implacable opposition to Communism. He has borne the brunt of criticism from the Left for his work in making our immigration laws the envy of the world and from the Right for his fairness in safeguarding civil liberties. In spite of the critics, he has made it possible for the down-

## Jack Eddinger

trodden of the world to find sanctuary in this country. With his help and support in Congress thousands of oppressed peoples; Hungarians, Czechs, Ukrainians, Poles, who have fled the Iron Curtain today are free; free to earn by hard work and achievement the fruits of democracy. Ladies and gentlemen, a great American, a great Democrat, a great friend. I give you the Freedom Fighter of 1956, the Honorable Zachary Taylor Harris!"

Even before Steckel pronounced the congressman's name, chairs rumbled. The gathering rose in sustained applause. Zach Harris stood beaming at the rostrum. He spoke in smiling asides and animated hand gestures to his head table admirers. He let the wave of adulation break over him.

The applause subsided. The diners took their seats. Men began lighting cigars. Congressman Harris put on his reading glasses, spread the text of his speech across the rostrum and raised his right hand in the familiar gesture that was both a salute and a call to order. He was the man of the moment. He would send his legions forth with a spirited speech that would vibrate all the strings of the Democratic lyre: Wilson's public morality; FDR's rescue of the nation from depression and war; Harry Truman's republic for the common man and Adlai Stevenson's vision of an optimistic and moral future.

Midway through his arm's downward swing, a stabbing, burning, suffocating pain shot though his chest, up through the jaw and across his shoulder blades. He fell backward pulling papers, centerpieces, water goblets and ashtrays down with him behind the dais. The crowd's singular "Ohh, No" ripped away the ambiance.

"Jesus Christ!" Charlie Miller shouted from the press table. "Zach Harris collapsed." Arnold Mason, rising volcanically, tipped over the table, sending crockery, glassware and dishes to the floor in a resounding crash.

"Is there a doctor here?" Barney Steckel shouted at the microphone. "Get a doctor up here fast ... Congressman Harris ...." A man in a tuxedo vaulted over the head table and threw himself on the congressman's chest. "I'm a doctor ... Call an ambulance ... Get back ... Give me room!" He ripped off the silk bow tie, tore away the collar and pounded the inert chest with his fists, as if inflicting a severe beating. Seconds later the body heaved. A faint pulse returned. Breathing, though fitful, relaxed into a steadiness that told the doctor the crisis had passed. Two stretcher bearers appeared. They eased the congressman's limp form onto the stretcher, and with the physician accompanying them, bore him across the ballroom as if on a bier. The crowd buzzing with gay conversation only moments before formed a corridor through which the congressman was borne. The men were silent. Women sobbed. Father Cavanaugh solemnly made the sign

# INQUISITION

of the cross, as Zach Harris was slipped into the back of a hearse-like ambulance. Marion Harris stood alone, clasping herself as if exposed to a wintry blast. Women rushed to her.

"Is he dead? ... God dammit, is he dead? ... Can somebody tell me whether he's alive or dead?" Charlie Miller shouted.

"No, he was breathing. I saw him breathing." Miller wrote down the quote then dashed to the ambulance. The hotel driveway was blocked by a tow truck maneuvering a Buick convertible out of the way. Policemen blew whistles and stopped traffic on the street. Men cursed.

"I'm riding with you," Miller told the driver as he got into the front seat of the ambulance. He wrote furiously on a book of folded copy paper like a young reporter covering a fatal accident. Sirens screamed, tires laid down a streak of black rubber as the ambulance finally got underway. A black and white police car, its red dome light flashing furiously, whooshed past the ambulance. Charlie Miller spotted Marion Harris in the rear seat. He turned and looked back through the partition window of the ambulance. An attendant snaked a plastic tube through the congressman's nostrils. Another shot a hypodermic solution into his right forearm. The tuxedo jacket had been stripped off, the black silk cummerbund removed and the sleeve of the formal white shirt had been sliced with surgical scissors. Charlie Miller saw Zach Harris open an eye from a cyanotic trance. It fluttered then closed. A small green ball traced peaks and valleys on an oscilloscope screen alongside the stretcher. Cardiac activity appeared weak but stable.

"Stop the presses, you assholes! This is MacManus, dammit! Stop them right now! Oliver get on rewrite and take Charlie Miller from St. Helena's. Zach Harris collapsed with a heart attack. Saxon, pull the Harris clips and get to work on the offlead. I want history and color. Moses, get the hell out to the hospital. Get me a shot of Harris. I don't care what you have to do. Just get it. Mrs. Batt, get over to the McKean. No the emergency room. Put a full nelson on Mrs. Harris. Don't let her talk to anyone till you've plucked her clean. I want quotes. Franklyn give me two sidebars, one on Harris's record, the second on his congressional career. When's the last time we ran block type? Hand set it." Rufus MacManus mobilized the *Star-Times* news room in seven minutes. Only a perplexed copy boy stood next to him at the city desk. "Of all the damned luck. We shoulda had an obit set in type a month ago. Miller warned me," MacManus, chain-smoking a Pall Mall, cursed himself. He had only an hour to pull the story together otherwise he'd be the laughingfuckingstock of the Lenape Valley and if *The Sentinel* beat him, maybe out of a job. He'd not get another crack at the story for 24 hours.

# Jack Eddinger

John Oliver, the rewrite pro who wore his cardigan sweater draped over his shoulders - a trait which always bothered MacManus - began taking Charlie Miller's story over a phone cradled between his shoulder and cheek. Oliver never had to correct, re-section or polish Charlie Miller. He moved the story in two paragraph takes to the copy desk. The desk marked it up, put MacManus's eight-column banner over it and sped it by vacuum tube to the composing room. Linotypes clattered out the type. The makeup man ripped the steel form box apart and began remaking page one. When he was finished, it carried Miller's main story under the *Star-Times* flag, a three column six-inch photo of the ambulance backed up against the St. Helena's emergency room, two Harris sidebars and the offlead with a two-column four-inch cut of Congressman and Mrs. Harris taken at the ice sculpture earlier that evening. Within 25-minutes the *Star-Times* bank of Hoe presses two decks high picked up momentum then thundered like a diesel-electric locomotive, sending a wide white ribbon of newsprint slicing through giant stainless steel spindles. Readers of the *Star Times* hadn't seen a front page like it since V-J Day.

Miller's page one story read:

*Congressman Zachary Taylor Harris, one of the iron-men of the U.S. House of Representatives for more than 30 years, suffered an apparent heart attack last night while being feted by women Democrats as Man of the Year. He is listed in serious but stable condition at St. Helena's Hospital. Harris, 58, collapsed at the rostrum of the McKean Hotel at 9 p.m., as he was about to accept the award. He was to be followed by the main speaker Asst. Sec. of State G. Glenn Masters. Doctors at St. Helena's described his condition as "critical." He was rushed to the hospital by ambulance with Dr. Meyer Feldman, a guest at the dinner, attending the congressman enroute. Dr. Feldman described the situation in an exclusive interview, "as one of the most harrowing experiences I've ever faced. Thank God, we were able to get to him in time. What he needs now is complete rest. He is a strong man, but it is evident he is under heavy stress."*

MacManus's eight-column headline screamed:

RED-HUNTER COLLAPSES AT TESTIMONIAL
MD SAYS HEART ATTACK, WIFE AT BEDSIDE

The following morning Dr. Martin Blackman, chief of internal medicine at St. Helena's Hospital and Clinic, called a news conference. He read from

# INQUISITION

a prepared statement: "The news story relative to Congressman Harris's collapse and hospitalization, while not completely inaccurate, contained statements which are not in accord with the medical disposition." He complained about "errors of interpretation and omission." Charlie Miller heard the accusations a hundred times, mostly from plaintiffs' lawyers.

"Doctor, Miller of the *Star-Times*. Will you please describe for us precisely what is wrong with Congressman Harris?"

The internist launched into an extensive clinical description of pulmonary and gastro-intestinal physiology.

"Can't we just call it a heart attack, Doc? said Arnold Mason. "If you cut out the medical jargon, that's what we got. Right?" Dr. Blackman's face reddened. Dr. Feldman, the man who came to Zach Harris's aid at the dinner, smiled and took over.

"Mr. Mason, what Dr. Blackman wants you to understand is that the congressman did not, repeat did not, have a heart attack. In fact, the early tests show his heart to be strong and vital. What we apparently have here is an anomaly we've diagnosed provisionally as 'angina dyspeptica.' In a way, it seems nothing more than a very serious case of indigestion. The symptoms have all the earmarks of a coronary occlusion; in layman's terms a heart attack. But it was not. The stomach is distended or pushed out due to gas. It is manifest as a spasmodic, choking pain similar to that seen in a heart attack, but in fact, has nothing to do with the heart itself. Now, we're not precisely certain of this diagnosis. The medical staff is conducting a series of tests and examinations. It could be a number of other things. Congressman Harris is suffering from quite a heavy cold with some incipient pleurisy. We've ordered complete bed rest for the next few days until we have had a chance to evaluate the tests."

"Thank you, Dr. Feldman," said the internist. "Now gentlemen, if you will excuse me, I have rounds to make."

"And miles to go before we sleep," Miller quipped.

Miller, Mason and the crowd of reporters gathered around Dr. Feldman. He gave them a detailed description of the procedures used to resuscitate the congressman for their next-day stories. "I'll be available to interpret future findings in the case, gentlemen, but frankly I believe he will be all right. He's had a bad scare, and off the record, maybe this will put the fear of God into the old witch hunter."

Had St. Helena's medical laboratory been a first rate unit like those at Walter Reed or Bethesda Naval Hospital with equipment and personnel to conduct sophisticated blood studies the provisional diagnosis would be immediately revised. Hypoleukocytic angina was something else again.

# Jack Eddinger

Propped up in a hospital bed two days later, Zachary Taylor Harris, wearing a navy blue bathrobe looked a hundred years old. His hair stood in clumps, his face was pale and his long bony hands were almost transparent. He resembled a figure in a wax museum. He refused to accept his immobility and spent the morning on the telephone telling his staff and Steckel's campaign workers that he would be out of the hospital and campaigning by the end of the week. He called Charlie Miller and chatted for more than an hour, telling the newsman he thought the collapse would give him his biggest victory ever. "The way I figure it, I'll get the sympathy vote. After 25 years it's about time." Miller wrote a sympathetic election-eve column based on the interview.

The only phone call he postponed until the end of the day was to Robert Bird. He needed time to think it through. The coffee-stained penny postcard arrived with the day's get-well cards. The message bothered him all day. It read: "The bulls are jittery. It's feeding time." It was signed in pencil with Lloyd Kressman's spidery black monogram. There was no way out of the hospital, the doctors and the damned newspapers had seen to that. He had to get cash to Kressman immediately, or the big vote would come unglued. He decided to risk it.

"Robert," he told his administrative assistant in a barely audible voice, "I'm going to ask you to carry out a delicate task. Something I'd do myself, only I'm here and you're there."

"God, it's a relief to hear your voice, congressman," Robert Bird responded. "I want you to know you can count on me for anything. We've been terribly worried."

"No reason to worry. I'm okay. A scare, I'll admit, but I can feel my strength returning. I'll be out of here by the weekend. And that's why I'm calling. I've got to have the cash I've reserved for the final week in hand within 24 hours. It's locked in my safe, and I'll need you to go in there and get it. You'll find the cash box key taped to the ceiling inside the safe. Count out $25,000 and put it in my briefcase and lock it. Sam McBryan's on his way to Washington now. Give him the briefcase. McBryan thinks its official papers. Don't relieve him of that belief. To get into the safe, you'll need the combination. I want you to memorize what I'm about to give you, then disregard it immediately. Understand?"

He always kept large amounts of cash on hand in his office safe just as Hughie Long did with his "deeduct box" over in the Senate Office Building

"Absolutely, sir." Robert Bird never trusted his memory. Just in case, he'd write down the combination in his reporter's notebook, then rip out the page and burn it. That ought to satisfy him, I can be trusted.

# INQUISITION

No one had been in Zach Harris's safe, ever. "Robert, you are the only other living human being with those numbers. When you finish, I want you to purge them from your mind. Do you understand?"

"I do, Congressman. I'll take care of everything. You take care of yourself. Get some rest."

"Thank you, Robert. Remember, I meant what I told you about closing the book."

"I sure won't, sir."

Robert Bird dismissed the staff early. He spun the tumbler of the shiny black vintage Mosler safe in the alcove behind the Congressman's desk, removed the strong box and found the key. He put the box on the Congressman's desk and opened it. The amount of cash startled him. He'd never seen so much money. There must have been over $50,000 in packets of 50, 100 and 500 dollar bills. They looked as if they'd just come off the presses at the U.S. Mint. It bothered him, but then again the Harrises were rich people, and rich people do strange things with their money. He thought no more of it. Bird counted out $25,000 in $50s and $100s, then shut and locked the strong box. As he put it back in the safe, a large manila portfolio fell out. He examined it closely. The label "INS files" puzzled him. He acted on his curiosity and unwound the red string over the flap and rummaged through the papers inside. What he saw puzzled him even more: immigration documents and files of almost archival quality in a folder tabbed IMMSUBCOMM; officially engrossed congressional private immigration bills mostly dated in the 1930s; a letter of agreement, which looked like a typical lawyer's contract. It was on the stationery of Daley & Harris, Counsellors-at-Law, and bore the initials "T.A.D" and "SM."

Another file looked like notes at autopsy or a coroner's report. The title page was missing. Robert Bird scanned the clinically explicit report about the cause of death of a white male in his early forties. He glanced through assay notes of internal organs, and stopped reading when the report arrived at the victim's severely damaged head, or what was left of it. The conclusion: "Death by suicide resulting from a wound caused by a .32 caliber bullet. Weapon probably placed against subject's left occipital lobe." Slightly embarrassed at his intrusion and repelled by the autopsy notes, he carefully replaced the papers in the portfolio rewound the string and put it back in the safe.

Then he made another disturbing discovery: a nickel-plated Smith & Wesson revolver with a black bone hand grip lay tucked beneath a red and black account ledger. He removed the ledger first, and opened it. It

## *Jack Eddinger*

contained deposit and disbursement records written in French. Across the top of the first page in neat block European type stretched the legend, Banque Rahner & Cie. Privee SA, Rue de Hesse, 18 Geneve. Then he picked up the revolver. It was loaded. He held it in his hand for a long time, felt for the safety catch under the trigger guard. The safety was on. With great care, and not a little apprehension, he put the weapon back in the safe and placed the ledger over it, then returned the cash box to its place. He closed the steel door and spun the dial. He tore the page with the combination from his notebook, lighted it with his Zippo and watched it blacken and disappear in the ashtray. Robert Bird went to his desk and dropped into deep thought. His rendezvous with the safe, would occupy his thoughts for months. Try as he may, he could not augur its meaning. When Sam McBryan arrived at 7 P.M., Bird gave him the Congressman's battered leather briefcase.

Election day 1956 dawned bright and clear. It meant a heavy turnout. The Bessemer City *Star-Times* carried a four-column photo of Congressman Zachary Taylor Harris and Mrs. Harris waving from the portico of the big house on Prospect Hill. He was in his bath robe. She wore the same smart tweed outfit and feathered hat she wore the day he kicked off his reelection campaign. He had his arm around her waist. Both smiled broadly. The story by Charlie Miller noted the closeness of the race for District Attorney, and for the first time predicted that the incumbent might be in for a surprise. The pulse beat of Hampton County told him the Democrats were split on Daley's independent candidacy. The race between Rep. Zachary Taylor Harris and State Senator Henry Marcel, Miller predicted, was no contest. Harris would win big. Former Governor George Lerner carried too many stigmata to expect victory in Pennsylvania's senatorial contest against a tough incumbent, and Ike would carry precincts that no Republican had ever carried. As the day wore on, Zach Harris climbed out of his sickbed long enough to get his ceremonial election day haircut and to vote in his home precinct. By early evening Senator Marcel's campaign manager started issuing hourly forecasts of a close election. The up-county vote, he told Arnold Mason of *The Sentinel*, would swing it for their man.

"Bullshit," Mason snorted.

Daley for District Attorney Headquarters featured a Dixieland band serenading about one hundred campaign volunteers, both male and female wearing red, white and blue skimmers. Fishnets fastened high on the ceiling were poised to cascade balloons and tinsel down on the crowd. Since it was the only close race, it attracted most of the newspaper reporters. They quaffed free beer and wolfed down the ham and cheese sandwiches

# INQUISITION

prepared for the Daley campaign workers who were arriving from their assigned wards, precincts and election districts. Early returns showed they were in for a long night. The evening stretched into early morning in a blur of tobacco smoke and black coffee. Somnambulant workers chalked voting totals on a big blackboard, which broke down the returns for Hampton County District Attorney into columns representing each candidate: Daley (Independent Democrat), Parker (Democrat) and Knowles (Republican). Frank Comstock wore a campaign manager's frown and groaned each time a new tally showed Daley's lead trickling away. He sipped a cup of lukewarm coffee spiked with two fingers of Remy Martin and chewed on a burnt-out cheroot. He held the phone against his ear with his shoulder and entered numbers on the master tally sheet, swearing each time a new total came in from the field. He was paying a squad of MacManus's rewrite-men ten dollars an hour under the table to share the totals they were taking in the *Star-Times* city room from reporters in the precincts. The reporters got them straight from the election judges' tally sheets. He'd always admired MacManus' system for getting the election day edition on the streets with all the results. The *Sentinel's* report later in the day was at best a second-day mop up. The *Star-Times* coverage always led the state wires. MacManus gave Frank Comstock his secret over a beer one night at Adolph's Hofbrau Haus, the hangout frequented by politicians and newsmen a few steps from the newspaper's loading dock. Adolph's was a melange of bad art, antlers, black wrought iron, heraldry and the flags of Hohenstauffen principalities and grand duchies. The legend, *Fur Koenig und Der Vaterland Mitt Gott in Himmel*, arched across the entrance to the loud dining hall, which Frank Comstock called the Putsch Platz. Rufus MacManus held court in the dark cranny of Adolph's weine stube. Adolph's enjoyed a rebirth a few years after VE Day under a new name, Churchill's, and began to attract a younger clientele among reporters and would-be politicos. It reverted to Adolph's as the Second World War receded in memory.

Had MacManus known Comstock was getting the results before they were locked into type in the *Star-Times* composing room Rufus MacManus, Columbia Graduate School of Journalism '39, would have the desk men groveling for their jobs. "You'll be shoveling llama shit in the Andes before you get a crack at the obit desk of another newspaper," he'd have railed at them. The editors did it to supplement their meager wages.

At three a.m. Comstock put down the telephone, pushed his tortoise-rimmed glasses to the top of his head and massaged his watery blue eyes. "That's it. It's over. Knowles wins. The south county came up with a few hundred votes we didn't know were down there. Looks like he's got us by about 500 votes. Zach Harris carried him over. Just look at the vote

# Jack Eddinger

Harris rolled up. That's how Knowles did it. The rest of the county went solidly for us. Poor Henry Marcel. Harris buried him alive. No decency in politics!"

"Zach cut a deal with Kressman," Tom Daley countered, tipping his grey fedora back on his head. He was still wearing the unbuttoned trench coat, grey suit, white shirt and red foulard tie he'd donned fifteen hours earlier before visiting every ward and precinct in Hampton County. "Look at the local and county office figures. They tell the whole story. I'll bet when the certified figures are in and compared, Harris's vote will match the Republican registration figures less Marcel's numbers. It's clear to me. Kressman had his people take a walk on their own man to give Zach Harris that big majority. Hell, they never voted like that for anybody - not even in the Depression. Harris gave Knowles a free ride. Looks like he had this figured from the beginning."

"We've got to find a way to keep the pressure on," Comstock said. "You've got to contest this election. First we need to get a recount, and to do that we need an injunction. That'll keep you on the job for at least sixty days. If the court dismisses it, we can take an appeal. If we can shave the results down to under 100 votes, we can go into court and try to get a runoff. Failing that, you can use your subpoena power to investigate election fraud. We've got to use every resource at hand and then some."

"That might work, but you know I'm not a born optimist," said the lame duck D.A. of Hampton County. "Thing's got me puzzled is the size of Harris' vote. He never pulled those kinds of totals even in his vintage years."

"Looks like he bought it, don't it?" Comstock agreed. "But now you're just an ex pol looking for a job, instead of the man to change this venal system. The only way we can hope to get anywhere with this is to get a recount started. And we've gotta keep the files away from Knowles. If he gets a look at that material, no matter how thin it is at this point, he'll run to Kressman. *Der Alte* will go to Harris, and Zach'll put a match to it. We've got to secure those files until we can make a case."

"How do we do that, Mr. Genius? I can't even get us reelected let alone bring a case for election fraud. And we've got to assume Harris knows we know."

"I have an idea. I'd like to talk to John Maggio about it."

"But Maggio's no use to us. Besides, he's off the force. I understand he damned near gave DiLupo a coronary."

"Look, I know it's a long shot, but you can deputize him right now as a county detective, and we can stash the files in your basement and let him go through them. Knowles has no idea of what we've got. But I need time

# INQUISITION

to convince the good lieutenant to join our cause, and we'll need a court order to proceed."

"That means we've got to keep Knowles from taking the oath until there's a certified recount," Daley told his personal lawyer and confidante. "If the vote looks like it was stolen, we'll need an injunction to freeze the situation, then petition the court to hold a special election. No way we're gonna prove that. Better get out the law books, son. Buy me time. If we can tie things up for a few months, we ought to be able to finish the job. We got one thing going for us. The Superior Court moves slow. What's your thinking?"

"You're timetable's probably accurate, but more than anything else, get those files under a court order then padlocked."

"I think you better start drafting a petition for Judge Benson to sign in the morning. We need to see him in chambers."

"Let's not get too heavy handed," said Comstock, "Zach Harris has got to believe he's knocked us out. Right now, my guess is he's broke. I'm certain he's used up every penny he's got to pay Kressman to deliver that vote."

"Don't be too certain of that, my friend. He's got pipelines we'd need metal detectors to locate."

"Maybe so, but he's got to believe his gamble against you is worth it. Knowles can't take the oath till the vote's been certified. You gotta keep this moving through the courts. Benson's a good start. I'm afraid, Mr. Nice Guy, you're gonna have to be a sore loser in front of the press tomorrow. I think you ought to complain and stomp and tell them you think Knowles stole the election, and you're contesting it. I wouldn't get into too many details. Make them believe you're steaming mad. That'll give Knowles the public's sympathy, while we're in court."

"Okay, but you know how much I hate acting," Daley retorted. "Never could do justice to a performance that needs an Olivier. Oh, what the hell. I once swung a jury with the script of Mr. District Attorney, champion of the people, defender of truth, blah, blah, blah. Used to listen every Wednesday night when I was a kid."

"You can expect the newspapers to clobber you," Comstock said. "I hope you and Linda are prepared to live with the harassment. You're gonna find out who your friends are, real quick and Rufus MacManus isn't one of them. The crazies'll be writing hate letters. As I said, ain't no decency in politics."

"Somebody's got to take the heat, Frank. I've been applying it for eight years. Guess it's time I got a little singed. I like your idea about Maggio. What are our chances of recruiting him?"

# Jack Eddinger

"Real tough nut. He's been pissed beyond any sense of reasonableness ever since Fats Kourkorian got hit. Blames himself for getting mousetrapped. Plus it'll be far more difficult to persuade him now that you're not only the ex-DA but a sorehead, too?"

"Christ, don't complicate things any more than they are. Just get him to say yes. Tell him our plan. Give him everything we got. Right now he's flat out of a job and out of the BCPD. I think we can level with him. If we can't trust Maggio, who can we trust? Mean time we got work to do with Judge Benson. You think we can convince him the election is a fraud? All we got is our gut and some interesting voting patterns. Benson was a helluva lawyer before going on the bench, and if I know him, he'll support us as long as we give him good constitutional theory. Everything's got to be airtight. I know it's a lousy strategy, particularly the way it's gonna look in the press, but there's no time. Bring Maggio around as soon as possible. Find a way. Tell him we can't do it without him. Kiss his ass. Flatter him, but get him on board."

"Draw a petition. Impound the files. Confer with Benson. Kiss Maggio's ass! What the hell do you think I am, Daley, the god-damned 28th Infantry Division?"

Davis smiled. "Blondie, not only are you the Bloody Bucket, you're the entire Western Front. I'll draw the petition. I haven't argued constitutional theory since the ACLU opposed me in prosecuting the goons Harvey Gregovich brought in to organize the rolling mills. The whole thing taught me a lot about the Feds investigative machinery. Get some sleep. I'll see you at 8 o'clock."

"Eight ayem! God Dammit! That's three hours from now! Big-hearted sonofabitch."

The eight-column headline on page one of the *Star Times* read:

A RECUPERATING HARRIS BURIES MARCEL
WINS REELECTION BY LARGEST VOTE EVER

The off lead ragged deck headline read:

Daley Fails Narrowly For District Attorney
Local Vote Provides Margin Of Defeat
Knowles Ready To Take Up D.A. Duties

Two days after the destruction of the Blue Peacock, John Maggio strode tight-lipped into Rocco Di Lupo's office. In his years as a detective, he'd never been so thoroughly humiliated. Not only did Kourkorian's murder

# INQUISITION

bring accusations of incompetence and carelessness from Di Lupo, but the *Star-Times* launched an editorial campaign aimed at reforming what it called a "corrupt and ineffectual police department." The chief holding up a handful of news clippings told Maggio he was fed up with his inability to put an end to racketeering in Bessemer City. But more insulting to John Maggio's Roman pride was the barbaric and depraved way Anastas Kourkorian was whacked. Maggio vowed retribution.

John Maggio placed the gold detective's shield he carried with pride for nearly twenty years in the center of the chief's desk. With eyes blazing, he reached across the desk and grabbed Di Lupo's tie, winding it around his fist until tie and fist were knotted against the chief's Adam's apple. Di Lupo's slitted eyes looked like pieces of black olives floating in a plate of gnocchi. "I promise you this, you *buffo*," Maggio snarled into DiLupo's face, "I don't know who tipped them, but I'm gonna find out, and when I do, you, the newspapers and the politicians who put you in that chair and keep you there will never second-guess me again." Maggio shoved the chief back into his chair, turned and stalked out, slamming the door so forcefully the frosted window shattered. He considered a paralyzing grappa drunk as a rite of exorcism, but dismissed it.

Chief Di Lupo's news conference announcing the departmental shakeup turned into pandemonium when he told the press he fired John Maggio for failing to apprehend Anastas Kourkorian's murderers. Reporters fell over each other to get to the telephones. Di Lupo read his prepared statement to the news photographers whose strobe flashes never letup throughout the chief's monologue.

"The victim of this atrocious crime had a reputation for greed and when you play with fire you get burned," Di Lupo intoned. "Since the man who headed this investigation is no longer with the department, I have taken direct charge of the situation. Detective Sgt. Blendon will be my liaison with the higher authorities, into whose jurisdiction this crime falls. To this whole affair, the police department can only say, good riddance."

John Maggio tormented himself for letting his gut rule his head. After eighteen years of police work and three commanding a combat infantry outfit, his gut always provided unerring advice. He brooded over the way he handled the Kourkorian case. He was unfit to live with.

"Mr. Comstock," John Maggio said pushing his coffee cup to the center of the small table. "I know you didn't invite me here to test a new brand of coffee, and I know you have not come seeking my advice on copping a plea."

"Oh, you are a delight this morning, Lieutenant. I really came to get your nominee for the next Supreme Court opening, knowing how you support its views on the rules of evidence, defendants' rights and limits on police questioning. Correct me if I'm wrong. You are for abolition of defense counsel, declaring the American Civil Liberties Union unconstitutional as well as uncivil, separating rapists from their sexual organs, and capital punishment for all who defame the red, white and green, the Holy Roman Emperor and the people of Italy," Frank Comstock said, lifting his coffee mug up under his big blond mustache in a fake toast. "I got a job for you, sweetheart. That's what I want to talk to you about. Joe O'Neill asked me to see if you might be interested in going to work for him at Bessemer Steel. What do you say?"

"Plant security? Shit, I'll have desk-sergeant fanny and elephantitis of the brain within six months. No way you're gonna convince me the pleasures of command extend to running a brigade of flat-feet, hernias and hearing aids. I'm a police lieutenant, not a god-damned nurse."

"Lieutenant Maggio, you are an ungrateful man. Here I am making you an offer that will give you adventure, travel, riches and prestige, and I get nothin but disrespect. Shame on you."

"You know I respect you, counselor. Whenever you're up at the plate with one of your 'maladjusted unfortunates' whose lack of standing in society's caused them to rip-off 70-year-old ladies, or cut up their wife or split an eight-year-old kid wide open, respect just oozes out of me. You know how I bleed. Now, when you were on the other side as a prosecutor, that was different. Even I gotta say you showed me a few things in front of juries. Just like making a salami. I provided the raw meat and you stuffed the baloney. Then we hung 'em up on hooks to dry, *Si senore?*"

Comstock smiled.

"Madge," Comstock said, "One of the things that always got me about you besides being a hard ass was that you have outstanding instincts. Brains, guts, call it what you will, but its something a lot of us would kill for. You know how I know that? You could've been top wop on that animal farm, and you never went after it. You let Di Lupo take the credit. That told me either you don't have any ambition, or you're waiting to make your move. I discounted the former, because I know you too well. It had to be the latter. For one thing it told me you were not on anybody's payroll. I checked you out. No lines to Kourkorian or Maglie or anyone else. That's why I never held back when I prosecuted your cases as an assistant D.A. Maybe we learned something from each other. But, you know, I'm beginning to revise my estimate. Maybe it was just stupidity. John Maggio doesn't have any special instincts. He's just a dumb fucking guinea. I'm the one who's been fooled."

# INQUISITION

Maggio was out of his chair and across the table grabbing at Frank Comstock's tie and pulling the shabby blond head in tight. His Roman nose crushed Comstock's like a dent in a ball of mozzarella. "Knock off the genealogy, or I'll throw your ass into tonight's goulash" Maggio snarled.

"Hey! Calm down god-dammit or I'll call the cops," Comstock recoiled.

"You guys get yourselves appointed assistant DAs by the politicians for practice, like spring training." Maggio said, his ire diminishing. "The good ones - and I'll admit you were one of the best - use the system to shove the law up the cops' ass. You know who the tough judges are and you avoid them. You load juries with assholes, and you know when to postpone and continue cases. By the time anything comes to trial the statute of limitations has run out. Where's the justice? And what's worse is when you've sold out to private practice. We're left with some nitwit just out of law school who we gotta wet-nurse through grand jury presentments and trials. No sooner we got em working right, and they're joining you and screwing us. It's a vicious circle. I'm finished with the good-guys, bad-guys games. Your laws and my laws are different. You make a buck by twisting facts to fit the law. According to my reading, there are two sources of the word police. One comes from the Greeks and it means politics, political activity to you. That's not what we're talking about. The other comes from the Romans. It means control, to regulate, to keep order. That's what a cop's job is - keeping the jungle safe - keeping the animals from clawing us apart."

"John, if I had to live under that definition, there'd be no reason for lawyers. Now let me tell you about this opportunity. You'd be working exclusively for Joe on a special project. He's asked me and Tom Daley to participate. I think you'll enjoy the work, and it might even help you land the trio who hit the fat man."

"What does the job pay? John Maggio said.

"Eighteen grand and Joe'll guarantee that you'll be back on the force within a year with Di Lupo out."

"I don't trust anybody. Bessemer City and Hampton County are as corrupt as you'll find anywhere, anytime."

"Now **that**, Lieutenant Maggio, is what we want to talk to you about."

Joseph Patrick O'Neill, labor lawyer, lobbyist, and story teller *extraordinaire*, sat at the round table on the patio of his comfortable home on a golf course just outside Bessemer City with a small group of men. He wore rumpled weekend work clothes instead of the pinstripes which

# Jack Eddinger

normally distinguished him as Bessemer Steel Corporation's chief counsel. The group included his step-son, Tom Daley, Frank Comstock and former Lt. of Detectives, John Maggio. The muscular heft undiminished from O'Neill's days as Lenape University's All American tailback reduced his 56 years by at least a decade.

"Lieutenant Maggio," he began. "Tom and Frank here have asked me to sit down with you to see if we can't convince you to serve the cause of justice by helping us bring closure to a case that began nearly twenty years ago, and eludes us to this day."

"That's a long time," Maggio observed. "Statute of limitations ..."

"This is not an ordinary case. I wouldn't be talking to you if it were, Lieutenant. You might say there's no statute governing the corrosive influence of one man's unchecked power."

"How's that?"

"The story I'm about to tell you has its beginning in the careers of two ambitious men. One, unfortunately, went to an early grave by his own hand. The other is very much with us. In fact he continues to exercise far-reaching and seemingly permanent influence. No one has the temerity to question the motives of Zachary Taylor Harris or to investigate his sources of power.

"The Congressman? I don't know very much about him, but I've always regarded him as so high on the pecking order that local concerns are far beyond his interests," said Maggio.

"Not so far as you may think, Lieutenant. Unfortunately, you'll have to take my word for it. The suicide, as you are probably aware by now, was our late district attorney and Tom's father, Tad Daley. He was my good friend. He gave me a job in the depths of the Depression ... something I'm thankful for to this day. The day of his funeral has remained in the foreground of my memory.

"You may or may not know that when I returned from the Marines after the war, I fell in love with Anna Daley, Tom's mother. We were married in 1948. In addition to marrying a beautiful and intelligent woman, I gained a son. Tom was a freshman in college at the time. He missed his Dad badly, and I've tried to bring something of Tad Daley's generosity of spirit to bear on Tom's life. I hope I've been somewhat successful."

"More than successful, Joe. You've helped give my life direction and your constant encouragement supports my commitment to public service," Tom Daley said.

"Enough of this mutual admiration. Sgt. Maggio, the story I want to relate to you begins a long time ago. I got the highlights from Tom's dad, Tad Daley. Over the years Anna filled in the gaps.

# INQUISITION

"Zach Harris was just out of George Washington Law School. His father's old business partner, Mort Brodfield, who you might remember, was President Wilson's attorney general. He hired Zach as a very junior attorney in the anti-trust division. Zach was easily bored and wanted more action, so he switched to the criminal division, prosecuting moonshiners and tax evaders. When President Harding took over in 1921, Zach came home to the Lenape Valley. But through his Washington experience he'd contracted a terminal case of Potomac Fever. He decided that a career in politics beat everything else he'd ever before experienced. By then Brodfield was out of office, but as Pennsylvania's Democratic Committeeman, Mort still had plenty of influence. Zach prevailed on his old boss and mentor to have him appointed to the vacant office of Attorney for Hampton County. That raised a lot of eyebrows around the Court House, but he worked hard - harder than anyone else - and in 1926 won election as the state's youngest district attorney. His law partner and campaign manager was Tad Daley. Tad kept their law practice going with plenty of work from the county government. Harris and Daley soon earned themselves reputations as tough, smart and astute stars rising in Pennsylvania's political heavens.

"They helped to hold the Pennsylvania delegation for Al Smith through the final ballot at the Democratic convention in 1928. They won Al's notice and made a lot of important friends who proved useful for their own political ambitions. In November of 1932, Zach won election to Congress by the largest vote ever recorded in the 26th District - not quite as large a vote as this election just past, however. But that's another story. He soon became a reliable vote among the legion of Democrats pulled in with FDR. His experience and contacts in Washington going back to the Wilson Administration made him an insider from the start.

"The new congressman and his campaign manager plotted out their career goals with shrewd political insight. Tad succeeded Zach as D.A. Their timetable called for Zach to run for governor no later than 1942. In the meantime Tad would manage every campaign along with his own. The gubernatorial campaign, they reasoned, would give Tad the statewide experience and exposure he needed to run a strong campaign for the U.S. Senate two years later. After two terms as governor, Zach calculated that he'd be ready to step on to the national stage. He figured his experience as governor of a state with 34 electoral votes would make him a natural choice as vice president on a future ticket. According to their timetable, Zach'd be reviewing the inaugural parade on January 20, 1949, and delivering the State of the Union a week later. Senator Daley would be Majority Leader, moving President Harris's legislative agenda to enactment. That's the way they saw it.

# Jack Eddinger

"But by 1936, Roosevelt's magic faltered. Zach barely won reelection. His association with FDR became a liability. The newspapers flailed the court-packing gambit and strikes rocked the steel industry. The state constabulary was called out to put down a strike that threatened our property at the Lenape River works. Harris was caught between his ambition and the workers. He sided with the CIO. By this time, Zach found it advantageous to oppose Roosevelt just as he's opposed us on the merger. He voted against the Supreme Court bill, and introduced legislation to reorganize the executive branch of government, - a brash act for a young congressman - maintaining that the country was skirting dictatorship under FDR. That's when the southerners in the House adopted him as one of theirs."

O'Neill paused to ask if his listeners needed to refresh their drinks.

"No, but if I don't get to the can, this patio will float away," Maggio said.

"Ohh sure, Lieutenant to the right and down the stairs. Anyone else?" Maggio was back at the table in three minutes.

"Beautiful place you have here, Mr. O'Neill," he said as he took his seat.

"Now, as I was saying Tad Daley succeeded Zach as District Attorney. He was establishing a record as a strong D.A. His conviction of Johnny Campesino, aka Johnny the Wop, for murder earned him coverage in newspapers across the state. He was front page news from Philadelphia to Erie. Before Tad's crusade the situation here was hopeless. Prohibition brought in the likes of Campesino and bootlegging, and along with it came hijacking, numbers running, prostitution, extortion, the whole corrupt grab bag of which, I might add, the Blue Peacock is only the latest manifestation. Daley unearthed a level of corruption that shocked even the worldly press. Westbrook Pegler praised him for taking Campesino & Co. head-on. 'One honest man has the rats on the run,' he wrote in his syndicated column.

"Tad was a tough prosecutor, but he had a knack for tempering the hard-nosed cop approach with his charm and an ability to turn a phrase. He was a highly quotable news source and always available to reporters. Charlie Miller once told me Daley took calls from even the most inexperienced reporters, helping them understand the complexities of criminal law, grand juries and the processes of indictment and conviction. By 1938 District Attorney Daley's reputation across Pennsylvania began eclipsing the Congressman's. It gave Zach a fit. I remember hearing the two of them go at it in the DA's office. The argument got so heated that I was embarrassed and had to leave my office next door to the DA's. Harris told Tad he was moving up his timetable and would run for governor. That meant Tad would have to wait almost six years for the Senate. On the surface their

# INQUISITION

friendship looked solid, but fault lines were opening. It started with small things like whose name would appear first on political dinner programs or who would introduce the National Chairman at the Jefferson-Jackson Day Dinner. *The Star-Times* got into the act by predicting a bright future for Daley. I understand Zach was apoplectic over a particular column by Miller that promoted Daley as the state's strongest Democrat.

"When Hitler invaded Poland, everything changed. Harris knew instantly it would be a lifetime before the governor's mansion would be the route to the White House. As in 1916-20, Washington would be the epicenter of the universe. Experience in foreign policy and in shaping a war economy would be prime requisites for a national leader well into the future. He informed Daley that he, Zach Harris, would become Pennsylvania's new Senator. He would run with FDR on the Roosevelt dictum of helping our friends, but staying out of Europe's war. The Foreign Relations Committee would be his route to the presidency.

"The day before his tragic death, Tad called me into his office. Said he wanted to go over some cases coming up to the grand jury. When I walked in, I never saw him so agitated. He paced the floor, back and forth over and over. His face was red and puffy. That's when he told me about Zach's double-cross. He said his hopes and dreams were shattered.

"I tried to tell him that was nonsense and that his best days still lay ahead ... that he was twice the man Harris is. But he seemed inconsolable. To this day, I believe he wanted to tell me more; that he had something weighing heavily on his mind. He seemed to be on the verge of panic. I didn't know what to say, so I just sat there and listened while he bitterly denounced Zach Harris. I got up and left the room. I don't think he even noticed.

"The next day he was dead. I've chastised myself ever since for sitting there like a dunce, as he poured out his guts."

"That's an interesting story," said John Maggio when O'Neill finished. "But it just proves my point about trusting politicians, not even when they're best friends. What do you want me to do about it? This is ancient history."

"Lieutenant," O'Neill replied, "I believe Tad Daley was being blackmailed by Zach Harris. Harris knew something so sensitive about Daley that it drove Tad over the line. Politics doesn't lead men to suicide, even though we'd like to kill a few. Who's ever heard of anyone killing themselves because their timetable's been upset. Not grown men, professional men. Hell, no. There's something sinister in all of this and it's been gnawing at me all these years. I know I speak for young Tom and Frank here when I say we want to get to the bottom of it. Will you help?"

# Jack Eddinger

"Sure, but what can I do? Too much time's gone by."

"This item was found among his personal effects. It came to light earlier this year as Tom was reading through his father's files before announcing his own Senate candidacy. He brought it to my attention. Asked if I might know what it means. Maybe you can make some sense of it. I haven't been able to."

O'Neill handed Maggio a sheet of lined paper that appeared to be a page torn from a ledger pad, circa 1930s. Written in bold face block letters inside a box was the legend IMMSUBCOM. The page was otherwise blank.

"Looks like a military code of some kind, like unit orders. I issued and signed them every day. But this doesn't have the same ring. There'd be a USAR or AUS in there somewhere. More like a government code or acronym. But Mr. Daley died before the war, didn't he?"

"Yeah, 1938."

"Then it's not military; at least not of my era. How about one of those agencies - there was a lot of shorthand used at that time - AAA, NRA, WPA, NLRB?

"Too long."

"It's close to FBI telegraphic, but I'd recognize it if it came from the Bureau."

"Y'know, Lieutenant," O'Neill said. I've been staring at those letters and numbers for six months and this is the first time anyone has made any sense."

"Whattaya mean," Maggio replied.

"Well, I thought I'd covered everything - license plates, serial numbers, dog tags, registries, acronyms, chemical formulas. Never considered a federal agency, but as you say, this doesn't conform to any known system of nomenclature the Feds use.

"So if its government, but not federal what is it? What government organization or entity could those nine characters stand for?"

John Maggio narrowed his icy Siberian eyes.

"It's government all right. I'd say Congress. I've seen references like these in stuff backing up federal indictments. Usually a committee or subcommittee investigative referral. The "IMM" probably stands for the area of interest or inquiry. My guess would be 'immigration' - the subcommittee on immigration. I'd read it as files related to the subcommittee's activities from 1935 to 1938. That's just about when both of these men were making their reputations. Search the committee files for those years."

# INQUISITION

"But that material would be long gone," Tom Daley interjected. "The *Congressional Record* for those years might be the place to start." He had listened to O'Neill's story without comment. "But it won't give us details. Members of Congress keep their files as personal property. They leave them to libraries or university history departments after they've cleaned them up. That's how they establish their legacy, you might say."

"So, can we count on you, Lieutenant ?" O'Neill asked.

"Sure, but this doesn't sound like industrial security. Is this in my job description?" John Maggio replied coolly.

"You'd be working for me. That's the only condition of employment you need to understand. I've arranged for you to join the executive staff. I knew you'd be frustrated out in the plant. Hell, I was banking on it. Also, this business with the Blue Peacock raises a lot of unanswered questions. Pyrotechnics like that can't be attributed to a leaking gas line, by god. Why don't you sniff around? See what you can turn up."

"Now you're talking my language," John Maggio fairly chortled, struggling to hold back his emotions. "Tell you what, gimme a day or two a week on the Peacock, and I'll give you 16 hour days on the political stuff."

"Okay, you have a deal. But this IMMSUBCOMM business is priority number one. Understood?"

"Understood."

"Gentlemen," O'Neill said. "I want you to give me your best thoughts on where we go from here."

"I'll do that," said Tom Daley, "but I think John ought to know that I'm a significant part of this story. It's a pretty sensitive subject. You may not know this, but Mrs. Harris is my god-mother and paid my way to college. She wanted me to go to Princeton but I ended up at Penn. I don't think Zach Harris ever knew about it. My mother was almost penniless after Dad's death and before she married Joe. Her relationship with Mrs. Harris figures into just about everything that's happened since."

"Well, that's a whole other story and I don't want to bore you with it, John."

"No, no. Keep talking. You've got me interested. If I'm to be of any help, I want to know everything you can tell me about these people."

Throughout the lunch hour and continuing into the afternoon, beginning at the beginning, Joe O'Neill related the story of Zachary Taylor and Marion Hanson Harris and their rise to power and prominence in Washington. He had absorbed it over the years in bits and pieces in long conversations with his wife, Anna Lee Daley O'Neill, who seemed to want to exorcise it from her searing memories.

# Jack Eddinger
"It all began on a cold, wet day in March 1933 ...

# CHAPTER EIGHT
## *Years Of Power And Fulfillment*
### March 1933

Congressman-elect Zachary Taylor Harris standing on the rear platform of Bessemer Steel Corporation's private Pullman coach, stared solemnly down at the crowd assembled under the rain slicked canopy over the tracks outside Bessemer City's Union Station. He wore striped trousers, cutaway coat and black homburg, the ensemble evoking the sartorial seriousness of American public office. At his side in Chesterfield coat, white scarf and tall silk hat, his law partner, Tad Daley, the new Hampton County Democratic Party Chairman, was a fitting reflection of Charles Stewart Parnell, the 19th Century Irish political leader he hoped to emulate. Between them stood the Honorable A. Morton Brodfield, former Attorney General of the United States. He clenched a big black cigar between yellow thoroughbred teeth and leaned heavily on a polished mahogany cane. The radiant young wives, Marion Harris and Anna Daley, each clasping a spray of red carnations they laughingly called Depression roses, stood behind their husbands, beaming and waving to faces they recognized in the crowd. Frivolity played counterpoint to gravitas.

In a gesture that was both political and personal, Eugene Garrett Palmer put his private railroad car at their disposal for the trip to Franklin Delano Roosevelt's inauguration scheduled for noon the next day on the East Portico of the Capitol in Washington. Yardmen coupled the special car to the end of the Philadelphia & Northern Railroad's intercity passenger train, *The City of Brotherly Love*. In Philadelphia it would be shunted over to the Baltimore & Ohio's *Royal Blue* for the two-hour journey to Washington. Palmer augured that his gesture of friendship would be a good investment when the country's mood, as reflected in the incoming Democratic administration and Congress, might cause problems for his industry. In brief comments he saluted the former Attorney General, congratulated Congressman-elect Harris on his victory the previous November, and reminded him that the economy of the Lenape Valley would always spin in Bessemer Steel's orbit. A steward in white jacket and gloves offered flutes of Mumm's *cordon bleu* from a silver tray. Palmer declined, but suggested that everyone enjoy themselves. He recalled the Harrises wedding a decade before and told Marion Harris she looked younger and lovelier than ever - not easy words for a man accustomed to the rough language and earthiness of his mills. He excused himself and exited from the rear of the car, just as

# Jack Eddinger

Congressman-elect Harris strode to a microphone to deliver a five-minute, "Farewell and New Beginnings" speech.

Marion Harris went through a pack of *Tareytons* in a half hour. The champagne, the crowd gathering on the station platform and her own future in Washington brought her to a high pitch of excitement. She spotted Charles Miller, a reporter for the *Globe Post*, standing at the edge of the crowd with his big Speed Graphic, popping flash bulbs against the drab morning. She waved and offered her profile like a film star. Miller, smiling, waved back, cupped his hands over his mustache and yelled that he'd send her copies of the photos that would make page one that evening. Her life was about to take a major new turn. She pictured a bright future in the capital, something more than being helpmate to a new congressman; a future that rose above the country's dour mood and would mark her as a woman of independent mind as well as means. She'd take up a cause; one which she nurtured since first hearing its broad outlines articulated by President Wilson in a commencement address to the Bryn Mawr College Class of 1914. Settlement House work and Junior League projects held scant interest. Reviving the League of Nations before another conflagration burst on mankind became a consuming passion. She asked her husband to include a passage about the importance of the League - which she wrote - in his maiden speech to the House.

Anna Lee Daley, born in Virginia, educated at Mary Washington and former headmistress of Miss Renwick's Country Day School had all the brains needed to complement her husband's best friend's wife. But she lacked Marion's passion for causes. That was a Yankee trait to be shunned by a daughter of the South. However, her attitude toward Northerners did not keep her from falling in love with the handsome Yankee-Irishman law student from the University of Virginia. Ash-blonde, slender and green-eyed, Anna Lee fell in love with Tad Daley the first time they met. It was at a dramatized court trial conducted for young ladies from private schools throughout the Commonwealth of Virginia. Watching him argue constitutional law, the young headmistress perceived humor, insight and Gaelic charm, a combination which captivated her.

Their train arrived in the pharaonic mausoleum of Washington's Union Station at 11 a.m. They took a cab straight to the Mayflower Hotel. Early that afternoon former Congressman Brodfield, Zach Harris and Tad Daley went to the Hill to mingle with their fellow Democrats, now 313 members strong. Zach Harris attended the party caucus to select new leaders for the first time in nearly two decades as the minority party. Marion Harris and Anna Daley shopped on Connecticut Avenue and downtown, then called at Grace Brodfield's brownstone on F Street for tea. In the evening the

# INQUISITION

couples rendezvoused for dinner at the Mayflower with the Brodfields, and friends from Mrs. Brodfield's hometown on Maryland's Eastern Shore. Over rye highballs, the men chatted about Chesapeake Bay duck shooting and Governor Albert Ritchie's strange campaign for President the previous summer. The ladies talked about Eastern Shore recipes, antique collecting and how difficult it would be finding a place to live. It could mean being far out in Cleveland Park, Kalorama or Dumbarton Oaks. The ladies retired early to prepare for the long day ahead. The men talked politics over brandy and cigars until well past midnight.

At 11:30 the next morning at Tad Daley's suggestion and just for the fun of it, the Harrises, Brodfields and Daleys climbed aboard the Mount Pleasant streetcar. The old attorney general hadn't been on a tram in decades. They headed down Connecticut Avenue past Lafayette Park, turned right into the low canyon of 14th Street past the flag-trimmed Willard, made a screeching steel-on-steel left turn and swung up Pennsylvania Avenue. Along the inaugural parade route, they passed hundreds of men, women and children - three rows deep - holding small American flags and huddling against a strong wind. The motorman clanged the bell and waved to the crowds. The packed trolley carried citizens lucky enough to hold tickets for the ceremony. The new congressman's party got off at the foot of the graceful hill and walked up the winding footpath to the Capitol. All movement halted at the top of the hill. Police lines and saw horses cordoned off the rain swept plaza. Policemen admitted only those with the special credentials issued by the Senate Rules Committee. Red construction lanterns dangled from the center of the barriers. A beefy Capital policeman, looking like a Huey Long bodyguard in black jodhpurs with a light blue stripe down each leg, short black leather tunic and black boots polished to a high gloss, directed the flow. "Why, hello there, General," he said jovially greeting Mort Brodfield. "I don't suppose you remember me, but I was one of the officers who helped you round up all those Commies back in '20. You told us we did a damned fine job. The country needs somebody like you right now. Commies're stirrin up the niggers. Too bad you weren't around a few years back to handle that rabble camped down at the Anacostia Flats. They called themselves soldiers. Hah! MacArthur sure as hell showed them how to soldier."

Mrs. Harris handed him four blue tickets. Zach Harris and Tad Daley sported the red, white and blue floor-leader ribbons they wore at the Democratic convention in Chicago the previous summer. The badges distinguished them as foot soldiers like the World War veterans milling about in the crowd, wearing shoulder patches of the 82nd All American, Fighting 69th, Yankee and Rainbow divisions. The three couples went

# Jack Eddinger

directly to Statuary Hall in the Capitol, following the directions issued by the Rules Committee. They emerged from the rotunda with other members of Congress and their families, passing through the great bronze east doors. The Senate Sergeant-at-Arms greeted them and took their blue VIP tickets. He escorted the Brodfields to a second-row seat where a group of old Wilsonians sat. White-thatched Josephus Daniels sat next to the new Attorney General, Homer Cummings. Both greeted Brodfield as if he were a member of the Lost Battalion. James McReynolds, Brodfield's opponent in the struggle to be Attorney General thirteen years before and now an Associate Justice, sat stoically in black judicial robes. Wilson's last Attorney General and his wife took their seats among the ancients. The Sergeant-at-Arms returned for the ladies and escorted Marion Harris and Anna Daley, one on each arm, to their seats. Congressman-elect Harris and his campaign manager followed. They nodded to the Majority Leader, the Speaker and the team of House Whips who stood hatless and severe in the front row like platoon sergeants dressing ranks. Zach Harris made a mental note. It would be the first and last time he would trail behind anyone in Washington. That included the Brodfields, his own wife and his best friend's spouse.

"Look at the size of that crowd," he exclaimed to his companion with a low whistle. "A gathering of the elect," Daley smiled, surveying the crowd huddled under shimmering black umbrellas flapping against the cruel northwest wind. The crowd stood shoulder to shoulder, packing the asphalt plaza below. It stretched back for a quarter mile on the sodden lawn beyond the plaza. "I didn't expect to see anything like this till Judgment Day. There must be 10,000 people down there." An aura of hushed solemnity prevailed, as if the scene were a religious ceremony instead of the orderly transfer of secular power. Something powerful and anticipatory lay just below the surface. The iron forces of history signaling radical change were on the move once again.

Symbolism and pageantry moved Tad Daley's Irish soul. In his imaginings the Great Seal of the United States transfixed itself high overhead, settling above the Statue of Freedom at the pinnacle of the Capitol dome. The eye atop the pyramid, screened in mystery, beyond time and proclaiming *Novus Ordo Seclorum*, appeared in his imagination to scrutinize and approve the act that was about to unfold. Perhaps his sensitivity came from years of participating at Mass first as an altar boy and later as an influential layman. Maybe it originated in the obscurant richness of the Latin - *fiat voluntas tua sicut in coelo et in terra* - chanted and sung in the exquisite Celtic tenor of the priests of his youth. Or, perhaps it was encrypted in puffs of incense rising from the burning censor

# INQUISITION

he swung at high mass on Holy Days; or maybe it lurked deep within the colors of liturgical vestments portraying recurrent themes of birth, growth, decline and death; pain, suffering, sin and salvation. For him the spectacle was a glorious Democratic epiphany not without overtones of penance and atonement for the excesses of the previous decade.

Herbert Clark Hoover, the republic's rigid and correct thirty-first president, sat motionless in morning dress in a big leather armchair to the left of the metal lectern. His high, tight collar drained the blood from his face and pinched it into a lump of glazier's putty. John Nance Garner, the former Speaker of the House, stood red-faced and awkward in striped pants after taking the oath making him the new Vice President of these United States, as he always referred to his country. He smelled of cigar smoke and thought about the shot of bourbon he needed to brace himself against the penetrating cold. Chief Justice Hughes, white-bearded and looking like a Hebrew patriarch in flowing black robes and skullcap, waited impatiently. The diplomatic corps perched in avian splendor in a special section of the portico reserved for dignitaries and special guests. Crimson-lined capes chained at the breast covered exquisite uniforms of black and white with silver and gold piping. Scarlet sashes draped diagonally across their chests displayed rows of tiny medals and sunburst badges. Some wore jewel-inlaid swords in leather scabbards; others held white plumed headgear. En bloc, they resembled a bird of paradise, preening in Renaissance splendor.

At 12:35 p.m. sharp the President-elect appeared in formal dress on the short runway leading to the lectern. He stood achingly erect and moved very slowly. The silk top hat appeared out of place with his body teetering as if strapped to a pair of stilts. He was fixed in heavy steel braces from the hips down. His eldest son clutched his right arm, guiding him out on the podium. He smiled and shook hands with the Chief Justice, adjusted his rain-flecked pince-nez and with firmly set jaw waited for the cheering and applause to subside. The U.S. Marine Corps Band in white barracks hats, scarlet tunics trimmed in white over blue trousers rose in unison. Trumpets, tubas, trombones, oboes, piccolos and clarinets combined with clanging timpani and thunderous drum rolls electrified the gathering. *Hail to the Chief,* played at every inaugural since Abraham Lincoln's in 1861, brought the crowd to its feet, as if responding to Gideon's trumpet.

Looking over the gathering, Tad Daley thought about his father hiking barefoot across the treeless green hills of County Donegal six decades before, his only pair of shoes tied around his neck. He wondered what it was like riding steerage in the converted English merchant ship that carried him and other men of Donegal across the stormy North Atlantic. They thought they'd seen the last of English overlords and their surrogates

## Jack Eddinger

in the peat bogs and pits of their homeland. It was an exquisite irony for that race for whom irony forms a body of literature to find the same brutal tyranny. It gave character and profundity to their melancholy. He remembered his father's stories of the Molly Maguires and how their trial left a young Irishman in despair of improving the killing conditions of the mines, sending him down river to new employment at the Bessemer Iron Works. He exchanged the soul-penetrating darkness and piercing cold of the deep Appalachian rift for the searing, blinding fire of the Bessemer furnace and open hearth. It was an exchange arranged by *reull na maidne - the deahman* - The Evil One. He was proud that an Irish coal miner's son helped make Franklin Roosevelt President. Zachary Taylor Harris was deep in his own thoughts. How, he wondered, could this man he once knew from the Navy Department as a pleasant but snotty, rich man's son be standing up here taking the oath to preserve, protect and defend the constitution of the United States against all enemies, foreign and domestic? How could a damned cripple lead the country out of chaos.

A few weeks after the inauguration, Zach Harris began the privileged education that few first term House members received. It would lead to rapid advancement and establish him among the new members as one destined to play a major role in the future. His teacher was the Texas dirt farmer from the rich black earth country in the cotton lands along the south bank of the Red River, who was soon to become chairman of the most powerful committee of the House. Bonham (Ham) Clayburg had served in the House since 1912. After years of watching and waiting in the minority, this son of a Confederate cavalryman, was taking over as chairman of Interstate and Foreign Commerce. Zach Harris knew that Clayburg and his committee would set the agenda for the legislative combat which lay ahead for FDR's New Deal.

Ham Clayburg always took a position at the rear of the House chamber whenever the House was in session. He rested his chin on the polished brass rail that ran along the back row of leather seats with his eyes intently focused on traffic moving on the House floor. One late afternoon as Zach Harris was about to push through the swinging saloon doors to leave the chamber, Clayburg grabbed him by the arm. "Wait a minute young fella. It's time we had a talk. Mort Brodfield tells me you got a pretty good head on your shoulders. Now, I need a man who can be my eyes and ears with all of these new people in this House. I need somebody who'll listen and won't talk. I've been watching you for a few months now, and I ain't seen you yakkin about how Pennsylvania can't get on without you. I'm looking

# INQUISITION

for somebody who can stick up a wet finger in the wind and take a reading without spit blowin back in his face."

Zachary Taylor Harris of Pennsylvania thus began the apprenticeship which would, in a few years, turn him into a House insider. "There's things you gotta learn before doing anything else," Clayburg told him. "First, you gotta be a good listener. After you get good at that, then you gotta concentrate on the things that ain't said, because if you can't feel things you can't see or hear, you don't belong here. Second, you gotta go along even when you think you can make a name for yourself by opposin things. Now, that don't mean bein a rubber stamp for any man. I'd never ask a man to vote against his conscience or his constituents. Hell, when two men agree on everything, it tells me only one of em's doin the thinkin. There's only one rule you gotta make part of everything you do here: when you give y're word, never break it. Now I don't mean that because of concern for morality or Bible teachin. I mean it because it's the straw that makes the bricks, and you build one brick at a time. And it won't hurt none, if you get known for something nobody else knows. Maybe you plowed a line in a cotton field and know that different grades of dirt can make you rich or poor, or you know something about railroad laws, or corporation taxes. That can't hurt a'tall. When I came here back in 'nineteen and twelve, I didn't know my asshole from a coon waller. Mr. Champ Clark was Speaker, and taught me everything about this place. He was an expert on parliamentary procedure and the rules that govern this House. Why, he could talk the tits off a cow, make you believe they work the same way on a bull, then quote you five or ten lines from *Hines Precedents* tellin ya how you could pass a law - approved by the FTC - lettin you sell bull piss in milk bottles."

Harris learned quickly. Washington is a city defined solely by power, real or imagined. But you never know what real power is until you understand the inner workings of the House of Representatives. Ham Clayburg never asked a member for anything more than once, whether a vote or a favor. If you turned him down once he would never ask you again, for anything. He'd never ask a man to do anything against his own interests. "A congressman's first duty is to get reelected," he'd say. He advised young congressmen like Zachary Taylor Harris, "to always vote yer district." That meant if you told him a particular vote would hurt you back home, he'd always honor your decision. But you'd better be right, because he made it his business to know the details, every issue, every election result, every oddity, every political ingredient that make each of the country's congressional districts unique.

# Jack Eddinger

Zach Harris was on the floor the day Chairman Clayburg asked a new congressman to vote in committee for his railroad reorganization bill. When the congressman told Ham he could not vote his way because of public opinion in his district, Clayburg gave him an impassive look. After a second vote against a bill Ham wanted, the congressman approached him with a big smile. "I sure wish I could have voted with you, Mr. Chairman, but you know a yes vote can really hurt me with the voters back home." Ham waited a long minute as a grim scowl turned his ruddy face almost black. "You could have voted with me. I've known that district since before you were born, and that vote wouldn't have hurt ya one damned bit. Ya didn't vote with me because ya don't have the guts." The flush spread to Clayburg's bald head radiating like a burning coal pile. "Don't you come crawlin across the room tellin me ya wish ya could have voted for that bill. That's a damn lie and you're a damned liar. Ya didn't vote for the bill, 'cause ya have no guts. Let me tell you something, friend, all you represent is the business interests of your district, nothin else, and when the voters find that out, they're going to kick your ass." A week later, a chilling sight greeted the congressman as he walked into the House dining room. Ham and the chairman of the House Democratic Campaign Committee were deep in conversation with the congressman's opponent from the primary election. He never served another term.

A lesson in the use of skirmish tactics as a tool of House-Senate bargaining came when a conference committee met to work out differences on a bill to regulate securities trading. Ham asked Zach to sit at his right hand as the conference got underway across a big mahogany table covered by a smooth green cloth, giving it the appearance of a billiard table. Ham laid out the case against the Senate version of the bill, which he considered hopeless. Wall Street's voice in the Senate, Senator J. Livingston Butler III, of Virginia, known more for horses and bourbon than for negotiating skills, sponsored the Senate bill. Senator Butler, always condescending to the House, stroked his white goatee. Deference, Ham knew, never failed with a Senate grandee of Butler's inflated stature. Offer the honey pot and he'll fall all over himself to grant a concession.

"Would the Senator care to chair the conference?, Ham asked politely.

"No, Mr. Chairman, rules of procedure dictate that it ought to be your job," the Virginian replied. "Even though ours is the better bill."

"Thank you, Senator Butler," Ham responded with exquisite courtesy. "That brings us to the version for consideration. Do you care to make a motion, as to which bill you prefer Senator?"

"Why I certainly do, Mr. Chairman. I move the Senate version."

# INQUISITION

"Motion moved and seconded," Ham said quickly.

"Vote on the motion."

"Senate members for, eight. House members for, eight. Tie. Motion defeated."

That was that. Ham Clayburg had the legislative gears oiled and moving smoothly toward his version of the bill before all the conferees settled into their seats. He guided the Senators with care and deference. His tone, always conciliatory; his demeanor always casual. He solicited comments with courtesy and civility in all matters but substance. Within an hour the conference adopted the House bill without change. Ham stood to one side as Senator Butler in his most obsequious manner explained the bill to the press in the hallway outside the conference room. He'd been skunked and he knew it.

Walking back to the House side of the capitol through Statuary Hall, Ham threw his arm around Zach Harris's shoulder and chuckled, "Well now, Zach, waddya think about the august upper chamber?"

"A bunch of charlatans, if that old man represents the highest achievement of the six-year term," Harris smiled. "But I wouldn't have let him take credit with the press."

"Let him take the headlines, I'll take the law," Ham grinned.

Late in the day when substantive business of the House was finished, a scattering of members always headed to the small room directly below the chamber. The Department of Education, they called it. Sitting in big leather chairs, shiny and smooth like the saddles of range busters, they reviewed and scrutinized the day's work and fashioned new legislative strategies. Bourbon was the strong lubricant preferred by Ham Clayburg and his southern allies, who sat before the marble fireplace yellowed by tobacco smoke. They spent endless hours devising the calculus - some would say schemes - by which they ran their committees and distributed power in the feudal web of seniority and camaraderie which govern the House of Representatives.

During his first two years, Zach Harris came to know House precedents, rules and procedures as a rabbi knows the Talmud, and when he did not know he improvised. Few of the freshmen he led knew otherwise, and those who suspected never challenged him. He committed the 538-page book on House rules to memory, and followed that with a study of each of the eleven volumes of precedents and rulings, which form the arcane governance of the House of Representatives. He made himself indispensable to the chairmen. They came to rely on him. The knowledge he acquired became his mainstay, the pinion gear to propel him rapidly to a position of influence, for getting legislation enacted, or for devising a feint that got the same results. Soon he was attending the late afternoon meetings. It became common knowledge that he was a Clayburg protégé even though the two men were separated by age, experience and geography. Both liked poker and stories laced with expletives and barnyard imagery. They enjoyed the smooth feel of power; its subtleties and indirection; its extraordinary power to hypnotize, to galvanize, and to manifest its hold over men in manifold forms: the iron fist, the velvet glove; its irrationality and reasonableness; its pettiness and grandiloquence; its domination over the Babel of voices. The bond between them brought Zach Harris to real power in the House by 1936, and during that year into direct conflict with the President through his skillful management of the government reorganization act. The legislation was aimed by an envious and suspicious Congress at the growing executive branch and the new crowd of lawyers, academics and non-conformists that created and carried out the New Deal.

Zach Harris worked hard and listened. His reward was a seat on the immigration subcommittee, then secretary of the Democratic caucus and soon thereafter a member of the patronage committee, which gave him a hand in the party's national affairs. At the end of the first session of the 73rd Congress he stood next in line for a seat on criminal law and investigations. With his reelection in 1934, came an invitation to sit in on the vice president's Tuesday night poker games, which lasted till dawn. The grizzled Texan had stepped down as Speaker for a job he said, "ain't worth a pitcher of warm piss." Harris impressed Vice President Garner just as he had Clayburg and the other chairmen. All were puzzled to hear him describe his goal as running for governor of Pennsylvania rather than moving up to chairman of Judiciary.

### January, 1936

Marion Hanson Harris had settled into a satisfying new role; not as the wife of an obscure congressman, but as an independent woman with a mission that she believed to be every bit as important as that of her husband. She selected the house in Kalorama Circle, not for its Tudor grandeur, but for its strategic location near the embassies and missions of the countries that counted - Great Britain, France, Germany, Japan, the Soviet Union. She named their three-story residence with its leaded glass casement windows, turrets and stone-trimmed balconies Buchanan House in honor of her father, and as a subtle reminder to Washington that an earlier Pennsylvanian had captured the presidency, and another just might do it again.

# INQUISITION

She purchased the house and its furnishings outright, spending from her trust fund rather than from Zach's mundane salary. A congressman's salary simply was insufficient to entertain in the proper manner, let alone to live well on. While Zach Harris busied himself with his political and legislative education, she furnished the venue that would be the scene of future triumphs. She spared no expense: *Louis Quatorze grande ciecle* settees, chests and occasional pieces; Persian and Chinese-patterned rugs covering highly-polished oak floors; azure *trompe l'oeil* wall coverings trimmed in gold depicting vaguely classical ruins she had remembered from her trips to Tuscany with her father decades before; an entrance hall with carved oak-paneled walls and curving stairwell. The main salon was a blend of French courtesan and Tuscan classic with a fireplace trimmed in orange-pink marble. The dining room was a reflection of Philadelphia colonial elegance with floor-to-ceiling windows and French doors opening to a wisteria-vined patio. A long mahogany table stretched almost the length of the room with seating for up to twenty. A six-pointed star-within-a-star of rosewood marquetry radiated from the center of the table. On one wall over a hunt board, a mural depicted William Penn meeting Algonquin and Delaware chieftains under a spreading elm. The muralist was the son of a contemporary of Thomas Eakins, whose work was confined to the patronage of Philadelphia's gentry. The room would be the setting for influencing the influential; for late evening suppers with senators, committee chairmen, lawyers, professors, ambassadors and senior journalists and their wives. As one of Washington's accomplished new hostesses, Marion Hanson Harris would re-ignite Woodrow Wilson's torch of world peace and international accord. The country may be in the grip of the Depression but Buchanan House was an oasis of elegance, light and merriment amid the gloom.

By the fall of 1936 Marion had firmly established herself in Washington's imitation of Regency Society. Buchanan House events rapidly became *de riguer* for Democrats anxious to sample something of the high life - excellent food and wine, and in informed and animated conversation, to add their opinions to the national dialogue about the sorry state of the world. With each new season came the delivery of cases of superlative wines and cognac from the French ambassador's cellar, along with frequent deliveries of Scotland's finest whiskies from the Embassy of Great Britain to blot out the unpleasant effects of the silly Volstead Act. The Season at Buchanan House began in October and extended to just before Christmas, starting up again in the new year as Congress reconvened and the President reported on the State of the Union. Late January through April was a dead period with Republicans and Democrats alike raising

# Jack Eddinger

campaign funds at dinners across the land honoring Lincoln, Theodore Roosevelt, Jefferson and Jackson. Things picked up again in May before ending abruptly as the sultry Tidewater summer moved up the Potomac and Congress adjourned for the year.

While her husband immersed himself in his congressional and party politics, and with their daughter away at boarding school, Marion inaugurated *Les Affaires Internationale,* as she called her foray into world politics, promoting her favorite Wilsonian idea, the establishment of a single world government. It always headed the agenda she had prepared for intellectual survival in a city dominated by secretive and insular men who wore vests and crushed fedoras, smoked cigars and drank bourbon behind closed doors.

"Is it any wonder we're thought of as children by the Europeans," she complained to her husband shortly after settling in. "Our foreign policy, if that's what you call it, is conducted as background music to the whims of a handful of senators who want to keep us isolated and marginalized; who do not even begin to understand what a democratic society stands for. And what's truly pitiful, they have completely cowed Mr. Roosevelt, who says he's a Wilsonian, but relies more and more on that Tammany ward boss, Mr. Farley, who is more interested in handing out patronage and perquisites than in world affairs."

"Don't be ridiculous, Marion," Zach Harris told his wife. "Even though I disagree with him on some things, particularly his trying to stuff the Supreme Court the way Farley's man, Ed Flynn, stuffs ballot boxes in New York, he's doing a helluva job considering the obstacles he faces. I admit the isolationists in the Senate are obstinate on any issue if its not of American origin, particularly after Borah's speech the other day, but foxy old Franklin will give him and his other six irreconcilables whatever they want to get his domestic program through. Once he gets what he wants, he'll pluck their feathers clean. That is pure politics, my dear. Something you've got to learn before too long. Hell, I'm more worried about that rabble rousing priest out in Detroit. Whatisname? Coglin? His broadcasts could spell real trouble for the country with his class warfare nonsense. Things are touch and go in the automobile plants. It'll only take a spark to touch off an explosion. And Al Smith's behavior baffles me, consorting with plutocrats. I suppose he's still bitter about FDR's getting the nomination."

"Well, I think it's juvenile, and I intend to do my part to achieve President Wilson's noble dream," she rejoined. "By the way I've invited Senator Pittman and a few others to Buchanan House to see if we can change some minds about the World Court and re-igniting the World War.

# INQUISITION

What's happening in Germany scares me. When Fascism visits, it usually stays until it is dealt with forcefully and fully. I'm surprised that you don't see what's going on there and in Italy and now in Spain." Marion Hanson Harris wanted desperately to play a role in making America's most influential men see what the country was facing in Europe. She had no interest in the Far East. But how could she become involved in events occurring 5-10,000 miles from listless, self-absorbed Washington? Zach Harris was overseeing the implementation of the Government Reorganization Act, which he authored. He had no time to think about much else, and less than nothing about foreign policy, not one of his strong suits anyway. But a wealthy, determined and influential wife was something else again.

She plotted a one-woman campaign to turn Congress, if not the country, away from neutrality. She joined the Women's International League For Peace and Freedom. It's objectives were her objectives: membership in the League of Nations, admission to the World Court, and an objective she would take on personally: convincing someone in Congress to call for an investigation of the role of munitions makers and bankers in creating world conflict. This time she would not make the mistake she made as a college student in 1914, when she passionately believed as did her hero, President Wilson, that with the unfortunate exception of republican France, the war in Europe was a grand quarrel among decadent monarchies, and should be avoided at all costs. The World War, she believed like most Americans of her generation and social standing, would be a lark, something akin to the gentry riding out in carriages and coaches to witness the clash of armies from afar; like a cinema film or a painting of Napoleonic armies colliding on distant fields; or the frolic that preceded the rout in the Virginia countryside in 1861. She was sure that the conflict which had begun in her junior year would be resolved by the professional armies of the allies quickly and decisively. After three years of slaughter, mayhem and death emanating from places with unfamiliar names like Passchendaele, Verdun and the Somme, she, as did millions of Americans, came to support President Wilson's declaration of war. While many of her classmates remained pacifists and others joined the Socialist Party and protested, Marion Hanson decided to do something. She organized the first group of fifty women volunteers for the American Red Cross from among her Bryn Mawr classmates and friends from sister colleges. She personally paid the passage to Southampton of her Blue Serge Girls, as she called them. She carried a letter of introduction to Ambassador Walter Hines Page from Secretary of State Lansing. The ambassador in full morning dress and silk top hat, as if on an official visit to George V, addressed them at Waterloo Station:

# Jack Eddinger

"Welcome to London Miss Hanson and young ladies. I thank God for your safe arrival. You cannot begin to imagine what your presence means here, as you truly represent the humanity of the American people. For the past three years this has been a lonely and depressing outpost, but the president's war message and the declaration by Congress accompanied by the arrival of the first contingent of Americans, and delightfully and most importantly, a group of dedicated young women, simply lights up skies that have been too long dark and sullen. The English people, I know, join me in welcoming you."

It was Page who educated her about America's role in the world.

"We must make some expression of a conviction that there is a moral question of right or wrong in this war," he told her in a private conversation at an embassy reception in her honor. "A question of humanity, a question of democracy. So far we have spoken only of the wrongs done to our ships and citizens. Deep wrongs have been done to our moral ideas, our ideals. Every political and social ideal we have is at stake in this war. If we make them secure, we'll save Europe from destruction and save ourselves too."

"Simply put," the former editor of America's leading intellectual magazine turned diplomat, importuned his guest, "this is America's destiny."

### October, 1938

Marion's Washington dinner invitations were eagerly anticipated and always stimulated a lively stream of newspaper gossip about who was and who was not infra dig. Her 1938 season began with a celebration of American internationalism in spite of the Administration's proclaimed policy of strict neutrality. The guest list tilted towards ambassadors and assistant secretaries, but included long-experienced members of Congress. Senators accepting included President Wilson's son-in-law and her good friend from earlier days, William McAdoo of California; Sen. Key Pittman, chairman of foreign relations; the new senator from South Carolina and Mrs. Jim Byrnes, and the late Speaker's son, Bennett Champ Clark of Missouri and Mrs. Clark. Senator Clark came to honor his father's floor leader, A.M. Brodfield of Pennsylvania, now 70 and practicing international law with Harry Covington's new law firm on Connecticut Avenue. Zach insisted that Brodfield be guest of honor. As a special surprise for her husband from the House she invited Rep. Taylor Coburn, of Massachusetts, chairman of Foreign Affairs, the Hon. William Bankhead of Alabama, the majority leader, Rep. John McCormack, the Democratic whip, and their wives, and full time bachelor, Ham Clayburg,

# INQUISITION

chairman of Commerce. Speaker Robinson sent regrets. The Daleys drove down from Pennsylvania, as they frequently did, to be with their friends. It was a jovial evening marred only towards the end by a vociferous exchange between Byrnes and Coburn, which Clayburg quickly quashed by leading a rousing rendition of *The Eyes of Texas*. The evening ended around the piano with the rich tenor voices of John McCormack and Tad Daley rendering the mournful dirges of their ancestral homeland, ending with Tad's interpretation of *Danny Boy*.

Before retiring that evening, Marion Harris received a lecture on Congressional decorum. "God dammit, Marion, don't you know you can't put Byrnes in the same room with Coburn? They hate each other's guts. Jimmy served on that committee in the House for three terms and detested the Yankee snob every minute he was in office. And, seating the majority leader across the table from Clark put the two biggest speechifiers in Congress in each other's direct line of sight. Nobody had a chance to get a word in edgewise."

Marion Harris dismissed her husband's complaint. This was her domain and she let him know it with icy blue eyes and steely voice. "You, my dear, may be the pragmatic politician, but the personality quirks and petty grievances of the House are not going to spoil the larger purposes of our responsibilities to the office you hold. Besides, I have bigger fish to fry. You'll soon be reading about the new Senate select committee to examine the root causes of war and world conflict. Senator Pittman told me he's following my suggestion on the munitions industry. Your isolationist friend, Senator Nye will chair the investigation. That way there'll be no criticism from either side, and the President has already agreed to cooperate. Remember, darling, our investment in each other brought us here. Yours by considerable talent and determination, mine by fidelity to democratic ideals, which you seem to have forgotten, and shall we say, by not a minor financial investment."

The reminder froze Zach Harris's carping. Without his wife's money, he'd be scrambling for cases at the Hampton County bar. His reliance on her trust fund bothered him deeply. Something had to be done about it.

### December 1938

Joe O'Neill's disquisition on the life and times of Congressman Harris and his wife for Lt. John Maggio would have been superfluous if he had been privy to the confrontation between the partners of Harris & Daley, Counselors-at Law that December.

# Jack Eddinger

The opportunity to correct his embarrassing financial dependence came abruptly and unexpectedly to Zachary Taylor Harris one Saturday morning at home in the 26th District while reviewing a registry of financial transactions for the firm. The bank log had been left open on his partner's desk. He picked it up to return it to the files when a column heading caught his eye. It recorded deposits registered to the law firm, but allocated to a private account. Zach Harris never concerned himself with the firm's paper work. He trusted Tad Daley with the details of their joint practice. The firm was growing nicely under the arrangement. His duties in Washington kept him, thankfully, out of the day-to-day details. His partner handled the monthly summary of income and disbursements. He had not been aware of a special bank account. A closer scrutiny of the log showed details of deposits for the years 1935-38. The meticulous detail of the entries astonished him. It showed far greater amounts than the fees he believed the law firm to be earning. Payments appearing at regular monthly intervals were logged under the initials, "SM," fixing date of payment and invoice numbers. The payments were designated "consulting services."

He could not bring himself to believe what he was reading. It became clear to him that the source of the revenue was in some way related to private immigration bills. As chairman of the subcommittee, he had always recused himself from getting them approved. He left the filing of private bills to the subcommittee staff. Any special requests coming from his district, he put in the hands of his law partner. But, now he had the answer to a question that puzzled him for several years: Who are these people Daley wants brought in on private bills? Sometimes there were so many, he'd asked Johnny O'Hara or Charlie Muncie to sponsor a number. Some smart reporter going through the *Federal Register* line by line, he figured, might get the idea that Zachary Taylor Harris was a member of the Sons of Italy or of Palestine relief, or might get some other far-fetched notion that might not play well among the nativists who dominated parts of the district and were outspoken against foreigners. Aiding refugees at a time when many numbers of Europeans were trying to enter the country, is just good constituent service and had news value. But you can't overdo it. He had counseled his law partner to spread out the requests and suggested his next door neighbor in the Longworth Building, Johnny O'Hara of Jersey City, as someone who'd be more than glad to help. O'Hara picked up at least ten a year. Zach Harris never asked who or why, trusting his partner, the district attorney, as he would trust no other man. Appended to the record was a committee report listing bills introduced by the Honorable John P. O'Hara, of the Eighth Congressional District of New Jersey. Each entry contained the bill number and date of introduction. All were personal privilege bills.

# INQUISITION

The records began around the time Harris was managing the government reorganization bill. He had little time for the firm's business. He'd arranged a meeting between Daley and O'Hara, and had not thought about it again. Why are the transactions showing up in these deposit records? He closed the ledger and returned it to the office file cabinet. Riffling through the files, he came across a folder marked IMMSUBCOMM. It contained the original bills and supporting paper work. The figure next to each entry was $5,000. He sat at his desk for a long time pondering his discovery.

The file folder trembled in Tad Daley's hands. He immediately recognized the material his partner handed him. His eyes twitched as he read each page. He sighed deeply and slumped back in the chair. He covered his eyes with his right hand; the hand he had raised countless times pledging fidelity to the rule of law and to the Constitution he cherished. The pages were written in the broad, flourishing script Zach Harris had known intimately for two decades. It was on breezy post card quips in green ink Daley sent from Dublin, in marginal notes on a floor speech he wanted his partner's judgment on, and appended to a decade of campaign memoranda. The author was known instantly to Zach Harris by the graceful long-hand sentences he penned with the gold-tipped Waterman Harris gave his partner as a reminder of their first congressional victory in 1932. Invoices written by the same hand recorded payments to the account of Harris & Daley, attorneys at law. They totaled $80,000 and were accompanied by handwritten notes describing the origin of and method of payment for each entry.

The account book showed periodic withdrawals. Next to each were the initials "TAD."

"I had to force myself to read this." Harris's tone was tough, cold and brutal. "Never mind how I came by it. I was dumbfounded and still am. That a man of your ability would succumb to a scheme like this. Here, read it. And when you're finished, think again about your political future. We're finished. Your career, my friend, just turned down a dead-end street." Daley blinked reflexively, as his eyes passed over the tab at the edge of a file folder, which read, IMMSUBCOMM. "I ...I ... I can explain," he said mournfully. "It was a serious error of judgment. I ... I ... I'll make good." His voice trailed off.

So popular a figure had District Attorney Daley become throughout the Keystone State that his death could be fathomed by no amount of speculation, public or private. Zachary Taylor Harris, solemnly noting his friend's service to Hampton County and the Democratic Party, delivered the graveside eulogy. He told the throng of family, public officials, reporters and county workers who came to pay their respects, that psychological depression took a terrible toll on people's lives. Daley, the spirited Catholic layman, had been denied a requiem mass and burial in the ritual of his church. Harris complained to the Archbishop of Philadelphia to no avail. Church law, as interpreted, promulgated and decreed by Dennis Cardinal Dougherty was inviolate. Suicide denied a man burial in consecrated ground. Congressman Harris expressed his deepest sympathy to Anna Daley, and patted young Tommy's head. In his private thoughts about the matter, his partner's suicide was the ultimate expression of human weakness.

Only one obstacle remained in the path of Congressman Harris's financial independence and national ambition. He charted his course carefully. The route to national office would require the acquisition of significant financial resources from a steady and dependable source; a source now fortuitously available. No longer would he rely on his wife for the money his campaigns required every two years. The dependency that put Marion Harris in the middle of all his decisions, career and otherwise, could now be effectively terminated. He began making contacts which would lead to the monetary pact he had in mind. He presented selected copies of the papers to the well-groomed, sun-tanned businessman from Union City and to his equally well-groomed attorney, emphasizing the grave threat they posed in the hands of federal prosecutors. He proposed a simple solution. Investment plus frequency equals silence. To assure a permanent cash flow, the five thousand dollar monthly retainer would remain in effect, but beginning immediately would be wired to a bank in Geneva for deposit in an un-numbered account. In exchange, the Russo family would be free to expand their enterprises without the obstruction of federal investigations. It was an airtight deal from which both parties would profit handsomely. The paper trail would continue in the name of the estate of Thomas A. Daley, attorney at law. As executor, Zachary Taylor Harris, guaranteed that no a footprint remained to trace it further.

### Late Summer, 1940

By 1940 Marion's dinner invitations became imperatives. They were attracting New Dealers of divergent and interesting backgrounds, as well as an occasional appearance by a cabinet secretary or two. The field widened to include world federalists, left-leaning academics and lawyers and administrators toiling in the new agencies and commissions coordinating FDR's "Arsenal of Democracy." None of the newcomers,

# INQUISITION

however, was more attentive and engaging as was Hobart "Hobe" Tenley, executive assistant to the Secretary of State.

The gathering on an afternoon in late September at Mrs. Hull's annual tea for congressional wives in the ornate Indian Treaty Room on the second floor of the State, War and Navy Building next to the White House went just about as Marion Harris expected. It was all small talk about children, schools, fashions and recipes. Not a word about the deteriorating international situation the President was confronting in the Oval Office just out the window and a floor below them. She longed to be in the middle of it, but on such occasions, she had to be the dutiful congressional wife; listening but never participating. To do so might draw attention to her and raise questions about her husband's celebrated autonomy. Only when Secretary Hull entered the gilded room did her mood shift. "Mr. Secretary, I can't for the life of me understand why we simply cannot be more supportive of England," she said, as the Secretary of State greeted her. He was accompanied by two aides.

"Well now, Mrs. Harris the president feels the same way, but he's not comfortable having members of Congress reminding him of his responsibilities to the Neutrality Act. It's damned if you do and damned if you don't, as he sees it. Perhaps you can ask Mr. Harris to help us put some iron in the backbones of his colleagues on Foreign Affairs. That's where the rub is. But we're working on it, aren't we, Hobe?" Hull said turning to one of his aides.

"Permit me, Mrs. Harris, to introduce you to Mr. L. Hobart Tenley, my eyes and ears on the Hill and chief counselor on things British and Russian. In spite of the first initial, which incidentally stands for Livingston, I presume, we call him Hobe. Princeton, Harvard Law, Oxford."

"Delighted to meet you, Mrs. Harris. Your husband's one of the Department's best friends on immigration. I trust he'll be even more of an asset as Pennsylvania's next Senator," Tenley said, taking Marion Harris's gloved hand. His light brown eyes, expressing the ease and intelligence of a professional diplomat, met hers. He looked to be slightly older than Zach. Tall with a powerful physique accented by broad shoulders, he looked like he had just walked off a tennis court. He held her hand for an instant too long, but Marion Harris didn't mind. She held her breath for but an instant, returning his smile. She'd never reacted that way before, even when introduced to the president. The words "school girl" flashed through her mind.

"Hobe's just back from London, and I'm ordering him to sit you down on that settee over there and give you the same briefing he gave me yesterday," the Secretary of State said in his courtly Tennesseean manner,

## Jack Eddinger

his gray eyes looking directly into her light blues. With his hands on each of their shoulders, he steered them across the room as if they were his most intimate friends. "I've got Stalin's new Foreign Secretary coming in an hour, and that means a long Bolshevik harangue," said Hull. "Damn, how I hate these commissars in striped pants. If I had my way, he'd be on the next boat to Leningrad. I won't need you till he arrives, Hobe. I'll entrust this lovely lady to you in the meantime."

Marion Harris flushed ever so slightly as Tenley sat down close to her, their thighs almost touching. They sat beneath a mural in hues of blue, green, red and gold depicting a tribe of Plains Indians accepting a treaty, ceding their hunting grounds to accommodate a continent-spanning railroad. It covered the entire length of the wall, stretching to an interior point of infinity and dissolving into the ocher, purple, tan and earth tones of a southwestern desert sunset. He packed a well-seasoned briar pipe, lit it and puffed up a pleasant woodsy cloud. She always liked a man who smoked a pipe - smart, introspective, someone who thinks before acting. His accent, she augured, was Northeast, possibly Connecticut. Midway between New Yorker and Brahmin. He reminded her of a taller, muscular version of George VI, complete with tweed jacket and tortoise-rimmed glasses - the king as he appeared in newspaper photographs visiting bombed-out London neighborhoods.

"Well now Mrs. H., where shall we begin?"

Marion wanted him to call her by her first name but thought the better of it. At least for the moment. "It's been an exceptionally difficult few months." Tenley spoke in a firm resonant baritone, which radiated easy self-assurance. His informed understanding of the faraway conflict and his precise vocabulary in describing it induced a state of near trance in Marion Harris. Her pulse quickened as he put his hand on her arm approvingly in emphasizing his first-hand knowledge of England's lonely battle for survival.

"You can stand almost anywhere along the coast south of London and hear the invasion fleet being assembled," he told her. "Transmissions grinding and Panzers clanking up the ramps of cargo ships put the Nazis a heck of a lot closer psychologically than Napoleon ever got. Between the debacle at Dunkirk and the nightly bombing raids, Britain seems to be moving closer to the precipice. At least that's the consensus around Grosvenor Square. Our people from the ambassador on down seem to believe defeat is inevitable in spite of Mr. Churchill's leadership. That's a far cry from Ambassador Page's wise counsel and tenacity in 1917. I think it's downright unworthy of us."

# INQUISITION

A thrill rose in her at the mention of Page. Nearly forgotten scenes of 1918 London; of long conversations at table in the dimly-lighted embassy; of her blue serge Red Cross girls spread out at hospitals around London and down through Kent to Dover and Folkestone, consoling badly mutilated, blinded and psychologically ruined men.

"I spoke with a family in London just a few days ago about the bomb that crashed through their roof," Tenley said. "Luckily, it was a dud. They invited the neighbors in for a look. They told me the Jerries were getting as sloppy as the Japanese! Imagine that. The projectile crashed through three floors and buried itself in the basement. And, they're talking about poor quality! What a fierce and imperturbable race, the English. I admire them greatly. You can't begin to believe what's happening to the center of London. It's worse than criminal - it's barbarism."

"Oh, Mr. Tenley. Your description puts it so vividly. "

"Please call me Hobe."

"Well all right. Hobe," she said hesitantly. "Did you know Ambassador Page? I consider him the finest diplomat America has produced in this century. He was a very special and warm friend. He towered above everyone in the diplomatic corps, and certainly was made of sterner stuff than that man Kennedy. Lord Grey and Mr. Aisquith, then Mr. Lloyd George himself told me England would not have survived without Ambassador Page and his direct link to President Wilson."

"No not personally," Hobe said. "But I'll never forget the ambassador's words as the 82$^{nd}$ Infantry Division stood at attention on the dock at Le Havre. He came over to France to meet the AEF as we disembarked. My men were in the first echelon. He addressed us briefly. He spoke like an old-fashioned orator - in the truest sense of that misused term, Bryan perhaps or Charles Sumner. He showed us his knowledge of Shakespeare and editor's skill for choosing the precise term. It reminded me of Henry's speech before Harfleur." Tenley quoted several lines from *Henry V* ending with a rousing, "Cry God, for Harry! England and St. George!"

People in the room turned their heads.

"The ambassador put on quite a performance. Very unlike a public official let alone a diplomat."

"Well, speaking of performances, Mr. Tenley ... My word. Your recitation was simply extraordinary. Have you been an actor?"

"Everything but, he replied. Journalist, sea-dog, non-practicing lawyer, teacher, political strategist ... you name it. But never an actor, although I wouldn't mind giving it a try."

"I must say, I am impressed. But getting back to the present ... we've only heard reports on the radio here, nothing first hand," Marion

# Jack Eddinger

Harris said. "My impression is that Mr. Murrow on CBS is being a bit melodramatic, but your account certainly verifies his reports. Those poor people. I've always loved London. It's crushing to hear that its beauty is being destroyed; so many beautiful places and architectural treasures. Westminster Abbey, St. Paul's, the National Gallery ... even the Houses of Parliament. What can anyone do? We're so far away and there's simply no motivation here to intervene."

"President Roosevelt wants to help, but his hands are tied by the Neutrality Act," Tenley responded. "Lend Lease is about as far as he can go, and that's stretching it. What's more, his reelection is not guaranteed, you know. I fear for this country. The newspapers are all lining up for Willkie. America First has recruited Eddie Rickenbacker, Al Smith and Alice Longworth to join Lindberg. These are dark days, Mrs. Harris. But Secretary Hull has one of the best political barometers I know of, and assures me that Roosevelt and Wallace will prevail. I hope he's right."

Hobe was a frequent dinner guest at Marion's soirees throughout the fall of 1940. Zach was off in Pennsylvania campaigning for the Roosevelt-Wallace ticket and gearing up for his campaign for the Senate, only a year away. Their daughter, Pamela, now 13, was off at school. The interval without her husband's presence gave Marion Harris her longed-for opportunity to establish full independence and her own reputation among Washington's new women epitomized by Eleanor Roosevelt and Frances Perkins. She began having a small group calling themselves World Federalists to dinner. With them she believed that a single world government was the answer to global conflict and future harmony among the world's nations. Hobe was among its quiet promoters in the State Department.

Zach Harris chuckled when he learned of his wife's new interest, and dismissed it as a harmless, if zany, cause cooked up by Ivy league professors and the New York intellectual crowd; a fringe movement at best with no chance of gaining a place on the national ballot. "Sounds like one of Eleanor's causes," he chortled, "Right up there with Negro rights and working women."

Marion Harris shared many interests with her new friend, the handsome lawyer-diplomat. More and more she caught herself thinking of him. Her daydreams often started with the sound of a refined manly voice stirring in her sub-conscious. They shared an interest in everything English - the Romantic poets and Shaw's dramas, country houses and gardens, the Cotswolds, Oxfordshire and Derwentwater. She learned that like her younger brother, Alec, Hobe's wife, Clare was killed in an automobile accident. They had no children. Hobe banged around Europe

# INQUISITION

for a few years trying to forget and writing freelance articles for American and Canadian newspapers, and an occasional piece from Spain for the *Manchester Guardian* and *The Nation*. He came to Washington directly from assignment in Spain in 1938 to be counsel to the Senate Foreign Relations Committee. He moved over to State in 1939 when the chairman recommended him to Secretary Hull, who like most Americans except for the Guernica bombing, knew very little of the brutal clash on the Iberian Peninsula. Having tried to educate his fellow citizens with his writings about the underlying war between fascism and communism in Spain, he was eager to take on educating the Secretary of State.

### September, 1941

A wave formed far out on an otherwise calm sea. It rose and fell in swells, stirred by currents running in towards the shore at depths they had only begun to perceive. Then it broke upon them suddenly with unrestrained passion. Nothing else mattered. By the late summer of 1941, they had fallen daringly, provocatively and forbiddingly in love. It began when he asked her to come over to Annapolis with him for a long weekend at the end of August. He was lecturing First Classmen in diplomatic history at the Naval Academy. At first she said no but reconsidered when Hobe told her others would be staying with them at the rambling oyster-tonger's place he'd turned into a bayside cottage not far from the ferry landing on the Eastern Shore. He told the guard at the academy gate that Mrs. Harris was representing her husband, Congressman Zachary Taylor Harris. His jocular staccato pronunciation made the congressman's name sound like a drum roll. The marine gave them a crisp white-gloved salute and sent them to the VIP parking lot in front of Bancroft Hall.

"We've got to do this more often. They usually make me park this jalopy down by the water, where no one would mistake me for brass," he said, grinning. He studied the windshield permits on every car parked at Bancroft then backed into a space between two shiny black sedans, each with four gold-star permits.

"Navy Department stickers," he grinned wryly. "Leahy and King, I'll wager. I'll send the boss a memo Monday morning, complaining that there's so much Navy brass around here that an ordinary sailor can't even find a place to park his car! The Secretary will phone King to rag him a bit. Ernie's ornery as hell, and if I know him, he'll tell Hull to go to hell, and chew out the superintendent for letting my wreck on the academy grounds." Marion Harris loved Hobe Tenley's smart-alecky irreverence. A

## Jack Eddinger

big small boy, she thought. Zach would want a car, a driver and an honor guard to greet him.

Hobe opened the driver's side door, got out and came around to Marion's door of the beat-up Ford coupe. Her slender legs were already emerging, one foot touching the running board. She smiled a big blue-eyed smile at him. She looked stunning in a stylish two-piece pink suit and white blouse open slightly at the neck. She wore silk hose and carried a stylish black paten leather handbag that matched her shoes. In honor of the occasion a little white sailor's hat was pinned her short shiny brown hair in place.

"Please remove the headgear, Hanni. No formality in this man's navy. We're from State, remember? No need for regulation dress."

"Hanni? Is that a German diminutive … like Shatzie?" Marion said puzzled.

"Oh what's in a name, my dear. I can't call you Marion. Too formal, like your husband's. And Hanson sounds too masculine. So why not, Hanni? Hanni darling. Sounds just about right. Besides it was my grandmother's nickname and she taught me everything I know, including skeet shooting. We shot up a raft of clay pigeons along the Connecticut shore when I was growing up. She lived alone near Essex after my grandfather's death. He taught her how to shoot. She was a pistol with a shotgun," Hobe said playfully.

Marion Hanson Harris, daughter of an industrial titan, wife of a powerful congressman, sister of a would-be novelist slipped off her white gloves and wound her slender, shapely fingers around his. *Oh Hobe ... Hobe, darling. You're just what my heart has been yearning for all these long years.* The words echoed in her deepest psychic recesses, as she listened to his lecture on seapower and diplomacy in rapt calm and radiance.

He made it sound as if it was happening right there in the classroom, describing how bitter enmity among willful men scuttled the centuries-old dream of a world organization devoted to the peaceful resolution of grievances among men and nations. President Wilson and Senators Henry Cabot Lodge of Massachusetts and Nelson Aldrich of New York came alive for the ensigns-to-be that last late summer of peace. When he ended, the middies stood up to a man and applauded. Hobe's vivid lecture contrasted with their daily academic fare of super-heated steam boilers, angles of fire, instrument navigation and the rules of engagement at sea, making naval academics sound like Scholastic metaphysics. As they drove down to catch the Chesapeake Bay ferry near Sandy Point, Marion Harris could not take her eyes off him. He had removed his seersucker jacket, pulled

# INQUISITION

his tie askew and rolled his white shirt cuffs midway between wrists and elbows. She wanted to move towards him and caress his powerful thigh. Damn! She thought. Why must there be others.

As if reading her mind, Hobe grinned, crinkling his eyes. "Alone at last. Now we can enjoy each other without the navy, the marines, the state of Maryland or anyone. Just us."

"But, I thought …"

"Never mind. You'd never have come."

"What is a lady supposed to say or do?"

"Nothing sweet, lady. Allow your gallant knight to spirit you away to the timbered walls of Buckinghamshire."

On the way to the ferry, Hobe took the shore road down to a cove which opened to the bay. "Beautiful sight out there. That regatta is actually the middies sailing team moving into the wind. Just a bunch of kids, but complete pros with those sailboats. They're going to need all the skills they can muster if we go to war with Japan. The Jap Navy's twice the size of ours and they've been practicing how to use it against us for the last decade." He pulled up by a jetty and put his right arm gently around her shoulder in a half embrace and with his left pointed around her to the swift-moving sailboats rounding a buoy in the distance. His elbow rested on the steering wheel. His body was bent ever so slightly towards her. A ray of sunlight caught a few gold strands amid a shock of shiny chestnut hair, putting a youthful angle on the mature countenance of his 52 years. He was so close that she could detect the faint fragrance of *eau de cologne* that he had splashed on his face that morning. He pulled her to him in an embrace so strong, yet so tender it caressed her in a haze of unmistakably erotic masculinity.

They were jolted from their embrace by two short blasts of the Bay ferry's klaxon. "Hold on Moses we're a'comin," Hobe chortled, starting the motor. They were at the ferry slip in two minutes, then out on the Chesapeake as the setting sun thrust long fingers of gold, salmon, pink and purple into the sky to light the way across. Within minutes of driving off the ferry, they turned into an unpaved road leading to the water's edge. A white clapboard cottage stood alone in a copse of tall pines. Hobe drove around a circular driveway paved with crushed oyster and clam shells, stopped just beyond the doorway, got out and helped Marion alight. He noticed that she had removed her wedding ring. He pulled her to him and held her tightly. She took a breath and felt him hard against her. Then she did something wildly exciting. Sliding her hand down his trousers, she squeezed him, kneading and rubbing until he murmured.

"Not here. Let's get settled."

# Jack Eddinger

He took her hand, and led her through the doorway, down a short hall and into a big comfortable living room with a large window that looked out over the water. He removed her jacket, unbuttoned her blouse and turned down both straps of her slip until her white brassiere was rubbing up against his hairy chest. She wriggled out of her girdle, stockings and skirt, dropping them on the floor along with her slip. She was moist and tumescent and ready for him. He removed his things. They stood in their undergarments, pressing against each other tightly. They dropped to the floor. She slid off his boxer shorts and took him in her hands. He helped her slip out of her silk panties and unhooked her bra. Then she lowered herself onto him to receive his throbbing and thrusting, long, slow strokes. They were a single body undulating in carnal rhythm, when he exploded in her. His mouth muffled her groans and shrieks as the wave broke over her. She'd never felt anything like it and wanted it to last forever. It was deliciously, illicitly licentious and she craved it. They made love as the soft summer nightfall descended, turning the cottage into a secret and enchanted place. The only sound came from a very gentle surf and the intermittent clank of a bell on a channel buoy. Reflections of red and green running lights far out on the water mingled with bright starlight filtering into the room.

He fixed a special dinner of oysters, blue crab, clams and rockfish. They dined by candlelight on the small screened-in porch and sipped a well-chilled Muscadet. They talked about novels they read that year, and Hobe read his review for *The Nation* of Ernest Hemingway's new novel, *For Whom The Bell Tolls*, which was on best-seller lists around the country. He also read from his review of William Shirer's, *Berlin Diary*, which he praised as, "the best non-fiction book of 1941 and a wake-up call for Americans who believe the country has found a sanctuary in neutrality."

By Sunday morning after another night of love-making, shortened by a furious electrical storm that lashed the small cottage, shadowy thoughts about the consequences of her behavior began to blur Marion's desire. She thought of her mother's affair. Thoughts of her father's wrath chilled her. Zach would be unforgiving. They sailed to a small island near the Chester River during the afternoon. A change of weather brought a strong wind out of the northwest. It lashed the small sailboat, churning up an incessant chop that left her queasy and slightly irritable. He brought the sailboat around and headed downwind toward home. "You've been very quiet, Hanni," he said, as they drifted towards the marina. "I'm sorry that you're not feeling well. The bay gets rough now and then, especially this time of year. Maybe too much of a good thing made its contribution, too, eh?" She smiled, her blue eyes sparkling.

# INQUISITION

"Now that's more like it, Hanni," he said, reaching for her hand. Both were looking across the Narrows toward the western shore. His eyes were focused on the *verdigris* dome of the Academy chapel. Hers remained unfocused as she peered across the darkening expanse, as lights began to come on along the distant, dusky shoreline. She took his sun-freckled hand and put it around her waist. They waited until the last streaks of daylight disappeared in the western sky. Then they drove back to the cottage and packed up Hobe's Model A coupe for the return ferry crossing and the nearly two-hour drive back to Washington.

Only the few lights she had turned on around mid day on Friday remained burning, as they walked up the flagstone walk of the stone mansion in Kalorama Circle. She had dismissed Hattie, their cook, and James, her driver and house man, Thursday evening, telling them she'd be away the entire weekend, and they needn't report till Monday morning. The congressman was in Pennsylvania politicking. This was often the case, as both Mr. and Mrs. Harris led independent lives.

"Hanni, darling," Hobe said to her as they walked up the driveway hand in hand. "I think you ought to divorce him."

"Oh, Hobe, it's not that easy," she replied trying not to reveal her anguish. "There's so much to consider, and this is so sudden. I simply haven't had time to gather my thoughts, darling. I love you. You know that now. I've loved you from the day we sat together and you brought me into your world. I love you deeply, my darling … but I just need time to let my heart come to terms with itself. If it were my decision alone, you know I'd run off with you anywhere, but I must consider consequences - a word I've always hated. What will it mean for Pammie; for all of the warm friends I've made here. If it were only Zach, it would be easy. Hah! That's a lie! There's no simple yes or no answer that I can give you. Please understand, Hobe darling."

"Don't be foolish, Hanni. You'll regret it. I love you more than my life, and I want to spend the rest of it with you." He took her in his arms in the softly lit alcove in front of the big oak door and kissed her passionately.

She tried to turn away. "No, please, Hobe. Let me do it my way."

She kissed him gently, turned and fumbled with the key. He pushed the door open. Her high heels clicked on the cold marble floor. She smiled at him then hesitantly closed the door. He waited until he saw a light come on in her bedroom above the driveway. She came to the window and blew him a kiss.

He considered the irony, as he walked to his car:

*O! For my sake do you with Fortune chide*

# Jack Eddinger

*The guilty goddess of my harmful deeds*
*That did not better for my life provide*
*Than public means which public manners breeds.*

"Public people, bah!"

He got in and drove off. Marion, watching from her window, listened as the sound of Hobe's jalopy with its throaty, slightly raucous vibrato receded into the night. "Sounds just like him," she smiled.

She set the Christmas holidays as her self-imposed deadline for a decision. There would be time to consider everything. Pammie would be home for the holidays. And Zach. God, won't he be stunned when he realizes he'll have neither the money nor the wife he needs to get the office he's lusted for all these years since Tad's death. Prepare for a hurricane, she told herself.

But in the waning afternoon light of a Sunday in early December events taking place on an island far beyond the North American continent warped all plans, all hopes, all desires, all longings. The seismic forces of history erupted for a second time in a century. Titanic explosions and billowing clouds of burning oil commingling with the stench of seared flesh, carried all of humanity before it.

At noon on Monday December 8, 1941, Zachary Taylor Harris listened as Franklin Roosevelt, speaking deliberately and firmly from the well of the House to a joint session of Congress and to all America, proclaimed a state of war between the United States and the Empire of Japan. Two days later in one of the most reckless acts of a reckless career, Adolph Hitler declared war on the United States. In 24 hours time, the United States of America was fully committed to winning the conflict its people desperately wished to avoid. A day later Congressman Zachary Taylor Harris announced that he was withdrawing from his campaign for United States Senator from Pennsylvania, and would be sworn in as a Commander in the U.S. Navy. He would go on active duty at the Navy Department immediately and with the Speaker's permission would retain his seat in the House.

Before the month was out, the State Department announced that L.H. Tenley, executive assistant to the Secretary, would head a special mission to His Majesty's government. He would be posted to allied headquarters London effective January 1, 1942.

# CHAPTER NINE
## *Irreversible Reality*

Pan American Clipper No. 676, *The Atlantic*, rocked gently against the big hemp mooring lines that held her in place against the harsh wind of early January. Baltimore's harbor lined with ramshackle corrugated tin wharves built on ancient and dilapidated piers was crowded with sea borne craft of every description. Freighters and colliers pitched and rolled in their berths. A motley collection of craft, large and small - tugs, barges, lighters, including the ancient stern-wheeled Baltimore-Norfolk ferry - churned up wakes of slimy green murk going about their appointed tasks.

"Well, Hanni, I guess this is it," a raspy-voiced Hobe Tenley shouted over the whining roar, as each of the clipper's 4,000-horsepower Wright engines, began to rev. Two of the monsters were perched on each wing above the fuselage of the silver flying boat sitting low in the water at the pier. An American flag emblazoned each side of the big pelican mouth. Pan Am's winged-globe was printed above the flag under the flight deck. The U.S. Navy had taken over the *Atlantic* and other clippers from the Pan-Am fleet for the duration of the war. The State and War Departments were ferrying personnel to England, now that the United States was firmly in the fight. Hobe had his arm wound tightly around her waist. She pressed into the comfortable angle between the epaulets and belt of his sand-colored trench coat. She wore a mink coat, a red, white and blue scarf, and had a veiled, navy blue hat pinned securely above her short brown hair, smartly coiffed for the new year by one of the Shoreham's less conventional hair stylists. He pulled down the brim of his brown fedora to keep it from blowing off. "It's a damned pity. You never looked brighter, younger, lovelier. If it were in my power, good lady, I'd whisk you straight uptown to the Belvedere for martinis at the Owl Bar then a deliciously warm bed. We'd never get up," he said feeling himself go hard under the two layers of clothing he'd need in London. She pressed even more tightly against him.

"Now I want you to make me one promise," he told her, lifting the small veil, revealing her tear-stained face. "I know. I know," she said. "But it is so difficult getting his attention. I had myself steeled to bring it up between Christmas and New Year's, but he was gone all week, and when he did come home, it was nothing but war talk then he went straight to bed. In the morning he was gone by five-thirty. I realize there's a war on, but you'd think he was fighting it himself. He hasn't the slightest inkling about us."

# Jack Eddinger

"The man's a perfect scoundrel. The only war he'll see is from behind a desk. What a cushy deal he made for himself. How'd he do it?"

"As I understand it, he told Secretary Knox, the Navy owed him a commission, because he personally cut through the red tape holding up delivery of two aircraft carriers built by Bessemer Steel," she explained.

"I really despise politicians," Hobe spat. All engines were humming now. They embraced. He kissed her passionately. She never wanted it to end.

He was the last to board. The steward pulled down the big overhead door and spun the locking mechanism, as if battening down a storage locker. Hobe was securing his seatbelt and leaning toward the small porthole next to his seat, as the Clipper, free of its mooring, taxied to a position in mid-harbor, past the star-shaped battlements of Ft. McHenry. The flying boat sped out over open water, shooting twin white geysers skyward and trailing a long silvery wake. It lifted off gracefully, made a climbing turn over the pier and harbor below, then headed northeast. The flight would take him over New York, Boston, Halifax, then to Botwood, Newfoundland for refueling. In the air again, the clipper would head out across the vast black expanse of the North Atlantic towards landfall and another refueling stop at Foynes Island, Ireland. Aloft again, the silver aircraft banked northeast over St. Alban's Head, flying low over the Isle of Wight then dropped quickly to the surface of Poole Bay, spewing great spouts of briny foam as it headed into a slip at the Royal Naval Base at Dorset.

Hobe's first Letter from Britain, as he promised, arrived at Buchanan House a week later. It was delivered by a courier. Hobe included it in the London-Washington diplomatic pouch and had it stamped, "Hand Deliver On Arrival."

*London, January 12, 1942*
*Somewhere in Knightsbridge*

*Hanni, Darling*

*This war is so entirely new that any explanation I might give you would be as speculative as a theologian wrestling with the forces of darkness and light. Civilization has progressed so far that it will have to begin again, when this conflict is over - though how and with what kind of devastation we would be at a loss to contemplate. In this conflict the lessons of the last war are as obsolete as medieval weapons and chivalry. There are no front*

# INQUISITION

lines as at Hastings or Waterloo or Ypres. Just as you're thinking the trouble is nowhere near you, explosions begin without prelude. Down you go into a ditch, or flat on the pavement. The front line stretches to the limit of the skies and runs across the rooftops of this tormented city.

Today, I was in a street in Shepherd's Market when the Nazi bombers dumped their cargo. I watched an antiquarian shake his fist at the sky and shout, "They shall pay for this!" as he emerged dazed from the plaster and broken glass, china and smashed brass - all that was left of a fine Georgian antiques business. This war is a direct outcome of the last one, and for the men of Britain - those surviving from blood and mud of the Somme - it's a grim and bitter harvest. Yet, a new generation fights on. They've passed the decisive test of what it means to be free men; they've blasted the Wagnerian myth out of the skies; their resolve has put the lie to the Nazis romantic nonsense. I don't know how to write about these fellows, who so few in number, went up on wings to throw back what seemed to be the oncoming age of darkness. Mr. Churchill has said all there is to say.

These thoughts are about all I can put down. I wanted to share a few of them with you, Hanni darling, from this forlorn and grieving patch of good green earth, this once happy island. As sure as I know there is a God in heaven, this torment will end, and the outlines of victory will emerge, my dearest, slowly at first, then with a growing retributive fury. Perhaps then Woodrow Wilson's vision of world peace, justice and order will prevail.

Well, Hanni, the all clear sirens have sounded. It's time to shake off the dust and get back to work. My love for you will outlast all of this, and all of the confusion to come. I love you, my dearest, and long for your warmth and sweet caresses.

Till next time,

Passionately,

Hobe

PS  I've asked Andy Burnham, my good friend at State I told you about, to get in touch. He and Elaine will help you keep the flame burning. I trust them completely - H.

# Jack Eddinger

Marion kept Hobe's letters tied with silk ribbon locked in a drawer with her prettiest lingerie where they'd be safe from snooping. Her letters to him were always written in blue ink in the elegant handwriting she had perfected since her days at boarding school. For Hobe Tenley something exceptionally erotic lurked in the graceful, cursive pen strokes that painted word pictures, even if they were only about Broadway's latest drama, or the spring fashions or *The Evening Star's* social pages. She also kept him up with "The Movement," as they referred to advancing the cause of a single world government that would make war obsolete and rescue humanity from destruction.

Capt. Zachary Taylor Harris, USN, impeccable and handsome in his tailored and braided naval officer's uniform, cracked the shell of a softboiled egg and slipped its contents onto a slab of buttered toast, as he had for countless mornings during their 20 years of wedded life. He looked up from the portfolio stamped "U.S. War Department" in gold leaf toward his wife, seated at the opposite end of the long table. She was in a pink satin dressing gown and looked radiant in light makeup and small diamond ear studs. "Well, my dear, you're going to have to get on without me for an indeterminate time," he said without looking up from his papers. "The Secretary has asked me to scout out new ship-building sites on the Gulf and West coasts, then go out to Pearl to give him an assessment of what it's going to take to rebuild and expand the naval base. I'm afraid I'll be gone for some time."

Marion Harris tried not to show her exhilaration. "Duty always, darling. What would you be without answering the call," she said trying not to be sarcastic.

He stared at her blankly, attempting to fathom a deeper meaning in the slight smile she suppressed with fluttering eyelashes. She took a cigarette from the gold box, snapped the striker of the table lighter and inhaled deeply, blowing a wisp of blue smoke toward her husband.

"Well now, nothing that heroic; no combat assignment. Not that I would turn one down," he said. "Just getting the job done for this man's navy. Might be a helpful career move in the long run."

"There's something we need to discuss," she said offhandedly, as he snapped his briefcase closed, drained his coffee cup and let his driver help him on with his overcoat. He headed towards the door. "It'll have to wait, my dear, and speaking of waiting let's go Seaman McBrien. I've a briefing at the War Department in 10 minutes. So long, Marion. Don't wait up for me. I'll be late as usual then out to Bolling Field for an early flight. I'll see

# INQUISITION

you when I return and we can discuss whatever's on your mind." He was out the door before she could rise from the table.

"Well, of all the thoughtless, uncaring, conceited ..." she said to an empty room. "I hope he never comes back."

Several weeks passed before she received the hand-delivered note inviting her to dinner in Georgetown. It was signed "Elaine Burnham" in purple ink in the broad strokes of an artist's brush. The friends Hobe told her about. She recalled him describing Andy Burnham, head of the Soviet desk at State, as his closest friend and confidante. She found it somewhat strange that the tweedy professorial type that Hobe described Burnham would have an obviously flamboyant artist for a wife and live in a part of town that's always been slightly dishabille. Oh well, I guess intellectuals really are different.

The rambling brick townhouse on P Street was equal parts art studio and antiquarian bookstore. Stark white walls were hung with the screaming colors, androgynous shapes and contorted figures of 20th Century painting. Two large Diego Riviera market scenes hung on opposite walls of the book-strewn living room. A small black and white rendering entitled, *The Trial of Sacco and Vanzetti*, accentuated a hallway lined with small paintings of a decidedly proletarian world view, and signed "ERB" in flared slashes. The monogram appeared as a single brushstroke, as in Japanese calligraphy. They were the same as those on the dinner invitation.

"Welcome, Hanni. Andy and I are just dying to meet you. Hobe's told us all about you," said Elaine Burnham, extending a paint-mottled hand out of a paint-mottled smock.

"My God, Joseph's multi-hued coat," Marion thought.

"Sorry for the messy greeting, but the turpentine we're getting nowadays, doesn't get it all. It's thin as water," Elaine Burnham responded with a slightly warped smile and a decidedly New York accent. She had dark skin, almost Asian features, deep-set black eyes, prominent nose and long black braided hair with streaks of grey. Marion Harris could not quite categorize her; Navaho Indian perhaps. From a certain perspective, she could be man or woman. She certainly did not look anything like the wife of an Assistant Secretary of State and the government's leading expert on the USSR. And worse, she knows about us. How much has Hobe told them? She began feeling a vague sense of embarrassment, as their eyes met, and quickly looked away.

"Oh, don't let Elaine's disguise trouble you, Hanni." The rich baritone boomed from a room somewhere down the hallway. "She's actually quite

## Jack Eddinger

normal; could almost pass for a congressman's wife when she dresses up."

There was the name again. What did Hobe tell them? Why? It is our secret. She felt perplexed and slightly put out.

Andy Burnham's athletic frame nearly filled the doorway. Quickly noting her discomfiture, he gently eased her out of her coat. He was just over six feet tall and wore steel-rimmed glasses which magnified his friendly brown eyes. His grey-black hair was cut short in the same brush style she'd seen in photos accompanying an article in *Life* about the first days of U.S. Army recruits. The only un-military aspect of his appearance was the short, clipped mustache and beard the color of salt and pepper, which gave him the look of a Renaissance nobleman. He wore a light blue shirt, and green and gold striped bow tie, which she later learned was his way of taking a small, but characteristic, liberty from standard American male sartorial identity. He wore a brown tweed jacket with leather arm patches - the quintessential professor, she mused. His gray flannel slacks were sharply creased and just touched the tops of his highly-polished black shoes. He looked younger than his 51 years. She felt immediately at ease. There was something charming about his easy friendliness and mock-heroic demeanor, as if he were a kind uncle or older brother.

"Now don't blame Hobe. He's never been good about keeping secrets. As his friend and longtime co-conspirator, all I can tell you, Hanni, is that he loves you. You've raised him out of the terrible depression he's been fighting off ever since Clare's death. You're both fortunate and all the better for finding each other in these despairing times. Now let's get you out of this clutter and into a sanctuary where we can get to know you." He guided her down the hallway and into his study, a softly lighted room with comfortable leather chairs, a flickering fireplace with an enormous white bearskin covering an Astrakhan carpet. Above the fireplace hung a pair of crossed, highly varnished wooden skis with straps, wires and steel boot plates. A pair of bamboo poles with leather baskets stood next to the firewood box. An autographed photo of Lenin haranguing the St. Petersburg crowd hung next to FDR's. The latter signed by the president with the message: "For Andy Burnham, bear-baiter par excellence! FDR."

As her eyes became accustomed to the soft light, she watched him stretch for a silver-framed photo on a shelf high in the wall of books that reached the ceiling. He ran it over his sleeve in a quick dusting and handed it to her. It was of two young men, and appeared to have been taken many years before. She studied it for a very long moment. Her heart raced. She was overwhelmed. A flood of memories rushed at her. Could it be ... could it possibly be?

# INQUISITION

"That's why I feel I've known you so well, Hanni," he said gently. "He was just like Hobe."

She examined the photo for several minutes. A tender emotion with a tragic edge welled up inside her. Her eyes filled. Two young men with their arms over each other's shoulders like childhood pals smiled at her. One was a very much younger, athletically built Andy Burnham. She knew him by his wire-rimmed spectacles and wispy Leon Trotsky beard. The other was her brother, Alec Hanson, looking more relaxed, more debonair, more animated than she could ever remember. She thought immediately of Scott Fitzgerald with his sandy hair, light eyes, big smile and handsomely-tailored suit of summer white linen.

"It was taken the summer between our junior and senior year at Princeton. We'd just spent two months as copy boys on the old *New York American*. I wanted to write news stories like Richard Harding Davis. Alec wanted to create fiction like Stephen Crane. What a writer he would have been. I want you to have the photo and this."

He handed her a slim leather-bound volume with gilt-edged pages.

"They are all here. Alec's short stories. Axel Hammond at Knopf was going to publish him before graduation. I believe your father prohibited posthumous publication. I asked Axel to put them together for me a few years after Alec's death. They've been with me all these years."

"Ohh, Mr., Burnham ... Andy ... You don't know ... Does Hobe know?"

"No, not really. I felt I wanted to share them with you, no one else. I never expected to give them up. Hobe provided the link. I guess they've been waiting for you to claim them." Marion Harris held the slender book to her breast. Tears came easily. Then she regained her composure and smiled.

"How well did you know Alec? Have you known Hobe for a long time?"

"Well enough to envy Alec Hanson's extraordinary talent as a writer, Hanni. We were close at Princeton. I remember many a night putting the newspaper to bed. He was editor and I was his ace reporter. We were going to own the literary world in a few years. As for Hobe, about five years. Helped him get started on the Hill, then at State. I consider Hobe Tenley to be a pretty extraordinary and capable fellow. If he were at all political I'd expect he'd be Secretary of State one day. And, by the way, from our first meeting in Barcelona, he always reminded me of Alec. Honest. Talented. Smart. Self-assured. Completely without guile, a commodity in very short supply around this town. In short, a serious man. I consider it a privilege to know and work with him. We met in Spain in '37. He was writing for the

# Jack Eddinger

*Manchester Guardian*. He helped me publish a number of freelance pieces under a *nom de plume*, or should I say *nom de guerre*? He was trying to get a handle on the Loyalist forces in Galicia. When he told me he admired the reporting of Richard Harding Davis, I felt I'd met a long lost member of the tribe of Hearst. We've been good friends and co-conspirators for a united world since those days. He tells me you have a similar interest and are willing to help."

"All right. Okay. Now," he shouted down the hallway to his wife who had discreetly left them alone in the library.

"What's the big kurfuffel? I'm coming," came the response from a far off room. "So I should get with the martinis?"

"Come now, sweetheart. How do you expect to pass your orals at the Sorbonne some day? Franglaise maybe they'll understand, but Yiddish? Never," her husband growled. "I've just told Hanni we've got the whole evening to get acquainted. It stretcheth before us, *mein kinder liebling*."

Elaine Burnham set out on a cocktail table a pitcher of ice, glass stirring rod, a fifth of Gordon's gin and a small bottle of vermouth. She spread canapés out on a tray and added a large chunk of cheddar and soda biscuits. Her husband poured half of the gin into the pitcher, carefully squeezed a few drops of vermouth like a chemist with a pipette and stirred the mixture slowly.

"I really don't know why I'm stirring," he chuckled. "Ritual, I suppose." He strained the contents into three glasses, each with a small white onion. "Ahh, nothing like the bite of a Gibson to loosen the tongue, eh Elaine?" He leaned across the table to light the cork-tipped cigarette Marion Harris slipped from an engraved silver case. "Elegant cigarette case, Hanni. A gift from the Congressman?"

"Actually, no. Hobe gave it to me at dinner the night before he left for England. Something to remember quiet evenings and better days he said." Andy Burnham took two Camels from a pack, lighted one and handed it to Elaine. He lit another for himself.

"Tell me about your interest in the movement," Marion said inhaling deeply. "Hobe tells me your interest goes back to protesting the World War. I remember many people our age were against our involvement. But they didn't actually protest out on the street or that kind of thing. That was more for the bohemians and radicals. Hardly the stuff of patriotism I'd say. After all, the president had no other choice."

"It depends on how you define the word 'patriot,' Hanni. We believed it was our patriotic duty to exercise our right of free speech by expressing opposition to sending young Americans to what was, in its essence, a

# INQUISITION

capitalists' war, as our hero, Gene Debs, described it. I still believe that by the way."

Marion Harris had to suppress a smile. Her husband would be apoplectic. Consorting with sedition. If he only knew, she thought. She wondered what Eugene Palmer would say having supplied the U.S. Navy with most of its ships and armament. They're certainly different from us.

"Fellow traveler you're thinking," Andy Burnham grinned. "Oh, I go way back - long before that label had any currency. Elaine's the newcomer. I inherited my political views from my parents. Both had soft spots for the cause of industrial workers, not to mention the outcasts of society. Mother was a school teacher and the only child of Christian missionaries. She was an activist for suffrage in her teens. She worked in Bryan's campaigns for president. Before he died at the age of 28, father was an organizer for the old Western Federation of Miners, and one of the earliest converts to the IWW. He never lived to see the Wobblies lead the way to the dawn of Socialism, but mother took his place, traveling around the country - with me in tow - lecturing about workers rights to lead and copper miners, railroad laborers, factory hands, women in sweatshops - anyone who'd listen. This was long before FDR's conversion. After Bryan, her favorite, believe it or not, was Theodore Roosevelt. She met a whole new crowd when she became a Progressive. Many were school teachers like herself. It was quite a mélange. All true individuals - and I stress individual. They were appalled by working conditions in the mines, mills and factories, not to mention the exploitation of our natural resources to make a handful of the rich plutocrats even richer. They were civic reformers, naturalists, public health and land preservation advocates who considered Teddy's job unfinished. Then you had the far outs - the nudists, the promoters of free-love, family planning advocates, a handful proclaiming the rights of Negroes and dreamers propounding the theories of Sigmund Freud. The musk of the Bull Moose still hung heavy. And let's be frank, Woodrow Wilson, an unlikely hero, rode reform all the way to the presidency.

"Where did you fit in? And what about Elaine? Did she share your radical theories? And please show more respect for President Wilson. He's certainly my hero," said Marion Harris, wondering what she had gotten herself into. It was strange. The man speaking to her was not some wild-eyed, bearded bomb-throwing type, as she had always pictured left-wing activists, but an intelligent, well-spoken and impeccably attired individual very much at ease with himself.

"That's another story and I'll get to it in a minute," he said. "You may not believe it, but we also had a few millionaires in the ranks, mostly women, except for Alonzo de Rochemont whose Calvinist ancestors

## Jack Eddinger

endowed him with a social conscience. Alonzo was a character. He waxed the tips of his mustaches, wore a *pincenez*, carried a cane and gave huge amounts of his family fortune to the cause. Many of the women were soon to be widows. They spent their husband's reserves to start or resurrect magazines and intellectual journals. When their husbands bade farewell to this vale of tears to enter the great celestial counting house, the wives spent every waking moment divesting themselves of their ill-gained wealth. They supported settlement houses, education, infant health and nutrition, Margaret Sanger's birth control crusade, temperance and, in 1916, protesting against sending Americans to fight in Europe. Mother was involved in every cause it seems."

Marion Harris considered what her own mother might have done with Buchanan Hanson's fortune and shuddered. Yet, she regretted that her only experience of proletarian existence came on Saturday morning forays from Bryn Mawr to the river wards of Philadelphia, and then only for a half day during her junior and senior years. The children of the city's Irish were an ill clad, snot-dripping, foul-tongued lot. They despised any woman teacher not garbed in black habit and white wimple. How Medieval she remembered thinking at the time. Andy Burnham lit another Camel and continued. He spoke of New York in the 1920s, post-graduate work at Columbia, speaking Russian on the East Side and trying to break in as a writer with a proletarian outlook.

"We were all smitten with the Bolsheviks. Lenin was our deity. That sounds morbid today with his corpse on display in the Kremlin. Trotsky was our intellectual lodestar. Malraux's brilliant man of action sweeping away the corrupt system of capitalism. For us it was imperative not only to protest the war, but to help overthrow Kerensky and the Mensheviks. The monarchies and democracies were doomed to lie exhausted and depleted in their own ashes. As we saw it, the capitalists would move into the vacuum and add to their obscene profits. Fifty years after our own Civil War American workers remained enslaved. Only a national movement captained by men like Big Bill Haywood, Jim Cannon and Jack Reed could overthrow the rotten and repressive system we lived under. We were a raging army of Christian socialists, orthodox Marxists, trade unionists, suffragists, immigrant workers and intellectuals and, as I said, a few millionaire social reformers. We were proud to proclaim ourselves Socialists."

"What on earth prompted you to enroll at Princeton, that fortress of capitalism?" Marion asked bemused.

"Princeton was grand-father Mills' alma mater. He studied for the ministry at the theological seminary. I guess it's the only way a grandson

# INQUISITION

of radical stripe would be accepted as an undergraduate. Of course, neither they nor I knew that at the time. I enjoyed my four years in Tigerville. As for Elaine and me, we met - appropriately at the Intimate Gallery - in 1925. I was writing freelance pieces for Max Eastman at *The Liberator*. She was a student at CCNY and spending all her free time at the Metropolitan studying color and form. Walter Steiglitz was lecturing on Jean Arp, if I'm not incorrect. I was doing a retrospective piece on the Dadaists which Max published that spring as, *Ten Years Beyond Zurich*. Elaine was quite shy then and absorbed in courses in abstraction. We didn't have much time for romance. I was finishing up my dissertation on Ferdinand Lassalle at Columbia and spending most of my time at the N.Y. Public Library. We decided to marry after a date or two. We agreed there would be no children, so we could pursue our careers. She continued painting and work toward a degree in fine arts. I ended up at the New School, teaching the theory and practice of Marxism and the rhetoric of fiction. Quite a combination wouldn't you say? The Rubenstein's - that's Elaine's family - kept us alive during this time. Sunday nights at the flat in Brooklyn became the week's central activity; good food and deep discussions of society's ills long into the night. Her father was a syndicalist. Her brother, Jay was an anarchist, and 'what was your mother, anyway, my dear?'

"Mama's father knew Frederick Engels," replied Elaine Burnham. "Grandfather loved professor Engels, as he called him, but he couldn't bear Marx - too imperious and set in his views. Typical German, even though a Jew. So, I don't know … if she wasn't for Marx, who she was for, maybe Utopian? They were all some kind of socialists, but she had such a good heart. And what a cook!"

The Burnhams fascinated Marion Harris. She suspended disbelief and spent more and more time with them.

From Pearl Harbor Zach Harris went directly on active duty without so much as a leave after his assignment for the Navy Department. He joined Admiral Nimitz' staff at CINCPAC, and was in the thick of planning naval support for the islands campaign. From his desk in London, Hobe Tenley had a unique view of the war. He reviewed the Department's top-secret cable traffic, earmarking the messages essential for Secretary Hull's daily briefing of the President. He could foresee a long, drawn-out war. Only daring action could reverse the grim news trickling out of the continent; news so dire it didn't need Goebbels' Propaganda Ministry's sneering embellishment. He wanted badly to get involved, and volunteered for a new action group to conduct clandestine military operations in advance of the allied re-conquest. The operations included espionage, sabotage and

# Jack Eddinger

special reconnaissance behind enemy lines, working with every type of group whether monarchist or communist.

At about the same time in Washington, Andy Burnham was commissioned a Lieutenant Colonel in Army intelligence and psychological warfare. He was posted to Room 31338 in the War Department's dilapidated World War I buildings lining Constitution Avenue between the Washington Monument and the Lincoln Memorial. One of the rooms on his floor housed an embryonic organization known only as the Office of Strategic Services. Reporting directly to the President, the unit was commanded by Colonel William Donovan, a hero of the World War. Veterans of the International Brigades formed the nucleus of the new organization. Because of his experience in Spain and his fluency in Russian and several Slavic languages, Andy Burnham was seconded to the secret group within weeks of its formation.

Marion began attending meetings of a group calling themselves United Federalists. In the beginning it consisted of several elderly ex-congressmen and their wives, two or three former missionaries to China, a group of middle-aged women with husbands serving overseas, two New Deal George Washington University professors and Andy and Elaine Burnham. Andy attended irregularly, but maintained a keen interest in their activities. He encouraged Marion to support the cause financially, which she did with enthusiasm.

With Elaine as her teacher, Marion also began to sketch and paint - something she had not done since her junior year at Bryn Mawr. She invited a group of Elaine's fellow artists to use the basement recreation room of Buchanan House as their Washington studio. With them, she began to explore the themes, images and abstractions of 20$^{th}$ Century painting. A new world of color without form was opening to her. Elaine invited her friend the art critic, Morris Hertzog, to review their work. Hertzog became more than a passive critic. He gave weekly lectures on non-objective art, tracing its roots in Cubism, Expressionism and Fauvism; discussing elements of form, color, line, tone and texture, and how the sub-conscious could be penetrated and made objective. They shared a deep interest in the irrational and fantastic; in abstraction that probed far beyond familiar and representational imagery. The surfaces of their canvasses, angles of light, qualities and textures of paint; the penetration of the deep subconscious actualized what Hertzog held to be the ultimate definition of their art, the "cool, non-referential ideal."

The new experience intensified Marion's emotional life. Painful familial memories emerged as she probed and explored the subconscious, bringing them to the surface where they could be objectified, interpreted

# INQUISITION

and healed. Exhilarated, released and thrust upon a new self-awareness sparked intense creativity in her. She felt the old inhibitions that had sealed her off in a loveless marriage fall away like scrapings from a palette knife. She was free to experience reality for herself and to forget her responsibilities to her marriage vows and an uncaring husband. Now she knew what Hobe had called that quiet place within, which one must return to again and again to drink as from a fresh running spring.

Hobe's letters came in swarms, stopped and started again. Zach wrote occasionally, usually complaining of the tropical heat, mosquitoes and routine of CINCPAC Headquarters. Without the diplomatic immunity of Hobe's letters which were untouched by the censors' black ink, Commander Harris's correspondence was black-lined like every other soldier's and sailor's stationed in or near a war zone.

Marion wrote to Hobe about her painting and how it was taking her deeper and deeper into the realm of the subconscious; how her newly-discovered medium was having a refreshing effect on her work and on her feeling, how she felt release and rebirth in spite of the gloomy war news and the drab routine and the hordes of regimented and unimaginative people descending upon wartime Washington. She told him she had crossed the river and would demand a divorce, even if she had to send the separation papers to her husband by air mail special delivery.

One night in late fall, while Marion was hosting a lecture to a group of new recruits to the one world cause in the library of Buchanan House, she was startled by the confusion of sound coming from the stately door chimes. The notes struggled to recognize an alien ring pattern - the insistent beeping of an ancient automobile horn. She left the group ran to the foyer with her heart pounding and threw open the heavy oak door to a smiling and slightly thinner and grayer Hobe Tenley.

"Oh my god," she gasped. "Hobe. Darling. I must be dreaming."

"Hello, you beautiful temptress. I've flown for two days and nights and would fly a thousand more to be with you," he smiled. They embraced in the doorway, holding each other tightly. "I've about used up the 72 hours the U.S. Army has vouchsafed me just to get here. I've got to be back at Mitchell Field and on a plane tomorrow night. We've no time to lose. He was removing his brown officer's tunic with gold leaves on each epaulet.

"Your arrival is a godsend, darling. I'm meeting with a group of very confused people. We were just discussing what will be needed to rebuild the world after the war, and how peace can be assured. They're bogged down on post-war organizations."

# Jack Eddinger

"The post-war world can wait, dammit. We've got a lot of catching up to do, Hanni, and only a few hours to spare."

"Well, you know law professors," she smiled. They're going into detail far beyond anyone's comprehension. Now's an opportune time to break it off. I'll tell them something urgent's come up and get rid of them. You can hide here in the hall closet."

"No. No. Wait. Let me help," he said. "Introduce me as a mystery guest just in from the battlefront and I'll give them some news to get their blood moving. A little real world experience ought to keep them in the movement for life. Besides, I'm too big for that closet." She straightened her hair, checked her makeup and smoothed out her skirt. Together they entered the library where the group was in deep discussion about how to assist Jewish refugees, and whether there was a moral issue to be raised publicly calling on President Roosevelt to release the ships to get them to the United States. She introduced them to Major Tenley of Army Intelligence, who she said would speak to them about the war in Europe. She made it sound as if Hobe's appearance had been in the works for weeks. Hobe described the situation in general terms, telling them an invasion would take place in the coming year. It would begin the long campaign to free Europe from Nazism. He did not tell them the invasion would be a small one and limited to North Africa, which he had a hard time justifying in his own mind. He spoke of the effort beyond fighting and winning the war - repatriation, rebuilding, civil government, de-Nazification - all the things that had to happen before the concept of a single world government could take hold.

His audience listened intently as he spoke forcefully, extemporaneously. "Major, I hope you run for president after the war," said an ancient ex-GOP congressman who'd once been a missionary in China. "I would be pleased to offer you my full support. Just the other day I was telling Mme. Chiang that we need young men of high moral character and vision to lead the country when this war is over - I trust you are a Republican, sir." Marion almost choked in suppressing a guffaw. She wondered what the man might say if he knew the truth about Hobe's and Andy Burnham's service in Spain.

"I'm not cut out for elective office," Hobe told his admirer. "The State Department's my bailiwick and I hope to return to it to help shape the post-war world along the lines of your discussions tonight."

A half hour later Marion Harris and Hobe Tenley were just beginning to relax into a long night of love-making. "Oh, my darling I've so much to tell you. I don't know where to begin. This is so sudden … so unexpected,

# INQUISITION

so wonderful. You're the most marvelous thing that's happened in my life … and the Burnhams are just delightful. They've given me so much."

"Didn't I tell you that? I knew you and they were a group, Hanni."

They made love, awoke then made love again. Never once did Zach's name come up, or the divorce. They enjoyed every caress, every movement, every level of love driven by their hunger for each other. Both knew this would be the last time they'd be together for a very long time. In 24-hours he would be flying eastward across the Atlantic. Beyond that, he could only conjecture. He casually mentioned that he'd volunteered for a new assignment, something he'd wanted ever since he'd seen what the Fascists did to an unarmed population in Spain. He was ready for it, he told her without detailing what the "it" would demand of him and where it would take him.

He did not tell her he would be transferred from a British submarine to a fishing dory ten miles out in the Gulf of Salerno. Fisherman from Minori would drop him on the Amalfi coast. He was to pinpoint parachute drops of radios, weapons and ammunition and get them to the Committee of National Liberation in Naples. She'd never know him as, Aldo, a slender mule driver who lived on a ridge above the mountain town of Ravello, where the Fascists had a radio transmitter directing air and naval activity in the Western Mediterranean. Disabling the transmitter and broadcasting phony information to the Italian Fleet would be Act One in the coming invasion of North Africa. His assignment in Southern Italy was the prelude to something far more dangerous.

Act Two brought Hobe and Andy Burnham together in the spring of 1943. The President wanted hard intelligence from the Balkans as to which of the opposition forces - the Chetniks or the Partisans - the United States should recognize and support with arms, equipment, food and medical supplies. Outwardly, FDR recognized the 18-year-old Yugoslav king, but was uneasy supporting a monarchy. He needed a candid assessment from American sources rather than having all of his decision-making filtered through the British Special Operations Executive (SOE). The Brits had been operating with both sides in the Balkans since the combined Nazi and Italian invasion of Croatia, Serbia, Bosnia and Montenegro.

Slavic-speaking operatives, Colonel Burnham and Major Tenley, carrying Swedish passports, parachuted into Montenegro. At the drop zone they were met by a British agent named Peter Randolph, a major in the SOE, and a young partisan named, Veljko.

Hobe, accompanied by a Chetnik officer, went south in a commandeered Italian army truck over the mountains to Serbia to the headquarters of

# Jack Eddinger

General Draza Mihjalovic. His guide wore a Fascist uniform. Hobe was attired as a Swedish businessman traveling through Serbia to Bulgaria for the international Red Cross.

Andy Burnham, Maj. Randolph and Veljko set off with a mixed group of Croats, Montenegrins and Slovenes armed with machine guns, mortars and rifles for Partisan headquarters in the mountains above Foca by mule caravan. Zigzagging around boulders sent down the mountain by winter avalanches, they plunged into deep almost impassable ravines cut by foaming green torrents thundering off the blinding white snow field above a tree line of fire-blackened spruces, their spikes and pinnacles forming an abstract tree line. They climbed endlessly. Looking back and down the long narrow valley carved by glaciers, they espied minarets and the red-tiled domes of mosques sticking up out of the fog rising off the Drina. At rest stops during the treacherous climb, Veljko conversed in Serbian with Andy Burnham. He had been a journalist in Zagreb before the invasion of the Balkans and was a novelist serving as propaganda officer with the Partisans. He was fascinated by Andy's stories of working in New York. Around their campfire after a day of particularly rugged climbing and short-circuiting squads of Mussolini's troops, they found time to discuss the philosophical and literary merits of Andre Malraux's novel of socialism, *Man's Fate* and George Orwell's and Arthur Koestler's reportage from Spain. Maj. Randolph fraternized minimally, spending daylight hours catching whatever sleep he could, and nights calibrating and testing the vital radio equipment being hauled by one of the mules, which kept them tied by an umbilical of electrons to SOE headquarters at Uxbridge Common outside London.

Peter Randolph reminded Andy of the sons of those English working class families who adopted leftish ideas at university in the period just before Neville Chamberlain became prime minister. His rimless eye glasses and thinning hair accented by a plunging widow's peak made him appear older than his age. He was tall, gangly and sardonic, and to Andy Burnham, at least, seemed more European than English. He had the vague feeling of having met him previously. His accent was not public school; Midlands perhaps or Scot. There were echoes of mid-Europe in his pronunciation, maybe Czech or Hungarian. Burnham could not quite put his finger on it and was surprised when Randolph explained that he grew up on the Isle of Man, whose original settlers were Celts from Central Europe. He'd been recruited by Scotland Yard out of Cambridge to infiltrate the IRA before the war. The major was a superior radio operator, and could find and hold a frequency for as long as required, as German army signals

# INQUISITION

experts tried to ascertain and triangulate migrant radio waves bouncing off the ionosphere.

Meanwhile, Hobe was gaining insights into Chetnik operations in Serbia. The Monarchist Army's approach to command, he observed, was precisely how not to fight a guerrilla war. The soldiers were eager, but were disorganized and poorly led by Mihjalovic. He radioed a caustic report to Andy Burnham via Major Randolph, quipping that with Mijailovic in command of Union forces at Gettysburg, Lee would have rolled to Washington and we'd all be talking like rebels. His assignment completed, Hobe and his Croat guide started out on a long and circuitous trek over the barren mountains of Macedonia and northern Greece to Kavala on the northern Aegean coast. There he was to be met by Greek fishermen to be taken across the Aegean Sea in a *kaikia* to Alexandria. From Egypt, he would fly back to London for debriefing at Uxbridge and reassignment to Washington.

In the mountains above Foca Andy Burnham and Maj. Randolph were escorted by Veljko to a camouflaged command post dug into a hillside. Partisan guards ordered them to surrender their side arms and ammunition belts, an unexpected and unpleasant move that made a tense situation menacing. Veljko, surmising their wariness, smiled and assured them their safety was personally guaranteed by the commander-in-chief of all Partisan forces.

They were led to a clean, austere and well-lighted dugout with a corrugated sheet iron door. It was burrowed into the mountain side behind the observation post and covered with fir branches. From behind a scarred and battered desk that looked as if it survived the Bolshevik Revolution, a powerfully-built man of about fifty with blond hair going gray approached in a manner that was intimidating in its absence of intimidation. Veljko quickly introduced them to the leader of the Partisans, whose only description in the outside world came from vague, mainly royalist, reports from Croatian and Serbian exiles. The muscular, ursine man with a flashing smile brightened by several gold teeth offered Andy a powerful paw hardened by life on the run. He wore an olive drab mountaineer's outfit - rough wool trousers, khaki shirt, green tie and wide green suspenders. A small gold star on the lapel was the only indication of rank. Andy could think only of the Norse god of war, but unlike Odin, the man standing before him was very much the stuff of humanity with piercing blue eyes and a sun-tanned complexion. His biceps and thighs looked as if they would burst through the seams of his homemade uniform. He was known to his followers only as, Tito, the old man, a *nom de guerre* befitting his

## Jack Eddinger

reputation as an original Bolshevik. He spoke no English. Veljko translated from Croatian to Serbian, which Burnham could follow.

"So comrades, Veljko tells me your President Roosevelt wants advice, eh?," the Partisan leader spoke forcefully, his blue almost violet eyes flashing a penetrating and cunning intelligence; the measured wariness of a man accustomed to being on the run, a fugitive from an aborted *coup d'etat*. But Andy Burnham also perceived a certain openness and courtesy countering the raw animal power of his physique.

"You tell him please this; Josip Broz sends greetings. Tell him he knows the United States will do the right thing to support the people of Yugoslavia. How do I know this? Tell him in Russia, before Stalin, I worked with Americans to build the tractor plant at Omsk. Two brothers - Victor and Walter - we became good friends. They showed how to set up the lines of assembly. They were good mechanics like me. We were three brothers in a few months, instead of two. We worked hard, drank vodka and had plenty of women. They told me when I come to Detroit, they will build me a motor car at Mr. Henry Ford's automobile plant and get me drunk. I loved those fellows ... I love Americans. You tell that to your President Roosevelt. After the war, I want the people of Yugoslavia to be friends of America. Give him that message. I want his help and support. I do not trust Mr. Churchill. He wants to return to the monarchy. But we want no more king. We want to govern ourselves. Now, Veljko take these comrades to the mess to enjoy the strongest Slivovitz and finest roast goat in Bosnia-Herzegovina."

After a grueling month among the Partisans, Col. Burnham and Maj. Randolph had learned enough about guerrilla heroism, deprivation and leadership to return with a strong recommendation to throw U.S. support behind Tito. With Veljko guiding them, they made their way back over the mountains to the coast to be picked up by a British submarine operating in the Adriatic near Ulcinj.

Back in Room 31338 near the Lincoln Memorial on a rainy windswept evening, Colonel Burnham and Major Randolph, were interviewed separately by OSS debriefers and told to prepare for an appearance at the White House at 9 a.m. the following morning to repeat their findings and recommendations for the president. From the East Portico of the White House at 8:30 a.m. sharp Andy Burnham was escorted by a marine guard with a .45 on one hip past the East Room and down a set of low stairs leading to a long, carpeted hallway to the Situation Room. He wondered what had become of Major Randolph.

# INQUISITION

Colonel Donovan, now a general, greeted him. "Welcome home Colonel Burnham. You are to be congratulated on the completion of a very, very tough assignment." Donovan, always a no-nonsense commander seemed even graver in his greeting. "The president asked me to extend you his deepest personal thanks and good wishes."

"But General, Major Randolph and I are to brief the president personally we were told," said Andy Burnham with more than a little disappointment in his voice.

"Yes, that was the intention, Colonel. The president, I'm afraid, cannot spare a moment today. But, as I said, he wants you to know how critical your mission was. He intends to follow your recommendations about Broz." The silver-haired investment banker looked every bit as dashing in civilian clothes as he did when he commanded New York's Sixty-Ninth Infantry Division, the fabled Fighting 69th as the press labeled it in 1918.

"Excellent, sir. Broz will not disappoint. He's a strong leader. When he gives his word, he keeps it."

"Your report certainly supports that fact. Now, regrettably I have some bad news to report," Donovan said maintaining unflinching eye contact.

"What's that, sir?" As Andy Burnham responded, his mind raced through scenarios ranging from death through sickness to injury of one of his many friends and colleagues in Washington.

"It always comes in pairs, I'm afraid, Colonel. I'm sorry to inform you that we lost Major Tenley. I know you two were close."

"Damn! Damn! Damn!" were the only words Andy Burnham could utter.

"He was betrayed by one of Mihjalovic's lieutenants, a Croat. The sonofabitch was working with the SS, as best we can tell. We got it from one of our plants, a Hungarian woman, who was seeing the SS leader in Skopje. Hobe was a true hero. He acted with great courage and honor, sticking to his story to the end we were advised." Donovan said he was recommending Hobe for several posthumous medals for his exploits in Italy as well as Serbia. His actions and the intelligence he produced in Italy, the general said, were invaluable to the success of the invasion of North Africa. Andy Burnham breathed heavily throttling back anguish rising from deep within. "Poor Hobe, poor bastard," he choked. "I got him involved in this thing."

Donovan led Andy Burnham to a small office the president frequently used to rest after long and intense war room briefings. There he recounted the story of Hobe Tenley's last days. Hobe's guide was a member of the Ustashe, Croatian collaborators with the Nazis. He turned Hobe over to the SS in Skopje for $1,000 in gold coins," Donovan explained grimly.

# Jack Eddinger

"The SS executioners tortured him in the basement of a bombed out Serbian Orthodox church before putting a .9 mm bullet in his brain. He gave them no information, insisting he was a Swedish businessman on his way to Sofia. The German propaganda machine broadcast the death of a British spy named H. Livingston. OSS headquarters at Uxbridge knew otherwise.

"We're all brothers in this thing, Andy," Wild Bill Donovan, the consoler, said putting a sympathetic hand on Burnham's shoulder.

"What's the rest of the bad news?" Andy asked. "You said it came in twos."

"Bad news for the enemy, Colonel." Donovan said sharply, divesting himself quickly of any semblance of priestly or humane ministrations. Your companion, Major Randolph has exchanged his life for Hobe's."

"What? What in God's name do you mean?"

Donovan described the special executive action, which took place in a suite at the Hotel Bellevue on E St. the previous evening. Randolph, he was shocked to learn, was an NKVD double agent sent by Moscow to assess Tito's strength.

"He had orders directly from Stalin to let you make your report to the President, because the Soviets needed Tito to keep the Wehrmacht tied down in the Balkans as the Red Army battled von Manstein's panzers at Kursk," Donovan told him. "Your presence frustrated any chance of this. His orders were to liquidate you at the first opportunity after you briefed the president. We terminated him instead. Made it look like suicide. Veljko works for us via Uxbridge."

Suddenly, Andy Burnham remembered Randolph. But in Spain, he was a younger and heavier Russian adviser serving with the Loyalist brigades on the Ebro.

War news dominated the front pages of Washington's dailies. News, features and wire stories accompanied by photos and maps from the various theaters of global war pushed all other news to the inside pages. Local stories that would have made front page news, such as a police report of a shooting death - an apparent suicide - of a middle-aged man in a hotel room near Union Station, were relegated to a line or two in roundup stories in the back pages. The military draft assured that there'd be few reporters to cover local news, so the police blotter was reproduced verbatim, set in agate type and buried in the back pages. Old school city editors at *The Evening Star, The Post, The Daily News* and *The Times-Herald* would never consider assigning a female reporter to crime coverage. That's precisely the way the men involved wanted it. Gen. Donovan told Col. Burnham he was sworn to secrecy on both counts under the new National

# INQUISITION

Security Act passed unanimously by Congress to protect American secrets and clandestine personnel.

Reclining on a divan in a blue pastel lounging robe, Anna Daley was reading the *Post* that Saturday morning in the bright sunlight filtering through the solarium at Buchanan House. She and Tommy, now 14, were spending the weekend as they had so many times since her husband's sad death a few years before. She regarded herself not just as Marion's closest friend, companion and confidante but as her female soul-mate; someone who thought, cared and felt the same way. When she was at home in Bessemer City, they spoke almost every day by long distance in spite of the wartime limitations on telephone lines. Anna and the boy drove to Washington at least once a month, staying at Buchanan House for days at a time, particularly when Marion was alone in the big house in Kalorama Circle. Anna participated in the art classes, avoiding the premises and forms of modern art the women were exploring, but relying on her own superb sketching and drawing skills with water colors. She worked mostly in pastels, concentrating on sunny land, sky and seascapes. Tommy was a precocious young man. On every trip to Washington he would head down to the Smithsonian or across the Mall to the Museum of Natural History. But most of the time he could be seen wandering the halls of the Capitol. The House Doorkeeper let him sit in the family members' section of the balcony above the House floor. The FBI's crime laboratory also fascinated him. He became a kind of mascot and occasional errand boy to the men running the lab, who knew his "uncle" was an important member of Congress. At the Department of Justice, he began noticing the comings and goings of the stately and proper Francis Biddle, the Attorney General. He watched intently as Biddle emerged from the chauffeured black sedan. He even managed to sneak into the Attorney General's press conferences. Combined, these experiences intensified his interest in the national government, and inspired a serious attraction for law enforcement. Tommy Daley knew that one day he'd be riding in a black sedan and holding press conferences. He vowed that he would be U. S. Senator from Pennsylvania.

For Marion Harris their companionship was no intrusion. She was completely relaxed in Anna's presence. Moreover, Anna was an agreeable and undemanding relief from Elaine Burnham's intensity, however inspirational and imaginative. Marion had confided in her about her love affair and how her thoughts of Hobe Tenley were seldom out of mind, something she could never confide to Elaine. She told of their intimacy, and her plan to divorce Zach and marry Hobe, on his next leave. Anna kept Marion's secrets and encouraged the divorce with no reservations believing it long overdue.

"Ohh, my God!" Anna gasped. " No. There's some mistake. It can't be." She clambered up two flights of stairs and went straight to Marion's bedroom. Marion Harris was sitting at a boudoir table putting the finishing touches on her makeup and listening to the war news on the radio, when Anna Daley, her face twisted and ashen, appeared in the doorway.

"Oh, Marion. Oh, my God. Oh dear Lord."

The name appeared in agate type on the daily list of war casualties - the killed, wounded and missing on an inside page of the *Washington Post*. Officers surnames appeared in capital letters.

**TENLEY, Livingston, Hobart. Maj., U.S. Army 060363442, KIA**

The sudden irreversible reality of Hobe's death boiled up from the deep recesses of Marion's being in a prolonged anguished cry from the heart, as if she were a doe standing at the edge of a clearing watching her offspring being consumed in a holocaust. It plunged her into prolonged despair. Her grief overwhelmed her formidable self-control and paralyzed her capacity for the artistic expression that had re-defined her existence. All was lost. All joy; all tenderness; all spontaneity; all intimacy. It was as if her soul had been ripped from her, rendering her incapable of emotion. Not her father's death, nor her brother's, nor her best friend's husband's evoked the same isolation and pain. She could do nothing to reverse it.

The U. S. government's official recognition of Hobe Tenley's death was a brief, private memorial service at the Department of State for Foreign Service officers killed in the line of duty. She did not attend. National security saw to it that there would be no obituary, no news story, no announcement of any kind. In the ensuing days and months of her grief, she began feeling angry, bitter and betrayed further isolating her from her friends. Even religion's ordinary rites of exorcism and catharsis were denied her by her own despairing disbelief. She felt cut off from existence, adrift in a black, suffocating vacuum. In spite of the constant presence and attentiveness of her two dearest friends, Anna Daley and Elaine Burnham, a void opened within her; a void bereft of all thought, of all feeling, of all human emotion. She no longer wished to live. Only the soothing capacity of alcohol seemed to deaden the pain and to diminish her anguish. A profound depression settled upon her bringing disaffection and anomie.

# INQUISITION

Captain Zachary Taylor Harris had a politician's distaste for diplomats, particularly for diplomats in uniform. He was clearly puzzled when the State Department's liaison officer to CINCPAC, Lt. j.g. Walter Powers, USNR, called to request an appointment. With the Coral Sea, Guadalcanal, Midway and Rabual campaigns firmly enshrined in its annals of heroic exploits at sea, the U.S. Navy had turned its strategic and logistic wizards led by officers like Zach Harris loose on assembling the ships, men and materiel to support the liberation of the Philippines.

Lt. Powers was announced by a yeoman over the intercom, as Capt. Harris sat at a large metal desk preparing to dig into the pile of manila personnel folders, logistics and ordnance reports and loading schedules. The liaison officer from State saluted his senior officer. Reaching for the coffee pot on the edge of the desk, Harris remained seated and returned the salute sideways. He was feeling good after just being handed the ultimate compliment by Adm. Halsey following his briefing for Task Force commanders. Halsey called it the congressman's, "State of the Fleet Address," which, he said, might serve as inspiration for a post-war speech Harris might one day deliver to a joint session of Congress. Zach smiled and cleared his throat as the tough old admiral perched on a leather deck chair listened intently to the presentation.

"At ease, Lieutenant. Join me? How do you like it?"

"No thanks, sir, had more than my daily fix over at the BOQ. Quarters here are pretty Spartan, I must say, sir."

"Yeah, well. I guess they don't quite measure up to the officers' mess at State, eh? I understand you've taken over the Mayflower back in Washington. What's on your mind Lieutenant? Just let me warn you in advance that I hope this is fleet business, because Bull Halsey's an extremely impatient man, whose time frame doesn't recognize the 24-hour day. Please state your business. I've no time to waste."

"Yes sir, Congress … I mean captain. I'll be as brief as I can be. This is an extremely sensitive subject, sir, that's why Secretary Hull sent me out here to brief you personally. He thought you would want to know about it immediately. It concerns Mrs. Harris …"

"Mrs. Harris! You mean to tell me you came all the way out here to bring me a message from my wife. I can't believe this. Don't you know we're at war, son?"

"Well, it's not quite that simple, sir. We're well aware of the extraordinary work you've been doing. It's just that …"

"C'mon, lieutenant. What's this important information that brought you 5,000 miles to relate to me personally? Oh I get it, this thing she has about getting me transferred back to Washington. Don't tell me you have special orders to that effect, Lieutenant? You know I haven't seen her in nearly a year, and I'll bet she's gone to the top to arrange it. It would be just like her to have Cordell Hull intervene directly. She's a personal friend of the Secretary, you know? I can't say that I wouldn't mind some stateside service, but we've got too much going out here. Nimitz will countermand orders to that effect. Sorry Lieutenant."

"Sir, I received Admiral Nimitz's permission to speak with you. I realize this is a very delicate matter but we have reason to believe Mrs. Harris has put herself in a position which may have compromised state and military secrets."

"What?," he said with a laugh that was half sarcasm, half amusement. "What do you mean 'may have compromised secrets'? Why that's absolute nonsense. Rubbish. Marion compromising military secrets? Whatever the hell they served up at the BOQ this morning must be damned intoxicating. Have them send over a case. Why Marion wouldn't know a battleship from an aircraft carrier. Besides all of my correspondence with her has been through the censors. This is preposterous."

"This has nothing directly to do with you or your correspondence, sir. You see, we have hard evidence that your wife ... that Mrs. Harris, had been indiscreet in a relationship with one of our most important clandestine operatives in the European Theater ... and that state and military secrets may have been compromised. Not willingly perhaps, but certain things have been exchanged between them which could put imminent military campaigns in jeopardy. Moreover, we have reason to believe that several of her associates in an organization she supports are suspected enemy agents."

"Wait ... wait just a minute. Just what do you mean by 'indiscreet in a relationship,' Lieutenant?"

"Well sir, I'm afraid I can't put it with more sensitivity ... an extramarital affair, sir. Suffice it to say our evidence is ironclad, sir."

"That's arrant nonsense, Powers. I don't care what your so-called evidence is, but I do know this, you have insulted a senior officer and I will personally see that you are severely disciplined. You go back and tell your boss, Mr. Hull, that if he does not desist, I will go directly to his boss." He flipped the intercom switch. "Better still, Yeoman, put me through to Washington to Mr. Cordell Hull at the Department of State. I don't care what time it is there, get him on the phone! Whose your commanding officer, Powers?"

"I report to the Secretary Captain Harris, and as you know, he reports directly to the Commander in Chief."

# INQUISITION

"This is an outrage. It's a slander which I cannot let stand. Even if it were true, why would she do it? She knows full well that any such conduct would destroy both of us. She knows that. What's this so-called hard evidence you have, Lieutenant?"

"Well, sir we have letters that have been exchanged. The man in question had long been using the diplomatic pouch to bypass Army censors. Unfortunately, he was killed in action. One of his last missives ended up in a security officer's "eyes only" material. He was immediately suspicious of personal correspondence routed through diplomatic mail channels. A request for permission to examine the contents went all the way up to the Secretary. I have to tell you, Captain Harris, Mr. Hull was flabbergasted. He hesitantly approved monitoring the situation after discussing it with the Commander in Chief. The President very reluctantly approved only after an investigation by both Army and Navy counter-intelligence."

Stunned and speechless Zachary Taylor Harris felt as if he were engulfed in the shock wave from a salvo off the battleship Missouri.

A Navy motorcycle courier delivered the cablegram to Buchanan House in the late afternoon. "High Priority telex for Mrs. Marion Harris, please sign right here, he said, handing a clipboard with the yellow envelope stamped, "U.S. Navy Official Business" in black letters to Anna Daley. Through the cellophane address window, she could partially read the sender's address, "CINCPAC, Honolulu." For a blinding instant the official disclosure of Congressman Harris's death in action flashed through her mind. The potential irony of it sent a shiver through her .

Two weeks earlier Anna Daley had rushed to Washington after an anguished phone call from Hattie Brown, the Harris's housekeeper, with the news that Mrs. Harris had been taken to the hospital that morning after swallowing a bottle of sleeping pills. Marion had survived the initial crisis, but was unconscious and confined to a room at Columbia Women's Hospital in guarded condition when Anna arrived. She stayed with her friend as Marion moved in and out of consciousness. When the initial crisis had passed Anna was confronted with a medical decision that no one else could make. The emergency staff had recommended that Marion be transferred to St. Elizabeth's for further evaluation and treatment. Marion's condition remained critical with the diagnosis inconclusive. A few days after Marion was transferred to St. Elizabeth's, the District of Columbia's principal mental institution, Anna was contacted by Elaine Burnham, who after hearing of Marion's hospitalization, suggested that she could arrange for Marion to be seen at the Johns Hopkins Hospital's Phipps Clinic by the chief of psychiatry, Dr. Adolph Meyer, a friend of her mentor, Hertzog.

# Jack Eddinger

On a cold, overcast winter day which duplicated their common mood, Anna and Elaine drove Marion to Baltimore. Anna had taken over all of Marion's affairs, including the responsibility for signing the papers to have her friend admitted to the psychiatric facility, which while perhaps one of the world's great centers of healing, remained a hospital for the mentally ill. The Hopkins physicians, who examined her, assured Anna and Elaine that Marion's condition was not uncommon in cases of severe stress, particularly in wartime with little or no family support structures. The therapeutic program they prescribed would require a full regimen of psychotherapy and treatment accompanied by several months' residency at the Hopkins supervised by Dr. Meyer.

Anna's anguish for her friend ran deep. She thought about Marion's spiritual calamity, as she opened the cablegram. It read:

**ARRIVE WASHINGTON DAY AFTER TOMORROW STOP MUCH TO DISCUSS STOP. - Z.T. HARRIS, CAPT., USN**

"Good God," she said. "What a time for this." The brusque message left her with a feeling of hard indifference.

Zach Harris had flown for nearly 36 hours; first from Hawaii to San Francisco aboard an Army Air Corps B-17, then a long cross country flight on a commercial DC-3, taken over by the military, which stopped at Denver, Chicago and Pittsburgh to refuel before arriving in Washington. Zach Harris arrived at Buchanan House in an official sedan the State Department sent to National Airport.

"Why wasn't I informed of her condition, Anna?" Zach Harris demanded even before removing his overcoat. The suntan he had gained from months in the South Pacific made him appear fit and somewhat younger. It did nothing to conceal the old arrogance and self-importance that Anna despised in her friend's husband. "Why am I the last to know anything? When can I see her?"

Anna Daley responded with studied coolness. She told him that she had nothing to impart as to the cause of his wife's mental breakdown, only that Marion had been depressed for some time, and her condition had worsened in recent weeks. She told him Marion had been feeling despondent and lonely and had no one with whom to share her feelings. Anna told him about the phone call from their housekeeper, and how Hattie and James, the handyman and driver, called the police who contacted the DC ambulance service.

"You can thank their quick thinking for saving Marion's life. I got down here as soon as I received the news," Anna explained. "I approved her

# INQUISITION

transfer to St. Elizabeth's for observation and tests following emergency treatment for a drug overdose. She'd been taking sleeping pills for years, or didn't you know that either? She lapsed in and out of consciousness, and when she was conscious wavered between anxiety and submissiveness. I was upset and very concerned that she would not receive the best possible care in a place like St. Elizabeth's. I took it upon myself to have her seen by Dr. Meyer at Johns Hopkins. He's the world's most eminent authority on depression and mental illness, you know. I signed the admission papers, knowing that you would want me to. She is now under Dr. Meyer's direct care, but is still in a state of confusion and depression." Anna Daley did not speculate about causes. She was not about to reveal the reason for her dearest friend's breakdown.

"This is all very strange, Anna," said Zachary Taylor Harris somewhat subdued. "I've been informed of an accusation of infidelity … that this situation has arisen from some form of relationship she established with another man while I was away; that it involved some sort of affair. Is this true, Anna? Have you two colluded to keep me in the dark about this?"

"That is a completely callous remark and totally uncalled for," Anna said with rising indignity. "You have no idea of Marion's distress, because you never cared a whit about her. I know nothing of such accusations. You should be ashamed of yourself at a time when your wife is going through mental torture to the point of complete breakdown. You are a self-centered, disingenuous and selfish man, Zach Harris, and I do not care to honor your remarks with a response." Anna Daley's contempt had been simmering below the surface of her outwardly cool demeanor towards him for decades. She always believed, but could not prove, that Zachary Taylor Harris had something to do with her husband's suicide. Now, the break was complete. She felt relieved and justified.

The next morning the battleship gray U.S. Navy Plymouth sedan stripped of its chrome and familiar three-ship hood ornament, pulled into the circular driveway at the Johns Hopkins Hospital. Zach Harris was met by a hospital official, who escorted him through the main door into a dark lobby. He was taken somewhat aback to see in the wellspring of the behavioral sciences, Thorvaldsen's immense statue of *Christ the Consoler* in white marble, arms outstretched, looking down upon him. The official took him through several corridors to the Phipps Psychiatric Clinic and to the office of Dr. Adolph Meyer. It was Meyer who had treated Zelda Fitzgerald for a combination of stress-related psychiatric ills compounded by alcohol abuse.

"Please sit down, Congressman Harris. It is a pleasure to finally meet you. May I offer you a smoke." Adolph Meyer MD, the dean of American

## Jack Eddinger

psychiatry, held a box of small fat cigars out to Zach Harris. Now retired from his longtime position as chairman of the department of psychiatry at Hopkins, Adolph Meyer looked like a Zurich banker rather than the world's foremost psychiatrist. Instead of the standard white lab coat, he was dressed in a dark suit, bright red tie and vest with a gold watch chain stretching across a slight paunch. His short grey beard, trimmed in the manner of an Austro-Hungarian archduke, full mustache and dark eyes conjured up the disagreeable image of Sigmund Freud to Zach Harris.

"No thanks, but I'm sure you won't mind my having a cigarette." He produced a pack of Camels, tapped one on his navy Zippo lighter, lighted it and inhaled deeply, as the old man puffed the corona to life.

"You know Congressman," Meyer said with a slight trace of a Viennese accent and a twinkle in his eyes, "I once had a great interest in American politics. Does the name Giuseppe Zangara evoke any memories for you?"

"Sounds vaguely familiar. Sacco-Vanzetti case?" Zach Harris guessed. He spoke guardedly, trying to figure out why he was being confronted with an Italian surname in a famous hospital. An image of the New York hotel room flared like a shooting star across his mind for a nanosecond then burnt out.

"One of your patients, perhaps?"

"In a manner of speaking, you might say," Meyer said suppressing a chuckle. "I won't mystify you further. Mr. Zangara was the gunman who fired on President Roosevelt, but instead killed the mayor of Chicago. Now you remember, no?"

"Sure, sure, Mayor Cermak. Tony Cermak. It happened down in Miami. FDR was making a speech in an open car, and the mayor happened to be standing between the gunman and the president. Before he died, his last words to Roosevelt were, 'I'm glad it was me instead of you'."

"I was brought in to examine the brain of Mr. Zangara at autopsy to determine if there was a relationship between his brain type and the homicide. *Nein*, nothing, zed, but that was the way forensic pathology was practiced by some in the field. We've advanced far beyond this method of investigation. Today we rely upon a deep understanding of the whole person; we look at family background, external environment, character; we employ the richness of the biographer's art rather than the scalpel in attempting to assemble a complete picture."

"That's very interesting, doctor, but what about Mrs. Harris? I'm certainly here to do everything I can to assist you in your diagnosis, but I want to see her immediately." A hardship discharge was unthinkable. He'd lose out on the climax of the war.

# INQUISITION

"Your wife is a very depressed woman," Meyer began. "It is going to take a great deal of care to restore her mental balance. There is no doubt in my mind that she will recover from this episode. However, it is going to take time and patience and in-depth treatment. I take it that your time is severely restricted, yes?"

"That's right, doctor. Unfortunately, I've only a few days for this. I'm on a week's emergency leave, and must return to my command just as soon as we've made some decisions about her case. I'll make all the necessary arrangements for her care when she leaves here. Our daughter is unattached and can certainly help with her care. Now, when can I see her?"

"I would first like to prepare you for your visit with her. Our provisional diagnosis is acute dysthemia. In layman's terms, it is a condition not uncommon in individuals experiencing extreme depression. Your wife remains at the acute stage of anxiety-depression, Congressman Harris. In this state she remains exceptionally vulnerable to outside stimuli and must be carefully prepared before she can interact with others. Family visits must be carefully planned so as to maintain the equilibrium brought about by the course of therapy she is undergoing. We must take exceptional care so as not to trigger a more profound depression. I realize that what I have just said may be a substantial obstacle given your military responsibilities, but I am confident that Mrs. Harris will make a full recovery. It is going to take time, however. Can you give me any specific insights into your wife's background that may help us in her treatment? Has there been any recent trauma - a death in the family, a serious disappointment, a terminal illness - anything - that might help to explain what might have precipitated the onset of her depression? I realize that this may seem an impertinence, or in the least an indelicate question, but has she had prior difficulty with alcohol?"

"Absolutely not," Zach Harris responded indignantly. "Mrs. Harris is an accomplished woman of high intelligence and grace. She is widely known and admired in Washington as a hostess of impeccable taste and gentility. She has never. I repeat, never, used alcohol in excess. Like everyone else, she engages in social drinking, but is too much the lady to take it to excess. I resent the insinuation."

"I was insinuating nothing. I believe it only wise that you be given some insight into your wife's condition. Mrs. Harris is a very sick woman, sir. We have begun intensive psychotherapy, and it is unwise to break the spell, if you understand what I mean. I cannot emphasize strongly enough that she must be approached with consummate sympathy and understanding. "Please, now come with me."

# Jack Eddinger

Marion Harris was sitting alone in a corner of a large, windowless but well-lighted room, which seemed to shrink her to a minor presence. She wore a white hospital gown, in which she appeared pale and withdrawn. Her brown hair, always neatly coifed, showed streaks of grey and hung limply almost to her shoulders. Her face was puffy; her eyes glazed and focused on a non-existent object across the room. Zach Harris could not believe the change that had taken place since he last saw his wife. He knew instantly that Marion was adrift and beyond ordinary communication.

"Marion, my dear. It's me, Zach. Everything's going to be all right now. I've come all the way from the Pacific to see that you get better," he said, trying to summon compassion and understanding which seemed beyond his psychic reach. He took her hand and looked into her eyes. She gazed at her husband with a puzzled, quizzical look; a frightened and defenseless animal caught in the headlights of an onrushing vehicle. "Oh officer. Have I done something wrong? Did I have too much to drink at Andy and Elaine's last night? I don't remember ... Are you here to arrest me? I must call my husband. He's a congressman, you know. He'll explain everything." Dr. Meyer and a nurse entered quietly.

"Hello, Mrs. Harris. How are you today?" the nurse said with the faux geniality medical personnel affect with defenseless patients. "Are you ready for your chat with Dr. Meyer? He's right here, and wants to take you to the garden with him to enjoy the sunshine. It's a beautiful day and the flowers are beginning to bloom."

"You must ask this nice policeman," she said with a vacant expression. "He wants to arrest me, but I told him my husband is a powerful man and will report him to President Roosevelt."

"May we walk out to the garden together officer?" the nurse said to Zach Harris. He held his white officer's hat with gold braid on the visor under one arm. "Her treatment program," she said in a low voice, nodding towards the doorway. She took Marion's arm in hers and walked slowly with Zach Harris and the psychiatrist behind them. She guided Marion to a small garden filled with green plants. A fountain bubbled into a small, rock-rimmed pond. Goldfish darted under pink and yellow water lilies.

"It is imperative that the session be conducted between the physician and patient alone, Congressman Harris," Meyer said. "Therefore, I must ask you to remain in the waiting room. I will let you know when the session is concluded."

"What are your expectations, doctor? How long will this process take? What if she does not respond to this approach? What is your back-up plan? Zachary Taylor Harris pressed the psychiatrist. "Let me tell you here

# INQUISITION

and now, there will be no surgery, period. This new lobotomy business is barbaric. There will be none of that."

"That is not a consideration, sir." Meyer replied. "However, we have had success with mild electro-shock therapy and I would not want to rule out such a procedure. True, there may be some memory loss, but it would be a mild effect over the long term of her illness. The prognosis is for full recovery."

"Memory loss? Mild effect?"

"Yes. However, patients undergoing this therapy tend to lose only those memories associated with the immediate onset of the anxiety-depression or the precipitating event. In laymen's terms, the causal circumstances. Should this obtain in your wife's case, I believe it a small price to pay for her recovery. There is no question in my mind that she will return to a normal, healthy mental state. The obliteration of any such memories, however important and personal to both of you, would be central to full recovery. I expect her to return to a normal life."

"Well, I appreciate your frankness, doctor. You have my approval to proceed."

On his return to San Francisco, Zach was reassigned as a staff logistics expert at Yerba Buena naval base, a job he despised. A phone call to the new Secretary of State Edward Stettinius, whom he had known from the Secretary's days as chairman of U.S. Steel, landed him a staff position with the American delegation to the United Nations Conference convening in San Francisco in the spring of 1945. In the intervening period, Dr. Meyer reported to him twice a month about Marion's progress. He read the reports thoroughly, made notes and placed them in a file marked "Marion's Illness." The psychiatrist described the warm relationship being reestablished between Marion and their daughter, Pamela, who had left college in mid-semester to join her mother in Washington. Marion had progressed significantly by late spring of 1945. Her doctors suggested a change of place for the next phase of treatment. Mother and daughter journeyed across the country by train for a stay at a new treatment center near Santa Fe, which employed alternative approaches to mental and psychic dislocation, including ancient Asanazi healing practices being investigated by psychiatric researchers.

Andy and Elaine Burnham arranged artistic sessions and conversations for Marion and Pam at the nearby Ghost Ranch studio of their old friend from the Twenties, Georgia O'Keeffe. Elaine knew the artist and her husband, Alfred Steiglitz, from their days at the *Intimate* and *American Place* galleries in Manhattan. Under Miss O'Keeffe's instruction Pamela was becoming an emerging artist in her own right. Her mother reveled

## Jack Eddinger

in Pamela's success, and found new sources for exploration in Miss O'Keeffe's desert-light and sun-baked forms, but more deeply in the artist's unique and imaginative forays into the nature and essence of the American southwest.

Zach visited once, driving across the desert from the Bay Area. He complained of the heat and what, he mused, was Miss O'Keeffe's, "weird and decadent work, which some people call art." Shaking his head, he took particular offense with the themes of Eros and death embodied in her work.

At the end of a year and a half Marion had recovered nearly all of her mental capabilities. Her short term memory loss, however, proved resistant to amelioration. She could not remember anything from the immediate past. Their sojourn in the desert complete, Marion and Pam boarded a train for Los Angeles then the *West Coast Limited* to San Francisco to attend the opening Conference of the United Nations Organization at the invitation of Secretary of State and Mrs. Stettinius. Marion and Kathryn Stettinius had been classmates at Bryn Mawr and passionate devotees of the Wilsonian vision that was now finally to be fulfilled after nearly a quarter century. Pam and Marion were put up in a suite at the Mark Hopkins, courtesy of the Secretary. Zach groused. He was quartered at the Presidio with military personnel attending the conference as advisers to the U.S. delegation.

Tinged in rose, violet and gold, the normally fog-wrapped city glowed in the morning sunlight. Angular shadows spread across rectilinear buildings climbing the terraced volcanic hills above the turquoise bay, summoning images of Matisse and the Grande Corniche. On Union Square across from the St. Francis Hotel, news stands were plastered with front page photos from the *Chronicle* and *Examiner* of the men and events making news at the Opera House a few blocks away. Black paint peeled from the second and third floor windows of stores and office buildings flanking the square, a reminder that Japanese aircraft had once threatened the city.

"Mother's making a wonderful recovery, Dad." Pam Harris confided to her father across breakfast in the Mark Hopkins dining room. Marion usually slept until noon, using eye shades and drawn curtains to seal out the dazzling white light of a San Francisco morning. Except for the brief sojourn in the desert, Zachary Taylor Harris had not spent serious time with his daughter for over four years. He was startled at her beauty and poise. She reminded him of himself as a young man twenty five years before. Her grey eyes exuded a certain capacity for mischief, and her blonde pageboy hair style, dark eyebrows and peachy complexion lit up her face. The eyes of every man in the room were transfixed, as she spoke animatedly. Zachary Taylor Harris, aware of the attention his daughter

# INQUISITION

was attracting, glowed with pride. "We've been invited to the Secretary's reception tonight, Dad. I hope you are coming."

"I'm afraid that's a tough one, my dear, I will present my study on the decommissioning of the Japanese fleet - what's left of it - to the military affairs council tomorrow, so I'll be up late putting the finishing touches to it. I'm still on active duty, you know. But I want you and your mother to have a good time. Heaven knows, she's earned it. Be sure to give the Secretary and Mrs. S. my very best regards. Now, tell me about all the young men you've been seeing. I'm envious of 'em all."

The Secretary of State's reception that evening in the penthouse suite of the Mark Hopkins was a gathering of nations. Military attaches from 50 nations, resplendent in polished brass and fringed epaulets, even a few sporting ceremonial sabers moved about stiffly in a sea of robes, turbans and a fez or two accented by colors hitherto unseen away from their habitat by diplomats in western-style business dress. Marion and Pam Harris, looking like sisters in matching sapphire off-the-shoulder gowns and upswept hairstyles, circulated in the room after being introduced to the Secretary by Mrs. Stettinius, then to Foreign Minister V.S. Molotov and Ambassador and Mrs. Gromyko of the Soviet Union, and Lord and Lady Cadogan of the United Kingdom. Except for an inability to put names on faces of people she should know, Marion felt buoyant for the first time since the onset of her depression. Kathryn Stettinius with Marion and Beth in tow, moved around the room introducing them to the leaders and delegates representing the nations at war with the Axis, and to the staff the Secretary brought with him from Washington.

A bearded man in his mid-fifties wearing a black eye patch, smiled broadly as he approached. "Well hello, Hanni, so good to see you looking so well. It's been a long time." The voice sounded vaguely familiar, but she could not summon a name from her memory bank. Even though his black eye patch appeared vaguely menacing to Marion Harris, the man was warm and sincere, sounding as though he meant every word of greeting. But she was more puzzled by the strange name he used in greeting her."

"I'm afraid I must remind you of someone," she told him. "I'm Marion Harris and this is my daughter, Pamela. Have we met?" She felt terribly uncomfortable as the stranger's eye patch left one piercing brown eye focused intently upon her. The minute the words left his lips, Deputy Assistant Secretary of State Andrew Burnham knew instantly that he had confused her. "I beg your pardon, Mrs. Harris, I thought you were someone I hadn't seen in several years." He took exceptional care not to open a door that had been tightly sealed. He nodded slightly then moved towards a knot of Americans standing near the bar. Marion was perplexed, as she moved through the crowded room. She felt slightly disturbed, even annoyed that a stranger would approach her in this manner. And that silly name; where did it come from? Strange. Later that evening, the Secretary of State took Marion aside. He told her that the country would be honored if she would accept an appointment to one of the new organizations that would be formed by the United Nations to relieve the problems of hunger and poverty in the post-war world. It would not be an honorific position, he said, but one that would require significant work and travel. He asked if she felt up to the job. Without hesitation, she accepted.

"That's quite a story," John Maggio said, as Joe O'Neill finished his portentous tale. _____

"But let me ask you this, why did she stay with him?" It was late afternoon. The O'Neill's house man arrived to take orders for drinks. Joe O'Neill had a gin rickey, John Maggio a rye highball and Frank Comstock, scotch and soda.

"Ambition is a powerful opiate, John. In a few months Marion was spending much of her time at Lake Success on Long Island. She still battled valiantly against depression and alcohol. Zach returned to his seat in the House. They went their separate ways, but both realized they needed each other, if only for cover," O'Neill said.

"Well, I'd like to see that S.O.B. get what's coming to him. I'll take the assignment." Maggio responded.

"Good. Come down to the office Monday morning and we'll get things moving."

# CHAPTER TEN
## *Philadelphia, 1957*

A Department of Justice manila envelope stamped, "Hand Deliver To Addressee" arrived on Zachary Taylor Harris's desk within a week of his meeting with the Director. It contained a type-written memorandum headed, *Re. Mills Andrew Burnham, Ph.D.*, along with copies of personnel and military records, photographs, newspaper clippings, wire service copy, magazine articles and editorial cartoons. It read:

> "Reference is made to the above-captioned individual. A search of Bureau files indicates that subject had been under surveillance periodically as possible Comintern agent and associate of Igor Fitkin, aka J. Peters, a Soviet agent found dead under suspicious circumstances in room at the Bellevue Hotel, 450 E. St. N.W., Washington, D.C. on or about June 30, 1943.
>
> A highly confidential informant of complete reliability associated with the American representative to the Comintern reported in March 1937 that subject Burnham entered Spain under the cover of journalist accredited to left-wing Intercontinental News Service (INS), to covertly act as liaison to Trotskyite elements in Barcelona.
>
> Informant notes that Fitkin-Peters was double agent with the rank of colonel of GRU, later NKVD. Known to be in Spain with INS at same time as subject, Burnham. Served in Balkans (1943) under alias, Maj. P. Randolph, British Special Operations Executive (SOE). Informant attests that subject Burnham also suspected of being Comintern double agent. While surveillance of subject continued during 1938-40, a gap exists due to subsequent military service in Balkans with the Donovan organization. No useful evidence yet exists tying subject to Fitkin-Peters (aka Randolph) death or to <u>visible</u> Comintern activities in U.S. However, Bureau continues believe subject Burnham has long been Soviet sleeper agent in position to exert a pernicious influence on U.S. foreign policy.

The Bureau concluded from its intercepts of Comintern radio traffic that Burnham and Randolph initiated their conspiracy in Spain.

After reading the material, Chairman Harris stamped it "Eyes Only" and had the package delivered to committee counsel Robert Sterling with the handwritten note: "The Smoking Gun. Please proceed."

Andy Burnham regarded SUBACK's invitation to testify as another petty annoyance and an unnecessary intrusion into his academic routine,

# Jack Eddinger

notwithstanding his reputation as one of the country's leading experts on the history, structure, objectives and assets of the American Communist Party. Had he been aware of his dossier in the Bureau's files, he'd have protested at the highest levels of the United States government.

He'd been following each session of the Committee closely in *The New York Times,* in Philadelphia's newspapers and occasionally on the evening news programs. His instincts told him that the Subversive Activities Committee, removed from the confines of Capitol Hill, was moving with uncharacteristic independence.

His long held cynicism about the Committee's political purposes was confirmed by a feeling that the hearings now three weeks into the new year were moving in a troubling direction and reopening old wounds. He was baffled by the hearings, inasmuch as the Chairman was quite firm in declaring SUBACK defunct just three months previously. Why these particular hearings? Why now? Why here? Why only the chairman and chief counsel in attendance? Testimony about CP influence in Pennsylvania's industrial unions, research institutions and academia, he felt, was setting the stage for a new onslaught; one aimed not at uncovering the true nature of soviet Communism's malevolence to its fellow Russians, but one which put ordinary citizens - some his colleagues - in SUBACK's telescopic sights. He feared that the Committee in spite of the chairman's disavowals, could easily be on its way back to the truculent days of witness badgering and contempt citations. His appearance of the previous fall, seemed at the time to indicate a change of direction away from the sins of the past. He certainly had no intention of whetting the Committee's appetite by adding his expert testimony about the motivations and recruiting techniques of the CPUSA. He was mystified when Harris elevated Ronald Sterling to chief counsel, and allowed him wide latitude in questioning witnesses. Perhaps it was a *quid pro quo* to keep his publicity-seeking colleague, Ray Nelson, out of the first hearings broadcast outside Washington. The amicable, high-minded exchanges of his last appearance, he feared, would be lost to Ronald Sterling's prosecutor's style: demands not queries; heat not light, acrimony not counsel. He was further baffled by the Chairman's demeanor. Harris appeared distant, detached, remote, looking tired and bored at the same time. He did not understand why Harris allowed Sterling to usurp the chairman's prerogatives. It was as if the congressman were flying on auto pilot. Harris appeared indifferent to the proceedings, yet Burnham assured himself that the chairman always appreciated his incisive testimony. He gave no further thought to his appearance, and arrived at the hearing room in the United States court house on Market Street a few blocks from Independence Hall fully prepared to deliver a compelling lecture, which

# INQUISITION

would re-affirm his reputation as the best informed and objective observer of the American Communist Party.

Andy Burnham would have been astonished to be privy to the extraordinary exchange that took place in the Speaker's chamber in the Capitol the week before the hearings opened. Zach Harris had to once again reach deep into his psychic vault to summon the qualities of character required to challenge Ham Clayburg's knowledge and authority in interpreting House rules and precedents, but even more in overcoming, or at least bypassing, the Speaker's ability to bend and hammer men to do what they don't want to do.

With a sharp rap of the gavel the Chairman continued the committee's inquiry into subversive activities in the country's third largest city. With a history extending to the nation's colonial and patriot beginnings, Philadelphia, seemed an unlikely venue for Red hunting. But the city's true character owes less to the good works of the Penns and the constitutional framers than to a 19th Century patrimony distinguished by strikes, riots and civic agitation by an assortment of anarchists and utopians of every stripe - Populists, single taxers, Bellamy nationalists, Wobblies, Millenariansts, and later, homegrown Communists. Andy Burnham sat in the hearing room confident that his knowledge and real world experience would help to shorten the inquiry. Instead, he sat through a long day of bluster and belligerence as Sterling tangled with Red Mike Mahone, leader of Local 8 of Philadelphia's Maritime Transport Workers Union. Sterling's opening question and Mahone's response set the tone:

"Now, Mr. Mahone, isn't it a fact that Local 8 is under the direct influence of Communists ... that you and your cohorts actively conspired to block access to the Port of Philadelphia at a time of national emergency ... that the MTW rendered the port inoperable as Soviet forces shut off access to Berlin and the anthracite coal needed for survival during the harsh winter of 1947. Isn't it a fact, sir, that through the action of you and your fellow conspirators the Delaware shipping channel was blocked for 20 miles down river, so that nothing could move through this strategic port?"

"I ain't answering no questions from an illegal scab committee, mister, and stand on my rights under the Fifth Amendment," was Mahone's monotonous answer to every question Sterling put to him. By mid-afternoon Mahone's belligerence provoked the Chairman to issue a contempt citation and had the Longshoremen leader removed from the hearing room. It was a trying day. Andy Burnham enjoyed it immensely. About 3 p.m. in a voice of barely concealed anger and exasperation Sterling announced, "the committee calls Professor A.M. Burnham."

# Jack Eddinger

"Dr. Burnham in your last appearance before this committee you testified as an expert witness did you not?" the chief counsel asked.

"That is correct, Mr. Sterling. "But let me correct the record. You have my initials backwards. They are 'M.A.' not 'A.M.' Now, if memory serves, there was a somewhat spirited exchange with the ranking minority member, Mr. Nelson. Be that as it may, I am pleased to say that I am once again at the committee's disposal. However, I must say Mr. Chairman that I have been somewhat apprehensive about the general thrust of these particular hearings. One needs to be vigilant, but at the same time cognizant that civil liberties must not be sacrificed to expediency," Burnham said unemotionally. "Given the scope of testimony both of today and during the past few weeks, I can readily see why the committee requires further perspective. I am pleased, Mr. Chairman, to once again offer you a detached and objective view of the so-called communist threat, particularly as it applies to our institutions of higher learning here in the Keystone State. I would not, however, venture into the thicket of organized labor."

"I realize the hour is late, but you may begin, Mr. Sterling." The chairman nodded toward his chief counsel. "Thank you, Mr. Chairman." Ronald Sterling began. "As you are aware, Professor Burnham, the committee has heard a great deal of testimony over the past few weeks about the infiltration of unions in defense facilities here. I would now like to turn the committee's focus in another direction, sir, and that will require your sworn testimony. Please rise, sir, and raise your right hand."

Taken aback Andy Burnham looked directly towards the Committee counsel then at the Chairman. "Pardon me, Mr. Chairman but do I understand that I am not to be queried as to my expertise related to the issues raised in these hearings … that I am to be an ordinary witness?"

"You are hardly ordinary, professor," Sterling rejoined with irritation.

Zach Harris said nothing. He sat at the dais expressionless. "Clerk, please swear this witness."

"Mr. Chairman, if I am to provide testimony beyond my expertise, I respectfully request an adjournment, so that I may retain counsel. This is not at all what I anticipated, sir." Burnham sat in stunned silence while the chairman and his chief counsel huddled - a priest listening to the sins of a penitent. Harris motioned with his head to Sterling. Both men retired through a doorway behind the dais for several minutes before emerging grim-faced. "Counsel has acceded to your request, Dr. Burnham." Zach Harris spoke for the first time. His voice was thick and husky, as if awakening from a deep sleep. "Meanwhile, I note that you are currently not under subpoena. I ask Counsel to correct this oversight and issue a

# INQUISITION

subpoena to compel your testimony if necessary. The committee will stand in recess until notice of continuance is issued."

Two weeks later at 9 a.m. sharp an unsmiling Zach Harris gaveled the committee to order. His meeting with the Speaker during the committee's adjournment still rankled. It troubled him more than anything in his years as a member of the House leadership that the Speaker would question his judgment, let alone challenge his prerogatives as a chairman. But, goddammit, if he wants a showdown, that's what he'll get. They'd met in the ornate, faintly Byzantine chamber cordoned off from the public with a velvet-covered brass chain on the second floor of the Capitol, where the Speaker receives VIPs. Both men had an implicit understanding of the application of power in the affairs of men and how to make it stick. They were a pair of menacing bulls, pawing the turf, snorting, eyeing each other carefully; ready to charge at the first sign of provocation.

"I see you've taken it on yourself to change House rules, Congressman." The Speaker, wearing ancient horn-rimmed glasses with one ear template missing, the lenses magnifying a set of brown almost black irises, was reading from a press release issued by the Committee on Subversive Activities. His voice was low, steady and edged in steel. "That coon ya think ya got by the scruff of the neck ain't comin outta his hole. Not as long as I'm here. Now, you just call your friends in the press and tell em there won't be any further hearings broadcast off this Hill." The Speaker's resolve momentarily stunned Zach Harris. He suppressed his disdain for the Speaker's Texas vernacular.

"Now just a minute, Ham. This is purely committee business. I am in violation of no rules or precedents. You are well aware that as chairman I have every right under the rules of this House to pursue my oath of office as I see fit without interference." Harris said. "Cite me a rule that prohibits me or any chairman from exercising his responsibilities, and I will, of course, desist. Give me that citation."

"I thought I've interpreted House procedures clearly," the Speaker said in a calm, measured voice that became firmer as the seconds ticked away on the wall clock. Then he slammed his fist on his ceremonial desk. "There'll be no broadcasting of any committee hearing in Washington or anywhere else without my okay. You went ahead without asking for my O.K."

"Well now, that's a problem. As I read House rules and precedents there's no specific rule to that effect. As chairman, my interpretation is somewhat different," Harris said suppressing a twinge of nervousness. " I am simply doing the job I am sworn to carry out. There is no rule ..."

# Jack Eddinger

"In the absence of a specific rule general rules apply," the Speaker interrupted with some heat. "You know how I feel about this business of uncontrolled coverage of our proceedings. I have no complaint about TV itself. Hell, I enjoy watching a good ballgame and the news programs. I've done my share of interviews. But TV people look for drama, and there is no drama in fashioning good law. There will be no committee or sub-committee hearings in Washington or anywhere else televised or broadcast by radio without my say so. Is that clear?"

"There is no such rule," Harris shot back curling his lip.

"I appointed you to chair this committee to protect the good name of this House and I won't have you or any member thwart my purpose. If these hearings you're conducting in Philadelphia on your own authority continue," the Speaker warned. "I will personally see to it that you'll never chair a full committee. Is that understood, sir?"

"Threats are unworthy of you, Mr. Speaker. With all due respect you cannot thwart progress. I am willing to put this to a vote of the caucus. Meanwhile, I must go about the business of oversight that I'm sworn to conduct; the business of the House of Representatives is bigger than any one man. I'm sorry, Ham. I trust you will not let your personal interests or predilections defeat our legitimate purpose or color our proceedings."

The Speaker glared at him with cold fury, fully aware that Zach Harris had the votes in the Democratic Caucus to support his gambit. A deep crimson flush settled on his face and moved slowly over his forehead and across his bald dome.

"We'll see about that," Clayburg said and stalked out, leaving Zachary Taylor Harris without second thoughts. He'll get over it.

The Speaker stalked past a group of members gathered in a knot just outside the House chamber and pushed through the elegantly frosted glass saloon doors without lifting his head.

"Ouch! Ham's on the warpath," one of the members said in a low voice. I feel sorry for whoever provoked him. That man's not worth coon shit."

Late that afternoon, the Speaker put through a call to the chief counsel for Bessemer Steel, Joe O'Neill, whom he'd known since his days as chairman of Interstate Commerce. He asked O'Neill to drop into his office for a talk over bourbon and branch during the next few weeks and to bring along, "that young fella who lost the Senate primary up your way. I'd like to get to know him."

Zach Harris left the meeting agitated but righteously indignant. He went immediately to his hideaway office and put through a call to Ronald Sterling. "I want you to press Burnham without letup. I want every piece

# INQUISITION

he's ever written analyzed and read into the record. Then I want you to get into his personnel record in detail, with particular emphasis on Spain and his clandestine service in the Balkans. That ought to lead us somewhere. We need to push him aggressively on his journalistic output and ties to Red propaganda."

For the next fortnight Ronald Sterling led the most thorough research project in his long career as a congressional staff investigator and committee counsel. It involved the analysis of newspaper, magazine and journal articles, Bureau reports, declassified State Department and OSS cable traffic, Army radio intercepts and British SOE operational intelligence from Eastern Europe and the Balkans for the period 1943-45.

Andy Burnham was confident, almost jaunty as Zach Harris slammed down his gavel to renew the hearing. He riffled through his papers and smilingly stroked his neatly-trimmed, grey beard. He abandoned the black eye patch, substituting dark glasses. No reason to give SUBACK a pretext for considering him offbeat, he told his counsel. A tall man wearing wire-rimmed glasses and a grey pin-striped suit and vest sat at his side, scribbled a few notes and smiled confidently at the two-man panel.

"We are prepared to testify, Mr. Chairman. But allow me to introduce my counsel, whom I believe is well-known to you and to many Americans, Mr. Alexander Marbury. As you know, Mr. Marbury is a distinguished member of the Philadelphia Bar and has had an illustrious career both in government, particularly as former Attorney General of the Commonwealth of Pennsylvania, and as the current chairman of the Philadelphia Chapter of the American Civil Liberties Union. He is no stranger to constitutional guarantees." Marbury nodded to the Chairman and chief counsel.

When Andy Burnham received the subpoena to appear before the committee, he wanted to call a press conference to denounce the hearings as a trivial fishing expedition, but Alex Marbury counseled against it. Instead, Marbury helped him prepare a detailed opening statement.

"Mr. Chairman, before I begin. I wish to read a statement?"

"Professor Burnham," Harris said, "This committee's ambit is restricted as to subject and time. Your statement will be included in the record. Please tell the committee about your background and professional credentials."

"If I might, Mr. Chairman?" Marbury interjected. "My client wishes to cooperate fully with the committee, and, I submit, should be extended the simple courtesy of reading his statement."

"Mr. Marbury," Harris rejoined. "My consistent rule throughout these hearings is no statements are to be read aloud by witnesses. All statements, however, will be incorporated in the record. This ruling has been made both in the interests of time and of propriety. I will not permit even the suggestion of a media circus to prevail. That is final."

"Yes, Mr. Chairman. I'd like a word with my client."

Burnham and Marbury chatted with their heads together for several minutes. "We're going to have to back and fill here, Andy. I suggest that you affect as genial a disposition as possible without being evasive. The professorial style always fit you well."

"Wear the bastards down, eh?" Burnham chuckled. I'll try to be Mr. Unflappable."

"Precisely."

"Very well, Mr. Chairman, Dr. Burnham has consented. We are ready to proceed."

Zachary Taylor Harris nodded to the witness.

"My name is Mills Anson Burnham. I reside at 323 Dartmouth Drive, Wynnewood, Pennsylvania. I am professor of international diplomacy at the University of Pennsylvania, where I hold the Robert Morris Chair of American Studies. I am also adjunct professor of International Studies and Slavic Language Studies at Bryn Mawr College.

"Just a minute professor," Harris interjected. Will you repeat your full name?"

"Why certainly. Mills Anson Burnham, as I said.

Harris, a stickler for detail, whispered to his chief counsel: "This report refers to 'Mills Andrew Burnham,' not Anson. Could we have the wrong man here?"

"No sir, Mr. Chairman. That's a Bureau typo. I've verified his full name as Mills Anson Burnham."

"Professor Burnham there is some confusion about your middle name," Harris said. "Are you not referred to as 'Andy?'"

"That's correct, Mr. Chairman. Anson's my mother's maiden name. I changed it to Andy as a young man - less uppity."

"Very well, you may proceed, sir."

"I received my bachelors and masters degrees in history-philosophy from Princeton University and was awarded the doctorate of philosophy by Columbia University. I was a fellow in Merton College Oxford University 1935-37, taking time out for a tour of duty as a journalist during the loyalist war against fascism in Spain. I was invited to join the Department of State as a Slavic language specialist and advisor to Secretary Hull on the USSR and Southeastern Europe issues. During the war, I was detailed from State to the Office of Strategic Services for special assignment in the Balkans. I returned to the Department in 1945 and served as Deputy Undersecretary

# INQUISITION

through 1945-47. I joined the university faculty here in 1947 where I have remained to the present." Burnham turned and smiled broadly. Elaine Burnham sat in the first row behind the witness table with members of the press. Her grey hair was pulled back and gathered in a pony-tail, which dangled to the middle of her back. She returned his smile and continued drawing in charcoal in a large artist's sketchbook.

"Dr. Burnham the Committee's interest extends to your service with the Department of State," Ronald Sterling began. "Your personnel record here shows you began employment in 1938 as an adviser to Secretary Hull. Your specialty is listed as, and I quote, "an expert on the operations and objectives of the Communist International Movement, otherwise known as the Comintern. Is that a fact, sir?"

"Before answering directly, let me provide some background, Mr. Chairman. By 1935 the Comintern, as put forth by Lenin in 1919 was thoroughly reorganized by Stalin and his man, Dimitrov. This was the period marked by the Sixth World Congress, when it was thought capitalism was disintegrating - the period of the People's Front Against War and Fascism, otherwise known as the Popular Front. Following the Nazi invasion of Russia the Comintern, as we knew it, was dissolved to support the Allied war effort and later reappeared as the Cominform. Is your question related to the Comintern or Cominform, Mr. Sterling?"

"The Committee does not require a history lesson, sir. We are well aware of the distinction. What we want is straightforward answers not digression into your interpretation of history," Sterling snapped.

"Comintern or Cominform. What will it be?"

"I believe I made myself clear, professor. Comintern. Do you want me to have the clerk read the record?"

"That won't be necessary, Mr. Sterling. Just trying to be a responsive witness. But to answer your question. Under-Secretary Welles recruited me from among a group of journalists, writers and others with first-hand knowledge of the War in Spain and its relationship to the international movement i.e., the Comintern, if you please."

"You say you were, 'recruited' by Under-Secretary Welles. What was your special relationship to Mr. Welles that prompted him to go outside regular personnel channels, sir? Would you consider yourself one of his – unh – boys." Sterling's dour demeanor turned into a deprecating smirk.

"Let me say, Mr. Chairman, that I had known Under-Secretary Welles since my postgraduate days at Columbia. He taught diplomatic history and international diplomacy, and encouraged many of us Wilsonian Democrats to pursue careers as internationalists. The tragedy which occurred later in his career can only be attributed to mental and physical exhaustion. He

## Jack Eddinger

was a faithful and loyal American and outstanding public servant. I would challenge the Chairman to condemn the insinuation behind Mr. Sterling's statement. "

"I am unaware of any insinuation, Mr. Chairman, perhaps the professor would like time to explain," Sterling responded with a grin.

"Let's get on with the questioning, Mr. Sterling," said Zachary Taylor Harris. "Our time is limited and the subject too important for side issues. Proceed."

"Yes, Mr. Chairman. Now Professor I asked why the State Department with a multi-million dollar budget was so in need of expert knowledge that it required outside resources?"

"It had been my understanding, Mr. Sterling, that the Department lacked sufficient depth - expertise if you will - in gaining on-the-ground intelligence and all-around general knowledge of the Comintern position *vis a vis* the growing threat of Fascism. As you know the Nazis and Mussolini's Fascists were supporting Franco heavily with guns and planes. There simply were no specialists on the war in the Department due to the U.S. government's strict neutrality. As a journalist accredited to POUM, I was in a position to assist in the Department's policy-making process."

"Excuse me," the Chairman interrupted. "What is that word you used?"

"Pardon me, Mr. Chairman. POUM. It is an acronym. It stands for *Partido obrero de unificacion Marxista*. Roughly translated it means "Workers Party of Marxist Unification" but like all such shorthand the acronym has gained a life of its own, connoting more than the literal translation. At the time, our interpretation was the Party of Freedom and its members, Freedom Fighters. As objective observers, journalists always like to simplify concepts, you know. Some of our colleagues like George Orwell, put their objectivity aside and took up arms. But for the most part we put our professions first to cover the war for news organizations around the world. Mine were the *Manchester Guardian, The Christian Science Monitor* and Intercontinental News Service. When Americans and Canadians began arriving in numbers, I moved on to cover their involvement ... "

"Let me stop you right there. Professor," Ronald Sterling interjected. "However much the committee appreciates your seemingly bottomless knowledge, sir, we want to focus on facts here. Were you not aware that the Cominterm raised 30,000 quote 'volunteers' enquote to fight for the so-called International Brigades? Furthermore, that 80 percent of these 'volunteers' were hard core Communists?"

# INQUISITION

"Mr. Sterling, my experience in Spain begins and ends with the written word. I wrote volumes about this experience from Tarragona and Ebro to the retreat from Gandesa to Castelldefells prison camp, where many idealistic young Americans paid the full price for freedom. Some 3,300 Americans fought as soldiers or served as ambulance drivers in the International Brigades. Communists or not, the American public demanded the coverage we supplied. Several of my colleagues lost their lives getting their stories."

"Thank you, Dr. Burnham. Now, Mr. Chairman I would like to turn to the witness's so-called expertise and how it was acquired above and beyond what he calls journalism and his fellow travelers call *agitprop*, agitation and propaganda. Are you with me, Doctor? By the way I believe one of the publications you wrote for was the *New Masses*? Is that not correct?"

"Yes. However, by that time TNM belonged to Max Eastman, who had repudiated his earlier flirtation with the CP. You are probably referring to its predecessor, *Liberator*, which I must say was quite rabidly red."

"Answer the question, professor. Were you not a contributor to *New Masses*? Yes or no?"

"Like many others, yes. All of us espoused some form of theoretical socialism back then."

Marbury put his arm across Andy Burnham's sloping shoulders and whispered in his ear.

"Pardon me, Mr. Sterling, counsel has asked for a brief *tête-à-tête*. With the chairman's permission ..."

"This could be tricky, Andy," Marburg advised his client. "You'll need to proceed carefully. We do not want to get into Fifth Amendment territory. I don't quite know where he's going with this. Just respond naturally and as casually as possible. Don't let him think he's in any way drawn blood."

"As I've indicated Mr. Sterling, my academic credentials, contributions to scholarly publications, government service and popular journalism may have had something to do with my being considered an expert. I believe the chairman himself would support me in that claim."

The chief counsel took a file folder from his briefcase and held up a fistful of news clippings and editorial cartoons made yellow and brittle by time. "Let me read what Mr. Burnham refers to as objective journalism, Mr. Chairman. From Intercontinental News, the foreign press arm of the *Daily Worker*, under the byline of M.A. Burns:

"I quote, *'Some of POUM'S adherents in this savage war within a war want to advance the ideology of Leon Trotsky – even with that laudable goal, internal struggles are afoot - to bring Communism out of the dark*

# Jack Eddinger

*night of Stalinism into the broad daylight of acceptability in a world of divergent cultures'* "What do you mean by, 'laudable goal ... broad daylight of acceptability?' Mr. Burnham?"

"The article, as anyone can see, Mr. Sterling is an analytical piece written for a readership that still does not understand the Trotskyite schism. This was 1936, not 1956, sir. Intercontinental picked it up from the *Guardian*. I had nothing to do with its publication by the *Worker*."

Ronald Sterling held up a file folder for the TV and still cameras. "Now, Doctor, I would like to pass you some editorial material. Please identify this photograph for the Committee."

"Well, that's quite easy. Leon Trotsky addressing the Sixth World Congress."

"Did you write a favorable story for Intercontinental about the speech?"

"I would not classify anything I wrote at that time as either favorable or unfavorable, Mr. Sterling. I was reporting on the Congress with objectivity and insight. I think the article speaks for itself."

"Indeed it does, professor. You refer to Trotsky as, and I quote, 'perhaps the most heroic of all the old Bolsheviks .. a man of destiny, without whom there would have been no revolution in 1917 and no Soviet Union today' Mr. Chairman I ask that the article in its entirety be included in the record."

The clerk handed Burnham two additional 8 x 10 photos.

"Please identify these photos, Mr. Burnham."

Andy Burnham studied the photos for less than a minute. "This is - let me think a bit because the face is familiar ... Yes, yes. It is Jay Lovestone. Expelled from the party in '29 for supporting Michael Bukharin."

He studied the third photo very closely. He recognized the face immediately. He barely concealed his surprise. Where the hell did they come by this?

"I cannot say I am able to identify the third man," Andy Burnham dissembled. "The face looks vaguely familiar, but I wouldn't hazard a guess as to who he is."

"Think back to those Comintern days you seem to regard so highly and know so well, professor. Does the name, Randolph, stir your memory?"

"Randolph? Is that a Christian name or surname?"

"A surname."

"No. I have no recollection of anyone named Randolph from the period."

"How about Peters? J. Peters?"

# INQUISITION

"That's a fairly common name. I'm sure I knew someone back then named Peters. Perhaps a graduate student or onetime colleague, but then again that is, as you would say, ancient history."

Zachary Taylor Harris was getting impatient. He beckoned his counsel to a huddle.

"When are you going to get to the core of his Red activity?" he asked Sterling over his reading glasses. "All of this is too slow and tedious. We need something more specific, and we need it soon. Otherwise we're going to lose our friends in the press. They're already shifting in their seats."

"Bear with me just a bit longer, Mr. Chairman," Sterling whispered with a tinge of exasperation. "I'm laying the groundwork to show Burnham's been an active Comintern agent since his involvement in Spain, then joined Donovan's crowd when the only qualification required was an Ivy League degree and a summer in Europe. The key here, I believe, is this mystery man, Randolph. The Bureau reached a dead end in the homicide investigation, but subsequent wiretaps led them to conclude it was a Donovan operation with Burnham deeply involved."

Andy Burnham turned to his counsel. "This is going to get sticky, Alex. The photo could open me to very serious questions that have nothing to do with this charade. Any information I might divulge involves top secret OSS activities conducted on the direct orders of President Roosevelt which are still classified. Responding materially in any way potentially opens an area of substantive testimony and subjects me to violation of the National Security Act. If I don't respond, he can cite me for contempt. Either way, I can go to jail. I'm caught between what I know and what I cannot say. I'm sure, given Sterling's thrust for the jugular, I'll bleed for this. They also could lead into other, more personal areas that I would rather not have to bring out in a public forum. We need to discuss them in detail and develop a strategy."

"Mr. Chairman, with all due respect, sir, my client requests a recess in order to respond fully and factually to Mr. Sterling's questions. Classified State Department files which require clearance are involved. We will need time to discuss the levels of clearance with the Department, then have an opportunity to review them in order to respond intelligently to the Committee."

The Chairman beckoned Sterling to yet another huddle. "God-dammit, I don't want to get into security clearances here. I'm in enough difficulty with the Speaker over holding these hearings away from Washington. They're not producing the national press coverage I anticipated. I need to reconsider this whole thing before proceeding down this road. As a Democratic leader, I cannot afford to be seen attacking FDR."

# Jack Eddinger

"The committee will stand in recess for exactly one week," Zachary Taylor Harris declared. "All subpoenas will remain in effect."

In the days that followed Andy Burnham confided to Marbury things he never told anyone. There were far more than journalistic activities in Spain the committee could turn against him. He described his wartime clandestine OSS activities in the Balkans with Hobe Tenley; how they parachuted into Montenegro together on a presidential mission to scout out the guerrilla movements. Relating the story of Hobe's murder by the SS opened a wound that had never properly healed, and brought him to the verge of tears. He told of his own escape from assassination after returning to Washington accompanied by a British SOE agent named Randolph. Only later was he told by Donovan that Randolph was a Cominterm alias used by a Soviet NKVD officer named Igor Fitkin, who also used the cover name, Peters.

"Randolph briefed Hobe and me when we jumped into Yugoslavia. After Hobe went off to reconnoiter Mihjalovic, Randolph and I set out for the Partisan sector. He was with me all the way. We ate together, slept on the bare ground, drank Slivovitz with the Partisans and we both took the measure of the Partisan leader, Tito, who at the time, was unknown in Britain and the United States. We compared notes on the flight home and found almost perfect agreement that, Broz or "Tito," as we came to know him, was going to be trouble for the Soviets after the war. Little did I realize that Randolph was in radio contact with Moscow every day we spent with the Partisans. I learned of his mission and identity after he failed to show up for our briefing of the President. Gen. Donovan told me about the delicacy of the situation. Randolph/Fitkin had orders directly from Stalin to liquidate me after briefing the president," Burnham told his lawyer.

"Stalin and Tito were in a Siberian labor camp together before the Soviet Revolution. During the Twenties, Broz was the Comintern's man in Belgrade. He was a ruthless and single-minded provocateur. Stalin murdered any potential rival, but could not afford to upset the Allies by liquidating Tito, who was tying down twelve Nazi divisions, divisions that Hitler could otherwise deploy on the Eastern Front. Instead, he sent his assassin to silence the messenger, me, but we got him first. Termination with extreme prejudice, as it appeared in the mission report. Randolph's elimination was our first wet operation. A bullet to the side of his head delivered in a Washington hotel room reduced the NKVD's ranks of assassins by one. The Bureau knew of our involvement and didn't want any part of it. The Director hated Donovan. He considered him an upstart and cowboy. The Bureau turned it over to the Metropolitan Police who ruled it a suicide. I'm beginning to get a whiff of the Bureau in this contretemps."

But more important, there was Hobe's love affair with Marion Harris to explain to Marbury, along with the story of his and Elaine's complicity, which in the current climate would be hard to justify should it become widely known. Then there was the exceptionally delicate problem of revealing the details of Marion's breakdown, and the necessity of safeguarding this knowledge from her husband not to mention from the public. It could also involve Marion's close friend, Anna Daley, who would probably break if the situation got out of hand, and it could even extend to her son. Harris would be remorseless in taking his vengeance. Finally, he believed Sterling to be perverse enough to drag Elaine into the hearings. Her onetime membership in the Young Communist League and the anti-capitalism cartoons she drew for *New Masses* and other left-leaning publications would be too tempting to ignore. Plus, there was enough in all of this to have the committee fingering him as the key man in losing Yugoslavia to Communism just as they hung losing China around Owen Latimore's neck. He visualized the headline:

**'Professor Played Key Role in Red Takeover of Balkans.'**

"I don't see how I can proceed without pleading the Fifth Amendment, and that's as good as a conviction in these grotesque times. That's how they got Bill Remington and we all know what happened to him in federal prison. Hiss was different. He'd have been home free if he hadn't challenged Chambers in the defamation lawsuit."

"The Committee will come to order. Call your witness, Mr. Sterling."

Ronald Sterling slipped a clipping from the morning Philadelphia *Inquirer* across the desk to the chairman. The headline read:

**Medical Scientist Takes His Life,
Note Blames SUBACK Hearings**

The news story described the suicide of a Jefferson Medical College biochemist, employed at the Oak Ridge National Laboratory during the war, whom the Committee had subpoenaed to testify at its next session about espionage during the Manhattan Project. A suicide note blamed Harris and the Committee for, "opening old wounds that have been discredited in the past." The note went on to castigate the Committee for preventing him, "from doing the kind of science I do best, which is aimed at saving rather than destroying lives. All I've ever asked for is to be left alone. I had hoped to spend my life in the laboratory here in the City of Brotherly Love, and with my family. Now, I will be able to do neither."

Zachary Taylor Harris read the news story with no display of emotion and passed it back to the chief counsel.

"Conscience is a demanding mistress. I feel sorry for the man's family. He was obviously guilty. Traitors deserve the fate they've chosen."

Having spent the previous weekend in Georgia with Lenore Price following a speech in Savannah to the Navy League and improving his 10-stroke handicap at the Cloisters, Zachary Taylor Harris, appeared relaxed, almost amiable, and free of the rattling cough that he had battled for more than three months. A light suntan had chased the pallor of previous weeks. The only indicator of less than perfect health was a blood pressure of 220/150, except he was unaware of it.

"The committee calls Mrs. Elaine Burnham," Ronald Sterling announced. "The clerk will deliver the subpoena directly to the witness." Sterling's words stunned Andy Burnham and threw Elaine Burnham into a state of shock and bewilderment like a small animal caught in powerful headlights. Alex Marbury immediately moved for a recess, but Harris denied his motion. "Mr. Chairman, I strenuously protest this completely irregular and unconstitutional assault on my clients' civil liberties."

"I will judge what's unconstitutional before this committee, Mr. Marbury. Mrs. Burnham has been called and will testify. I would like to hear her defense of this piece of slanderous garbage." Harris held up an editorial cartoon ripped from the weekly edition of the *Philadelphia Worker*. It depicted a figure dressed in the menacing black uniform and cap of an SS officer. The word "SUBACK" ran down one leg of his black knee breeches above shiny knee-high jackboots. The boot was on the neck of a cringing figure of a man in a professorial gown bearing the legend, "American Academe" across his back. The title "Freedom in the Cradle of Liberty" stretched across the top of the cartoon in block lettering. The lower left corner contained the monogram "ERB" in broad brush stokes.

"We take strong exception, Mr. Chairman, and insist that the record show that we are proceeding only under the most extreme protest," Marbury stated.

"Mr. Marbury, this committee is charged with finding the truth. Mrs. Burnham has long been her husband's willing accomplice, if not an outright subversive. Her record of mockery of American values as depicted in this crude drawing and through the clever innuendo of malicious political cartoons says more about her loyalties to Bolshevism than the entire record of these proceedings," Harris responded. "Moreover, this committee has

# INQUISITION

reviewed her so-called modern art and finds it decadent and morally degenerate. Proceed with swearing this witness Mr. Sterling."

Andy Burnham exploded from his seat like a super nova bursting across inter-galactic space. "I will not let you and your executioner destroy us," he shouted. "We will not testify before this rump of a committee. You make a mockery of justice and civil liberties. You, sir, are a pernicious threat to the Constitution and a malignancy on the body politic."

"And you, sir, are out of order. Sit down or be cited for contempt," Harris fumed.

As the Burnhams counseled with their lawyer, Zachary Taylor Harris beckoned to a Federal marshal seated at the rear of the hearing room. "If there is another outburst from these witnesses, marshal, I want you and your men, on my command, to take them into custody," the chairman ordered.

"Yes sir," the marshal nodded. "We'll handcuff them and escort them out. I'll have a van waiting in the garage to take them over to the Federal Detention Center for photographing and fingerprinting."

"Good. Move on my signal."

At the witness table, an exasperated Alex Marburg scolded Elaine Burnham. "That cartoon is a serious setback to Andy's cause, Elaine. If you had only told me you were submitting it, I would have counseled you to publish it after the hearings. Instead of being able to go over to the attack, as I planned, we've an extremely angry chairman to deal with. But go on we must." Marbury briefly went through the options available to his clients. Elaine could testify, but that would open both of them to an array of unwarranted side issues, as any student of the committee's history could attest. She could invoke the Fifth Amendment, which in the Committee's eyes was tantamount to an admission of guilt, not to mention the ensuing media circus that would envelop them. She could refuse to testify, but that would lead to a contempt citation.

"My advice is to decline to testify on the basis of your Fifth Amendment rights, Elaine." Marburg counseled. "That will stalemate things for the moment. We need to establish a firm record to take to Federal Court in a civil liberties complaint. Just remember though that the Courts have not been cordial to that approach. We'll have to find a logical and consistent way of arguing our case. Andy, you must constrain yourself. I know this is very traumatic for both of you, but we can gain both time and leverage. Moreover, you must consider what this might do to your professional careers."

"This is an absolute outrage," Andy Burnham burned with rage and disgust. "I don't like any of the options. We're damned by all three."

# Jack Eddinger

"Unfortunately, the approach will work only for Elaine," Alex Marbury could barely conceal his chagrin. "You're already on the record with your prior testimony, Andy. You cannot plead your rights under the Fifth Amendment, because they've been waived by your substantive testimony on the other matters. This, of course, compounds the dilemma."

"Well, what the hell am I suppose to do, counselor, throw myself off a cliff?" Andy Burnham was shaking with rage. "The god-damned newspapers have already convicted me. Think of what they'll do to both of us! It's not only my good name and loyalty Harris is dragging through the muck; it's my job. The faculty Senate's meeting next week to consider a resolution of suspension and the AAUP will wash their hands of me if it passes. So I can count on no help. They've got me by the testicles. It's the Rosenbergs all over again."

"Let's just get through Elaine's testimony. I have a few ideas I want to think through on your testimony, Andy," the civil liberties lawyer said. Elaine Burnham steadied herself and in a shaky Brooklyn accent repeated the oath, stating her name, address and employment - freelance artist.

"Now, Mrs. Burnham, Ronald Sterling began, "I have here three cartoons from three, shall we describe them as, 'unusual,' publications? Each bears the monogram ERB in the lower right corner. Please tell this committee, Mrs. Burnham whether you are familiar with these items and with the monogram. For the record, Mr. Chairman, the publications I am referring to are *The Daily Worker, The Industrial Worker* and *La Batalla*. Two are listed on the Attorney General's list of subversive publications. The third, now defunct, was the official propaganda organ of the Spanish Communists to which this witness has contributed subversive materials."

"I respectfully decline to answer on the ground of refusing to testify against myself," she responded tentatively, in that hesitant, skeptical way a Brooklyn inflection bestows uncertainty on the English language.

"Mrs. Burnham," the chairman interjected, "the only legal ground on which you can refuse to answer that question, the only ground recognized by this committee is the ground of self-incrimination. If you wish to plead self-incrimination, you may, but if you refuse to answer on some other grounds, you will be held in contempt of the committee and of Congress. Will you answer the question or do you decline to answer?"

"I would decline to answer the question on the ground of refusing to testify against myself," she responded nervously.

"Do you mean by refusing to testify against yourself that the answer to the question asked would tend to incriminate you? Is that what you mean to say; that it would put you in jeopardy?" Ronald Sterling asked.

"It might tend to do so, yes."

# INQUISITION

"Were you ever at any time a member of the New York League for Peace and Freedom? The Young Communist League or the New York Artists For Social Betterment?"

"I will have to give you the same answer to that, Mr. Sterling. There is no use of my going through the procedure again."

"Very well, Mrs. Burnham. You may step down."

"The committee calls, Mills Anson Burnham."

Andy Burnham strode to the witness table with fire in his eyes and took a seat behind a metal stalk sprouting microphones. He was still unsettled from his previous outburst but was determined to assail the committee for maximum effect in the press.

"I will remind you that you are still under oath, sir." Ronald Sterling ran his index finger down the transcript of the previous week. "Mr. Burnham, in your response last week to the question, 'Are you familiar with the name Randolph, your initial answer was, 'No.' I then handed you a photo and asked you to identify the individual in the photo. Your answer was, 'I would not hazard a guess as to who he is.' I will now ask you once again, are you or are you not familiar with the individual in this photograph?"

"Mr. Chairman, I strenuously protest the use of this committee to smear and intimidate me and my wife and to blacken our names with this bogus line of questioning," Burnham said steadily and soberly. "I have nothing more to say to you or Mr. Sterling. My record of public service on behalf of our nation speaks for itself. The so-called information counsel so recklessly injects into this proceeding stems from highly secret operational intelligence activities I conducted as a military officer in wartime. The records associated with that assignment remain under seal and are protected under the National Security Act that I have sworn to uphold. I, therefore, refuse to respond in any way to this asinine attempt to use me to further your reactionary agenda of fear and coercion to enforce uniformity and curtail freedom of speech. Furthermore, this committee has no jurisdiction over the intelligence and security policy of the United States, and is arbitrary and illegal. You have brought dishonor to the Congress and to the people of the United States, who have honored me with the Distinguished Service Cross. I welcome your contempt citation as a badge of honor like the DSC, awarded to me for the very action this committee has taken on itself to impugn. I guarantee you, Mr. Harris, that you will regret conducting this shameful exhibition."

Harris and Sterling were momentarily thrown off guard by Andy Burnham's vehemence. Never before had the words of a witness shattered the committee's composure so thoroughly.

# Jack Eddinger

"Mr. Witness, the committee has tolerated your dissembling and has granted you your right to free speech," Harris squinted with waspish bitterness. "Now, it is the committee's turn to exercise its constitutional duty by citing both you and your wife not only for contempt, but for conspiracy to violate the Smith Act of 1940 to wit: 'whoever, with intent to cause the overthrow or destruction of any such government; prints, publishes, edits, issues, circulates, sells, distributes, or publicly displays any written or printed matter advocating, advising, or teaching the duty, necessity, desirability, or propriety of overthrowing or destroying any government in the United States by force or violence, or attempts to do so upon conviction shall be subject to ten years imprisonment.'

"Additionally, the committee charges you with perjury for false testimony, as it relates to photographic evidence this committee has presented. Let me also remind you that upon conviction of a felony, you will be compelled to surrender your medals. Marshal, place these individuals under arrest."

The hearing ended in a loud scramble by reporters yelling questions at the departing couple. Harris and Sterling quickly left through the door behind the dais.

At a preliminary hearing before a U.S. Magistrate, the Burnhams posted $50,000 bond. Elaine was charged with contempt of Congress. Andy was charged with perjury and conspiracy to violate the Smith Act. They pleaded not guilty to all charges and were bound over to appear before the federal grand jury. Their bail was posted by the law firm of Marbury & Franklin.

Alexander Marbury told them he believed that the statute of limitations applied to all of their activities of the 1930s, that the Smith Act violation and perjury charge were incorrect in that the legislation was not passed until 1940 long after the alleged acts took place and that, regardless, the government could prove none of the charges and the committee would be ridiculed if their case went to trial.

"It's ass backwards and Harris is enough of a lawyer to know it," he told his clients. Elaine, however, may still have a problem with the contempt charge, he explained and said Andy's career would undoubtedly suffer, but as a liberal institution with a pedigree extending to the American Revolution, the University of Pennsylvania might declare his a *cause celebre* and keep him on the faculty. "We'll soon see what kind of stuff Ben Franklin's university is made of."

# CHAPTER ELEVEN
## *The Perfect Stratagem*

Since Congressman Harris's return to Washington, the small red light on Robert Bird's interoffice phone, indicating the boss's presence, glowed incessantly. Zachary Taylor Harris was in prolonged conversations with Ronald Sterling. He told his chief aide that he was not to be disturbed. The professor has clearly perjured himself on the photo. He would electrify the hearings the following week by citing Burnham for perjury. The Justice Department will take it from there. Then he would turn the proceedings over to SUBACK's chief counsel to go after the State Department's grandmotherly passport control officer for her leniency in approving passports for leftist artists, writers and entertainers for travel to the USSR and Soviet bloc countries. Sterling would relish the job. He'd bask in the national publicity.

With the Burnhams indicted he could count on the Director's full support and deference. Moreover, his overwhelming victory in November guaranteed Kressman's bank charter, putting *Der Alte* at the head of the long line of individuals permanently in his debt. With young Daley's name now lastingly engraved on a headstone in the Lenape Valley's political graveyard, investigations in Hampton County had reached a dead end. Only one issue remained. He had kept the file the Navy CID had compiled on his wife locked in his office safe awaiting an opportune moment. He could easily make the case for divorce on the grounds of infidelity. Her long slide into alcoholism provided a companion charge of equal merit. He'd have one of the young lawyers over at Harry Covington's law firm file the petition in the D.C. courts, where it would be buried among hundreds of similar cases. The decree should be final in a few months. Press coverage would be minimal - a few lines of agate type in domestic court roundups. Nobody reads Saturday's boiler plate.

Lenore will be rapturous. They discussed their future together on the trip south. Flying away from the dismal Washington winter to sunshine, sandy beaches and aquamarine water with the man she loved not only buoyed her spirits, but sent them soaring. He figured that a month in Lugano after the hearings will give him plenty of time to convince her that the nomination and confirmation of ambassadors are two different things. There were many other ways to enjoy Switzerland. One was, as he promised her, the International Commission on Eastern European Resettlement in Geneva. One of the three positions on the commission reserved for members of the House of Representatives was his for the

# Jack Eddinger

asking. With his seniority an appointment to the staff for Lenore would be easy. They'd have the best of both worlds - a chic apartment off the Quai du Mont-Blanc overlooking the waterspout on Lake Leman at government expense, and her cozy place in Cathedral Heights the rest of the time. She'd love it. But he'd hate Geneva's disagreeable winter weather, darkness and dank cold. It would aggravate the persistent hacking cough that had hung on longer than he anticipated. Fortunately, the week of love in the sun also foreclosed a recurrence of the incident which sent him to hospital two months previously.

All in all, he was feeling good, not excellent, but solidly good. The outlook was splendid. The hearings put the Director firmly in his debt. Daley's investigative machinery clanked to a standstill and would now be given the coup de grace by his new, hand-picked D.A. The divorce would remove once and for all the impediment to marrying Lenore Price. He would also begin to enjoy the capital that had been accumulating in the account at Banque Rahner et Cie. Zach Harris considered his good fortune and smiled benignly. He had devised and executed the perfect stratagem. Exhilaration pulsed through his bloodstream.

Robert Bird hesitated and took a deep breath before knocking on the varnished mahogany door to the Congressman's suite. He'd been mentally rehearsing the scenario for the past month. The chairman's long absence in Philadelphia and sojourn in the sun added to his anxiety. The time to act had come.

"Come in Robert."

Robert Bird entered the softly-lighted room. Congressman Harris was bent over his desk, his reading glasses perched on the tip of his nose. The administrative assistant stood before the Congressman whom he had served faithfully over the past five years since leaving the newspaper job he had traded for an insider's role in politics. His hands trembled slightly as he handed Zachary Taylor Harris the single page, single-spaced letter he had spent the last few weeks writing and revising.

"Don't tell me you're handing me your resignation now that the election's over, Robert. I won't hear of it," Harris said, skimming the page.

"Well, not exactly, Congressman. I'd like to think of it is as fulfilling the compact we agreed to last November before the election."

"Compact? What compact?"

"The agreement that I would run for your congressional seat in two years, as you yourself told me, Congressman," Robert Bird responded. "I'm ready to apply all my knowledge and everything you've taught me. I

# INQUISITION

sincerely believe I am the most qualified individual to wear your mantle, and I'll wear it with all the dignity and pride you've brought to the job. With your help, I ..."

"What is this, Robert, some kind of joke?"

"I realize your shoes will be difficult to fill, sir, but I'm convinced I can carry on your leadership."

"Robert, I'm surprised. No, I'm flabbergasted," Harris said, slightly embarrassed at Bird's naïvete "Do you think in your wildest imaginings that with no electoral experience, no political base, no appreciation of the historic roots of the 26th Congressional District and the forces that make it unique, that you can come in here and confront me with this so-called 'compact.' Look, you are a very good aide, Robert. But that's all you are. I made you. I gave you birth. I have had you baptized and confirmed by the House and I'm not about to place my hands on your head in Holy Orders and anoint you my successor. Why Lloyd Kressman would turn you over his knee and the Lenape Valley political brotherhood would hand you your ass in a ballot box."

"But Congressman, you explicitly told me from your hospital bed that you were retiring after this term. You confirmed to me that I could expect your support in the future," Bird said with undisguised shock.

"Oh that's it. Dammit Robert you've been around here long enough to understand the language of politics. There's the future and the Future. I needed your help when I was incapacitated. You know better than to interpret a few words of encouragement as a commitment. A compact! I haven't heard that term since the Pilgrims. The future is a long way off, mine and yours. Now, please excuse me. I have work to do."

Robert Bird turned sharply and shambled towards the door.

"Now, Robert. Don't sulk out of here. There's still plenty I can do for you, if you'll let me," Harris said recognizing his aide's deep distress. "The Public Works Committee needs a staff director. It's the perfect place for you what with your analytical and PR skills. Do you want me to talk to George Forney? He was a newspaper man in Maryland before his election."

"Thank you, sir, I'll consider it. But I am really not interested in gaining more staff experience. I want to be a member of Congress. I, too, have a future to think about ..."

Robert Bird sat at his desk in the cramped cubicle just outside the Congressman's door and sunk into deep thought. Disappointment knifed into his psyche. What a fool he had been. What a damned fool. He'd made an ass of himself. He remained in a near-trance for more than a quarter hour, staring blankly out the window towards the Capitol, brilliantly

## Jack Eddinger

lighted and stark white in the pale light of early evening. He ended his introspection abruptly then rooted through his desk drawers until he found his green spiral-bound stenographic notebook marked, "Election, 1956." He flipped through it carefully then put it in his coat pocket and switched off the light over his desk. He let the office door slam behind him as he exited, sending an echo reverberating through the dimly lit and vacant corridors on the third floor of the Longworth Building lined by the offices of the men he admired most and craved to emulate.

Charlie Miller rolled the last take of his weekly column out of the battered black and gold Underwood and called for a copy boy. He was stretching both arms overhead, when the gooseneck phone next to him jangled its brassy 1930s ring. He put on the battered headset, stroked his mustache and puffed a small Vesuvius of sparks and ash from his MacArthur corncob.

"Miller."

"Charlie, this is Bob Bird down in Washington."

"Hi Bob, good to hear your mellifluous baritone. What's on your mind? Zach still running your ass ragged?"

"I can't go into it on the phone. I'd like to get together - just you and me - next week when I'm in the district office." How about around noon on Wednesday at Adolph's?"

"Sure, sure, Bob. Actually, I should have called you. I'd like to get your view of what Zach's long range plans are after the SUBACK hearings." Charlie Miller clicked off the phone and removed the headset wondering what the congressman's top aide would come all the way back to the district to discuss with him. Must be important. Maybe something about Zach's health.

Robert Bird was one of the few political operatives Charlie Miller trusted, mainly because he had trained Bird to be a meticulous reporter and first-rate writer. He knew Bird wasn't happy working for MacManus on the *Star-Times* court house beat, and recommended Bird to Zach Harris as a professional he could trust to handle press relations. While they spoke frequently, Miller relied on the Congressman himself rather than on Bird for insider political stories, or to get the skinny on state or national developments. It was not unusual, however, for Bird to call him with announcements and releases on Lenape Valley issues or to point him in the direction of an agency snafu. They developed a close working relationship, and often had a beer together.

# INQUISITION

"Let me get this straight, Bob, you're telling me Zach Harris has been keeping secrets from his friends in the press? Now fancy that." Miller queried his former protégé, pulling his chair closer to the battered, carved-up table in Adolph's noisy rathskeller. He listened as Robert Bird described the chance discovery. He said nothing about his run in with the congressman, or his interest in the office.

"Charlie, I know you're a born skeptic, but I've seen things - documents, files, records, cash money - stuff nobody's ever seen. Last November when he was laid up at St. Helena's after the heart attack or whatever it was, he asked me to get twenty-five grand in cash from his office safe, because he couldn't leave his sick bed. He sent Sam McBryan down to pick it up. We packed it into the congressman's briefcase and he drove right back."

"So, what's new? Politicians attract big time cash. They need it to pay off the street guys on election day, buy drinks at the taverns on the South End, pay for signs and palm cards, print ballots. They all do it. Mostly it's legit. You and I and the editorial page wouldn't call it kosher, but its legit nevertheless. Zach's never had a problem with money. Mrs. Harris is loaded. He's a lot of things, Bobby, but I don't believe he's stupid, taking dough on the sly. That office means too much to him. I know, I've covered him for longer than I care to remember."

"It's not money, Charlie, but other stuff. I only had a fleeting look, but I saw Swiss bank account books and circa 1930s ledgers and agreements, contracts, immigration files, a U.S. Navy background report on Mrs. Harris. How about an autopsy report on his law partner, and a loaded .32 caliber pistol?"

"All I see is smoke, Bob and the detritus of politics. Granted, thick smoke and probably embarrassing detritus. But Zach's a prominent member of Congress who serves on committees with wide jurisdiction. Take the subcommittees on criminal law or immigration. Most of what you saw could very well be associated with legitimate congressional activity. Except for the gun. I wouldn't have expected that. Has it been fired?"

"I don't know. What if I told you I have the combination and can get into the safe? I destroyed my original notes as the congressman directed, but I realized that the combination I wrote down would reappear as an impression if I rubbed it with a little cigarette ash. Sure enough, it came back. Would you be interested in taking a look at some of the stuff in the safe? Maybe you'll change your mind. He'll be occupied next week in Philadelphia with the hearings, so why don't you come down. I'll spread it all out for you. Then you can judge for yourself."

"Now that's interesting. Sure, I'd love to have a peek. What's Zach done to you, Bob?"

# Jack Eddinger

"Let's just say the emperor's clay feet walked out on a commitment and leave it at that. You trained me well, Charlie."

The following Monday Robert Bird gave the office staff the afternoon off. The congressman was in Philadelphia finishing the SUBACK hearings. Charlie Miller left Bessemer City at 6 o'clock that morning on the long drive to Washington made longer by his leisurely route through Harrisburg and Frederick - plenty of time for thinking. He stopped at Gettysburg in mid-morning and walked the half mile, as he often did, from Seminary Ridge across the route Pickett's Virginians trod before being cut to pieces by Union howitzers atop Cemetery Ridge. He was always fascinated by the merciless savagery American men inflict on each other. He wondered if something buried deep in the genetic or psychological makeup of American males had not unleashed the fury on that scorching afternoon in July of 1863; something which boiled up from primal depths and overflowed into a thing at once instinctual, implacable, unremitting; its meaning encoded in the mists of history. Not every man possessed the warped gene, but some did, and, in abundance. He'd always thought Zach Harris expressed it singularly. It made him tick. It gave him the hard edge, the acute instincts, the rough jocularity, the intense intellect. It is what made him a quintessential, dominant American male, and a total sonofabitch.

Charlie showed up on Capitol Hill in late afternoon. Robert Bird used his pass key to open the polished door to the holy of holies and went straight to the safe in the alcove behind the congressman's desk. He started laying out its contents on the green baize-covered table the congressman used to conduct meetings with colleagues, staff or visiting constituents. "We need to catalog this," Miller said. "Why don't you start making a list, so we know what's what in this pile." Robert Bird made notations in his steno pad as Charlie Miller carefully examined and evaluated each item, like an antiquarian pricing treasures from a moneyed household.

"First, you can return this file on Mrs. Harris. I'm not interested in personal information. I'm not sure I want to read the autopsy report either. It's the public stuff I want. If there's anything in this agglomeration that ties Zach Harris to malfeasance, misfeasance or collusion, we'll need to verify it. Remember the three vees I taught you when you arrived at the *Star-Times* out of J-School, Bob? Verification. Verification. Verification. Everything else is secondary."

"It's a tenet I live by, Charlie."

"Where's the Swiss bank records?" Bird handed his mentor a large manila envelope with the congressman's frank in the upper right corner. It contained the deposit and disbursement records Bird had described at Adolph's. Charlie Miller examined the records and made notations on the

# INQUISITION

folded copy paper he used to take notes in his scratchy shorthand. He was interested in dates. The amount of deposit was always the same, $5,000 per month. The first record was dated July 1938, the last, December, 1956. "Geez, that's more than a million dollars over the past eighteen years. Compute the interest. Even at Swiss bank rates that's one helluva fine investment. Deposits during the war, too," Miller noted. The bank of origin for each deposit was listed as the First Federal Bank, Union City, N.J. Disbursements were few - a thousand or so a year. There were recent withdrawals paid in Swiss francs.

"What do you make of this?" Bird said, handing Miller a file folder marked IMMSUBCOM 1935-38 filled with personal privilege immigration bills initiated by Rep. Harris and ex-Congressmen John B. O'Hara and the late Charles Muncie, both of New Jersey. Each was accompanied by a transmittal letter from the Harris & Daley law firm signed by Thomas A. Daley, Esq. "Judging by the surnames, Harris & Daley seem to have had a trans-Atlantic pipeline from Italy. Look at this one, 'The Hon. Frank Della Notte. We are pleased to inform you that your client, Giuseppe Maria Zaccardi, of Reggio de Calabria, Provincia di Calabria, Italy, has been granted a waiver of immigration procedures and is admitted as a citizen of the United States by Special Act of Congress with all rights and privileges appertaining thereto, effective January 1, 1934.' Signed Thomas A. Daley, Esq."

"There must be a hundred of these."

"Didn't I tell you, Charlie?"

"Still mostly smoke."

"How about this file?"

One page caught his attention immediately. Miller's eyes narrowed as he read intently. Judas Priest, he thought, there it was all spelled out. He was looking at a contract made between T. A. Daley Esq. for Harris & Daley, Attorneys at Law and Cavalier Construction Inc. of Union City, N.J. The law firm was to be paid a $5,000 monthly retainer from the company's disbursement account at First Federal. The contract was initialed "SM" for Cavalier and "TAD" for the law firm.

"I think I've seen enough," Miller told Bird. "Put this material back in the safe. I'm driving back to Bessemer City tonight. There's someone I need to talk to. I'll be back to you. Be sure to return everything precisely as it was and wipe down the safe for fingerprints. If Zach even dreamed someone was in this safe, he'd have the FBI up here instantly. We'd both be on our way to Allenwood on the morning train. And by the way unload the gun before you put it back."

# Jack Eddinger

On his long solo drive back to Bessemer City Charlie Miller puzzled over the material he'd seen, but more fundamentally, how to deal with it. How much of it was potential evidence? What was beyond the Statute of Limitations? Does it in any way implicate Harris directly? Why would he keep an ancient document initialed by his law partner and the mob's top *consigliere*, which in no visible way involves him? You'd like to think the chairman of Criminal Law would have turned it over to the authorities. You can understand keeping it from the Bessemer City Police even the State Police. But this is Federal. The FBI or the U.S. Attorney would be interested. Is he protecting his late partner's memory, or Mrs. Daley, or Tommy or what? Charlie Miller did not sleep well. He tossed until dawn then headed to the *Star-Times*. He arrived before MacManus to an empty and unusually quiet city room, got himself a cup of coffee and dialed a private number he had not called in recent weeks.

"Good Morning, Angie. It's Charlie Miller. *Ist der Leutnant* up yet?" he said in mock German.

"Hi Charlie. Yes. He's right here. Getting ready to leave for the office. He loves his new job."

"Charlie Miller!" John Maggio boomed into the phone. "To what do I owe this distinctive honor? You guys find the fat man's missing hairpiece?"

"Madge, I need your advice. How about grabbing a bite of lunch. *Trattoria Positano* still makes the best calamari in town. I'm buying."

"Say no more. The *frutti de mare* for me. At what hour do you request my presence at the esteemed Posi?"

"Noon."

"See ya then, *paisan*."

Charlie Miller motioned to John Maggio from the rear of the restaurant. The ex-detective moved swiftly through the lunch time crowd, stopping to say hello to Bessemer City businessmen and their once-a-week paramours crowded into the soft leather banquettes. He made his way towards the newsman who waited in a private alcove off the main floor of the restaurant. They often met there to exchange confidential information. He'd known Miller longer than any journalist. They started their careers around the same time. Charlie covered the police beat back then and helped raise Maggio's profile. Miller's stories describing Maggio's exploits guaranteed him the post of Chief of Detectives. But the negative polarity of Maggio's rapid rise in the Department assured the unrelenting enmity of Corporal Rocco DiLupo, head of the BCPD's motorcycle brigade.

"*Ciao, amico.* You're looking pretty dapper for an ink-stained wretch. Is that a new sport coat or did you just replace the elbow patches?" John

# INQUISITION

Maggio slid his muscular frame across the leather banquette and picked up the menu. "I've already ordered. *Carpaccio di spada, insalata di carciofi, calamari fritti, frutta di mare.* Everything to your palate's delight. I thought I'd leave wine and dessert to you."

"Keep up the good work, my friend, and maybe one of these days I'll get you an honorary membership in the Sons of Italy. What's up?"

"I need your guidance, Madge. Conspiracy comes in many variations and I'm trying to get a handle on the one that fits a story I'm on to. Suppose I can produce documentary evidence of a collusion which took place a number of years ago - not ancient history, but a few years in the past. Only one of the conspirators is still alive. The main co-conspirator is dead and the organization he worked for, which entered into the conspiratorial act and on which the principal evidence is based, no longer exists. The nature of the conspiratorial act itself? Well, it's pretty much circumstantial. What appear to be the fruits of the conspiracy are sequestered in a private Swiss bank account to which cash deposits from the conspiracy are still being made monthly. Withdrawals are being made, I have to assume, by an individual whose name appears nowhere in any of the documents except on the letterhead of the extinct business entity, a once prominent law firm. I'm trying to filter out fact from fantasy, and what verification procedures law enforcement agencies require for making conspiracy charges hold up."

"Confirms my opinion of lawyers," Maggio joked then became serious. "This is tough terrain, Charlie. What you're talking about probably doesn't amount to anything indictable. Give me the specifics - names, dates, numbers - and I may be able to give you some answers. You can forget the Swiss bank account."

"I figured you'd ask for details. This story is so sensitive that I got to have your word that none of what I tell you will ever leak to anyone, and that includes law enforcement agencies. I'm not doing this to protect my sources, but to determine whether or not there's a case. So I'll need full confidentiality."

"Now isn't that a complete role reversal? It used to be me swearing you to secrecy," John Maggio laughed. "We've always trusted each other, Charlie. If we can't trust each other after all these years, then there's no such thing as trust." Miller described his meeting with Robert Bird and the trip to Washington, leaving out no details. Maggio listened intently to Miller's story. The pupils of his icy Siberian eyes narrowed. He could not believe his good fortune.

"Now, I'm gonna let you in on a secret, *amico*. Coincidental that you should bring this to me at this time. I haven't spoken with you since taking

## Jack Eddinger

the security job with Bess Steel. I know everybody thinks I'm a duck out of water, but Joe O'Neill convinced me that I wouldn't regret it. He's a man I know well and respect, Charlie, and he hasn't let me down. All of what you told me fits directly with an investigation that until this minute was going nowhere."

"What do you mean?"

"The connection involves the Daleys. You know that Joe married Mrs. Daley after the war."

"Of course, everyone knows that."

"And it also makes him Tom Daley's stepfather."

"Sure."

"Well, just before the last election, the kid was going through some of his father's old files and came across a piece of paper - a cover page of some kind - marked, lo and behold, IMMSUBCOM 1935-38. When he interviewed me for the job, Joe asked if I knew of any law enforcement agency by that name. It didn't dawn on me then and there, but I recalled seeing similar references at FBI school. We figured out that it was an immigration subcommittee file. By the way, I gotta tell you that Tom's partner, Frank Comstock, is also privy to this information."

"He's a good man. I'll trust him on your say so," Miller said.

"I'm not sure how to go about this, Charlie. Conspiracy cases are the toughest to make, and federal conspiracy's even tougher. Wiretap information is inadmissible, even in cases of suspected treason or national security violations. And we have no grounds for a warrant or a subpoena to get our hands on those files. A grand jury needs prima facie evidence to indict, and it don't sound like you got it. If you let me, I'll be happy to explore this with my FBI contact in Newark, Al Foster. He's an expert in this area. I worked with him on the Fats Kourkorian hit. Anything with Maglie's name on it he's interested. But now I have a double interest, *capische*?"

"We've got to be careful about widening the circle, Madge. But if you think Foster can be of help, we ought to bring him on board. Damn, this isn't my field. I'm a reporter not a cop. By the way, anything new on Operation Fats?"

"One of my conditions for taking the Bess Steel job was to continue investigating on my own. The Bureau keeps me posted via Foster. They want Maglie almost as much as I want the ginzos who terminated Fats with extreme prejudice, as we used to say in the infantry. I'm headed across the river this afternoon. There's something I want to follow up on that might lead somewhere. Never would have given it a thought if I was still on the force. I'll let you know if anything pans out."

# INQUISITION

"How do you think we ought to proceed with Bob Bird's information?"

"Let me talk to my guys and to Foster in the next day or two and I'll get back to you."

"Just a note in passing, John, one of those files is marked IMMSUBCOMM," Charlie Miller added.

"Shee-it! This could be bigger than all of us Charlie. Once in a lifetime."

Later that afternoon John Maggio emerged from the New Jersey Toll Bridge Authority's windowless blockhouse on the Jersey end of the Memorial Bridge over the Delaware River. He squinted into a blinding sun. He had been sitting in a darkened basement room for three hours watching a parade of cars and trucks crawl across a small TV monitor as they rolled through the tollgates. Each vehicle stopped long enough to pay the toll and to be recorded by the Authority's security cameras. He let out a triumphant yelp when he found the frame he was looking for. At precisely 3:30 a.m. on November 17, 1956, according to the date and time stamp, a Cavalier Refuse Company eight-wheeler trundled through the toll plaza. The camera caught the faces of three men crowded into the cab. A hatless young man with his collar pulled up against the cold sat between the driver and two older men both wearing cloth caps pulled down to eye level. Maggio went to a public phone booth and called Special Agent Al Foster in Newark.

John Maggio introduced Agent Foster to the assembled group, consisting of Joe O'Neill, Tom Daley and Frank Comstock. They were meeting in O'Neill's tenth-floor office suite overlooking the Lenape River on *Iron Mountain*. Daley, Comstock and O'Neill were eager to share their information with the Federal agent in the outside hope that the Bureau might be able to shed further light on the cover sheet found among Tad Daley's papers. Maggio was holding back the details of his meeting with Charlie Miller until his new associates met with the FBI man.

"So you have a single page with no accompanying documents," Foster said. You brought me all the way over here to tell me this? I could've told you it's worthless over the phone, Lieutenant. You need a lot more than this to start thinking conspiracy even if Maglie's name's on it. It's meaningless."

"That's exactly what I told these fellas, Al. I know how hard it is to make a conspiracy case. But that was before I stumbled into a shit hole and crawled out perfumed and looking like Liberace. Let me tell you about it."

241

# Jack Eddinger

As they listened to Maggio recount Charlie Miller's description of Robert Bird's discovery, Tom Daley became more and more agitated. He walked across the room, and stood in silence before the floor to ceiling windows with a sweeping view all the way to the haze-tinged Lenape Mountains. His father's life and exceptional achievements had energized him from his youth and motivated his choice of a career in public service. Now, a trap door had sprung open, plunging him into free fall. It bent the bright light from the guide star on which his career ambitions were fixed and sucked it into a Black Hole. He had built his career on the premise that a life of public service leading to high office would finally and forever erase the stigma of his father's suicide. He'd vowed to take up his father's fallen banner and one day carry it to the summit of the United States Senate. That goal now seemed as remote as light from an undiscovered galaxy.

Joe O'Neill approached his stepson and put a fatherly arm around his shoulder. They stood at the window in silence, looking down on a pair of fisherman paddling their canoe upstream against the Lenape's hard current. Tom Daley thought how much he envied the oarsmen. Frank Comstock fought against an impulse to say something consoling to his friend. The three men stood together in silence, looking into the distance but seeing nothing. Each knew what the other was thinking.

"Now I know what Tom Paine meant when he wrote about times which try men's souls," Daley faltered. "I guess I'll just have to face the hard fact that all men - even those we hold in highest esteem and on whom we bestow super-human attributes - are mortal with all of the flaws and failings mortality confers. In retrospect I have to honestly say that I thought something was amiss in Dad's papers. Too many unanswered questions."

Maggio and Foster sat at the glass-topped table in desultory conversation as the three men continued their quiet conversation by the window. Maggio puffed on a big brown Cuban cigar. Foster lit up a Camel.

"I'm sorry I'm the bearer of this news," Maggio said as the three men returned to the table, "… like getting run down by an 18-wheeler."

"Not your fault, John," O'Neill said quietly. "The task ahead is going to require our best thinking and most astute judgment. We can't let emotions, however noble, deter us. In view of the information the lieutenant has shared with us, what's your advice, Agent Foster?"

"First thing, we need hard proof. So, I suggest that we have Mr. Miller arrange for Mr. Bird to return to the scene of the crime, so to speak, and get us some photographic evidence." Foster said dryly. "He's going to have to get back into the congressman's safe with a Leica and shoot every page of every document. This will take some doing entailing a considerable amount of risk. Is he up to it?"

# INQUISITION

"I don't know the man," John Maggio responded. "The best judge of that is Charlie Miller. Charlie trained him and tells me he trusts him."

"OK, but I can't move on your say so alone, Lieutenant. I'll need to get approval from my SAC, and he'll need approval from Washington. Irrespective of that, all of you must understand that the Bureau can in no way be associated with this venture without going to the top. If we acted independently in this situation, I assure you the Director would banish us to oblivion and have our wives and children sold into bondage. You can count on us, but we're strictly in the background at this point. Our role in this must be solely investigative and informational. What you do with our information is on your own initiative. We will vouch for whatever we give you and make sure it stands up. I'm too old for reassignment to sitting in parking lots waiting for two-bit hoods to crawl out of the local bordello. And speaking of hoods, I brought you a present, lieutenant." Foster handed Maggio a file folder containing photo copies of the FBI's records related to the activities of Robert Basilico, Joseph Zaccardi and Dominic "Little Mimi" Di Francese, along with mugshots of Di Francese and Basilico. Reading the files thoroughly like an exegete studying the scriptures for levels of meaning, John Maggio fixed his attention on Bobby Basilico's photograph. He recognized him as the loony bird between the two apes in the Cavalier Refuse truck. This guy I can break, he thought.

"Well gentlemen, there's enough here to occupy us a fortnight or two. Oh, and by the way Mr. Daley, may I suggest that you shelve your plans for an electoral recount. We don't need further attention drawn to the election, and besides you wouldn't want to tarnish your armor now, would you?" Foster said with a wry smile, snapping down the brim of his gray fedora. Maggio accompanied Foster to the agent's car. On the way, he described the surprise he had in store for Bobby Basilico and how it would raise havoc in the environs of Cavalier Enterprises.

"I like the way you think, lieutenant. That is a brilliant ruse. I never heard a word you said. We could use your talent in the Bureau," Foster smiled.

Maggio caught up with Bobby Basilico as Bobby was getting into his red T-Bird around 2:30 a.m. in a deserted alley in back of *Il Ceppo's*, his hangout on Manhattan's East Side.

"Hey Babalu," a deep voice that Bobby Basilico did not recognize greeted him from behind, "You keep late hours." John Maggio pressed a nickel-plated .38 caliber police special hard against the back of Bobby's head. "Next time I'll make an appointment, *cacasotto*."

"Who the fuck are you? Waddya want?"

# Jack Eddinger

"Waddya, waddya, shit face? Maggio shoved Bobby's head down hard on the T-Bird's low roof, starting a gushing nose bleed. Bobby struggled to turn around. His assailant had his shirt collar in his fist and his knee in the center of his spinal column, applying agonizing pressure. Blood ran down Bobby's chin onto the lapels of his silk sport coat and down the front of his white shirt. Long strands of oily black hair covered his eyes, blinding him. He was confused, disoriented, dazed. He knew he'd be stopping a bullet in the next few seconds and was terrified. Why this shit? He carried out every detail the Duke requested. The fire took out the wires and all the other stuff he used. Maglie even congratulated him on a perfect job.

"I did every fuckin thing the Duke asked for, plus I made fuckin sure nothing could be traced. Mimi and the Calabrese will swear to it," he pleaded.

"Open the trunk!"

Fumbling and terrified, Bobby sprung the trunk. His assailant pushed him to the ground, his knee pinning Bobby's shoulders to the asphalt pavement grimy with crankcase oil. The stench of garbage overflowing from cans at the rear of the restaurant permeated the humid night. Then he handcuffed him face down and pushed him half way under the car, planting a foot on Bobby's buttocks. He rummaged through the trunk before ripping out the carpeting. He dragged Bobby from under the car, threw him into the trunk, slammed the lid down and locked it.

After an hour of silence Bobby Basilico could not believe he was still alive. The blood was sticky on his face. He began kicking at the trunk lid and yelling. Two Latinos from the nearby kitchen heard the commotion and called the police.

The experience brought Bobby Basilico to the realization that if he were to reach the age of 30, he had better start looking for a new line of work. He was smart enough to realize that what happened in the alley behind Il Ceppo's was the Duke's one time warning. That's how he owns you. Why else would he be alive? When a wise guy fails to whack you, the message is last chance, wise up. Except, wisdom told him there would be no opportunity to redeem himself. When The Duke puts out a preliminary contract, the rule is simple: you're destined for a one way swim. Bobby decided he needed to alter his destiny.

It was only natural for Bobby Basilico to seek out the Feds. They'd make a deal and provide protection if they think you're giving them what they want. Since he was not yet a made member of the Duke's organization like his two compadres, *omerta* didn't apply to him. At least that was the thinking that brought Bobby Boy to the FBI's field office in Newark.

# INQUISITION

"We're interested, Mr. Basilico, and we want everything. I mean all of it! So let's have it from the beginning." Al Foster offered Bobby a cigarette.

"This is Special Agent-in-Charge Jordan. He has an interest in anything you can tell us about the Blue Peacock and your employer Cavalier Enterprises." Foster hit the "record" button on the portable tape recorder between them.

Frank Jordan made no acknowledgment and stared coldly at Bobby Basilico until Bobby dropped his eyes to the table. Both agents had their jackets off. They wore black shoulder holsters holding .45-caliber Browning automatics big enough to take down a platoon of hit men.

"Before you begin, Mr. Basilico, Agent Jordan and I believe it's only fair to tell you that you face a number of felony charges - first degree murder, arson, interstate transportation of explosives, conspiracy, not to mention breaking and entering, malicious destruction of property and other local charges," Foster pushed an FBI Wanted circular across the desk. Bobby was surprised to see his picture. It was a mug shot from a DWI arrest in South Jersey. "In order for us to convince the U.S. Attorney to consider any form of leniency, you will answer every question we put to you. We know you want to cooperate. We are in a position to help. I don't think we need to spell out that murder one buys you a ticket to the gas chamber."

"I didn't murder nobody," Bobby Basilico told the FBI men.

"Prove it!" Jordan barked, speaking for the first time.

Bobby Basilico reluctantly and with sweat beads glistening on his upper lip and forehead described the special orders he received and how he purchased the materials to complete his assignment. He did not mention the meeting at Cavalier Construction Co., Gaetano Cavalieri Russo, Stefano Maglie or his two associates in the torching of the Blue Peacock. Nor did he mention Anastas Kourkorian. He told the agents he received his orders from an anonymous caller as he had received all of his assignments. Payment in cash came by special delivery mail the following day. He said he could not identify the source of the message. He said he knew the two men accompanying him only by the names, Little Mimi and Joe Calabrese. He said he did not know the victim, but was just doing his job.

"You call this information?" Frank Jordan bellowed at Bobby Basilico. "You expect us to keep the goons away on the basis of this flimsy stuff? I can take you down right now for mail fraud. That's ten years. Sorry, my friend, no deal."

# Jack Eddinger

"I didn't have nothin to do with killin the guy. Swear ta god. The others did it," Bobby blurted out. "Mimi and the Calabrese hit Fats. I just did my job."

"You were there, Bobby," Foster said. "You saw everything. That makes you an accessory to murder. Tell us exactly what you saw that night at the Blue Peacock. We want the whole score and on both the black and white keys. Play it, Bobby."

"All I know is Mimi was inside Fats's office. Joe was waitin in the truck. Then I heard a shotgun blast. I didn't see nuthin. Joe got outta the truck and him and Mimi dragged Fats's body to the back of the truck. I don't know what happened after that. I went inside the place and rigged it. I don't know nuthin about what went on when I was inside. I got into the truck. Joe gunned the dumpster engine and we waited for Mimi. He was tellin Fats's driver something. Then he got in and we drove away."

"I think we should charge him," Jordan said. "Let's get an assistant U.S. attorney up here right now. Y'know my friend, when the word reaches the street that Bobby Basilico's a canary, your ass won't be worth pigeon shit."

"I told you everything I know," Bobby wavered. "I don't know no more than that."

"You better think again, my friend," Jordan warned. "You come in here and tell us a story which reaches the stratosphere of bullshit, and you ask us to believe you? I think we ought to see what kind of balls Bobby Boy has, Al. Put the word out that a new tenor just made his debut singing *Pentito*. I don't think he'll survive opening night. For a wise guy, you're not too smart, Mr. Basilico. Interview ended. Get your ass out of here!"

Bobby Basilico considered his options and realized he had none. The Duke would see to that, quickly and effectively. And no way he was gonna take the rap for a hit he didn't make. He was being set up by the Duke and Maglie and left to hold the shit stick. Well, fuck them!

"Okay. Wait ... wait. I'll tell you everything I know," he faltered.

"Now if it isn't everything, fella, I can guarantee you a short, unhappy life," Jordan scowled. Bobby described the meeting in Union City. He told them why Anastas Kourkorian had to be hit; how he purchased the ammonium nitrate, the blasting caps and wiring he used to torch the Blue Peacock and the role of each of his accomplices in carrying out their orders from Gaetano Cavalieri Russo.

"What about Maglie? What was his part in all of this?"

"Nothin, other than I was to report to him about the job, and pick up my pay. I ain't seen him since then. He's *consigliere* and reports directly to the Duke. I never seen him before this."

# INQUISITION

"O.K. here's the deal, Firebird. I want you to continue serving Russo as a good soldier. But from now on, you are my eyes and ears inside Cavalier Enterprises, Inc., *capische*?" said Jordan. "I want a report on every job; every hit; and the name of every wiseguy involved, and I want to hear the play-by-play in your golden voice on the phone every week. You play ball with us, Bobby Boy, and a year from now, you'll be a free man in sunny California with a new apartment, a new job and a new face. Take it or leave it."

Bobby Basilico cringed when Jordan mentioned the nickname he used in the organization. It was the second time the Feds used it. A warm sensation spread down his legs and soaked his trousers. He shoulda never come here.

# CHAPTER TWELVE
## *The Incorruptible Man*

Waiters in starched white jackets were wiping down tables and polishing silverware in the House dining room as the last of the breakfast crowd filed out through the big arching doorway, too busy or too much in a hurry to notice the three men at a table in a distant corner of the room. The Speaker, as always, sat with his back to the other diners. Knowledgeable members of the House could tell he was conducting important business by the laconic manner, the arch of his back and the firmly planted feet encased in worn and dusty cowboy boots.

"I believe the last time we visited was when you and Mr. Palmer came to see me 'bout that merger you were pursuin.'" Ham Clayburg was speaking to Joe O'Neill but leveled his penetrating dark eyes on Tom Daley to see how long it would take the young man to look away. Daley knew he was being clocked by one of the most powerful men in America, so he dropped his gaze politely and offered the Speaker a firm right hand.

"Mr. Speaker, it's an honor to meet you, sir. You've always been a leader I'd be privileged to emulate," Daley said.

"Yes, Ham," Joe O'Neill said, "I remember it well. Gene Palmer was awfully upset that we couldn't get that merger through Congress, but I told him that you always kept your word, and when you gave it to me on seeing to it that Bessemer Steel would be awarded the Texas-North pipeline contract, it took some of the sting away. And the help you gave us at Galveston Ship Yard to build those missile frigates has certainly kept our business healthy. We can't thank you enough, Ham."

"Well, Joe, you're one of the few men I've known to keep **his** word, and that goes back a ways to when I was Chairman of Interstate and Foreign Commerce and you were lookin to get those destroyers Mr. Churchill had built by your company out from under the Neutrality Act embargo - that was back in '38-39, as I recall. Your idea to dismantle them and send the parts to Canada then convoy them over to England for re-assembly saved a lot of lives and allowed me to report to Mr. Roosevelt that we'd untied his hands. That was before we passed Lend Lease. The president was very gracious to me when it came to handin out credit."

"Yes, that was quite a coup. Those were interesting times, Ham. Every plant we owned was operating around the clock 365 days a year. I like to think we had something to do with winning the war."

While the two men reminisced, Tom Daley dug into his briefcase and produced a copy of *A Cavalryman's War* by Lt. General Richard Taylor,

# INQUISITION

CSA about the exploits of the Confederate cavalry in the Red River Campaign. The book had been out of print for nearly half a century, but Joe O'Neill, found a copy in an antiquarian bookstore in Philadelphia. He pushed it reverently across the table to the Speaker. "Please accept this book as a small token of mutual interests, Mr. Speaker. Not many people know about the campaigns in the southwest. General Taylor's history is one of the best," Tom Daley said, noticing a glint of approval in the Speaker's dark eyes.

"Well now, young fella, that's mighty nice of you. This is what you'd call a well-timed gift. I was giving a lot of thought to certain matters recently, and remembered General Taylor's disagreement with his commander, General Kirby Smith. It's funny you brought me this particalar book. Y'know General Taylor was the son of President Zachary Taylor? My pappy rode and fought with him down in Lousiana at Crump's Hill and Sabine Cross Roads. I genuinely appreciate having Gen. Taylor's history. It will make a fine addition to my collection on the War Between the States. Been out of print for years. General Taylor, y'know got into an argument with his superior officer, General Smith, near the end of the campaign over whose brigades were doin all the fightin. It got so bitter that General Smith had to relieve General Taylor of command, a decision that's never easy, 'specially when it's the son of a president who was a national hero himself. It set me to thinkin. Must be somethin with men carryin that name that they just let their pride get in front of their duty," the gnarled Texan said with an uncharacteristic tinge of resignation in his voice. His two guests were mystified by the cryptic remark. He quickly surmised their bafflement and without a prelude began relating the story of how an old friend and trusted confidante had let him down and had put him in the same position as General Taylor put General Smith.

Joe O'Neill and Tom Daley listened in silence, as the Speaker described Zach Harris's defiance of House procedures. Neither was prepared to believe what he was hearing. So powerful was the public perception of Zachary Taylor Harris that nothing short of death, terminal illness or resignation, they believed, could weaken, let alone remove him from the central position he had held in the Democratic Party, Pennsylvania and American public life for nearly a quarter century. Yet, this information was coming not from a press report or rumor, but from a man whose credibility was legendary and whose word was faultless. "I asked you to come down here today, so's I could determine for myself the kind of man you are, Mr. Daley, and to see whether you got what it takes to beat Zach Harris."

Tom Daley slouched back in his chair, pondering the Speaker's words. This was something he never remotely considered, as he charted his political future. It was unthinkable to consider that Zach Harris could be dislodged from the 26th Congressional District. No, it would be political suicide to try. Joe O'Neill with his eyes fixed on the Speaker's firm visage instantly grasped the immense and singular opportunity being handed to his step-son.

"I'm overwhelmed, Mr. Speaker. I've just never in my wildest dreams considered anything like this," Daley said. "Congressman Harris is part of the fabric of life back home. Running against him would take uncommon organizational, intellectual and moral resources."

"Well now, you've met my first criterion by not putting money anywhere on your list. If you think you possess the other qualities you mentioned and are willing to work hard, there are plenty of ways we can help you. "There's another reason Mr. Harris has to go, and I believe you know what I'm referrin to. My friend downtown has informed me of your meeting with one of his agents. Matter of fact, he gave me a full briefing. As I understand it, you've come across some very interesting information. I urge you to go wherever your findings take you, Mr. Daley. However, I advise you to terminate your pursuit of a recount. It'd be long, tedious and unfruitful. But I would encourage you, as a private citizen, to look into corrupt practices in the 26$^{th}$ District. I realize you no longer hold the investigative tools you had as District Attorney, but I can arrange to have many resources placed at your disposal. If you need staff investigators from any appropriate committee to help in any way, feel free to ask. I don't need your answer here and now. I want you to go back home; talk it over with Joe here and your wife and your closest friends, then come back and we'll talk about how to win elections. Zach Harris may think he's god-almighty but he ain't. He can be beat."

On his return to Washington from Philadelphia, Congressman Harris went directly to his Capitol hideaway office from Union Station to phone Lenore Price with the good news. The divorce would be final in two months and he'd need a temporary place to stay. She'd be ecstatic and he would not have to suffer the humiliation of having to find a place to live. Damned real estate agents'll have it all over town. He tried the key several times but the door failed to open. Puzzled, he checked the key then tried again, but the lock would not click open. He walked down a flight of stairs to the building superintendent's office and asked a secretary for a pass key to H-420.

"I'm sorry, Congressman, H-420's been vacated," she replied. "The Sergeant-at-Arms had everything moved to the basement storage room last week. They said you were getting a new office during the recess."

# INQUISITION

"New office? Nobody told me about a new office. What' here?" Harris demanded. "We were just following orders, Congr. Harris. You'll have to talk directly to the Sergeant-at-Arms."

"Damned right I will!"

Zach Harris caught up with, the burly House sergeant-at-arms, Harley Hattaway, as he ambled through a long darkened corridor leading to the empty House chamber. The halls of Congress in recess are like an empty tomb; no sounds, no lights, no sign of human activity.

"God dammit, Harley, just what the hell is going on with my office?" Harris demanded of the gregarious red-faced Georgian, who'd been on the House staff for a quarter century and knew every member by their first name.

"Speaker's orders, Zach. You'll have to take it up with him," Hattaway drawled. "He came to my office last week and ordered me - I say he ordered me - to have that office vacated before he left town. Didn't give a reason, but I can tell ya, he was madder'n hell."

"What do you mean before he left town? He never goes anywhere."

"Went back home for a few speeches around the Fourth District and to hunt bird down on the ranch. Told me he'd be out of touch but that he'd be back next week sometime. Said he'd have me over to his place for some tasty pheasant and chili he'd be cookin up. That's all I know."

His grey eyes blazing with fury, Zachary Taylor Harris brushed past the receptionist in the Longworth Building, slamming the door behind him and startling his office staff and two constituents waiting to see him. He slumped into the leather armchair next to the fireplace without removing his overcoat and hat. Through his simmering resentment, he tried to discern the Speaker's motivation. As he sat looking out the window towards the Capitol, he remembered the confrontation over televising the Philadelphia hearings and the Speaker's undefined threat. Why? he thought. What does the man want? He'd never crossed him on anything. He gave him countless votes over the years and never turned down a fight in his behalf whether with a committee chairman, the Administration or with the Senate. It was an unfair and ugly reprisal for a trivial violation - if that - of House protocol; pure chicken shit and he wasn't about to put up with it. He could not let this challenge pass. His integrity was at stake. How would his colleagues interpret it? His staff? Lenore? It bit sharply and unbalanced the psychic machinery he relied upon to confront difficult situations and resolve vexing problems. He felt stymied. He could usually dominate any member, or at least finesse them into agreement on just about any reasonable proposal. But the Speaker was different. He was not a man of the 20$^{th}$ century. He belonged in the ruts and furrows of a forgotten

# Jack Eddinger

America; in a time of corduroy roads, wagon tracks and uncleared land. He possessed personal qualities and quirks Zach Harris could never fathom, regardless of how close he had become in the early days, as one of Ham Clayburg's bright young lieutenants, and later as, if not an equal, then as a respected chairman and senior member of the House hierarchy. To Zach Harris the Speaker was a puzzle his Northerner's mind could not decipher. The man embodied something strong and primitive; a character formed by that antique sense of America embodied in the expression, "these United States," which had all but vanished from the nation's political vocabulary. He was a child of that pastoral America crushed and beaten in the Civil War; an anachronism, a displaced heir of Clay, Jackson and Calhoun, yet a formidable antagonist. Zach Harris owed him a great deal. But he did not know how to reach out to him. The man was beyond influence. He could not be touched. He had no use for money and rarely carried more than a five dollar bill in his pocket. He was the unique American, the incorruptible man.

As he pondered his options, a powerful thought struck him. The Speaker, he knew, had an eye for beautiful and stylish women at ease in the political atmosphere, particularly an intelligent, well-dressed, well-spoken woman who could talk knowledgeably about public affairs and the Democratic Party. The route to exoneration, he concluded, was through Lenore Price. Lenore was the ideal go-between. Like the Speaker she was passionately committed to the ideals of the party and adored the Speaker's favorite politician, Adlai Stevenson. She was completely comfortable in the world of men, something the Speaker admired in a woman. She would have no trouble winning his confidence, and reminding him that Zachary Taylor Harris was too good a Democrat to banish from his inner counsels for so frivolous a lapse in judgment. He would ask her to intercede with the Speaker. But it had to look right; as if being proposed solely on her initiative. That way, he would not appear to be groveling or to be seeking misplaced clemency. His dignity and self-respect would remain undiminished. She'd ask him to forgive and forget for the good of the party and the man.

With his new stratagem in place, Zachary Taylor Harris took up his proposal with Lenore Price, as they lay in bed in the semi-darkness of late afternoon post-coital rapture, the best time to ask her for a favor. He described his run-in with the Speaker, the petty vindictiveness over his hideaway office, and how he could not bring himself to placate Clayburg's misplaced animosity.

"I know he holds you in high regard, Lenore, ever since the convention when you got the California women's delegation to start the demonstration

# INQUISITION

for Stevenson," Harris told her. "That kept things moving for Adlai. It saved Ham from having to gavel down the other candidates. He'd grant you any favor you requested."

"He's just an old-fashioned man, darling, with old-fashioned notions," she told her congressman. "He's really very soft-hearted and sweet and doesn't hold grudges. He's probably already regretting this petty disagreement. I completely understand that you can't afford to have him as an enemy, but at the same time, cannot lose face as a chairman. It would diminish your stature as a statesman. And, of course, he mustn't know about us. At least not until the divorce is final."

Zach told Lenore she should casually approach the Speaker at the Democratic leaders conference scheduled for the following week. She should tell him of hearing rumors that he and Congressman Harris were quarreling, and that she hoped they weren't true, because if they became public, the Republicans would exploit them in the midterm elections. They'd say it shows that the Democrats are soft on communism, because they want the Speaker to muzzle the one man who has removed the House of Representatives from the national spotlight on this divisive national security issue by conducting business seriously and intelligently outside the overheated atmosphere of Washington.

"He likes women who are direct, smart and think like men. Tell him he and Congressman Harris should quietly put their disagreement to rest for the good of the party and our candidates. He'll thank you for your good common sense."

By now, he reckoned, Marion had received the decree. He was, for all practical purposes, a free man. After moving in with Lenore Price, Zach Harris took time out during the recess for a routine checkup at Bethesda Naval Hospital. He'd seen more than a few of his older colleagues collapse of heart attacks in their mistresses' apartments and wanted medical assurance he'd not share their fate. Moreover, he was bothered by intermittent bouts of coughing, which still left flecks of blood on his handkerchief. He attributed the condition to Philadelphia's winter dampness aggravating the condition that had sent him to the hospital three months previously.

The Congressman's absence had created the opportunity Robert Bird was waiting to exploit with more than a little anxiety. Shortly after his meeting with Charlie Miller a Bureau courier delivered the special Leica to Bird's apartment in Arlington, along with detailed instructions for obtaining the best images in photographing documents. It was the same type of camera U.S. clandestine agents used to photograph Politburo documents in the Kremlin. On a midweek night around ten o'clock he

# Jack Eddinger

let himself into the Congressman's office and once again carefully dialed open the safe. He spread the materials out on the table top and went to work under the intense light of a sun-lamp he bought at Walgreen's. By 4 A.M he had everything on film. Miller's instructions were to deliver the film to the Bureau's Special Operations Division in the basement of the Justice Department. He was to be met by the head of the photographic analysis unit. He turned over the film and the camera, but not before he was told that all further contact, including a witness interview, would be through the criminal division. Robert Bird had not counted on being a witness against his boss. The encounter left him agitated and acutely nervous. He began to have second thoughts about what he had done.

Three days later, John Maggio convened the group he christened "Task Force Red Man." It comprised the originals - Maggio, O'Neill, Daley, and Comstock - and two new members, Charlie Miller and Special Agent-in-Charge Frank Jordan, chief of the FBI's Newark field office. Jordan replaced Foster by direct order from Washington. Miller, in return for confidentiality and the information he provided Maggio from Robert Bird, would be given an exclusive on the story. Anticipating Jordan's concern about having a reporter present, Maggio explained his and the group's long relationship with Miller. "Besides," he told Foster, "Charlie Miller is the institutional memory of the Lenape Valley, and will be very helpful in any initiative aimed at cleaning up the public stables."

Jordan regarded Miller skeptically without commenting on the arrangement. There was no way a jerkwater newsman would be given an exclusive story with the Director now fully involved. Lou Richards, the Director's PR man, would see to that. Maggio can break the news to Miller when it's time.

"Before we get too far down the avenue, gentlemen," said Jordan. "You all need to know that this matter is now fully under federal jurisdiction. The Chief is intensely interested in every aspect of the situation and has ordered me to inform you of that fact. So there's no room for amateurism. Any investigative initiative; any discussion of charges; any prosecutorial strategy must meet his approval. His ground rules are clear. We don't go forward unless and until he's satisfied with the evidence. He has seen the photographic material the Congressman's man produced and was unimpressed. There's no evidence of wrongdoing on Harris's part - at least nothing admissible in Federal court or that will stand up to a forceful defense. I know you believe Harris's guilty as hell, and you may well be right, but everything on that strip of film is inadmissible, plus it was obtained surreptitiously - no writ, no court order, no warrant. No dice."

# INQUISITION

"What can this group do to assist you, to advance the cause?" Tom Daley asked. "There's a great deal of talent in this room. I'd hate to see it wasted."

"Tom's right, Agent Jordan, we can advance the investigation by doing a lot of the grunt work that your agents would be required to perform," Joe O'Neill added. "By the way, Tom has dropped his pursuit of the recount. But that means we'll lose access to the DA's active and historic files, which admittedly contain raw investigative material, but nonetheless could be a valuable source of information that can provide perspective to keep us focused."

"You have a point there," Jordan responded. "I'll send a squad of agents in to comb through the files. They'll know what to look for. I'll get the most promising material under federal subpoena. What's this new DA like?"

Politically connected to Harris but indirectly," Comstock said. "His ass is owned by the Hampton County GOP chairman, Lloyd Kressman, a shifty old Dutchman, who's had a long, and we believe conniving relationship with the congressman. Trouble is, there's no proof."

"That's no good. Too loosey, goosey. When are you guys going to produce something tangible?" Jordan complained. "Look, here's the way we're going to proceed. Frankly, I'm far more interested in what Lt. Maggio has given us than information about an allegedly corrupt congressman. Besides, as I said, the Director's handling that aspect in Washington. It's too political. The lieutenant here has presented us with a live singing turkey in the person of one Bobby Boy Basilico. Maggio accomplished more in one evening with this junior thug than an army of cops. He's given us our first material witness for putting the Russo crime family in federal prison. And its ramifications don't end there. This is off the record, Mr. Miller."

"Like you. I've heard nothing tangible, so there's nothing to write about," Charlie Miller retorted.

"There are two men I want, and you gentlemen can help me," Frank Jordan told his listeners. "Daley, you must have a dossier on Stefano Maglie's activities in Hampton County. Anything you can provide would be welcome."

"Maglie's a very cool operator. There's not much on him in our shop, is there, Frank?"

"Nothing of any consequence, but in my judgment the initials 'S.M.' on those private immigration bills from the IMMSUBCOM files belong to him," Frank Comstock noted. "If Maglie's on the scene, then Russo has to be lurking nearby. Maglie's his *consigliere*."

# Jack Eddinger

"Good thinking, Comstock. Maglie will take us to Russo. What do you know about The Duke?" Jordan asked.

"Madge can tell you more than I can. He's my source on anything involving the brotherhood."

"Well then we've come full circle. I'd like to have Lt. Maggio's service for the duration. If you agree to releasing him to me and my colleagues for the next few months, Mr. O'Neill, I'll do all I can to convince the Director to move Congressman Harris to the top of the Bureau's political watch list if it's not already there. But for public consumption Maggio stays on your payroll."

"The decision is the lieutenant's to make. If he agrees, we agree," said Joe O'Neill. "What about it, John?"

"I'm half way there now. Might as well go the rest of the way," John Maggio agreed. "Very well then Agent Jordan, unless there's an objection from my colleagues, we'll follow your lead."

"Tom?"

"No objection."

"Frank?"

"Second that."

"Charlie?"

"I'd follow John Maggio into mortal combat."

"Good. Let's get started."

# CHAPTER THIRTEEN
## *Confrontation*

In the days and weeks that followed, Zachary Taylor Harris received a brutal education in the exercise of power. His travel and personal expense vouchers were returned unpaid; his privileged parking space in the House garage was revoked and assigned to a chairman he particularly despised; his name was conspicuously absent from the State Department's list of members of the Commission on Eastern Europe Resettlement; members seemed to turn in another direction when he approached - his own committee colleagues were polite but non-committal to his recommendations for new inquiries - and his repeated phone calls to the Speaker's office were not returned. The daily calls to his office from Lloyd Kressman, badgering him about the bank charter, especially irked him. But one call on his private line from the Dutchman one late afternoon caught him at his desk and threatened to be far more menacing than the Speaker's sadistic little caper. Kressman informed him that federal agents were all over the Lenape Valley asking questions about the election.

"Vats more, Zach, I got a subpeenie today from the federal bank examiner in Philadelphia, wanting me to turn over all my account books," the Dutchman said. Zach Harris immediately picked up the apprehension in Kressman's voice.

"Don't worry, Lloyd. That's just routine. I've started the process to get your bank chartered," he lied. "They're just doing their homework to make sure everything's in good order."

"Like hell, they are," the Dutchman shot back. "They told me I was being investigated for some kind of fraud involving an elected official. I figured it was you, Zach. That's why I'm callin ya. Ya gotta call them off, Zach. We may be friends, but I ain't stickin my neck out for nobody."

A rasping cough erupted from deep in the congressman's chest cavity and shook him violently. He choked on yellowish sputum. The coughing continued for several minutes, but went unheeded behind the heavy oak doors which sealed him off from his staff. He lay with his head on the desk waiting for the spell to pass. Kressman's voice cackled on about scapegoats and fall guys heedless to what was occurring. Zach Harris pushed himself away from his desk and staggered to his private washroom a few feet away. He cupped cold water from his hand to his face, clutching the wash basin for support and straightening himself up, panting and wheezing like a marathon runner. He staggered back to his desk, clicked down the receiver, breaking the connection, and left the phone off its cradle. The rotten feeling he attributed to bronchitis and finally prompted him to undergo the physical at Bethesda Naval Hospital. The examination by the hospital's chief of internal medicine confirmed the earlier blood pressure reading of 225/115. Palpation and auscultation revealed an overworked heart and heavily congested lungs. The diagnostic tests ordered for him included an EKG, chest X-rays, pulmonary work-up and the full range of blood studies. He dreaded his next appointment, which would present the findings. He had no interest in learning about them. He attributed his latest malaise to the pills he was given on his previous visit to lower his blood pressure. They made him dizzy, nauseous and depressed. And now with Kressman the target of a federal investigation, the command and discipline he could normally summon to control events were slipping away. To remedy it meant he'd have to put his ace into play. His personal relationship with the Director had passed the *quid pro quo* test. As promised, the Director had provided him with all the investigative material he required to make the Burnham hearings a personal triumph. The telegram congratulating him on the Philadelphia hearings proved the Director's loyalty and stood as testimony to their compact. In return for keeping him on top of federal investigative activities in the 26th District, he would give the Director a free hand in all future hearings conducted by the Committee on Subversive Activities. Kressman's anxiety notwithstanding, he needed another meeting with his new ally downtown to assay the situation. It would not ease the Dutchman's distress, but might scare him into backing off the bank proposal if the federal investigative heat was something that he, Zach Harris, could channel into a palpable threat.

    Had he been informed of the Director's conference with the Speaker while he was in Philadelphia assailing the Burnhams, Zachary Taylor Harris would be far less sanguine in his expectations.

    Ham Clayburg, always distrustful of authoritative figures, listened carefully but skeptically as the Director briefed him about information the Bureau had received from a congressional staff member, whom he characterized as "a confidential informant" without identifying Robert Bird. The Director had requested the meeting and startled the Speaker's office staff when his compact frame and immediately recognized visage appeared in the doorway. Three staffers nearly collided to be the first to greet him.

    "Don't get up. Please don't. Forgive the inconvenience. I hope I'm not intruding," he announced with obsequious courtesy.

    "Right this way, sir. The Speaker's waiting for you in his private chamber down one flight. He told me to escort you there as soon as you

# INQUISITION

arrived," said the office manager, an ancient grey-haired woman with a Texas drawl, who'd managed the Speaker's affairs since his election to Congress in 1912. She led him down a stairwell to the Speaker's hideaway office below the House chamber.

"Well hello Mr. Speaker," the Director said jauntily. "It's a pleasure to visit you here in your native habitat - the lion in his den so to speak."

Ham Clayburg stood behind his desk with his jacket off. The sleeves of his white shirt were held up at the biceps with elastic bands. A black silk tie with gold stickpin peeked out above his black vest. His face was set in a somber grimace like a mortician viewing a corpse. The Speaker won his first election the same year the Director, at the age of twelve, was entering fifth grade in a District of Columbia public school. Ham Clayburg was the only man with more tenure and more knowledge of Washington's mythology than the Director. He was the kind of man an entrenched bureaucrat regarded with extreme wariness; a man beyond intimidation; a man like his patron, Judge Stone, to be both feared and admired.

"Sit down, sit down. I hope it wasn't inconvenient for you to come up here." The two men were alone. "Now, what's all this hush hush information you talked about on the phone."

"Mr. Speaker," the Director began without preliminary niceties, "I have the very unpleasant duty of bringing to your attention information and documents regarding the activities of a member of Congress, which I believe you will want to study closely and take appropriate action. I, of course, am prepared to offer the full investigative resources of the Bureau should you decide they would be applicable, and to hold all such information privileged and confidential."

The Director took a fat dossier from his briefcase and handed it to the Speaker. Ham Clayburg put on his horn-rimmed spectacles and scanned the covering memorandum. He was dumbfounded to read the caption centered at the top of the document under the Bureau's letterhead:

**Re: Zachary Taylor Harris,**
**Investigation of Government Employees - C,**
**(Bureau File 100-26126)**
**Summary of Evidence In Support of Statement of Alleged Violations**

As he reviewed the summary of allegations, including the 8 x 10 photographs produced by Robert Bird, his face flushed and a deep crimson wave crawled across his sun-freckled scalp. "Where'd this stuff come from?" he demanded angrily. He had seen files compiled on members in the past. While some were straightforward and factual, most contained

# Jack Eddinger

considerable hearsay, unsupported conclusions and conjecture supplied by so-called well-placed informants. But this looked different. Photographs don't lie.

"As you can see, the photographic evidence would appear to be overwhelming," the Director noted. "Rather than have the Bureau initiate a criminal probe, you may wish to turn this information over to your own investigators. That way you will have the invaluable resource of congressional subpoena power, which we do not have. Furthermore, you will be in a position to claim full credit for turning a discreet internal investigation into national news. We will, of course, brief your people. I am fully aware of the sensitivities involved."

The Speaker said nothing, but inside he was seething. His resentment at the Director's suggestion that he ought to use a public relations gimmick, however, was more than eclipsed by his outrage at the perfidy and deceit of a man he'd known and trusted for nearly a quarter century.

"I need to digest this, and the only way I can do that is to sit here and go through it page by page," Clayburg said. "Let me do that, then I'll decide how I want to proceed."

"Your decision, of course, Mr. Speaker. "But you'll note that a majority of what you will be reading is raw investigative information. Nothing strong enough to indict. Our evaluation is that because the photographic material was gained surreptitiously, it would not be admissible under current law. You may wish to handle this as an internal House matter with your own remedial proceeding, if you get what I mean."

"I'll be the judge of that." He resented the Director's non-committal demeanor and his use of the passive voice to relieve himself and the Bureau from the responsibility of supporting and authenticating the material he was presenting as if it were fact. Dissembling was the one characteristic he abhorred. He measured a man by his ability for straight-talk, eye contact, veracity and openness, the bedrock of honesty. He had no use for ass kissers, lickspittles and PR games.

"To be sure," the Director agreed. "Thank you and a good day to you, sir. And by the way, you may want to close those investigative loopholes I mentioned with new legislation. They're big enough to drive a Sherman tank through."

Ham Clayburg spent the rest of the day absorbing the information in the dossier. He pondered various courses of action with great care. He decided to apply the kind of indirect pressure that he was sure would bring Zachary Taylor Harris to his door, rather than to have the story leak out piecemeal to House members and to the press, thereby assuring a fiasco. He gave his man, Harley Hattaway, precise directions for carrying out

# INQUISITION

his wishes without giving the Sergeant-at-Arms his reasons. Heading the list was removing the furniture from and changing the locks to Zach's hideaway office.

The celebratory birthday dinner at *La Salle de Bois* to confirm his freedom and the new life they'd soon be enjoying was for Lenore Price anything but festive. In spite of her best efforts to lift his spirits, Zach Harris remained in the morose, resentful state that had descended upon him since his unpleasant discovery that he'd lost the Speaker's trust and esteem for willfully violating House rules. She was alarmed by his drawn and haggard appearance and his incessant, rasping cough, but tried to put the best face on the situation. When she approached the Speaker the previous week at a Democratic party function to gently chide him about the undeserved treatment being shown his good friend, Congressman Harris, Ham Clayburg turned his back on her and walked away, something he'd never done before. She was uneasy with the Speaker's snub, but attributed it to his dark side, which she'd heard stories about and to his being a lifelong bachelor who lived alone and had no other life than the House of Representatives. He'll get over it, but it will take a little time, she reflected. He must be quite upset.

"Darling, as we both agree, the Speaker's an old-fashioned and formal man," she told the man she loved. "He's really a sweet person. His authority means everything to him. His pride's been hurt by someone he admires greatly, but he's stubborn and cannot find a way to tell you that. It would be too difficult, even embarrassing, for him. I think you should take the initiative."

"What do you mean?"

"I think you should go to him with hat in hand and apologize," she said firmly. "Tell him you made a big mistake; that as chairman, you truly believed you had the authority to do what you did; that you had no intention of breaching his trust and that you have deep regrets for any difficulty you may have caused. Keep it on a personal level and show your genuine remorse. He'll admire you all the more for it, because it's true. Your friendship is too valuable to let something so small come between you. I'm sure he'll forgive and forget."

He coughed weakly but listened carefully as she continued. "You are just as proud a man as he is, Zach darling. I know this will require forbearance, but I just know that a heartfelt apology will be accepted. Will you do this one thing for yourself, Zach; for me; for us? I can't stand to see you tortured this way. It's taking a toll on your health."

# Jack Eddinger

Zach Harris, the man who kept his own counsel in all things and took advice grudgingly, knew hers was the right approach to a problem that could be resolved in no other way. He would meet with the Speaker, admit his error and seek exculpation ... forgiveness was something he could never ask for. He would make a convincing case for himself based on his interpretation of House rules of procedure, admit his mistake and offer to accept whatever disciplinary action the Speaker would exact. This was the manly way to handle the situation and the Speaker would appreciate it.

A day after requesting a meeting, Zach Harris approached the Speaker's small office in the Capitol hesitantly, as if he were about to make a weak and uncertain summation to a jury. The Speaker, his countenance stern and somber, pressed Zach Harris's hand firmly. He invited the congressman to have a seat in front of the big oak desk that members lounged around at the Speaker's late afternoon post mortems. To Zach Harris, who often attended the meetings which always ended when the Speaker took a bottle of bourbon from the washroom cabinet, sitting before him in the leather-padded chair like a schoolboy gone awry was wildly ridiculous. He remembered Lenore's strong advice, but had to suppress an ironic grin.

"Well, Ham, I've decided to see if we can't find an agreeable settlement to our little dispute," Harris began volubly. "I know I've offended you, and I've come down here to see if there's a way I can make amends for what I agree was a damned fool maneuver on my part. But in my defense let me just say that I thought I was doing the right thing for the country within the purview of my chairmanship and House rules. Now, I can see that I was clearly wrong and I'm here to ask for your understanding. I acknowledge that the fault was mine and mine alone, that I over-stepped my authority, that I committed a serious error of judgment. It was a mistake of the head not the heart and I take full blame for letting my aggressiveness - call it ambition - get in the way of my responsibilities. I plead guilty."

Throughout Zach Harris's monologue, the Speaker tilted back in his armchair and kept his eyes fixed on a spot on the ceiling. He was in his shirtsleeves. He listened, but made no effort to respond.

"Well aren't you going to respond, Ham?" Harris grumbled. "I admitted my mistake. I think I deserve a fair response."

In his long years as a chairman, majority and minority leader and as Speaker, Ham Clayburg found dealing with the frailties, foibles and human weaknesses of his fellow legislators to be among the most unpleasant and disagreeable burdens of leadership. Looking to the past as a guide to disciplining a fellow member proved uninstructive. Whether under Henry Clay, the most enduring and civil of House leaders, or under

# INQUISITION

tough Republicans like Czar Reed, Uncle Joe Cannon or Nick Longworth, members of Congress remained a class of men unto themselves. Sensitivity to and toleration of criticism was not their long suit. Reading them and leading them required a mastery of indirection, understatement, implied fear and an unmistakable resoluteness in carrying out the edicts of leadership.

Ham Clayburg listened carefully to the penitent then spoke:

"Back in '36 when you got yourself stuck up to your asshole with the executive reorganization bill FDR wanted killed, I pulled up your socks and got it straightened so you could take full credit for the reworked bill. I asked for nothing in return.

"When you gave that speech in support of the jury trial amendment to give you an advantage with the Dixiecrats without informing me, I let it pass," the Speaker said after a long silence. "I knew your purpose long before you requested floor time. It was one of the most stupid, most ignorant moves I've seen by a northerner since Reconstruction, but I said nothing. I knew you were currying favor with the Southerners to move yourself up in the leadership line. But I had the votes, so I overlooked your little scheme.

"When you asked me for military leave then later to restore your rank on committees after you came back from the service, I did so without hesitating, because I believed in you. I expected you to be our best postwar policy draftsman. I never asked you for payback of any kind.

"When you went off on this latest duck hunt and argued with me over whose authority, yours or mine, should prevail on televising the hearings, then went ahead anyway, I figured you might listen to reason after hearing me out as to why I insisted on taking a strong position against broadcasting out of town hearings that achieved no legislative purpose other than to prolong the distress they've caused. But you wouldn't listen. Your damned committee sent that young medical scientist up in Philadelphia to his death at the end of a rope the other day, because he feared for his family and his good name."

"I'm as sorry as I can be about him, Ham," Zach Harris said trying to show he cared. "But I can't help what men do. You know how things are. Look, I'm sorry for letting you down. I'll make it up to you."

"The sad part of this is that I've been the biggest damned fool of all. I made you what you are, what you've been and what you could have been. Down where I come from when you trust a man, you expect him to honor his oath to uphold the Constitution, to follow his conscience even when the voters say otherwise, and to do nothing to bring discredit to his office and to the United States House of Representatives."

# Jack Eddinger

"Wha...what are you talking about?" Zach Harris muttered, his voice laden with alarm. "I came here contrite ... to admit my mistake ... to apologize so we can move on. You're making an inconsequential thing sound like high crimes and misdemeanors, an impeachable offense like something short of treason."

Without comment or change in his grim facial expression the Speaker pushed the Bureau dossier across the desk to his visitor.

"What's that?" Harris rasped.

"Your biography, Mr. Harris. And to think Judas only got thirty pieces of silver."

Zach Harris lifted up the front of the folder delicately and began skimming the Bureau's transmittal memo. He stopped when he got to his name. He quickly opened and closed the folder marked IMMSUBCOMM. The visage of his old law partner, Tad Daley, flashed across his memory. He came to the documents Robert Bird had photographed and squinted at each carefully. It wasn't possible. No one ever penetrated his office, let alone his personal safe; no one would dare. In an instant, chagrin and disgust descended upon him as he remembered his hospitalization just before the election and his orders to Robert Bird. The thought of his aide rifling his safe staggered him.

"Wh-where did you get this material?" he demanded on the edge of panic. "It's all a fake. There's nothing of substance here. This is nothing short of attempted blackmail."

The Speaker did not respond. His face and mouth were pulled down in a somber mask. "I want your resignation on my desk forthwith," the Speaker told him. "I don't care how you handle it with the press. That's up to you. I want you out of this House within twenty-four hours. No ifs, ands or buts. Do you understand me, sir?"

Zach Harris trembled, unprepared to meet the Speaker's insistent demand. It went beyond any situation he'd experienced. Worst of all he had no plan, no allies. How did they get those files, the photos? His instincts told him attack!

"Oh no. I will not resign. If you force this issue, I will assure you that more than discredit will come to this House. I will demand a full investigation into how these materials were gained. These are illegal, surreptitiously-gained materials. Someone broke into my office ..."

Before he could correct his blunder and backtrack, Zach Harris knew the blurted admission had convicted him. Scenes from his long congressional career whizzed through his mind. It was the end. He sat before the Speaker's desk staring blankly at the files. The Speaker stood up and left the room.

264

# INQUISITION

Zachary Taylor Harris made his way back to his office through the dark and abandoned tunnel between the Capitol and the Longworth basement. No one was there to greet him. It was long after the staff had left for the day. He closed the door quietly behind him. In the center of his desk was a brown manila envelope marked "Official Business, Hand Deliver" with the return address of his physician at Bethesda Naval Hospital. He opened it and began reading the cover letter, which was backed up by clinical notes and laboratory data from his physical examination of the previous week. The physician's letter read:

*Dear Congressman Harris:*

*Results of the physical examination conducted on March 15, 1957 at U.S. Naval Hospital, Bethesda, Maryland, indicate elevated bilirubin levels, low serum haptoglobin, hemoglobin in the urine, an elevated reticulocyte count, low red blood count and low serum hemoglobin. Coombs test direct results indicate antibodies mobilized against red blood cells.*

*These test results support a provisional diagnosis of Autoimmune hemolytic anemia. In lay terms, this is a rare acquired disease resulting when antibodies form against one's own red blood cells. The diagnosis is also confirmed by the symptoms presented the day of the examination, including shortness of breath, rapid heart beat, continual coughing, yellowish skin and dark urine.*

*While I have every confidence in the care and treatment available here at USNHB, I must inform you that this disease has proved unyielding to contemporary medical research due to limited knowledge of the human immune system and the low volume of clinical cases. Unfortunately, this disease advances rapidly and offers limited therapeutic intervention and treatment options. In short, the symptoms you present indicate a condition for which treatment options are not ideal. A splenectomy (removal of the spleen) supported by blood transfusion have been found to arrest the condition in some patients. My colleagues and I recommend that this course be followed forthwith. I suggest that you contact me as soon as possible so that we may discuss both immediate treatment and options for long term management.*

*Be assured that the United States Navy will bring the highest level of professionalism and the very best medicine to bear on the care and treatment of a distinguished member of Congress and a former fellow officer.*

# Jack Eddinger

*Yours sincerely,*

*Robert L. Mahan,*
*Capt. USN*
*Chief of Internal Medicine*

He sat at his desk for a very long time. Then he dialed the tumblers of the safe in the alcove behind his desk until the heavy plate door quietly eased open. He put the file the Speaker gave him into the safe then fumbled through its contents until he found Tad Daley's revolver. He sat at his desk trembling and murmuring softly. He clicked off the safety and raised the pistol to his left temple. In the split instant - the interval between pulling the trigger and the descent into darkness - his eye caught the light from the desk lamp gleaming through empty bullet chambers. He held the pistol in front of him. Breathing heavily and in a state of blind rage and suppressed panic, he examined it closely. He discovered that all six chambers were empty. Wheezing and coughing, he let the weapon drop to the floor. "Bird, you dirty sonofabitch," he muttered before a convulsion of coughing and choking so violent that he could not catch his breath overwhelmed him. He felt as if he were drowning then everything went black.

The Intensive Care Unit on the 15th floor of the Bethesda Naval Hospital tower was one floor below the suite James V. Forestall, the country's first Secretary of Defense, had occupied in early May, 1949 before he jumped to his death. Had he been conscious, this fact would not have been lost on its current occupant. The congressman had been rushed unconscious to BNH by a District of Columbia ambulance minutes after he was discovered by a night watchman, making time clock rounds and checking suites in the Longworth Building. The watchman roused the Sergeant at Arms to report his discovery, taking pains to mention the open safe and the handgun. Hattaway immediately called the Capitol police and the DC emergency number. Then he put through a call to inform the Speaker. It was 4 a.m.

The taxicab carrying Lenore Price sped out Wisconsin Avenue. She'd heard the news of the congressman's collapse and hospitalization on the 8 a.m. newscast. Because of the congressman's grave condition, she was allowed into the ICU only at half hour intervals. She waited down the hall in a stark waiting room in a state of suppressed hysteria, oblivious to the monotonous entreaties of the black and white commercials flashing across the TV screen. She spent the anguished hours of her vigil praying and puzzling over the gravity and sudden onset of the affliction that struck

# INQUISITION

down the man she loved. She was unaware of the medical complications he faced, and chided herself for not urging him to seek immediate medical care when his coughing became uncontrollable. She had no intimation of his torment or the aborted attempt to end his life. She was bewildered and distressed. She wept softly when she saw him stretched out inside the transparent oxygen tent, his body limp and strung with tubes, straps and wires, a medical team hovering over his inert form.

"I'm afraid there's not much we can do," Dr. Mahan told her after checking his VIP patient carefully. "He may not make it through the night."

Lenore Price maintained her vigil outside the ICU throughout the next day and into the following afternoon and evening. At 3 a.m. a Navy officer gently awakened her from the fitful immersion that passed for sleep. When she saw the small gold crosses on the lapels of his blue serge uniform, she broke down and wept inconsolably. Exactly forty-eight hours after his admission to BNH, Zachary Taylor Harris, the man whose mental acuity, determination and supreme confidence never failed him departed this life at the age of 59 without regaining consciousness. Cause of death was noted as pneumonic suffocation triggered by an underlying condition of advanced Autoimmune Hypoleukocytic anemia. His body was released to the Williamson Funeral Establishment of Chevy Chase with funeral arrangements incomplete.

The Bessemer City *Star-Times* carried the story of the death of Congressman Harris under a headline on page-one in 36-point type. The news story was written by Charlie Miller. Miller also produced three sidebars from memory chronicling the life and times of the politician he had covered for a quarter century. Inside, two double-truck pages of photos presented the long political career of the Hon. Zachary Taylor Harris. The official obit by the skilled re-write man, John Oliver, noted that burial would be in Arlington National Cemetery, the grove of heroes and presidents. In Washington *The Post* and *The Evening Star* carried stories below the fold on page one accompanied by a single-column cut of the circa 1946 photograph released by his office. Neither mentioned funeral services or the place of burial.

A phone call from the Speaker's office to the Secretary of the Interior, bucked down to the National Park Service, denied burial at Arlington. No reason given. Instead, Zach Harris was laid to rest in the Old Congressional Cemetery out at the far end of Pennsylvania Avenue. It was within walking distance of the Anacostia Flats, where the Bonus Marchers, including many of his contemporaries, were driven out of their tar paper and cardboard shanties and dispersed with tear gas and fire hoses by troops

# Jack Eddinger

on the orders of President Hoover, the man that Democrats like Zachary Taylor Harris never let Americans forget. In supreme affirmation of life's insistent ironies, the congressman was laid to rest a short distance from the last resting place of Matthew Brady, the inventor of photojournalism. Brady's images of war and peace and public men made the extraordinary commonplace and changed forever the way American public life would be viewed, recorded and understood.

Only two persons attended the burial to hear the prayers of the chaplain of the U.S. House of Representatives. It took place on one of those warm and sunny days, which awaken the nation's capital to a new season. Spring had descended overnight, luxuriant with bird song, sprouting daffodils and the efflorescent greening of the equinox. One, a well-dressed slender and attractive woman wearing a veil, the other an awkward and rumpled man with a neatly trimmed grey mustache and a raft of folded copy paper stuffed into the pocket of his unbuttoned rain coat. Both knew the identity of the other, but did not exchange a word. Charlie Miller considered introducing himself to Lenore Price and inviting her to sit with him on one of the stone benches scattered about the handsome, venerable graveyard. He wanted to express his mixed feelings about Zachary Taylor Harris to someone who might listen. He wanted to tell her the truth about the man she thought she knew so well and loved so deeply. He wanted to touch her spirit, to reach out and enjoin her from investing too much of herself in the memory of a man whose ambition-misshapen character brought him the retribution the gods reserve for those who would befriend them. A fragment from T. S. Eliot's poem, *The Hollow Men*, circulated through his mind:

> *Between the idea*
> *And the reality*
> *Between the motion*
> *And the act*
> *Falls the Shadow*

Charlie Miller stood before the grave for a long time then walked slowly back to his car, completing the poem in his mind and leaving Lenore Price alone with her thoughts, her tears and her congressman.

> *This is the way the world ends*
> *Not with a bang but a whimper.*

# EPILOGUE

It has been many years since the divorce petition Zach Harris filed in the District of Columbia Superior Court arrived in the mail at the Georgian manse on the hilltop overlooking Bessemer City on Valentine's Day 1957. How typically considerate, Marion Harris mused at the time, as she read through the legalese. So, it all comes down to this after thirty-six years; a solemn commitment reduced to the stilted phrases of the lawyer hired to reduce their marriage to half-truths, lies and equivocation. She read on, more to absorb the irony than to grasp the meaning of the banal sentences. The lie, she thought, what a terrible affliction of the human heart - the dross of untruth that clings to every word of man - as a philosopher she once read put it.

Reintegration came to Marion Hanson Harris slowly and painfully over the length of a decade. Depression, alienation and anomie, the corrosives of the human spirit, the destroyers of hope had descended upon her in a long, heartless visitation, obscuring the artistic vision and emotional boundaries she had established. Her struggle with alcoholism added deeper misery, carrying her to the edge of the abyss. Only a woman of extraordinary courage and incandescent intelligence; one who had roamed the black corridors of depression could survive so searing a trial. She gradually came to the view that she and she alone could rescue herself, and she could do it only in powerful remembrance of the tenderness and affection that abided in the spirit of the two men she truly loved, her brother, Alec Hanson, and her lover of short but luminous duration, Hobe Tenley. Their stars, fixed forever in her firmament, helped her navigate the darkness. Anna Daley's presence and her own growing capacity to achieve expression through a fully developed artistic style brought her further along the path to wholeness. By the early sixties her daughter's marriage had produced a baby daughter, whom Marion adored. Although she still struggled, she had her drinking problem under control.

And with its control came the triumph of her work with the Washington Color School. A canvas entitled, *Balkan Dawn*, earned her widespread recognition among the art savants of Washington and later that year in New York City. She dedicated the abstract work, based on gradations of orange, ocher and brown transmuting into the gold of a sunrise enfolding the flags of proud Slavic kingdoms to the memory and gallantry of Major L.H. Tenley, U.S. Army.

She read her husband's obituary in *The Post* and *The Evening Star* with an admixture of shock and release ... shock, because Zach Harris always seemed to her indestructible; release because she was rid of the last vestige of the darkness that had smothered the light in her soul.

President Lyndon Johnson appointed her to the National Endowment for the Arts, where she continued to serve until her death in 1988.

Andy Burnham kept a low profile after the Philadelphia hearings but was quietly dropped from the Penn faculty. The AAUP voted against supporting his case. The ACLU took up his cause, which helped him land a teaching position at Swarthmore College through the intercession of some Quaker friends. He re-emerged in the mid-80s as a counselor to the State Department on nuclear non-proliferation and weapons of mass destruction issues. He was instrumental in having the Distinguished Service Cross, Silver Star and Navy Cross awarded to Major L. Hobart Tenley, posthumously. He, Elaine and Marion MacPherson Hanson (she had dropped the name Harris), attended the medal ceremony with President Reagan in the Rose Garden. At the age of 80, he completed a six volume history of dissent in America, which received the Pulitzer prize for history.

Elaine Burnham continued to paint well into her eighth decade. She first caught the interest of the art world in the 1960s with her geometric painting, *Chiliagon Perceived*. Later her work earned significant support from the U.S. government, which promoted Abstract Expressionism, because its radical character was considered to appeal to a Western European populace perceived by the State Department to be caught up in existentialism and socialism. She savored the irony.

Tom Daley was named an assistant attorney general in Robert Kennedy's Justice Department in 1962, specializing in organized crime. He moved to Maryland and in 1964 ran successfully for the U.S. Senate. He served on the Judiciary Committee, and was instrumental in the passage of the Crime Control Act of 1968 to curb organized crime in the United States and legislation to control the sale and possession of hand guns. President Johnson signed both bills into law. Daley was defeated for a second term in 1970 by a strident negative advertising campaign launched by the National Rifle Association ("If Daley Wins You Lose") and financed by the Committee to Re-elect the President (CREEP). He practices law in Washington with his longtime advisor and partner, Frank Comstock, in the firm of Daley & Comstock and raises funds for the Democratic Party.

Speaker Clayburg continued to lead the House of Representatives into the 1960s. As chairman of the Democratic convention, he was a major player in the party's victory in the 1960 presidential election and was instrumental in swinging Texas for the Kennedy-Johnson ticket. He surpassed Henry Clay's record as the longest-serving Speaker and was praised by both Democratic and Republican members of the House for his integrity, fairness and loyalty to the United States. He was awarded the Medal of Freedom at a White House ceremony just before his death of lung cancer in 1964.

Lt. John Maggio joined the Bureau in 1962, specializing in organized crime in Pennsylvania and New Jersey. He headed the Bureau's first RICO task force in New Jersey and Eastern Pennsylvania, which broke up the Russo, Strello and Buffolini families in the 1970s. Later, he was called to serve at national headquarters as an expert on the mob, which had metamorphosed into La Cosa Nostra. He retired in 1985. He and Angie built a small villa on the island of Monte Argentario, on the Ligurian coast north of Rome, and spend summers there growing tomatoes and enjoying their extended American and Italian families.

Special Agent Frank Jordan retired from the Bureau in the late 1960s and moved to the Phoenix, Arizona area to become a charter member of the Bureau ghetto in Sun City and a founder of the Federal Golf and Country Club. He made occasional forays to consult on casino security in Las Vegas, and assisted Phoenix police in their 1976 investigation into the car bomb murder of an *Arizona Republic* reporter.

Joe O'Neill succeeded Eugene Garrett Palmer as chairman of Bessemer Steel Corporation after Palmer's death in 1964. He engineered the merger between Bessemer and Overland Steel, which maintained Bessemer's rank as the world's second largest steel producer. He forged new long term labor agreements, which became standards for the industry. He retired to Ireland and tried his skills at forging an agreement between the Northern Ireland Provisional Army and the IRA to no avail. He died at Ballyronan on the west shore of Lough Neagh, County Tyrone, home of the O'Neill clan, in 1984.

Gaetano Cavalieri Russo was subpoenaed to testify before the New Jersey Crime Commission in late 1973 and seventeen times thereafter. In poor health from a heart condition, he established residence in Florida in 1976, but continued to return to Union City. His lawyer, Stefano Maglie, attempted to quash the Commission's continual subpoenas, claiming "harassment and oppression." An Appeals Court denied the claim and Russo was tried and found guilty of racketeering and mail fraud by a federal court in Newark. He was sentenced to three years in the U.S. Penitentiary at Danbury, Connecticut. He died of a heart attack at Captiva, Florida, in 1985.

Robert Basilico entered the witness protection program and was given a new identity after facial surgery. He lives in Southern California. For many years he operated a well-patronized and highly successful Italian-American restaurant in Mission Bay near San Diego.

Robert Bird joined the Washington bureau of the Associated Press to become the AP's man on the Hill, covering both the House and Senate. He left the wire service to become an on-camera TV news personality for CBS News in Washington. He has served as president of the National Press Club, the Capitol Correspondents Organization and the Overseas Press Club. Since his retirement, he does occasional commentary for National Public Radio.

Lenore Price remained in Washington with the Democratic National Committee for the next decade. In 1968, she headed Women for Humphrey-Muskie. She retired when the Nixon Administration came to power, and was an avid follower of the Ervin Committee's investigation into the Watergate affair. She lives on Social Security and a small pension from the DNC in the same apartment complex near the Washington Cathedral where she had lived since coming to the nation's capital.

Lloyd Kressman never received a bank charter. The death of Zachary Taylor Harris put an end to his dream, but had the beneficial effect of shutting off Federal investigations into political corruption in the Lenape Valley. He died at his desk of a cerebral stroke the day of Richard Nixon's resignation from the presidency in 1974.

Charlie Miller took a year's sabbatical to write a biography of Zachary Taylor Harris and his times. *The Chairman* received high praise from reviewers and remained on *The New York Times* non-fiction best-seller list for fifteen months. Miller, now retired, is writing a novel about the Lenape Valley and its role in America's industrial revolution.

Pennsylvania's 26th congressional district underwent considerable change since the death of Representative Zachary Taylor Harris. The seat was held until the early 1960s by Democrats with the interim appointment and subsequent one-time victory of Bessemer City's Mayor John Holland. As Pennsylvania began losing population, a new district was formed by combining the 26th and parts of two contiguous districts. The congressional seat, held for nearly 50 years of the 20th century by Democrats, became a swing district. In the 1970s, the District became firmly Republican. The GOP has held the seat ever since.

The unclaimed funds credited to the Daley & Harris Swiss bank account grew exponentially to nearly $10 million in the years following the Congressman's death, instigating a fierce legal battle between the United States Department of Justice and the Republic of Switzerland that has not been resolved to this day.

Printed in the United States
25920LVS00004B/13-39